Paul Fraser Collard
THE
TRUE
SOLDIER

HEADLINE

First published in Great Britain in 2017 by
HEADLINE PUBLISHING GROUP

First published in paperback in Great Britain in 2018 by
HEADLINE PUBLISHING GROUP

1

Cataloguing in Publication Data is available from the British Library

ISBN 978 1 4722 3906 8

Typeset in Sabon by Avon DataSet Ltd, Bidford-on-Avon, Warwickshire

Printed and bound in Great Britain by Clays Ltd, St Ives plc

MIX
Paper from
responsible sources
FSC® C104740

Headline's policy is to use papers that are natural, renewable and recyclable products
and made from wood grown in well-managed forests and other controlled sources.
The logging and manufacturing processes are expected to conform to the
environmental regulations of the country of origin.

HEADLINE PUBLISHING GROUP
An Hachette UK Company
Carmelite House
50 Victoria Embankment
London EC4Y 0DZ

www.headline.co.uk
www.hachette.co.uk

To David Headley

Glossary

crib	dwelling house for thieves and swindlers
Finn MacCool	Irish folk hero
gombeen	fool
hooplehead	idiot
Johnny Reb	Northern slang for a Confederate soldier
know-nothings	nickname for the right-wing American Party
langer	fool/bastard
lobster	British redcoat
longshoreman	docker
mofussil	country station or district away from the chief stations of the region, 'up country'
poke	bag or small sack
palmetto flag	South Carolina state flag; a white palmetto tree on an indigo field with a white crescent in the upper left corner
secession	act of separating from a nation and becoming independent
sechers	Northern slang for someone from the South who supported secession
shofulman	coiner or passer of bad money
trencherman	person who eats heartily

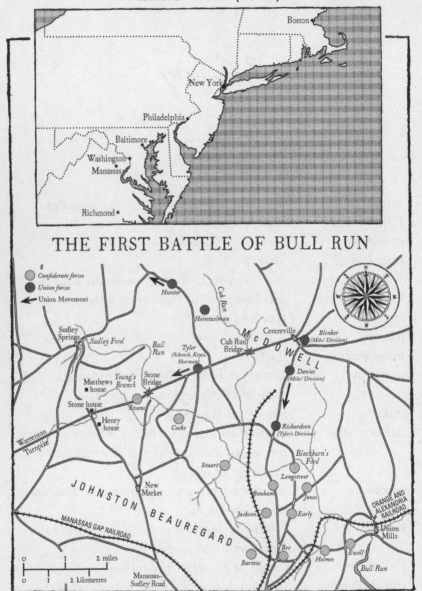

EAST USA (1861)

Boston

New York

Philadelphia

Baltimore

Washington
Manassas

Richmond

THE FIRST BATTLE OF BULL RUN

Confederate forces
Union forces
Union Movement

Hunter

Cub Run

Heintzelman

Centreville

Blenker
(Miles' Division)

Sudley
Springs

Sudley Ford

Bull
Run

Tyler
(Schenck, Keyes,
Sherman)

Cub Run
Bridge

M C D O W E L L

Matthews
house

Young's
Branch

Stone
Bridge

Davies
(Miles' Division)

Stone house

Evans

Cocke

Richardson
(Tyler's Division)

Henry
house

Warrenton
Turnpike

Stuart

Blackburn's
Ford

New
Market

Longstreet

J O H N S T O N   B E A U R E G A R D

Bonham

Jones

MANASSAS GAP RAILROAD

Jackson

Early

ORANGE AND
ALEXANDRIA
RAILROAD

Union
Mills

0   1   2 miles

0   1   2 kilometres

Bee

Bartow

Holmes

Ewell

Bull Run

Manassas–
Sudley Road

A house divided against itself cannot stand. I believe this government cannot endure permanently half-slave and half-free. I do not expect the Union to be dissolved – I do not expect the house to fall – but I do expect it will cease to be divided. It will become all one thing or all the other.

Lincoln's House Divided Speech, Springfield, Illinois, 16 June 1858

Chapter One

---◆---

Boston, Tuesday 16 April 1861

The Englishman strode down State Street. It had taken an age to get away from the wharf and the throng of longshoremen and officials who had gathered to welcome the latest swathe of immigrants come to Boston for a new life far away from their homelands. He walked away from the chaos with relief. The *Plymouth Rock* had been crowded, the demand for a berth to Boston far exceeding the carrying capacity of the steam packet, which had left Liverpool over a week before. The voyage had been miserable, his enforced incarceration with the horde made worse by the other cargo that had filled every nook and cranny of the vessel. For the *Plymouth Rock* had been carrying hope, a commodity the Englishman had left far behind on the blood-soaked battlefields of Europe and beyond.

He pulled his black pork pie hat down lower and quickened his pace as he reached the end of State Street. The ground pitched beneath his boots, his gait uneven as he became re-accustomed to walking on land. The rain might have made the cobbles treacherous, but they still felt wonderfully secure after so long on board the lurching uncertainty of a packet making the Atlantic crossing.

The smell of the place wrapped itself around him as he walked. The fresh, salt-laden air of the sea was replaced with the aroma of food and soot. Boston smelled of people. Not the rancid odour of too many souls kept together in a ship, but the earthy, meaty smell of life in a city.

A crowd of loud, brash stevedores hurried past. A few glanced at the tall Englishman, who met their stares calmly and with no hint of fear. The hard men who toiled in the docks did not worry him. He had fought the Russians, the Persians and the Austrians, along with mutinous sepoys and the army of an Indian maharajah. He knew fear, but he would not feel it standing in the rain on a grey Boston street.

The pause gave him the opportunity to look around and get his bearings. The sky was getting lighter, a brighter thumbprint behind the thick band of clouds indicating the chance of a change in the weather. But the sun would have to fight hard if it was to beat away the gloom, and as he waited, the rain grew heavier. Fine mist was replaced by a deluge, the water coming down in great sheets, bouncing high off the cobbles, the sound of the impact drowning out the noise of the city.

The Englishman shivered, then pulled his greatcoat tighter around him, the thick wool getting heavier as it soaked up the rain. The coat was not his. He had liberated it from a friend's pack, one of hundreds left unclaimed in the aftermath of the slaughter at Solferino. He doubted anyone in Boston would recognise that it had once been issued to a sergeant serving in the ranks of the French Foreign Legion. Yet that sergeant had been born in the city of Boston, and it was his death that had brought the Englishman to its shores.

It had been a long journey. It had started in a Lombard village crammed full of the dead and the wounded. In the aftermath of battle, he had made a vow to deliver the blood-stained letters of a dying man. It was nearly two years since he had left the battered French army in northern Italy; two years that had seen him journey across Europe before finally returning to his home city of London. He had planned to stay there only long enough to settle a score from his past before buying a train ticket to Liverpool and boarding a ship bound for Boston.

But fate had decided on a different plan. Her name had been Françoise du Breton, and she had been the wife of a French wine trader who spent much of his time travelling across Europe. The Englishman had lavished her with gifts whilst living the finest life London could provide. It had not ended well, and he had been left on the street with just enough money in his pocketbook to buy passage to Boston, and a sackful of regret at what might have been. His last English money had been exchanged on board the packet for dollars, the captain as deft as any shofulman at swindling his passengers with an outrageous rate of exchange.

His heavy carpet bag contained all his possessions. Its sides were stained with salt and darkened with damp, and its handle strained with the weight of the weapon hidden deep inside. His worldly goods had been reduced to the rumpled clothing on his back and the garments stuffed into the bag. He had once been a maharajah's general, living in a gilded palace and surrounded by beautiful objects. Now he was a near-penniless vagrant with a handful of dollars in his pocket and an unknown future waiting for him.

He pulled the collar of the greatcoat tighter and pressed on. A wagon approached, its horses' grey coats darkened almost to black by the rain. The Englishman caught the eye of the Negro teamster as he passed, then walked on, following the vague directions the ship's master had given him. He had been told that he would be able to find the address he sought unaided, the new buildings on Beacon Hill an easy enough saunter from the wharf.

The streets were busier as he approached the end of State Street. The locals, long used to the rain, hurried past, faces hidden behind collars and hat brims pulled low. A short, thickset fellow wrapped in a thick sou'wester knocked the Englishman's shoulder as he went by, his boots kicking up a heavy spray. There was no apology for the contact, the Bostonian moving away without even a grunt. The Englishman ignored the rudeness, just as he ignored the rain, which was beginning to show signs of lessening, and pressed on, passing by what looked to be a great covered market opposite a grand building with a fine cupola topped with a copper grasshopper weathervane.

After so long at sea, the crowd waiting at the wharf had been daunting. There were too many people, creating too much noise. Keen to avoid another crowd, he turned into a side street, thinking to bypass the busier streets altogether. At the next corner, and with the rain reduced to little more than a drizzle, he paused, dropping the heavy carpet bag to the ground and taking a moment to shake off the worst of the rain. Only when drier did he dig deep into a pocket and pull out the thick sheaf of letters that he had taken from the hand of the dying man.

The pages were crumpled and the string that bound them together was frayed. The text on the uppermost letter, written in pencil in a fine, sloping hand, was faded and part covered by a series of black stains. As the Englishman studied it, his thumbnail picked at the marks, scraping away some of the old blood. It did little to improve their appearance.

A lady of middling years bustled past. She was moving quickly, her dry cape an indication that she had waited for the rain to pass before stepping out. The Englishman saw her gaze wander over him, the rapid appraisal made in less than a second and without her losing a step. The contact was fleeting, but it lasted long enough for him to see her eyes widen just a fraction. It was a common enough reaction. The Englishman was no longer a young man. He was past his thirtieth year, and his lean, clean-shaven face bore a thick scar across the left cheek. The woman would have seen it, just as she would surely have seen the anger that simmered in his hard grey eyes. Some women were put off by the combination, but he knew that to a few he was still handsome, his steely expression and the blemish to his face only adding to his appeal.

He did not linger. He lifted his pork pie hat and ran his fingers through his close-cropped hair before picking up the carpet bag and moving on. For the next hour he wandered the streets of Boston, working his way past the great common and up the sloping streets where he had been told he would find the address that was just about legible on the bloodstained letters.

A watery sun was out by the time he realised he was thoroughly lost. It did little to shift the chill from the air. The Englishman found himself in a series of narrower streets, where the buildings pressed close together. Twice he had asked a passer-by for directions, and twice he had been answered with little more than a glare. On the third occasion he addressed a Negro woman carrying a bundle of sheets. She took one look at him before scuttling away without so much as a word.

He heard the sound of singing. Three men were walking along with arms interlinked so that they blocked nearly the entire width of the street. It did not take a great deal of experience to know that they had been drinking. It was still early in the evening, but the trio appeared to be three sheets to the wind already, the hour clearly no barrier to their excess.

The Englishman looked them over quickly, the appraisal immediate and instinctive. He did not think much to them. They were dressed in matching long dark-blue tunics with trousers of a lighter shade. None of the three were fine physical specimens and all bore the pinched, pale faces of men long used to life in the city.

If he hoped to let them pass without comment, he was to be disappointed.

'You looking at me?' The tallest of the three men spoke with a strong Irish accent. He was a long-faced, dark-haired man whose thin beard barely obscured skin covered with a thousand pockmarks.

'Excuse me.' The Englishman offered the apology with little sincerity.

'You're fecking English!' The reaction was immediate and it was loud.

'And you're a drunk.'

The three men came to a halt. It took a moment for the tallest to extricate himself from his fellows' arms. The Englishman stood and waited for him patiently. The Irishman paused, then slowly looked him up and down before his eyes focused on his face and took in the amused expression.

'You think this is funny?'

'A little.'

The Irishman was sobering up fast. He blinked, then took a

step closer. 'You want me to give you something to laugh about, you slave-loving English maggot?'

The Englishman smelled the sour stink of whisky on the other man's breath. He was given no time to find a reply.

'You heard the news, maggot?' The Irishman was forced to lift his chin so he could look the taller man in the eye.

'You care to tell me?'

'You don't know?' the Irishman sneered. 'Where've you been? Hiding in the dark, bothering little boys?'

'I just landed.' The Englishman's tone did not alter.

'And you never heard that those Southern langers have attacked Fort Sumter, I suppose?'

The Englishman raised an eyebrow at what he supposed was momentous news. He did not understand the reference to the fort, but there had been talk aplenty in the London papers of the growing conflict brewing in the United States, a country that appeared to no longer be so united. He had been aware that he was travelling to a place on the brink of civil war. The threat had not bothered him. It was not his fight.

The Irishman did not take kindly to his silence. 'We're at war, you dumb fecker. Like it or not, your Southern friends have started this thing. I reckon we're aiming to finish it. So why don't you get your chicken-shit English prick down south before one of us feels the need to cut if off and feed it to you.'

The Englishman laughed. He did not mean to. He was no fool. He knew the three Irishmen were spoiling for a fight. But there was something in the man's insults that he found amusing, and he could not hold back the short guffaw. He had met menacing characters before; men who would make the arsehole of the great Archangel Gabriel himself quiver with fear. This foul-mouthed Irishman was not one of them.

'You laughing at me now?' The Irishman's face twisted. 'You think I'm being funny, is it?' A hand shot out, palm first, and thumped into the Englishman's chest, rocking him back on his heels. 'You ain't laughing now, are you, you fecking pox-bottle?'

Another shove. This time it came with enough force to knock the Englishman back a pace. He had paused in front of a hitching post, and it caught him in the small of his back. Instantly, fierce red-hot pokers lanced up and down his spine and into his legs.

The Irishman saw his face react to the pain and laughed. He was still cackling when the carpet bag hit the floor.

'Back off, chum.' The Englishman hissed the words.

The warning was greeted with derision. 'Why don't you take yourself the feck away, maggot? This ain't no place for a mewling English eejit.'

The Englishman took a deep breath as he attempted to hold his anger in check. The temptation to fight was starting to mount. 'Go away. Now.'

'Why the feck would I do that? You think you can give me orders? We ain't back home. You English bastards don't rule the fecking roost round here.'

The Irishman paused to look around him. Already the first onlookers had been drawn to the prospect of a brawl, a rough circle of spectators forming around the three Irishmen and their English victim. The man's two cronies moved forward to take up position on either side of him. One pulled back his sleeves to reveal thin, pale wrists; he clearly thought to try to prevent blood from spoiling his uniform. The other merely grinned like a fool.

'Why don't you teach that English feck a lesson?' The first

catcall came from a fat, dumpy woman who was twisting her apron in her hands as if she were wringing the Englishman's neck.

'Shut his mouth, O'Dowd.' Another shout of encouragement sounded as more people gathered to watch.

The tall Irishman, O'Dowd, nodded in acknowledgement of the instruction. He glared at the Englishman, his mouth twisted. 'You want to fight, maggot? You want to fecking fight me?'

'No.'

'You a coward, then? You got yourself a yellow belly, maggot?'

The Englishman did not reply. He would not waste the breath. He would need it.

'I think that's what you are. Nothing but a yellow-bellied gobshite.' O'Dowd was playing to the growing crowd, which hooted and catcalled in encouragement. He turned his head, preening, enjoying the attention, acknowledging the people he knew with a smile and a wink. When he turned back, the sneer was on his face again as he prepared to insult his victim some more.

The Englishman did not wait to hear it. His fist rose quickly. The blow landed plum on the Irishman's mouth.

It was a fine punch. It was driven by weeks of frustration and it crushed O'Dowd's lips back against his teeth. The Irishman's head snapped back, his jaws cracking together with an audible click before he fell backwards and landed on his arse.

The crowd went silent. For a moment, all present contemplated O'Dowd. Then they went wild.

The smallest of the three Irishmen heard the call for violence. He stepped forward, fists swinging. He was no fool and he punched hard, each blow controlled. The Englishman was off balance and could not twist away. Both of the Irishman's fists connected with his chest, one after the other, and each hammer blow hurt. The pain was fierce, but it did not stop the Englishman, and he snapped his elbow forward. It was a vicious blow, the kind learned in the rookeries of east London, and it caught the shorter Irishman full in the throat. He fell like a sack of horseshit, hands clasped to his neck, his fighting roar replaced by a choking sob.

'Fecking hit him!' O'Dowd screamed the order through bloodstained lips. He was taking his time to get back to his feet, and it gave the third Irishman enough time to take two steps towards his opponent.

The Englishman made no sound as he faced the last man standing. Around him, the crowd bayed with anger, the street echoing to the snarls and cheers of the men, women and children drawn to the brawl. The feral roar goaded the last man into action and he swung at the Englishman, the blow powerful enough to fell an ox.

The Englishman saw it coming. He swayed back and let the punch wash past his face. Then he stepped forward. His fists did not miss, and the last Irishman went down to a short flurry of blows. Each one hit hard, and the last caught him on the point of the chin. He staggered backwards, but to his credit he stayed on his feet. The speed of the Englishman's fists, though, had near silenced the crowd.

'You useless feckers!' The dumpy woman with the twisted apron had seen enough. She had arms the thickness of a girl's thigh and she carried a pine dolly. It made for a fine weapon and she swung it like a quarterstaff. It hit the Englishman on the back of the head with a sickening thump.

He hit the cobbles without ever seeing who had felled him, blood hot on the nape of his neck as it poured from the back of his head. He barely had time to register what had happened before O'Dowd came for him again.

The Irishman's boots lashed out. The first caught the Englishman in the gut as he sprawled on the ground, driving the air from his lungs with a great whoosh. He was given no time to recover, and could do nothing but writhe in the dirt as the kicks rained down on him, one after another, blood splattering the rain-slicked cobbles as O'Dowd caught him on the skull.

'What the devil is going on here?' The voice silenced the crowd in an instant. It carried authority, its owner clearly expecting to be obeyed.

The Englishman barely heard it. But he did register that the kicking had stopped. He stayed down, the damp cobbles cold against his cheek.

'O'Dowd! I should have known.'

'Major, I—'

'Be quiet.' The stentorian voice silenced the Irishman. The crowd was hushed. The animal snarls had been replaced by the soft shuffle of boots moving across the ground, the onlookers melting away quickly now that someone had arrived to put an end to their entertainment.

The Englishman eased himself up. His chest hurt and one arm was numb from the pounding it had taken. He got to all fours, then paused, letting his head hang until the pain had receded enough for him to push himself to his knees. Once there, he stayed still, taking in the scene around him.

O'Dowd stood, head bowed, in front of the man who had come to interrupt the brawl. His hands were clasped in front of him so that he looked like an errant schoolboy. The shortest of the three Irishmen, the one the Englishman had felled with his elbow, still lay on his back, his sobs the only sound interrupting the silence. The third man was leaning against the wall of the closest building, his eyes opening and closing rapidly as he fought to stay on his feet.

The Englishman had seen enough and let his head loll.

'Let me help you.'

He felt strong hands take a firm grip on his upper arms. He was given no time to resist before he was hauled to his feet.

'Can you stand?'

The Englishman sucked down a breath, then nodded. His body protested, but he had known worse.

He turned his head. The man who had come to rescue him stood an inch or two shorter than the Englishman himself. He was old enough to have salt and pepper in his thick moustache, with more grey at his temples. He was wearing a uniform the same shade of blue as the three Irishmen, but where theirs were baggy and ill-fitted, his was smarter, with gold thread on the epaulettes and bright buttons running down the front.

'I can only offer an apology for my men's behaviour.'

The Englishman met the man's gaze. He noted the accent. His rescuer was American, not Irish, and clearly some kind of officer.

'Is this how you usually greet visitors around here?' He tasted blood as he spoke, so he turned his head and spat onto the cobbles.

'If they're English, then yes.' The reply was calm and measured. 'Here.' The American officer offered a handkerchief.

The Englishman took it and wiped his lips, streaking the

white cotton with red tendrils. He licked the last of the blood away, then ran his tongue around his mouth. A flap of skin had been torn from inside one cheek, the soft flesh caught by his teeth, but the back of his head hurt far more. He raised a hand and pressed the borrowed handkerchief to the wound.

'Does that hurt?'

The Englishman answered with a withering stare. He kept the handkerchief in place, hoping it would stem the flow of blood. He had seen enough head wounds to know they bled a lot even if the wound was small.

'Of course, that was a foolish question.' The American officer pursed his lips and his eyes narrowed. 'But perhaps it was foolish of you to venture into streets such as these at this hour.'

'I was lost.' The reply was clipped.

'I see.' There was a moment's pause. 'Where were you headed?'

The Englishman considered the question, then dug into his pocket with his free hand. He pulled out the letters and handed them to the American. 'I'm looking for that address.'

The American nodded. 'I know it.' He looked at the Englishman with a raised eyebrow. 'Are you a friend of the family?'

'No.' The Englishman did not say anything else. Instead, he pulled the handkerchief away from the back of his head, considering the amount of blood on it before clamping it back to the wound. 'I'm just delivering the letters.'

'You've come a long way to make a delivery.'

The Englishman snorted. 'You have no idea how far.'

The American's eyes narrowed. 'Well, I know the address and I know the family. I'll take you there.'

'Thank you.' The Englishman could not hold back a sigh of relief at the offer.

'May I know your name? I would like to know who I am taking with me.'

The Englishman offered a thin-lipped smile. And so it began again.

'My name is Lark. Jack Lark.'

Chapter Two

'What will you do with those three idiots?' Jack asked the American officer. He still held the borrowed handkerchief to the back of his neck as he nodded towards the Irishmen. The one whose throat he had crushed had finally lumbered to his feet and now stood next to his two compatriots so that they formed some semblance of a line. All three looked at the ground.

The officer chewed on the underside of his moustache as he gave the question serious thought. The silence built.

'Nothing.' He looked at Jack, finding his gaze and holding it. 'I am going to do nothing with them.' He spoke loudly enough for his men to hear.

Jack held back the words that sprang to his lips. He searched the American's face. 'Are you their commanding officer?'

'For my sins.'

'You ever heard of discipline?'

The American pursed his lips. 'I have no need to do anything more.' He raised a single eyebrow. 'You punished them well enough.'

Jack caught the hint of a glint in the American's eye. 'I'd barely got started.'

The American let out a short bark of laughter at Jack's boldness. 'I reckon you have that right.' He looked across at his recalcitrant soldiers. 'You hear that, boys? Mr Lark took all three of you down. If you hadn't had help, I reckon A Company could have lost three men.'

The trio looked down shamefaced as their officer scoffed at them.

'Why did you lose?' The American stood with his hands clasped behind his back. 'O'Dowd. Tell me why three of you could not handle one Englishman.'

O'Dowd sniffed. 'He didn't fight fair.' The words were mumbled. The Irishman's lips were puffy and already blackening.

'How so?' The question was snapped back.

O'Dowd struggled to find an answer. His mouth opened, but no sound came out.

'You lost, O'Dowd, because the three of you didn't work together.' The American officer filled the awkward silence. 'You need to learn from this. You attacked one at a time and so let Mr Lark fight you one at a time. Do that against the Confederates and you won't be nursing a sore lip. You'll be dead!'

Jack was hurting too much to find a smile. But he could only admire the American officer's attitude.

'Now get yourselves back to your barracks. If I hear you didn't report back immediately, then I shall let First Sergeant O'Connell teach you the importance of doing what you are told. You know what that means?'

'Yes, sir.' Two of the Irishmen murmured an affirmative.

The one with the crushed throat offered little more than a half-hearted sob. Then the three of them shuffled away, turning their backs on the Englishman who had knocked them on their arses.

'Now, Mr Lark.' The American officer returned his attention to Jack. 'Shall we find you your address?'

Jack made no attempt to move. 'Is that what the American army is like?' He glared at the officer. 'Is it really that soft?'

The American scowled. 'We are militia, not regulars.'

'That doesn't matter. My question holds.' Jack removed the handkerchief from his wound. He was pleased to see that the cloth came away with less blood on it this time.

'It is a fair question.' The American officer gnawed on the underside of his moustache, the gesture clearly a habit. 'I don't think I can explain easily. Not in a way you would understand. My men are volunteers. They have signed up for a cause they believe in, to fight for a country they have adopted and that they love, but not one that was theirs from birth. I admire them for that.' He fixed Jack with a firm stare. 'I will not crush such a fine and noble spirit.'

Jack did his best to understand the long answer, but his head was pounding and he wanted nothing more than to sit down and find someone to make him a mug of tea. 'Still seems to me like your boys need some discipline.'

'Perhaps.' The American officer treated Jack's opinion with respect. 'But we are not the British army. And this is not England. We do things differently here.'

Jack grunted. He would have said more, but he was painfully aware that he was among strangers. It was not for the first time. Experience had taught him to guard his thoughts and hold his opinions close. And he needed the American officer to show him the way to his destination, so he bit his tongue and forced something that could be said to resemble a smile onto his face.

'So will you tell me your name? You know mine. I'd like to know who I've to thank for rescuing me.' He asked the question as politely as he could.

The American officer gave his short bark of a laugh. 'We Bostonians are giving you a first-rate demonstration of Old Bay hospitality, aren't we just?' He offered his hand. 'Major Temperance Bridges of the 1st Boston Volunteer Militia.'

Jack did his best not to smile at the major's interesting first name and shook the hand offered to him.

'My parents were Puritans, Mr Lark.' Bridges was clearly well used to the reaction Jack had attempted to hide. He even offered a half-smile. 'They were fine people and I thank God daily for their upbringing. Now, are you hale enough to walk? It is not so far.'

'I'm fine.' Jack gave the lie easily. There would be time to sit and nurse his wounds, but that time would only come when the letters were delivered.

A Negro footman dressed in a smart dark-green livery opened the door to the fine red-brick townhouse. It was one of a dozen like it. All faced onto the small fenced garden at the centre of the square, where new-leafed trees rustled in the breeze. The houses were tall and clean, and each one was decked out in patriotic flags and bunting, the red, white and blue bright and spring-like.

'Good evening, master.'

'Good evening.' Bridges nodded a greeting at the servant. 'My friend is here to see your master. Is he at home?'

'He is, master.' The footman took a respectful step backwards, and Bridges turned and gestured for Jack to step inside.

'Are you not coming in?' Jack saw the officer hesitate.

'No, I shall leave you now.'

'Are you not welcome here?'

Bridges considered the question. 'No, I don't think I am.' He looked at Jack and offered his hand. 'I hope I shall see you again, Mr Lark.'

Jack shook the hand. 'Thank you for getting me here.'

Bridges waved the thanks aside. 'I hope your head heals.' He said nothing more before turning and walking back down the short flight of stone steps.

'This way, master.' The liveried footman had said nothing during the exchange. Now he gave a half-bow and gestured for Jack to enter.

Jack did what he was told and stepped inside. The hallway he entered was wide and welcoming. On the floor was a green carpet, and the walls were covered with a number of small paintings, each in a different style of frame.

'Let me take your bag, master.' The footman reached forward and removed Jack's bag from his hand before he could raise a protest. If he wondered at its weight, the thought did not reach his face. 'Please follow me.'

He led Jack down the hall before turning to his right and into a large, elegant reception room. It was perfectly symmetrical, with a single door opposite the one Jack had just walked through, and two more opposite the two tall windows that overlooked the square. The walls were painted in a mix of warm yellows and mellow greens. A fire burned merrily in the grate, the warmth a wonderful discovery after the damp chill outside, but the room did not smell of burning wood. Instead it smelled of flowers, a crystal vase on a curving side table full of bright spring blooms giving off a powerful aroma.

'If you will just wait here, master.' The footman pronounced each word deliberately.

Jack nodded in acknowledgement. His head throbbed with every beat of his heart and he dearly wanted to sit down, but he was wary of perching on either of the two elegant sofas arranged either side of the fireplace.

When the echo of the servant's footsteps had died away, the only sound left was the heavy tick of a long-case clock that stood against the room's far wall. To Jack's ear it sounded ominous, so he turned his attention to the portraits on the wall. He supposed them to be of members of the family, although closer inspection named one as George Washington and another as John Adams. Neither name meant anything to him.

Inspection completed, Jack circled the room before finally perching himself on the very edge of one of the dark green sofas. He felt intensely uncomfortable. He did not belong in a room of such elegant refinement. He might have impersonated a number of officers over the course of his career, but that had always been in an army on campaign. His only experience of such fine living had been as an officer's orderly, a soldier-servant pulled from the ranks to tend to a single officer's needs.

Time passed slowly, each second marked by a single somnolent tick. He still held Bridges' handkerchief pressed to the back of his head, and he suddenly felt foolish to be doing so. He pulled the sodden cotton away, thinking to hide it in a pocket. To his chagrin, blood dripped from the wound, a pair of glistening droplets landing on the seat of the green sofa.

He was given no chance to try to wipe them away.

'Good evening.' A tall gentleman limped into the room. Much of his head was bald, but a thick band of dark hair around the sides and back had been left long. His beard was neatly trimmed but more grey than dark. Despite his awkward gait, he carried himself with the authority of a man well used to his own power. He looked at Jack with eyes that were filled with a mix of interest and concern. 'I must admit to being intrigued. It is not often I am given such a cryptic summons.'

Jack rose to his feet and noticed that he was three or four inches shorter than the other man. The smile that greeted him seemed genuine enough. It sat well on the man's face, the fine wrinkles around his eyes creasing together.

'I should introduce myself.' The man shot out a hand. 'My name is Samuel Kearney, although perhaps you know that already, since you have sought me out.' He paused, and waited for Jack to react.

Jack hesitated. Perhaps the blow to his head had addled his wits, or else events were simply happening too quickly for him to keep up. Whatever the reason, he failed to find a reply, although he did manage to shake the hand he was being offered.

Kearney's brow furrowed at his guest's silence, but he filled it almost immediately. 'Please sit down. You look pale.' He craned his neck to peer at the back of Jack's head. 'And it appears you are injured.' He moved forward and placed a hand on Jack's elbow. 'Shall I summon a doctor?'

'No, I'm fine.' Jack spoke for the first time. His voice came out as little more than a croak.

'Then please, sit down before you fall down.' Kearney guided Jack back to the sofa. Only when he was satisfied that his guest was sitting comfortably did he move away to close the door before taking a chair opposite.

'So, will you tell me why you have come to see me, or must I tease it out of you?' Kearney sat back gingerly, as if the movement pained him.

Jack was still struggling. He had thought about this meeting for a long time. Now that it had arrived, he felt unprepared. He did not know how to begin.

'I understand it was Bridges who brought you to my door.' Kearney's mouth twisted down at the corners as he spoke the name, as if it were sour on his lips. 'It was good of him. He is a solid fellow, I'll give him his due, but rather dull. He has no conversation. A moment in his company can feel like a lifetime.' As he spoke, his eyes never once left Jack's face. He was clearly filling the silence to give his guest time to settle.

'I was set upon. He saved me from a beating.' Jack found his voice. 'Then brought me here.' He spared his host the details.

'Then that was indeed good of him.' Kearney found Jack's gaze and held it. 'You came to Boston to see me?' He spoke softly.

'Yes.' Jack fished the letters out of his pocket and looked at them, suddenly reluctant to part with them. His finger ran over the old marks, just as it had done a hundred times before. He had long pondered why his friend had taken the time to write the letters but never sent them. Once he had been tempted to read them, to discover more about the man he had only known for a short time. He had hoped it would help to assuage the burden of guilt he had carried since the moment he had taken them from his friend's hand. It was a temptation he had never succumbed to. Whatever was written in the letters had been saved for the man they were addressed to.

Jack felt little pride in his restraint. The memory of the

handing-over of the letters had escaped from its shackles and he felt nothing but shame. He no longer smelled the heady aroma of freshly picked flowers. Instead the acrid stink of fresh blood and spent powder filled the room. He was not in an elegant salon in the fashionable streets of Boston, but back on a gore-soaked battlefield.

'I brought you these.' He was surprised to find himself speaking, the words arriving on his lips unbidden. 'They are from your son.'

The silence stretched thin. He held out the letters, offering them towards Kearney. The older man made no move to take them. Instead he stared at the bloodstained bundle as if it were a snake about to strike out and bite him.

'We received a letter.' Kearney sounded old suddenly, his voice catching on the words as if they had been pulled from the depths of his being. 'From the French authorities. Of course, I couldn't read it. I had to ask my daughter, Elizabeth, to do that. It was in French, you see. I had no idea what it was about. When Thomas left . . .' His voice trailed off. 'We did not part on good terms. I had not known where he had gone, what he had chosen to do with his life. The truth came as something of a shock.' The confession was spoken softly.

His eyes never left the bundle of letters. Jack made no effort to pull his hand away, keeping them within the older man's reach. As he did so, he found himself almost smiling. He had fought alongside Kearney's son, enduring the worst of the brutal struggle against the Austrian army on the slopes around Solferino, yet he had never known his given name.

Kearney swallowed with difficulty before he spoke again. 'It was the only letter we ever received. He never wrote. Not once in all those years.'

Jack was transfixed by the change that had come over the man. At the mention of his son, his shoulders had slumped. It was as if he had aged a hundred years in the passage of a single second.

'Why?' He could not help the question. He knew little of Sergeant Kearney's past. Theirs had been a friendship formed and built on the battlefield. There had not been time to learn what had driven the American into the French army. 'Why didn't he write?'

'He didn't tell you?'

'No, he didn't talk of his past. He was in the Legion. It is their way. The man they are is all that matters, not who they were.'

Kearney's lips twitched as if he were about to smile. 'That sounds like Thomas; he kept his thoughts to himself.'

'You said you did not part on good terms,' Jack pressed.

'No.' Kearney's eyes closed. 'No, we did not.'

This time Jack said nothing. His arm ached from holding the letters out for so long, so he withdrew it and balanced them on his knee. He listened to the slow ticking of the long-case clock, allowing the sound to fill his mind. He would let Kearney take his time.

'You served in the Legion?' Kearney eventually broke the silence that had fallen over them.

'No.'

'But you were with him?'

'I was with him at the end.' Jack nearly choked on the words. He had told no one of the last moments of his friend's life. 'He gave me these.' He offered the bundle of letters for a second time. 'They were important to him. At the last.'

This time, Kearney reached out and took them.

The exchange was swift. There was a fleeting, clumsy touch of fingers and then the letters were delivered. Jack let out a sigh as they left his hand. He had waited a long time for this moment. Now it had passed so quickly that it took him a moment to realise that the task he had set himself was completed.

He heard Kearney's fingernail scratch at the black mark on the uppermost letter.

'Ink?'

'Blood.'

'His?'

'Mine.' Jack gave the lie quickly.

Kearney's fingernail did not still. It picked at the largest of the bloodstains, the sound of its scratching filling the silence.

'I took it badly when he left. I believe he took a part of me with him, a part of me that I shall never possess again. His brother, Robert, blamed me. Thomas was like a hero to him. Older brothers often are, aren't they?'

'I wouldn't know.'

'You have no brothers?'

'No.'

'Family?'

'No.' Jack looked deep into Kearney's gaze. 'I have nothing and no one.' He heard the coldness in his own words. It had not always been so. He had once had a family, but his mother was dead and anyone he had once cared about was lost to him. So he would admit to none of them. He was among strangers. His past would stay hidden.

'I would know what happened.'

Jack was wrestling with his emotions. The task of delivering the letters had sustained him, given him a purpose when he had none. Now they were in Kearney's hands and he no longer had a reason to be there, or anywhere. The realisation made him cruel. 'He died.'

Kearney winced. 'How?'

'You want me to tell you it was quick?' Jack could not hold back the bitterness. 'You want me to tell you he died easy?' His emotions churned inside him, mixing with his memories to create a volatile cocktail. He felt the stirrings of anger. He had done what he had set out to do, had brought the letters from the battlefield. He had not brought kindness.

'I would know how it happened.' Kearney's even tone was unchanged.

'You don't want to know.'

'I *would* know,' Kearney repeated, patient and calm.

'No.' Jack's tone was glacial. 'You want to know enough to ease your guilt. I came to deliver your son's letters. Nothing more.' He did not care that he was being callous.

'He was my son,' the words came back at Jack with more force, 'and he is dead.' Kearney reached out and took Jack's wrist. His touch was cold, but it was like iron. 'I would know how it happened.'

For a moment, Jack was tempted to unleash his demons. It would be easy to release the blackness hidden in his soul, to let the foul horrors have their head. But to do that was to unshackle them and set them free. If he let that happen, he did not know if he could ever force them back into their cage, and into the darkest recesses of his mind that he knew not to visit.

The long-case clock marked the passing of time as he controlled his thoughts. He did not know how long it took, but he felt Kearney's gaze on him the whole time.

'We were fighting the Austrians.' Jack was surprised at the calmness in his voice when he eventually started to speak. 'At a place called Solferino, to the south of Lake Garda.' He did not look at Kearney, but instead lifted his gaze and focused on the vase and its bright flowers. 'We had fought a few days before, at a place they told us afterwards was called Magenta. That was a nasty one. We had to fight in the streets, clear them out of the buildings.' For the first time his voice wavered; he paused and cleared his throat before continuing.

'After that, we marched east. No one expected another battle so soon. The Austrians were retreating faster than we could advance. But then they turned.' He paused again, taking time to slow his words. He had to release the memories more gently. If they came out in a rush, he would fail to constrain them.

'The Austrians held the high ground around Solferino and there were more of them out on the great plain to the south. That was where we started the day. On the plain.' He remembered the morning of the battle clearly. 'We were there until noon, doing nothing but waiting. Then we were ordered to attack the high ground.'

Once again he felt the fear of that moment. He swallowed it down with difficulty before he continued. 'It was hard fighting, but we captured our objective. Your son was in the front ranks the whole time. He knew what he was about and he fought like a devil. We all did. Those Austrians, they were just conscripts, yet no one had told them they should not fight hard.'

'When we were done, we were ordered back to the plain. The Austrians didn't know they were beaten, and they kept on attacking that flank. We pushed them back, but there were too many of them.' He looked away from the flowers. 'We broke.

There weren't many of us left, and we ran. That was when it happened.'

Kearney opened his mouth to say something, but he was interrupted by the sound of the door opening.

'Father! So this is where you have been hiding.'

Jack's breath stopped in his chest. His mouth opened of its own accord and he simply stared. The talk of death had chilled the room and cast it into shadow, but now it was filled with the light of the most beautiful woman he had ever seen.

Chapter Three

'Permit me; sir, to introduce you to my daughter. Elizabeth, this is . . .' Kearney had risen as his daughter entered the room. His introduction came to a premature end and he turned to Jack, his arm held out awkwardly in front of him. 'I am sorry, I don't think you gave me your name.'

Jack lumbered to his feet. He felt like a clumsy beast asked to hold the most delicate china doll. 'My name is Jack Lark.' He spoke gruffly.

Elizabeth Kearney looked back at him with the bluest of blue eyes. Her heart-shaped face was perfectly symmetrical, with a small, slightly pointed nose, and a wide, generous mouth that curled into a smile as she saw him rise. She wore her blonde hair in ringlets that bounced as she took a pace forward and offered him a slim, pale hand.

'I am pleased to meet you, Mr Lark.' She greeted the odd stranger she found in her parlour with politeness. 'It is typical of my father not to tell me that he was expecting a visitor.'

'He wasn't expecting me.' Jack's tongue seemed to be twice its normal size. He felt grubby and tawdry in front of such a perfect creature. His clothes were rumpled and smelled of damp, and the blood from the wound to the back of his head had trickled down one side of his neck to stain his jacket collar. Elizabeth Kearney, in contrast, was immaculate, perfect even. She was wearing a full-skirted dress of the palest blue that was gathered neatly around her waist and pulled tight across her chest. She was one of God's own angels, whilst he was a bloodstained and stinking beggar.

She could not have failed to take in his dishevelled appearance, yet she made no remark of it. 'Well, sir, I am sorry to have disturbed you.'

'Don't be sorry.' Jack was feeling dizzy. Elizabeth was beautiful enough to steal the breath of a saint. But it was not just her good looks that so captured his attention. Her accent captivated him too. It changed the way her words echoed in his head.

'Mr Lark knew Thomas.' Kearney cracked the veneer of politeness. 'He came to bring me these.' He held up the bundle of letters, then handed them to Elizabeth.

'Thomas wrote these?'

Jack watched her closely, following her eyes as they studied his face. He noticed the short pause as they lingered on his scar, the slight narrowing as she spotted the blood matting his hair.

'Did he give them to you?' She asked the second question a little more sharply, even as the first remained unanswered.

'Yes.'

'When?'

'At the last.'

'I see.' She looked at the letters, holding them in front of her as if they frightened her.

'He died easy, Lizzie.' Kearney glanced at Jack. 'Mr Lark here told me so himself just before you came in. Is that not so, Mr Lark?' It was not a question. It was a demand.

'I'm sure he did. Isn't that what people always say?' Elizabeth gave Jack no time to answer. There was a snap in her reply, a waspishness that sat at odds with the perfection of her face.

Jack spotted something flare in her eyes. He did not know what it was. Annoyance? Anger, even. Perhaps she too heard the lie in her father's words. Whatever it was, it was hidden quickly.

'Mr Lark, would you tell my daughter what you told me?' Kearney tried to force the issue.

'He . . .' Jack's voice tailed off before the first words were fully formed. It was as if his own tongue recoiled as it tasted the bitterness of his thoughts. He looked at Kearney and then at his daughter. Both were staring at him with intensity.

He cast his eyes downwards. He would not be the one to bring the filth and misery of the battlefield into their minds. It was not because they were kind, or because Elizabeth was beautiful. It was because they could never begin to understand what it was like. Only soldiers knew the true nature of such horrors. It was why so few spoke of their memories. Civilians, the men and women lucky enough not to have their souls sullied by the foul touch of war, could not hope to comprehend those moments that would haunt a man for a lifetime.

'He did not suffer, miss. I stayed at his side the whole time. He did not die alone.' He lifted his gaze and looked into her eyes before repeating the phrase that would give the comfort that was craved. 'He did not suffer.'

'Are you just telling us what we want to hear?' Elizabeth's tone was sharp.

'I did not come all this way to lie.' He forced down the guilt as he did exactly that. 'I was with him. He died as easy as any man I ever saw.' He spoke firmly. He had been an impostor for a long time. He was pretty damn good at lying.

Elizabeth did not reply. He saw her hold in a breath, her lips paling as she pressed them tightly together.

'What do you mean by *easy*, Mr Lark?' When she finally spoke, her words were as hard as iron. 'I cannot think that death comes easily to anyone, least of all a soldier on the field of battle.'

Jack did not shirk the question. 'He had been shot,' he lifted a hand and placed it over his heart, 'right here. There was enough time for him to ask me to deliver these letters before he passed.'

Elizabeth's eyes narrowed. 'That does not sound like a quick end.'

'No.' Jack stood firm. 'Not quick. But he did not linger. It isn't always like that, not for some. He was one of the lucky ones.' Again he saw something shift in her gaze. Whatever it was, it was unfathomable to him.

Elizabeth opened her mouth to speak again, but before she could do so, Kearney reached out to touch her arm. 'That is enough for the moment. Mr Lark was set upon on the way here. It took the timely intervention of Major Bridges to save him.'

'Temperance saved him?' Elizabeth could not help the exclamation.

'So it seems.'

'My, oh my, whatever next. You would think that man would know better than to interfere with this family.'

Jack caught the interplay. He was not given time to dwell.

'Are you badly hurt, Mr Lark?' Elizabeth asked.

'No.' He gave the denial immediately. The truth was that his head was pounding as if an entire corps of drummer boys was beating the *pas de charge* in the very centre of his skull. But he would not admit to it. Not to someone like Elizabeth. 'I am fine, truly.'

'You do not look so fine.' Elizabeth turned to her father. 'We should have one of the boys take Mr Lark home.'

'Of course.' Kearney accepted his daughter's suggestion without murmur. 'Where are you staying, Mr Lark?'

'I have yet to find accommodation, sir.'

'Then you must stay here.' Elizabeth spoke before her father could reply.

'I could not do that.'

'Of course you can.' She cut off his protest firmly. 'And you would be doing my family a great favour. You are the only link we have to my brother. We cannot let you leave so quickly. I hope you can understand that.'

Jack felt something akin to shackles being placed around his neck. 'I would not like to put you to any trouble.'

'It is no trouble. There is plenty of room. But I must warn you, I will pester you. I have a thousand questions. You may yet regret agreeing to this offer.'

Jack found it hard to imagine he would ever tire of being in Elizabeth's company. 'I'd be happy to answer your questions if I can.'

Elizabeth nodded at his answer. She did not smile. Instead she turned to her father. 'I will make the arrangements. I expect Mr Lark would enjoy a bath and then the chance to rest. I will send one of the boys to collect him when it is ready.'

* * *

Jack eased his shoulders beneath the water and let its heat envelop him. He felt the warmth soaking into his bones, the sensation sending delightful shudders through his entire body. He stayed there, eyes closed, luxuriating in the feeling, letting it force away the chill that had been buried deep inside him for so long.

All at once he jerked awake. For a moment he was not sure where he was, the strangeness of his surroundings overwhelming senses that had been dulled by the warmth of the bath. Then he let himself relax as he once again understood what it was that his eyes were telling him.

He did not know how long he had slept. He could hear the sound of movement in the house, the quiet murmur of voices in far-off rooms. It was a reminder that he was a stranger.

He took a deep breath, then slid his buttocks forward and submerged his head. The water was cooler now, but still it felt good as it wrapped its warmth around him. Carefully he ran his fingers over the back of his skull. There was a bright flash of pain as he probed the raw centre of the spot where he had been hit. As far as he could tell, the wound was not severe, but still he saw dark blood in the water that swirled around him as he pushed his head free.

With his doctoring complete, he rested the back of his head gingerly on the bath's lip and closed his eyes once again. He knew it was time to get out, but he did not want the moment to end, and so he lingered, lazy and content in the water's embrace.

He was half asleep for a second time when the door to the room was snatched open. He jerked upright, the water sloshing noisily onto the sheets covering the floorboards around the bath. A servant was bustling around, her actions purposeful.

She deposited a bundle of clothes on a wooden stool set near the window before turning and starting to gather the garments that he had discarded liberally around the room.

She looked up as she felt Jack's eyes upon her. There was no smile before she turned away to continue her task. Jack's hands slipped into the water to cover himself. He cleared his throat as he prepared to ask to be left in peace.

'There's clean towels on the dresser, master.' The girl glanced in his direction as she finished collecting up his things. Her wide brown eyes showed no hint of embarrassment at his nakedness. 'And I have put some clean clothes on the stool for you. They were Master Thomas's, but they should fit you well enough.'

Jack squirmed as he saw her eyes drop and roam over him, comparing his physique to the clothes she had brought in. He saw the pause as her eyes settled on the thick scar on his shoulder, then again on the wider one on his side. There were a dozen other smaller ones, and he knew she saw them all.

'Is there anything else?' he asked drily.

The girl stepped forward, unconcerned at the gruffness she heard in his voice. 'Would you like me to help you up? Master Kearney said you were hurt.'

'No.'

'As you wish.' She smiled sweetly, yet made no sign of moving away.

Jack saw a mischievous glint in her expression as she looked down at him. The water was cooling fast and was starting to feel clammy against his skin. He could feel his body reacting to the cold and knew he now barely needed a single hand to cover his dignity.

'I'll manage.' He spoke a little more firmly this time. He had no intention of getting out of the water in front of her and revealing the effect it had had on his body.

'Very good.' This time she did move away, but only to deposit his clothes in a basket in the corner of the room. 'We will wash your things. In the meantime, you will find plenty of clean clothes in your room.' She picked up the basket, then turned back to face him once more.

For the first time, he caught a glimpse of a thin line of scars that ran along one side of her face, just under her jawline. To his eye, it looked like the type of scar left by a knife, but there were too many in the same spot for it to be that. He saw her eyes narrow as she worked out what it was he had seen.

'Will that be all, master?' Jack heard the hint of anger in the question.

'Yes.'

The girl turned on her heel, as if finally eager to leave the room.

'Heh!' Jack called out to stop her. 'What's your name?'

She did not turn to look at him. She paused for a heartbeat, or perhaps two, then left the room, closing the door softly behind her.

Jack sat on the bed in the room he had been shown to and savoured the solitude. He had only got out of the bath when he had been reasonably sure that the Kearneys' maid would not return. In truth, he was rather disappointed to have been left alone. The girl's refusal to tell him her name spoke of an interesting character, whilst her scars spoke of a past. He found he wanted to know both.

He glanced around the room. It was homely enough. Though it was devoid of all personal effects, there was no doubting the quality of its furnishings. The bed itself was a fine example of craftsmanship. He could not name the beautiful honey-coloured wood it was made from, but he did recognise the skill and the countless hours that would have gone into its manufacture. The rest of the room was fitted out with matching furniture of the same exquisite standard. The ensemble looked new, and he doubted it had been shipped all the way from Europe. That meant it had been made locally. Clearly the folk of the New World knew what they were about, and it appeared that the Kearneys had the means to buy the best the local craftsmen could produce.

From where he sat, he could see out over a pretty courtyard to the rear of the house. Much of the view was of other, similar buildings, but through one gap he could see all the way down to the great common at the heart of the city. It gave him some sense of his surroundings. Boston was not large, and he felt foolish for having got so completely lost.

His hand rose to touch the back of his head. He had been here for barely half a day before he had been attacked and beaten. It was a chastening experience. Now he was living on the charity of the Kearney family. He did not think it would last. Once the impact of the letters had diminished, and the questions they inspired had been asked, he would be out on the street. In the past, that notion would not have bothered him. Back then he had been full of ambition and spirit, the kind that believed that someone with the balls to dare to really live their life could accomplish anything. Now he knew better, such naive ambition left behind on the battlefields of the Crimea and beyond.

Even with ambition lost, he still nurtured a single truth. He might have stolen lives that were not his to own, but he had never once failed to live up to the identity he had assumed. He had fought and bled for his Queen and country, fighting the enemies of the Crown on the field of battle. And he believed he was damn good at it.

In battle, men looked to him for leadership. When the die was cast, he had stood firm and fought for those around him. The price he had paid to stay loyal to his salt had been high. People he had cared for had been lost and he had been left alone solely down to the choices he had made; choices that had seen him do the right thing, no matter what it meant for his own future.

He held his ability in battle close. It was the one honest thing left after his long career as a charlatan and an impostor. He had once been told that his talent meant nothing. He was not good; he was just lucky. It had not been his aptitude for the fight that had kept him alive; it had been chance. He was not special. He was not a hero. He was just a fool with a sword and a gun.

He did not agree.

He knew the fate of soldiers. After Solferino, he had seen the dead piled into great heaps; hundreds of bodies thrown together so that all sense of their humanity was lost. One day he knew that it could well be his body in such a grotesque place, his staring eyes that would disgust an onlooker. Such a fate did not daunt him or even frighten him. If he were not a soldier, then he would be nothing. He might have a talent for battle, or he might be the luckiest son of a bitch alive; it did not matter, at least not to him.

His hand traced over the patchwork quilt that was folded neatly across the bottom of the bed. It sat at odds with the rest of the room and its expensive furnishings. It must once have been a beautiful creation, but now its colours were faded, with loose threads where some of the stitching had come apart. Some places showed the ravages of moths, the holes and gaps big enough to slide a finger through.

He found himself wondering about its tale. It would surely have started its life as a possession to cherish and enjoy. A young girl might have made it in the years before her marriage, her excitement and anticipation finding their way into its long and careful construction. Then perhaps it had watched children come and go, a silent witness to the ageing of its creator. What secrets could it tell? What life had it seen before it had been consigned to a guest room, to languish half-forgotten and good enough only for the occasional guest to make use of it for a night or two before it was ignored once again?

He smiled at his own sentimentality. It was certainly not like him to sit and ponder such frivolous things, but it was hard not to recognise something of himself in the quilt. Like him, it was useful only when someone had need of its shabby and faded services. No one cared what story it had to tell, or what past it had lived. The world had just one use for a battered and scarred soldier, just as the Kearney family had just one use for a moth-eaten quilt.

With a sigh he got to his feet, stretching his spine straight as he did so. The nagging pain in the small of his back was there, just as it always was. A childhood spent hauling barrels in an East End gin palace had given him the ever-present ache. Years spent fighting had done little to improve it, and now it felt as if the lower reaches of his spinal column had been tied into one tight knot.

He walked across the room, kneading his back, until he reached his carpet bag, which had been left beside a large dresser. The few clothes he had had with him had been taken away, and he now saw that his wash kit had been laid neatly on a side table. To his relief, there was a single bundle left inside the bag. He lifted it out carefully, grunting at the weight, then turned and laid it on the bed.

The bundle was made up of a faded dark-blue uniform coat, with green epaulettes decorated by red crescents. It was crumpled and creased, and covered with dozens of rents and tears. Much of the cloth bore dark stains, and it gave off a ripe aroma of mildew and old sweat. He was not surprised to see it had been left behind when his other clothes had been removed. Even the most diligent servant would hesitate to try to repair something that was now little more than an oversized rag. Yet there was no sentimentality attached to the legionnaire's uniform coatee. He did not linger to feel the battered fabric or to dwell on the memories that the sight of it stirred inside him. For hidden within its folds was his revolver.

He had maintained it every day since he had purchased it back in London, oiling the chambers and keeping the mechanism greased. It was not new, its barrel pitted and scratched from long, hard use, but it was serviceable and he knew it would work when he needed it. With the revolver were its leather ammunition pouch and a second, smaller one containing its firing caps. He had two packets of fresh cartridges and one of brand-new caps, enough to see him through until he could find a decent gunsmith.

Handling the gun led his thoughts back to his time in London. The intensity of the affair with Françoise had taken him by surprise. They had been together for over a year; a year that had been filled with every amusement and entertainment money could buy. What had started as flirtation and amusement had turned into something more serious. Her absent husband had made the affair possible, but its flames had been fanned by the fortune Jack had brought back with him from the East. The money had allowed him to live a life he would never have believed possible, and he had revelled in it. But even a stolen fortune had its limits. When the money had run out, he had discovered that Françoise's ardour had a price, one that a penniless rogue from the East End could no longer afford.

The return of the cuckolded husband had finished what was left of the relationship. Jack still replayed the night he had stood with the man in the sights of his revolver. The urge to kill him had been almost overpowering. Françoise had begged him to do it, telling him that the murder of her husband was the only way Jack could remain in her bed. It was a tempting prospect, but he had failed to do as he had been told. The cuckold was spared, and he himself had been turned onto the streets with nothing but the clothes on his back and another bitter memory to add to his collection.

He forced the reminiscences away and checked over the revolver with practised ease, then lifted it into a firing position. It was good to feel its weight again, and he held the pose, his finger curling around the trigger as if he were about to open fire. The familiar action served to remind him of what he was, something he had forgotten when living the high life with Françoise. He had only remembered in the moment when he was about to gun down a man whose only crime was to have married an unfaithful harpy. He was no back-street killer and he was certainly not a la-di-da toff with money to burn. He might have been an impostor and a thief, but he was also a soldier. There was nothing else he knew how to be.

Footsteps sounded from just outside the room. He lowered the weapon, then busied himself burying it back in the folds of the scruffy legionnaire's coatee. He had it hidden from sight before the first knock.

'Excuse me, Mr Lark.' It was a voice he recognised immediately. 'I wonder if you have a moment?'

He checked the revolver was hidden before he stepped forward to open the door. Elizabeth Kearney was standing outside, her hands held demurely in front of her. A liveried servant lingered in the background, standing against the wall like a living bronze statue.

'I am sorry to disturb you so soon, Mr Lark.'

'It's fine.' Jack stumbled over the simple reply. 'Do you want to come in?' The offer was made awkwardly.

'Thank you.' Elizabeth smiled at his obvious discomfort, then stepped past him into the room. She perched on the edge of the bed, clearly at ease with her surroundings.

Jack paused at the doorway. He had caught a whiff of her perfume as she passed him. The delicate fragrance spoke of decadence and sophistication, neither of which made him comfortable. He glanced at the servant left outside, but the man was staring directly ahead. Still he lingered, uncertain as to the etiquette of whether to close the door or leave it open.

'Mr Lark?' Elizabeth was watching him. 'Are you sure you are feeling quite well?'

'Yes, I'm fine.' Jack decided to pull the door almost closed. 'How can I help?'

'I would like to know why you lied to me.'

Jack was startled. He had not known what to expect from Elizabeth's visit, but the blunt question still foxed him. 'What do you mean?'

The smile had left her face. 'I asked you about my brother's passing. You made up a tale. I could see it in your eyes.'

Jack was not sure what to say. He was also not sure where to stand. He took a pace closer to the bed, then thought better of it and instead took up a station near the window. 'I don't know what you mean.'

'I think you do, Mr Lark. You strike me as a man who knows exactly what you are doing.'

Jack could not help a short bark of laughter. 'If only you knew.'

'So tell me what happened.'

'I did.'

'No.' Elizabeth's words came out bound in iron. 'I suspect you think the truth is not for my ears. I am, after all, a poor brainless woman who could not possibly begin to understand the complex events of battle.'

'No. That's not true.'

'Then tell me.'

Jack paused and took a deep breath. 'Your brother died at the end of a bloody, awful battle. It might not have happened quite as I told you, but I made sure he didn't suffer. It was quick enough.'

Elizabeth was searching his face with her gaze, her eyes flitting from side to side. 'My brother . . .' Her voice failed, and she swallowed with difficulty before trying again. 'My brother is dead.' She forced the words out. 'Yet I find it hard to comprehend that he is truly gone. I expect him still to return.' She shook her head. 'I expect that makes me something of a fool.'

'You're not a fool, Miss Kearney. I don't think anyone would say that.'

She looked at him sharply. 'You should call me Elizabeth. We should not be formal.'

'Then you can call me Jack.' He tried to sound gallant. The attempt fell flat as he saw the sadness in Elizabeth's eyes.

'So will you tell me what happened, Jack? Sparing no detail?'

Jack looked at the floor. 'No.'

Elizabeth studied him for several long moments, then got to her feet. 'My father has asked if you would join him in his study when you are ready.'

'Very well.' Jack forced his voice to sound level and calm. 'I shall be down shortly.'

Elizabeth nodded at the answer, her lips pursed. She said nothing more as she left the room, closing the door softly behind her as she went.

Jack listened to her footsteps as she walked away. Only when all was quiet did he let out a breath he had not been aware he was holding.

Chapter Four

---

*J*ack sat in the comfortable surroundings of Kearney's study. It felt strange to be wearing his dead friend's clothes. They were baggy and fitted him badly, his former companion's build, even in the years before he had joined the Legion, considerably more bulky than his own leaner frame.

It was hard to imagine the hard-fighting legionnaire sergeant calling this place home. Once Jack had asked him outright what he was doing so far from Boston. He could still remember the amused expression on the other man's face. Kearney had found his true home in the ranks of the French army, one that stood no comparison to the comfortable life he would surely have led in this fine Boston town house.

Sergeant Kearney had been one of the best non-commissioned officers Jack had ever come across. Calm and capable in encampment, yet brutal and uncompromising on the battlefield, he had exemplified all that was good about the hard-bitten Legion. It left Jack wondering at the events that had seen him forsake America for a life in the service of a foreign power.

Time passed slowly as Jack waited for his host to appear.

He did not mind the wait. The study was warm and comfortable. A fire was burning in one corner, staving off the chill of the damp spring evening. The walls were covered with dark-wood bookcases stuffed full of leather-covered books in warm red and green tones. A fine desk occupied much of the room, its leather blotter covered with sheets of paper.

Only when he gave them a closer look did he realise that these were the letters he had come so far to deliver. Clearly Kearney had wasted no time in reading their contents. It would be an easy thing to approach the desk and take up the sheets of paper that he had carried for so long, yet Jack felt no urge to read them. He had a feeling he would discover soon enough what they contained.

The warmth of the room was making him feel sleepy, so he got to his feet and walked to the tall window that overlooked the square to the front of the house. It was lit by tall, elegant gas lamps, and in their light he could just about make out the blossom on the many trees that filled the periphery of the square. It felt decadent to look out and study his surroundings. He was warm and comfortable, in good, clean clothes. Outside would be chill, the air still damp from the rain. He stared into the dark and wondered how long it would be before he would be forced to spend his nights out in the elements.

'I am sorry for keeping you waiting.'

Jack turned as soon as he heard his host speak. He wondered how long the older man had been there. How long he had been watched.

'How are you feeling?' Kearney asked as he settled in the chair behind his desk.

'Hungry,' Jack replied honestly.

Kearney smiled at the answer. 'Hunger is easily remedied.

But I would like to talk to you for a while before you eat. Would you mind?'

'No, sir, not at all.' It felt natural to Jack to address Kearney respectfully.

'That is good of you.' Kearney lifted a hand and gestured to a chair opposite his own. 'Please do sit.'

'Thank you.' Jack was closer to the letters now, but he did not try to read them, focusing his attention instead on Kearney's face.

'I must thank you for what you said to Elizabeth. It was a kindness.'

'For telling her the truth?'

'Please, Mr Lark, I think we both know that whatever that was, it was most certainly not the truth.'

Jack tried to read Kearney's expression. He failed. He was not good at understanding other people, unless they were trying to kill him. He was also clearly not as good a liar as he had believed, with neither Kearney nor his daughter taking his tale of Thomas's death at face value. 'I think it's what your son would've wanted,' he said, mounting what he hoped would prove to be a more resolute defence than the one he had presented when questioned by Elizabeth.

'I think you are very much alike.' Kearney smiled at Jack's answer. 'You remind me of him, Mr Lark.'

'Jack. You can call me Jack.'

'Thank you, I would like that.' Kearney steepled his fingers and looked at Jack over them. 'I am glad you came to me, Jack, truly. You have done this family a great service.'

'I wanted to do it. Besides, I'd nothing else to do. Bringing you the letters, well, it gave me a purpose.' Jack spoke deliberately. It felt good not to lie.

'A purpose?'

'Something to do. Something good. Something useful.' He struggled to find the right words. 'After Solferino, I had nothing.' He offered a half-smile. 'Except your son's letters.'

'Yet it took you two years to bring them to me.'

'It's a long way. And I was delayed.' Jack could not help a hint of a smile creeping onto his face. The affair with the Frenchwoman might have finished badly, and cost him dearly, but he did not regret it.

Kearney nodded. He appeared to be able to read Jack with ease. 'You said my son handed you the letters. At the end.'

'He did.'

'Of all the things you have said, that is the one thing that has stuck with me.' Kearney leaned forward in his chair. 'At the end, he thought of us, of me.' He sat back. 'That means a great deal. After all that happened, I was not totally lost to him.'

'Why did he leave?'

Kearney did not reply immediately. Instead he lowered his steepled hands and fiddled with the letters strewn across his blotter. Then he sighed. 'There was a girl.'

'A girl!' Jack could not help the exclamation. The sergeant had not seemed the type to be distracted by anything, least of all a woman.

'I did not approve of the match.' Kearney stopped his fiddling and looked directly at Jack. 'She was Irish, from the North End.' He paused, then ploughed ahead. 'She was not from the best stock. I forbade Thomas to see her.'

'What happened?'

'He chose her over me. I cut him off for it. No more money. No home. No contact. I pretended he was dead to me.' The words made Kearney shudder. He lowered his gaze. 'Only now do I see what a fool I was.'

Jack wondered at the sanity of families like the Kearneys. They had every advantage life could give them, yet still they contrived to find ways to make themselves utterly miserable. 'What happened to the girl?'

'She died,' Kearney looked away, 'in childbirth. The place they were living was not good. It was not clean. I only found that out much later, from someone who chose to interfere. By then, Thomas had already boarded a ship for Europe. I did not know where he was, or what he was doing. Until I got that letter from the French authorities.'

Jack said nothing as Kearney made his confession.

'Did he despise me very much?'

Jack heard the pain in the older man's words. His friend had not spoken of family, but then Jack had not known him for long. He did know that as the sergeant lay bleeding and dying, his last thought had been the letters. He had never sent them, but he had written them.

'I would know the truth.' Kearney was watching him closely. 'I am sorry to have forced your hand earlier, but Elizabeth needed to hear that Thomas died easily. The thought of his suffering has tormented her.' He paused to make sure he had Jack's attention. 'Now I want the truth.'

'I told you. He was shot. He died quickly.' Jack repeated the same hackneyed lines he had used earlier. 'He did not suffer.'

Kearney absorbed the words. His expression did not alter. 'I want the truth,' he repeated.

'The truth? The truth is that your son is dead.' Jack did not bite at the lure as he had before. 'Is that not enough?'

'No. Not for me.' Kearney's stare was intense. 'I know it

should be, and I thank you for being prepared to spare me the details. If you do decide to tell me what really happened, then I shall not share it. Elizabeth will never find out, nor Robert. But I would know.' The final words were delivered in little more than a hiss.

Jack did not shy away from the intensity in the other man's gaze. 'I'll tell you, if that's what you want. But all of it. I'll not hold anything back.'

'Very well.'

'So be it. I've told you much of it already. We were running for our lives. The Legion was broken by then; just scattered penny packets of men trying to stay alive. Their cavalry came for us as we ran. We lost a lot of men.' Jack spoke in an even tone. 'Your son and I were together. We both knew they had us, but we kept running,' he shrugged, 'as anyone would do, I suppose. Then we spotted this ditch, if you can call it that. It wasn't much more than a muddy puddle really, but it was enough. It saved us, just before two of the bastards would have cut us down.'

He was watching Kearney closely. He registered no change of emotion in the other man's eyes. 'We were in that bloody ditch and they were going to kill us as easily as knifing eels in a barrel. Then Thomas . . .' Jack paused and offered a tight-lipped smile as he used the name for the first time, 'Thomas shot one of them down. The other rider charged us. He hit Thomas before either of us could do a damned thing about it.' He paused and lifted a hand to the side of his neck. 'He cut him here.'

For the first time, Kearney's expression changed, the slightest tic moving one eye. Yet when he spoke, his voice was calm. 'Go on.'

'He fell. He was bleeding badly and struggling to breathe.'

'But he was still alive?'

'Yes, he was then.'

'What happened to the Austrian?'

'I chased him down.'

'How could you do that? He was mounted. You were on foot.'

'His poor horse was knackered. It was bloody slow. I killed it with my bayonet. Then I pulled the bastard out of the saddle and wrung his neck. When that was done, and it took a fair while, I went back to your son.'

'He was still alive?'

'Just.'

'How long did it take?'

'Not long.' Jack held Kearney's gaze, daring the other man to look away. 'The poor bastard was choking on blood, drowning in it. I could see it was hurting him. He tried to speak, but he couldn't; the blood was filling his throat, what was left of it. That was when he gave me the letters.'

He held his breath for the span of a single heartbeat before he pressed on. He had said he would tell the whole story. He would not hold back, no matter that he would be damning himself in the process.

'I put them away. I didn't think about delivering them then; that came later. I just sat with him, listening to him dying. He didn't cry out, even though that wound would've been agony. I wanted him to die. I just wanted it to be over. But he was strong and we both knew it would take a long time. That was when he asked me.'

All emotion had drained from Jack's voice, so the words were coming out cold and flat. 'I knew what he wanted me to do.' He felt a moment's anger at having to release his demons, demons that brought with them the stink of blood and the reek of powder smoke. 'He was dying and it was fucking agony.' He paused, a moment's hesitation before he gave Kearney the sordid truth. 'So I did what he asked. I took his knife and I sank it into his heart.' The words came out as hard as iron. 'You want the truth? Well, here it is. I killed your son. His blood is on my hands.'

He fell silent. He had not let his eyes move from Kearney as he spoke. He had not lost control, even when confessing to the killing. His emotions were mastered, the memories secure in their cages.

Kearney did not react for some time. It was as if he were carved from granite. Eventually he spoke softly. 'Thank you.'

Jack ran a hand over his close-cropped hair, moving it back and forth in several short, sharp gestures. 'You don't have to thank me.' For the first time a trace of bitterness crept into his words. 'I'll leave immediately.' He made to rise.

'Stay where you are.' Kearney stopped him before he could stand. 'You don't have to leave.'

'I killed your son, yet you would let me stay as a guest in your house?'

'You did what he asked of you. That was a kindness, a great kindness. I can see what it cost you.' Kearney looked at Jack and smiled. 'I am in your debt. I do not think I can ever repay you for all you have done.'

Jack could not speak. He had expected to be damned for his actions. He had not expected to be thanked.

'I don't know what to say.'

'Then don't. I often find that saying nothing is better than speaking for the sake of it. There remains just one question that you haven't answered.'

'Which is?'

'What are we to do with you now?'

'Nothing. I have always shifted for myself. I can do so again.'

'Where will you go?'

'I'm told America is a big country. I'll find someplace to go.'

Kearney eased himself back in his chair. 'When I first asked you if you had served in the Legion, you told me you had not. Yet you were fighting alongside my son. How can that be?'

'I was there in an unofficial capacity.'

'That is an enigmatic answer.'

'It's the truth.'

'So you were not a legionnaire?'

'No, not for real.'

'But you have served?'

'Yes.'

'When?'

'Before. I was in the British army. I was a redcoat.'

'A goddam lobster!'

'Yes. I fought in the Crimea, then in India and Persia.'

'So you have experience of war?'

'I've been around, yes.'

'Then I know what I can offer you.' Kearney's lips twitched. 'I can offer you employment.'

Chapter Five

'What do you know of our politics here, Jack?'

Jack noticed the way Kearney eased himself back in his chair and appeared keen to talk of something new. He supposed it was preferable to dwelling on the tale of a son's death.

'A little,' he answered with honesty. 'I read of your troubles in the London papers before I left.'

'Troubles? Is that what London thinks this is?' Kearney appeared affronted. 'That seems rather a small word to describe the strife of a country that is falling apart at the seams. Troubles indeed. But at least you do know that we are a country divided?'

'I know you stand at the brink of civil war. North against South, isn't that what you are calling it?'

'You have it. You said we are at the brink of war. Well, I fear that is in the past. Fort Sumter has fallen and the first shots have been fired. It took the rebels thirty hours of pounding to force us to drop our flag. Thirty hours!' Kearney slammed his open hand down onto his desk to emphasise the point. 'It is a sad day when men born under this flag find it in their hearts to fire upon it.'

Jack was interested. The gang of lacklustre Irish toughs had mentioned the attack on Fort Sumter when they had accosted him earlier that day. He had not appreciated the significance of it then, but now he understood that it appeared to mark the opening of the war between two halves of the nation the world had come to know as the United States.

Kearney turned to a rack beside his desk and fished out a newspaper, which he offered to Jack. 'The *Advertiser* gives a good account of the events.'

Jack leaned forward and took the paper. Kearney did not give him long to study the front page.

'We must fight this war. Not because we want to subjugate the South, but simply because we must preserve the Union. The world looks to us! Or at least we like to think that is the case. Our forebears fought to be free of you folk,' he raised an eyebrow at Jack, 'something that cost us dearly, but look what it made us.'

Jack kept his expression neutral. His natural reaction was to recoil from such fervour as Kearney was displaying. He did not have much time for politics. One of his former masters had worked for British army intelligence and had been only too happy to involve himself in the political machinations of the day. The man had proven himself to be something of a devil, and Jack had been inveigled into two of his schemes, neither of which had turned out to his benefit. Such experience had taught him to be leery of men who found passion in the affairs of state.

'We don't bow to people here.' Kearney continued without pause. 'We are free of the past, free from tradition. And we are succeeding. We are thriving. Oh, I know we are a young country, a mere babe in arms compared to the rest of the world, but we are prospering and growing, adding new land to the

Union and expanding west.' He paused, his eyes glittering, his pride in the Union obvious. 'We are growing up fast. We are building factories, railroads and ports, whilst new cities are establishing themselves in every direction.'

He had inched forward as he listed his country's achievements. Yet now he stopped and sat back, almost slumping in defeat as he contemplated what he had said. When he resumed speaking, the passion was gone. It was replaced by sadness.

'We call ourselves the land of the free, but we all know that's so much balderdash. Half the people in the South are slaves. Slaves, Jack, you hear me. We boast of modernity, and we take such pride in our founding fathers' message, but it transpires that the phrase of which we are all so proud, "we the people", does not include everyone in this land.' Kearney shook his head. 'Those fools in the South are staining our land with this great hypocrisy of slavery.'

Jack was intrigued. He knew so little of the state of affairs in the country he now found himself in. The notion of slavery had not even crossed his mind. It seemed so old-fashioned, an idea that he had believed had been cast into the darkness long ago.

'Those damn Southrons.' Kearney spoke with obvious distaste. 'Down South, it is just like the dark days of old Europe. If they are left to their own devices they will build a new aristocracy, one just as iniquitous and unjust as anything your forebears ever concocted.'

'There are no slaves in the North?' Jack used the term carefully. He was trying to remember what the papers had said about the gulf opening up between the Northern and Southern states. He did know that the two sides were labelling themselves North and South, the split geographic as well as political.

'Do you believe in slavery, Jack?'

'I've not given the question much thought,' Jack answered honestly. 'We don't have slaves in England.'

'You must think on this question, Jack, you must. I will tell you that I find the very idea repugnant; this notion that one man can own another. I do my bit to make things better. I give them jobs where I can.' Kearney pointed at Jack. 'Have you ever seen as many coloured servants as I have here?' He shook his head and moved on before Jack could form an answer. 'Beecher Stowe shamed us all. Have you read *Uncle Tom's Cabin*?'

'No, sir.'

'You should do so at the first opportunity. I shall lend you a copy.' Kearney paused and eased back in his chair. 'We are the best experiment in history, Jack. We must not lose that, not in some argument over states' rights. What we have in this country means too much for that. We are the United States. United we stand and united we fall.'

'You said the South has attacked one of your forts. Does that mean you are at war?'

'I believe it does. South Carolina, Mississippi, Florida, Alabama, Georgia, Louisiana and Texas have all seceded from the Union, and I can only imagine that Arkansas, Tennessee and North Carolina will follow, maybe even Virginia too. They have formed the Confederate States of America and have even named Jefferson Davis as their president. Their attack on Fort Sumter proves that the time for argument and discussion is over.' Kearney spoke quietly and with great earnest. 'The South will only listen to force, so we must go to war. We have no choice if the Union is to be preserved.'

'So what will happen?' Jack asked.

Kearney sighed. 'I think we will invade. I don't like it, but those Southerners are giving us no choice. They are raising their own army. If we don't invade, why then, I fear they will try to take Washington. We cannot allow that to happen.'

He sat forward, some of his former enthusiasm returning. 'One battle, Jack, that is all it will take, one hard fight to whip those Confederates back into line. President Lincoln has called for seventy-five thousand volunteers for three months' service, and he has called out the state militias. Here in Boston, all five of our regiments are preparing to fight, and men from all over the state have answered the call to arms. In our ranks we have farmers, blacksmiths, merchants, labourers, mariners, piano makers, gentlemen, fishermen, sailmakers, hack drivers, carpenters, telegraph operators, fish dealers, bakers – why, we even have a whalebone cutter. All united behind our cause.' For the first time in a while, he smiled. 'Together we shall preserve the Union.'

Jack was impressed by Kearney. He seemed to have a firm grasp on the facts and delivered them well. It would be easy to be swayed by his arguments, but Jack had long learned that there was more than one side to a story; his experience in India had taught him that. Kearney's arguments were too black and white, his solution to the fracturing of the Union too simple. And there was one thing Jack disbelieved totally.

'You really think there'll just be one battle?'

'I do. I hate the idea, Jack, and by all that is holy, I wish there was another way, but both sides have gone too far.'

'And you think everything can be sorted out in a single fight?' Jack could not hide his dubiousness.

'I do. It will all be over by Christmas.' Kearney shook his head with what appeared to be regret. 'It has to happen like this. Oftentimes, the hard choices are the right choices.'

Jack was not so sure. He had never heard of a single battle deciding anything. To his mind, the two sides were about to embark on what could only be a long, protracted and bitter civil war. 'Does the North just have these state militias, or do you have a regular army?'

'We do, and it is under our control. But it is small, fewer than twenty thousand men, if that, and it is spread all over the place. Many of its officers have left to join the South.'

Jack's eyes narrowed at the first crack in the certainty of Kearney's arguments. Clearly a number of the regular army's officers believed in the Confederate's cause sufficiently to forsake their commands. He also noticed Kearney's choice of the word 'our'. It was a reminder that he knew nothing about the man sitting opposite him. Clearly he was a man of means, but there was surely more to him than wealth alone. Somehow, Kearney had power, something infinitely harder to tally.

Kearney spotted his reaction. 'I see what you are thinking, Jack. I understand their choice, indeed I do. A man must do what he thinks is right, even if he is misguided, even if he is wrong. The pull of family and loyalty to one's home state is strong.'

Jack resolved to do a better job of hiding his response to the other man's words. 'So there is no regular army to speak of. Who'll be fighting in this battle of yours?'

'Some of the regular regiments will be available, and we have the state militia, but the bulk of the army will be made up of volunteers; men brave enough to stand up and fight for this Union. Why, if I were ten years younger, I would be joining them myself. All Boston, indeed all Massachusetts, is filled with enthusiasm. Men are coming in from Salem,

Milford, Marlboro and Stoughton, and there are already enough to fill two or even three new regiments. Men are being lodged all over the city, forming companies as accommodation allows. Soon we will have an army the like of which this country has never seen, the like of which this *world* has never seen.'

'You have it all in hand, then.' Jack could not help the wry observation. He was not swayed by Kearney's passion.

Kearney was watching him closely. 'No, not everything is quite as we would like it. Our men have enthusiasm. They have a righteous cause, and they are determined to do whatever it takes to preserve the Union.' He looked Jack straight in the eye. 'What they don't have is experience.'

Jack finally understood why Kearney had summoned him, why he had been treated so well, and why he was sitting here, late in the evening, listening to one man's justification of the North's cause. He wondered when the older man had first decided upon this course of action, when the notion of Jack's usefulness had first emerged in his mind.

'And I have.' He stepped ahead in the conversation.

Kearney raised an eyebrow. 'Colonel Scanlon commands the 1st Boston Volunteer Militia. He and I have known one another for a long time and he needs experienced men. I can arrange you a place, if you agree. But you will need to decide quickly. They will be under orders to march to Washington any day now. Richmond, the new Confederate capital, is just sixty miles to the south of Washington. The South are sure to mass their troops there, just as we must do at Washington. Our men are to be some of the first to protect the city.'

'Your friend Scanlon, what makes you so sure he'll take me?'

'If I ask it, then it shall happen.'

'Why?'

Kearney offered something that could be considered a smile. 'Scanlon owes me. He will do as I ask.'

Jack heard the certainty in his host's voice. It was time to piss on Kearney's parade. 'I'm not looking to fight in a war that's not my own.' He was deadly serious. He was a soldier, but not a mercenary. The war between North and South was not his war, and he felt no compulsion to make it so.

His comment fell on deaf ears. 'My daughter's betrothed, Ethan, commands one of Scanlon's companies. You can serve there alongside my son Robert, who is one of Ethan's lieutenants.'

Jack did his best to remain composed as he absorbed several pieces of news at once. He could not help but wince as Kearney pronounced the rank 'loot-tenant', and there was a moment's disappointment as he learned that Elizabeth was engaged to an officer in the regiment Kearney was proposing he join. He also caught a whiff of something odd in the way the man's tone had changed when he mentioned his other son.

'Your new friend, Bridges, will be there,' Kearney continued. 'He serves as second in command to Scanlon, can you believe. Bridges is a good man, but he is most certainly not a soldier. Still, Scanlon must take him, I suppose. The men chose him, after all. I pity poor Scanlon, although I am sure he will have the need of a solid administrator to help with the day-to-day running of the regiment. Just so long as Bridges leaves the soldiering to others. That man should have more sense and know when to hold his peace.' Kearney shook his head. 'He never seems to know what is and what is not his concern.'

Jack was barely listening as Kearney described Bridges'

failings. He was now certain he was not being told the whole story. Kearney was as slippery as an eel. 'I doubt they need my assistance,' he said.

'Scanlon would value the addition of a veteran soldier to his command. I would make sure that you would not serve as a common private. I am sure we could do better: a corporal, perhaps even a sergeant.'

'You can stick a feather up my arse and call me general, but I'm still not doing it. I didn't come all this way to fight in another war. Not for you. Not for anybody.' Jack tried to rile the older man in the hope that it would lead them to the truth, but Kearney made no remark at his choice language.

'You will be paid. As a sergeant, you will earn seventeen dollars a month.'

Jack grunted as he heard the first bribe. It was no small temptation. He no longer carried a letter of credit from Cox and Cox, one of the British army's most respected agents, that he could lodge at one of the local banks. His funds were running out, the valuables he had stolen in Bombay all those years before converted to cash; cash that he had lavished on the Frenchwoman. But money alone was not enough to change his mind.

'My answer is still no.' He held Kearney's gaze.

'Is it not enough that you would be supporting the Union?'

'No.'

Kearney smiled with what Jack took to be genuine warmth. 'You are a shrewd fellow, Jack Lark.'

Jack could not help but laugh at the comment. If only his former commander, Major Ballard, could see him now.

Kearney leaned forward and picked up one of the sheets of paper that was strewn across his desk. He held it for a second, then tossed it towards Jack. 'Thomas mentions you. In his last letter.'

Jack was surprised. He had not known the sergeant for long before the battle that had claimed his life. But it appeared that even that short acquaintance had been enough to warrant inclusion in his letters.

Kearney's smile widened as he read Jack's reaction. 'He says you are a danger to one of his men, that you are on some form of mission. He also says that you frighten him.'

'Bollocks.' Jack could not help the reaction. He had seen Thomas Kearney in battle. He had not been frightened of anything.

'You can read it for yourself if you wish.' Kearney gestured at the page. 'He writes that you have a relentless purpose about you and that you let nothing stand in your way.' His smile faded. 'He also says that you fight like the very devil.'

'That was nice of him.'

'I want you to look after Robert.' Kearney changed tack without warning. 'He is not like Thomas. He is not cut out for this. But I could not let him avoid it; it would damage his reputation after we have won if he were to shirk the call to arms now. He has to do this, but I cannot bear to lose another son. I will not let that happen.' He spoke slowly and forcefully.

'You want me to be a bodyguard?'

'Yes.'

'No.' Jack stood his ground. 'If there's a battle, then there's nothing I can do to keep your son out of harm's way. No one is safe. No one.'

'I appreciate that.' Kearney's eyes narrowed. 'But I think I know you now, Jack. If you accept this responsibility, you will make sure you live up to it. Thomas saw this in you too, and your delivery of his letters confirms it. I shall pay you well, but I suspect you know that already.' He paused. When he continued, he spoke softly. 'It will also give you something else.'

'And what would that be exactly?'

'Purpose.'

The single word was left to lie on the table between them. Jack lifted his chin. It would be easy to deny Kearney's assertion that he needed such a thing. A few words would end the conversation and let him go free. He could forget the Kearneys and the impending war, and go anywhere he chose.

'Robert must never know,' Kearney continued, his eyes fixed on Jack. 'He has his pride, and knowing that I paid for him to have protection would be too much, I think. I would not wish to turn my son against me, but if that is what it takes, I will pay that price.' He was watching Jack closely. 'You would be doing me a great service. I would be in your debt. Make this happen and you can name your price.' He fell silent, but his eyes never strayed from Jack's face.

Jack felt the pressure. He did not care for it. He was his own man. He chose where he would go, what he would do. Kearney's arguments meant little. Save for one.

He might no longer wear the famous red coat of the Queen's army, but at heart he was still a soldier. Nothing had dented his pride at what he was; not even battle. He was a redcoat, and he could fight.

'What do you expect me to do?'

'Do your best to safeguard my son. After the battle, I shall arrange for his transfer to somewhere far from any further danger. Do that and I shall pay you handsomely.'

'How much?' Jack was a boy from the East End. He knew the value of money.

'One thousand dollars.'

He made a quick calculation. It was a good sum, enough for a man to live on in comfort for a year, perhaps two. But he knew how to tally his own worth. 'Five thousand. Two thousand now and the rest after the first battle.'

'Five hundred now and three thousand after.' Kearney did not bat an eyelid as he named the sum.

Jack sat back in his chair. He had not negotiated for his services before. He had always done what he had been told. Now he would serve of his own choosing and on his own terms. He knew which he preferred.

'What if I say no?'

'Then you will leave my house immediately.'

Jack glanced over his host's shoulder. It was darker now, and the rain was beating steadily against the window pane. But it was not the fear of a cold, wet night that made up his mind. It was the chance to be a soldier once again. To be what he was meant to be.

'Do you accept my offer?' Kearney had seen something change in Jack's expression, and now he pounced.

Jack paused, a final moment's hesitation, before he answered in a firm voice, 'I do.'

He had just joined the Union army.

Chapter Six

Faneuil Hall, Boston, Wednesday 17 April 1861

The streets were busy, even early in the morning. Jack and Kearney had left the town house on Beacon Hill for the short journey down to the heart of the old city. The walk had made it clear to Jack that Boston was a commercial centre. Its inhabitants were workers and they got about their business long before the sun began another battle to fight through the gloomy, overcast skies.

'Here we are.' Kearney called for Jack's attention. They had arrived in front of the grand building opposite the covered market that Jack had passed the previous day, before he had managed to get lost.

'May we pause here a moment?'

'Of course.' The older man agreed to the request with a half-smile.

Jack suspected Kearney was perfectly capable of spotting his unease. He made a play of looking around him, as if getting his bearings. In truth, he was beginning to acquire some sense of where he was, but it was not geography that was making him pause.

It was not the first time he had approached a moment like this. He remembered arriving to take command of a company of British redcoats in the hellish conditions of the British army camp at Varna as his new regiment, the King's Royal Fusiliers, prepared to embark on the final leg of their journey to the Crimean peninsula; and again at a remote British cantonment far up in the mofussil at Bhundapur. He was no stranger to this moment of uncertainty, but still it troubled him. He was about to step over the threshold of a new life. No matter his experience, the moment still unsettled him.

At least Kearney had accompanied him, so that he was not totally alone. A servant had been dispatched ahead of them to warn Jack's new commander that he was on his way. As they walked, Kearney had told Jack that just a single company of the 1st Boston Volunteer Militia were barracked on the upper floor of Faneuil Hall, the building they now stood outside. The rest were spread around the area in meeting halls, houses and any other space large enough to accommodate them.

Jack also now knew that the 1st Boston, as they were more commonly known, was organised into ten companies, named from A to K, omitting the letter J. Jack would be joining Kearney's son, and future son-in-law, in A Company, one of the regiment's two elite flank companies.

'Shall we go in?' Kearney was leaning on his stick and was clearly keen to get inside. The air was chill, and although it was not raining, it was a damp and murky morning.

Jack nodded and let the older man lead him through a set of narrow double doors that opened onto a wide staircase up to the first floor. The moment they opened, he heard the sounds of the men he had agreed to serve alongside, the hall full of the noise of raised voices and boots thumping on wooden floors.

He sensed something of a holiday atmosphere, with the men upstairs catcalling and cheering. The bright red, white and blue bunting tied to the banisters and the large Stars and Stripes flag hanging over the doorway leading to the main hall enhanced the feeling that some form of celebration was in progress.

With Kearney leading, they walked into the hall. It was a splendid place, with a wide gallery running around both sides and the rear of the room. Kearney had called it the Cradle of Liberty, and had told Jack something of the role it had played in the country's formation. Now the large public auditorium on its upper floor had been pressed into service as a temporary barracks, the grand space filled with temporary cots and the materiel of war, rather than the voices and opinions of citizens forging a new country.

Their arrival was noticed immediately.

'Good morning, sir.' A tall, broad-shouldered man walked towards them, his handsome face fixed in a warm smile of greeting. It was plain he had been waiting for them to arrive. 'I was told to expect you.'

'Good morning to you, Ethan.' Kearney extended a hand that was instantly shaken warmly. 'If you got my note, then you must know who this is.' He gestured towards Jack.

'I do indeed, sir.' The man turned his attention to Jack. 'I take it you must be Mr Lark.'

Jack did his best to force at least half a smile onto his face. 'I am.'

'Ethan Rowell, and I am pleased to meet you.'

'Jack Lark. Likewise.' Jack shook the hand that was offered whilst doing his best not to bristle with jealousy as he met the man betrothed to the beautiful and intelligent Elizabeth Kearney. Ethan Rowell was a good-looking man. He wore his dark hair long enough that it could be tucked neatly behind his ears, and sported a thin moustache paired with a goatee that did nothing to hide the cleft in his chin and left his strong jawline free of hair. He was clad in an immaculate dark-blue uniform that was perfectly tailored to show off his muscular physique. If first impressions were anything to go by, then Elizabeth Kearney was fortunate to have such a fine-looking fiancé.

'Ethan commands A Company.' Kearney took over the conversation smoothly.

'For my sins.' Rowell had an easy charm. 'Not that they take a great deal of leading. They are a fine bunch of fellows. Johnny Reb will turn tail and skedaddle as soon as look at them.'

'I shouldn't wonder if you are right, Ethan. The rebels have no trained militia. They will not stand against the likes of you and your men.' Kearney clearly liked his daughter's intended, and reached out to clap his hand on the man's shoulder.

'Ah, there is Robert.' Kearney's face lit up as he spotted his son standing with another man wearing an officer's uniform. 'Robert! A moment, if you please.'

Jack watched Kearney's son approach. It was hard not to stare as he saw his face for the first time. His features were at once both familiar and different, the similarity to his older brother enough to send a jolt running through Jack's body.

'Jack, may I present my son, Robert.' Kearney, the proud father, ushered the young man forward.

'Good morning.' Jack went through the polite routine. He could see that Robert was leaner than his brother, his slight physique lacking the robust, muscular build of a soldier. He wore a beard, but it was patchy and thin, so that glimpses of pale flesh peeked through on his cheeks.

'Good morning.' The greeting was returned with little enthusiasm.

Jack smelled the taint of whisky on Robert's breath. The younger man's eyes were bloodshot, with puffy grey bags underneath, and his uniform looked like he had slept in it. He could only be nineteen, perhaps twenty. It made Jack feel every one of his thirty-one years. He had never felt stronger, but he spotted something in Robert's gaze that made him feel very old indeed.

'Kearney, you rogue, to what do we owe the pleasure this fine morning?'

Jack's inspection of Robert Kearney was brought to an abrupt end as someone else spotted their arrival. A short, rotund individual with a bald head, a pointed ginger beard and an impressive pot belly was striding towards the group. He was dressed in the same blue officer's uniform as Ethan and Robert, but with a silver eagle on his light-blue shoulder straps. Jack made a mental note to learn the markers of rank quickly so that in future he would know just who he was speaking to.

'Scanlon, I had no idea you would be here.' Kearney greeted the new arrival with gusto. Jack noticed the way he straightened his spine and stopped leaning quite so heavily on his stick as the commander of the 1st Boston came towards them.

'I'm just checking up on these hoopleheads. I need to make sure they're not sitting around on their backsides.' Scanlon chuckled at his own remark.

Jack was fascinated by Kearney's reaction to Scanlon's appearance. It was clear from his body language that he was trying not to look like an old man in front of the colonel. There was something intriguing in the byplay that hinted of a long history between them.

'May I introduce you to Jack Lark, the man I told you about

in my note.' Kearney gestured towards Jack.

'So you're the Englishman who wants to join us?'

It was Jack's turn to straighten his spine. He noticed Scanlon's eyes slide over the scar on his cheek before they settled on his own gaze. 'Mr Kearney gave me the impression you would welcome my experience.'

'What I would welcome, son, is some new rifles. What I would welcome is the chance to get out of this city and strike at the rebel army before they grow too bold.' Scanlon thrust his bearded chin out as he came to stand directly in front of Jack. 'What I would welcome is for the politicians to stop spouting hot air and let us soldiers get on with this goddam war.'

Jack could not help smiling at Scanlon's forthright language. The colonel stood at least six inches shorter than Jack himself, but his lack of height clearly did not matter to him. His red-veined cheeks were beginning to flush scarlet, a colour that did not sit well against the copper-coloured beard that jutted out from his chin. Still, Jack welcomed the change in tone. Kearney spoke like a politician. Scanlon spoke like a soldier.

'Jack is an experienced redcoat, Colonel.' Kearney could not help a hint of condescension creeping into his tone. 'As I explained in my note, I think you would do well to recruit him.'

'I have enough men. Why do I want an Englishman telling me what to do?' Scanlon watched Jack for a reaction.

'His experience would surely be useful to the men.' Kearney spoke before Jack could reply.

Scanlon grunted at the comment. His gaze never shifted from Jack's face. 'You're right, Kearney, I do need men who know what they're about. What experience do you have, son?'

'Enough.' Jack was taking a liking to Scanlon.

'Enough!' Scanlon shook his head at the evasive reply. 'You

expect me to take you on the back of that?'

'Yes.'

'Then you're a fool.' Scanlon made no move to turn away.

'I fought,' Jack spoke evenly, 'in the Crimea. I fought in India and then in Persia. I was at the siege of Delhi and I was with the French Foreign Legion in Italy.' He met Scanlon's beady eyes calmly. 'I've killed so many men that I've lost count. How many of your troops can say that?'

Scanlon half closed one eye as he considered Jack's words. 'You think you're better than us, son?'

Jack looked around the room. Most of the faces were turned his way and, judging by the expressions on many of them, few were impressed to hear an Englishman declaring his credentials. He spotted a familiar trio among the crowd. The three Irishmen who had accosted him the previous day were glaring at him. One sported a fabulous black eye, while the tallest of their number, who he remembered was called O'Dowd, had fat lips tinted black. Jack hoped the wounds hurt. He turned his attention back to Scanlon.

'Better?' He shook his head. 'No, I don't think I'm better than you or your men, but I do know how to fight. I know how to lead men in battle.'

'You think you should be leading my men? You want to be officering here?'

'I could do so.' Jack kept his tone even. 'If there's a vacancy.'

'We don't need officers.' Scanlon's steady stare bored into Jack's skull. 'Men don't waltz in here and just take command. We're not in merry old England now. This is the New World. We vote for our officers here, choose them for ourselves. In our army, you don't get the fancy braid just because you're some rich man's son.'

Jack could not help but smile at Scanlon's choice of words. He had stolen his first identity partly to prove that a man born in the grimmest rookeries of east London could lead men just as well as someone born with enough money to buy their rank. Yet something didn't ring true, and he looked at Kearney and then at his son. 'Your men selected him?' He nodded towards Robert.

'Isn't that what I just said?'

'So the fact that he's a rich man's son had nothing to do with it?'

Scanlon's eyes narrowed, but a flicker of a half-smile crept onto his face. 'What are you saying?'

'I'm just asking a question, Colonel. I'm new to this part of the world. I'm trying to find out how things work.'

'They work just fine. It may surprise you, but we know what we are about. We have veterans in our ranks. Men like me who fought the Mexicans, or who served with the regulars when they were fighting the Navajo.' Scanlon held Jack's gaze. 'We're not perfect, not by a long shot, and we have our problems just the same as any other army.' He glanced at Robert Kearney for a moment before turning his attention back towards Jack. 'I have enough men, Mr Lark. I thank you for your offer to join us, but I don't have a place for you.'

He turned to walk away. This time Jack stayed mum and did not try to stop him. He had no intention of begging for a place. As much as he wanted to be a soldier again, he would not serve a man who did not want him.

But Kearney was not to be denied. He raised his stick so that it was horizontal and blocked Scanlon's path. 'Do not be hasty, Colonel. I think Jack would be useful to you.'

Scanlon's whole body stiffened. But he did not push past, and stood stock-still as Kearney leaned forward and spoke quietly into his ear. The exchange did not take long. Then Scanlon turned on his heel and faced Jack once more, his cheeks redder than before, although whether coloured by embarrassment or anger, Jack could not tell.

'Forgive me, son, Mr Kearney here reminds me of a vacancy that I must admit I had forgotten.' Scanlon sounded tired, and the apology was delivered with little enthusiasm. 'Captain Rowell's company needs a sergeant on account of a man being demoted due to his overconsumption of alcohol.' He paused and glanced at the ceiling for a moment before looking back down and continuing. 'The position is yours if you will accept it.'

Jack could see Scanlon suppressing the urge to say something more. The man was positively vibrating with barely contained emotion. Jack could only wonder at the power of the few words Kearney had whispered in his ear.

Kearney caught Jack's eye and nodded his head. It was clear what Jack was expected to do.

'Thank you, Colonel, I accept. You won't regret this, I promise.'

Scanlon's expression did not alter as his offer was accepted. 'I'd better not, son. Captain Rowell will issue the paperwork.' He delivered the instruction, then turned so that he could address the wider room.

'Listen up.' The place had been quiet, but now it fell utterly silent as every man listened to his colonel. 'This fine fellow is your new sergeant. I trust you will give him a proper welcome and obey him in every regard.'

Introduction complete, Scanlon nodded once to Kearney, then bustled away. The silence was broken before he had taken more than two paces, the men reacting to the new arrival with murmured conversation.

Chapter Seven

'Robert, why don't you introduce Sergeant Lark to some of the men.' If Rowell felt any reservations at welcoming Jack into his company, he did not let them show.

Kearney's farewell had been warm, but Jack had a feeling that was more because he had been able to force his will over Colonel Scanlon, rather than due to any affection for the man who had brought him his son's letters.

'Do I have to, Ethan? You know I only just got in.' Robert wiped a hand across his face. 'O'Connell can do it.'

Rowell was clearly used to his subaltern calling him by his first name. 'Don't you think you should do what I say?' He glanced at Jack, who stood straight-backed and silent as he watched the interplay between the two Union officers.

'Surely I deserve a little rest? We have that farewell party at the Sinclairs' tonight, or had you forgotten? You cannot expect me to turn up looking like this.' Robert waved a hand in the general direction of his face.

'Right, damn, yes, I had forgotten.' Rowell cast his eyes about him. 'Where's Francis?'

'Having breakfast with the Sinclairs. Their daughter is mad for him. They'll be engaged before we leave, I reckon.'

'Poor fellow, that girl has the worst buck teeth I ever saw.'

'Her father owns nearly all the mills in Massachusetts. I reckon you could tell her to keep her mouth shut whilst you count the dollars that would be coming your way.'

Rowell guffawed at the remark before catching Jack's eye. Whatever he saw reflected there was enough to stop his laughter. 'Go on then, Robert, you get yourself some rest and I'll take him to O'Connell. Just make sure you look presentable for tonight. I cannot bear to see Elizabeth disappointed, and she surely will be if her brother arrives looking like he just got up.'

He turned to Jack. 'Come with me, Sergeant Lark.'

Jack did as he was asked. It felt decidedly odd to be addressed as Sergeant. It was a rank he had never assumed, his career as an impostor seeing him only ever pass himself off as an officer. However odd it felt, he was sure he could get used to it. In reality it was sergeants who ran infantry companies. Good officers knew it and left them to it.

'Morning, Thatcher.' Rowell nodded a greeting to one of his men as he led Jack across the hall. 'These are good boys, Sergeant Lark,' he observed. 'They are all volunteers, and boy, are they keen to take the fight to Johnny Reb.'

Jack watched the men as they reacted to their captain. Most smiled and nodded a greeting, a fair indication that Rowell was a popular officer.

'Many of my boys are of Irish descent,' Rowell continued as they started to climb one of the sets of stairs that led to the gallery. 'We have one German company in the regiment. They barely speak English, so we kept them together. Other than that, there are a couple of Englishmen, a Scot, a fair few Slavs and even one Swede.'

Rowell stopped both talking and walking as they reached the gallery. The cots were more widely spaced here, and each man had much more room than those crammed into the main body of the hall.

'This is where the sergeants have made camp.' He spoke more quietly, as if somehow nervous of straying into the domain of his non-commissioned officers. 'And here is First Sergeant O'Connell.' He gestured towards a thickset man who was working on his kit with his back to the two men. 'First Sergeant, a moment of your time, if you please?' He made it a request, not an order.

O'Connell did not turn round immediately. Instead he carried on with what he was doing; only when satisfied did he react to his company commander's summons.

Jack found himself looking at the man who truly ran Rowell's company. From the glare on the man's face it was clear he did not relish either being interrupted or the presence of a stranger.

'Captain?'

'This is Lark. Scanlon made him a sergeant.'

O'Connell gave Jack no more than a cursory glance. 'We already have enough sergeants.' He addressed himself to Rowell, cutting Jack dead.

Rowell's discomfort was clear. 'Colonel Scanlon appointed Sergeant Lark himself.'

'And my answer ain't changed.'

Jack studied O'Connell whilst the other man's attention was focused on Rowell. He had noticed the Irish accent, something that Rowell's comments had had him half-expecting.

The company's first sergeant was a tall man, with powerful shoulders and thick arms. His face was pugnacious, with a squat, crooked nose standing proud above a thick moustache. On the upper sleeves of his jacket were three thick light-blue chevron stripes surmounted by a diamond. Jack assumed these denoted his rank, and for the second time he regretted not knowing the insignia of the army he had joined.

'Scanlon has given him the place. There isn't a damned thing I can do about it now.' Rowell hissed his reply.

'Scanlon don't know shite.' O'Connell looked ready to spit. 'You tell him we don't need no gombeen we don't know getting in our way.'

'Sweet Lord of mercy.' Rowell looked to the ceiling. 'Can you not just do as you are told this once? You know Sergeant O'Rourke is moving to B Company after his troubles the other day. We have a vacancy. Give it to Lark.'

'Now why would I do that?' O'Connell did not give an inch. 'You tell Scanlon that this is my company and that I ain't taking some fecker who happens to have licked the right arse.' He turned his back on his captain and went back to attending to his kit.

Rowell's mouth opened to continue the argument, but no words came out of his mouth. Instead he looked at Jack as if asking for help.

For his part, Jack was surprised by the lack of deference O'Connell had shown his captain, especially in front of a stranger. He had known sergeants who had been allowed to get too big for their boots, but he had never seen any of them treat their commander with such obvious disdain. It did not speak well of Rowell's leadership. To Jack's mind, that was unforgivable. Soldiers deserved the best officers, not just those who hailed from the right background or who looked the part.

'First Sergeant O'Connell.' He called for the man's attention in the clipped tones of an experienced officer. It was not a request.

This time O'Connell whipped around sharply. 'You talking to me?'

'Yes.' Jack was not fazed by the belligerent reply. 'You don't want me here, that much is clear. But your officers have decided that I can help the regiment. I intend to do just that.'

'Help, is it now? How can a dry piece of English shite help me?'

'I've fought before.'

'Where's that exactly?'

'The Crimea, India—'

'India!' O'Connell interrupted. 'That weren't fighting. That was just English bastards murdering any poor eejit that got in their way.'

'I fought in Persia, and I was at Solferino.' Jack continued calmly despite the interruption.

'And it looks to me like you lost.' O'Connell cackled at his own humour. 'At least some beggar got close enough to wipe his sword right across your face.'

Jack lifted his chin as the Irishman mocked his scar. 'I've got more. You want to see them?'

'So you were in the wars.'

'I know how to fight.'

'So you're a murdering piece of English shite. I still don't want you.'

'You don't have a choice.'

'Of course I have a choice.' O'Connell took a step towards

Jack. 'This is my company, and if I don't want you, then you ain't stopping.'

'That's not how I see it. I think you're stuck with me.' Jack didn't so much as bat an eyelid as O'Connell came closer. He could feel the dislike emanating from the man like a physical force.

'Are you sure you have that right now?' O'Connell leered into Jack's face. 'Are you sure you shouldn't be down south fighting with your bastard friends from there? The last I heard, the fecking English are siding with the damn sechers.'

'I'm in the right place. I think you need me here.'

'Need you, is it? Let me tell you this, gombeen. I don't fecking need you.'

'How many of your men have fought?'

'They're Irishmen, most of them anyway. They were born knowing how to fight.'

'But do they know how to form line? Do they know how to fire three shots a minute when the enemy are firing back at them?' Jack snapped the words at O'Connell. 'Do they know what to do when the other bastards stop shooting and charge?'

'They know how to fight,' O'Connell spat.

Jack felt spittle land on his cheek, but he did not flinch. 'This won't be some brawl in a damn tavern. This will be war.'

'It's still a fight.' O'Connell shrugged off Jack's assertion.

'No. It's not. If you think that, then you're deluding yourself.'

O'Connell scowled. 'We aren't babes. We don't need an Englishman wiping our fecking arses for us.' This time the denial was delivered with less force. Jack's words were having an effect.

'But are they soldiers? Because they're going to have to be, otherwise a lot of them are going to die.' He saw O'Connell's jaw clench, but the Irishman said nothing. Jack lowered his tone. 'You want me to go someplace else? Fine. I'll leave right here and now. But can you afford to let me go?'

There was silence. Jack wondered why he was arguing. If he was not wanted here, he had a feeling that one of the other fledgling regiments would welcome him. If Kearney was correct, the Union was mobilising quickly. There would be plenty willing to take on an experienced European soldier.

He opened his mouth to say as much to Rowell, but the words would not come. Something was tugging at his pride. For a reason he did not fully understand, he wanted to be part of this regiment. Perhaps it was the connection to his friend, or maybe Kearney had sold him a line by persuading him to agree to wet-nurse Robert. Maybe it was just his own belligerence. Whatever it was, he wanted to stay.

'You knew Kearney's son?' Jack changed tack.

'Thomas? Sure, I knew him. He was a fine boy. Not like his fecking brother.'

Out of the corner of his eye, Jack saw Rowell wince, but this was not the moment to think about Robert Kearney's deficiencies. 'He was in the French Foreign Legion, you know that?'

'I heard as much.'

'We fought together against the Austrians. He was one of the best damn leaders of men that I ever saw. If he were here now, he'd be saying the same as me. Your boys need more than courage. They need to be drilled. They need to be trained. And they need men who know what battle is like to make sure they don't get bloody slaughtered.'

'And you can make sure that don't happen?'

'No, but you'll be better off for having me here.'

'And why *are* you here?' Some of O'Connell's vitriol returned as he spoke. 'Thomas died, God rest his soul, yet here you fecking are, telling me what's what and making out you're some sort of fecking Finn MacCool.'

'I'm only here because of Thomas. I had something of his that I thought his family should possess. So I brought it to them. It was his father who suggested I would be useful to his son's company. I happen to agree.'

O'Connell grunted. He looked at Rowell, who had kept well out of the matter. 'You say Scanlon wants us to take him?'

'He does.' Rowell nodded firmly.

O'Connell's face twisted as if someone was force-feeding him a turd. 'Then who am I to stand against the good colonel's wisdom?' He glanced at Jack. 'You give me any shite, and so help me I will feck you over. Is that clear?'

'Abundantly.' Jack heard the concession being given. For better or worse, O'Connell would back down.

Jack had his place in A Company.

'Listen up, all of you. This is important.'

Despite his words, Rowell sounded unsure that what he had to say would interest the audience he had assembled. The commander of A Company had rounded up his two subalterns and all of his sergeants, and had sat them down in an anteroom for a briefing.

'Is this going to take long?' One of the sergeants, a grey-bearded fellow with a thick head of hair, asked the question.

'No, it won't take long, Sergeant Doherty. But you'll want to hear what I have to say.' Rowell paused. If he hoped for a more animated reaction, he was to be disappointed.

Jack sat on a chair at the periphery of the group. The leader of A Company did not impress him. In battle, Captain Rowell would be the man the company would have to look to for orders. There would be no questioning him then. When the enemy was close, Rowell would make the decisions that would see his men live or die, and his sergeants would have to back him to the hilt. If they didn't, then the company was surely doomed.

'Spit it out.' O'Connell was the only one still standing. He was by the door, his arms crossed and his face set like thunder. 'We don't have time to sit around here with our thumbs up our fecking arses.'

Rowell's face coloured. 'We have our first movement orders.' He blurted the words out. 'We leave tomorrow.'

Robert Kearney had been sitting comfortably, his feet resting on an empty chair whilst he picked crud out of his ears with his little finger. Now he sat up sharply, his boots hitting the wooden floorboards with an audible thump.

'We're leaving?' It came out as little more than a whine.

'Tomorrow.'

'Hell, we only just got here.' Robert's feelings were clear. 'Where are they going to send us now? If it's that island outside the harbour, then I won't damn well go. How do they expect us to get into the city from there?'

'It's not Camp Wightman, Robert.' Rowell paused and looked around the room. 'It's Washington.'

'Well, I'll be damned.' It was O'Connell who spoke first. His arms uncrossed and he stepped forward before leaning his hand on the back of a chair. 'Tomorrow, you say?'

'Yes. Just ourselves and K Company for now. The rest of the regiment will follow. Colonel Scanlon and Major Bridges will be with us, whilst Lieutenant Colonel Murphy will have command here. We will travel with the 6th and—'

'Now why are we going with that bunch of langers?' O'Connell snorted with disdain at the idea. 'The 6th are nothing but a pile of shite.'

Rowell had to swallow hard before he dared to continue. 'Those are the orders. We parade first thing, with the 6th.' He paused and glanced anxiously at O'Connell before carrying on. 'There will be a ceremony. The Governor will give a speech. General Butler will be there too. We have the honour of being some of the very first regiments sent to secure the capital.'

Jack presumed the 6th were another regiment of volunteer militia. He was impressed. If he understood matters correctly, it had been just a few days since the militia had been called out, yet already they were ready to march to defend the capital against the Southern army.

'Why just two companies?' he asked. Every face turned to look at him.

'We're the best-trained companies in the regiment.' Rowell's chest puffed out as he made the bold claim. 'The enemy is just the other side of the Potomac river and could attack Washington any day now. If they do, it will be down to us to save the capital.'

'If we get there in time.' Jack could not help the laconic reply.

Rowell smiled any hint of doubt away. 'We'll be there in time, Sergeant Lark. The Governor has arranged for us to board a train in the morning after a little celebration on the common.'

Clearly, the idea of a grand send-off sat well in Rowell's mind. To Jack's eye, the commander of his new company looked the part, but he appeared to be lacking any substance behind the fine facade. His two lieutenants seemed even less ready to play the parts they had been assigned. Robert Kearney was more interested in what he had picked out of his ear, and the company's other lieutenant, a bespectacled young man who looked more like a clerk than a soldier, spent most of his time gazing wistfully out of the window. Only the sergeants had really given Rowell their fullest attention.

They too were a mixed bunch. First Sergeant O'Connell, the most senior non-commissioned officer in the company, had four other sergeants to assist him. Jack was now one of them. He had yet to be introduced to the other three, but judging by their expressions when they had turned to stare at him, not one of them was delighted to see him there.

'We'll travel to Baltimore overnight.' Rowell paid little attention to his two lieutenants and spent most of his time looking rather anxiously at First Sergeant O'Connell. 'From there we'll go to Philadelphia, then on to Baltimore and finally to Washington itself.'

Jack listened carefully. The place names meant little to him and he added a map to the list of important information he required. Already that list was growing. Yet he had no doubts. Despite the welcome he had received from O'Connell, it felt good to be back in an army, even if it was one that was foreign to him.

Rowell was still talking through the arrangements for the following day, but Jack found his attention drawn to Robert Kearney, who was now cleaning his nails. He worked methodically, moving from one to the next, but Jack could see his hands trembling. Only time would tell whether it was from excitement or barely concealed fear. Jack knew he would have to find out which. He had accepted the place in the company to comply with Kearney's request to look after Robert. He would need to know a lot more about the young man if he was going to have a chance of keeping him safe.

'Sergeant Lark?'

'Sir.' Jack had not seen Rowell's attention shift to him, yet he gave no hint of surprise in his steady reply. It had been a long time since he had served in the ranks, but he still knew how to deal with an officer.

'We cannot have you looking like that at the parade tomorrow. We've got plenty of uniforms in the store.' Rowell smiled. 'It's about time you were one of us.'

Jack stood in the side room and smoothed out the creases in the waist-length uniform jacket that he had just put on. It had clearly been in storage for a while, and it would take him some time to make himself look as presentable as he knew a sergeant should.

It felt good to be wearing a uniform again. The 1st Boston's was a smart dark blue, with a single row of brass buttons down the front of the jacket. Jack's bore the three light-blue chevrons of a sergeant on each sleeve. The trousers were dark grey, with a single red stripe running down the seams. He had kept his own boots, declining the chance to take a new pair, knowing full well that it would be impossible to break them in before they left. He had been an infantryman for long enough to know that of all his equipment, his boots were the most vital. He had no intention of starting his time in the Union army with feet rubbed raw.

The uniform was completed with a soft forage cap that reminded him of the kepi he had worn in the French Foreign

Legion. There was no mirror in the small room where he had changed, so he did his best to check his appearance in the reflection he could make out in the window glass. It felt odd not to be dressed as an officer, but overall he was pleased with how he looked. The uniform might not be as smart, or as well tailored, as that of a British army officer, but at least he looked like a soldier once again.

Chapter Eight

———◆◆◆———

'Are you ready, Sergeant?'

Jack smiled at the use of his new rank. Robert Kearney had arrived to collect him from his changing room. The young officer had attended to his own appearance and was wearing a clean jacket, his hair slicked back against his skull. He no longer looked like an exhausted rake come home from a night of debauchery. Instead he was the fresh-faced subaltern Jack had expected. He also looked dreadfully young.

'How old are you, Lieutenant?' Jack asked as he shut the door to the anteroom behind him.

'Nearly twenty.'

Jack smiled at the reply. At Robert's age, he himself had been a redcoat for over a year. They had been good, simple days, when his life had been mapped out for him. He did not regret the chaotic world he had lived in since, but a part of him longed to be back in a time when past decisions did not dog his every step.

'So tell me about the company.' He shook off the musings and focused his attention on the business at hand. It was time to get to work.

'Well, we have eighty-one privates.' Robert led them into

the main body of the hall. 'We had eighty-two, but we lost one when his mother came to take him home.'

Jack nodded. He was slowly becoming accustomed to the nature of his new unit. It was a homespun affair and little like the company of redcoats he had first joined as a fresh recruit over a decade before.

'We have two musicians. Then there are eight corporals and four of you sergeants.'

Jack was keeping tally. With O'Connell, the two lieutenants, and Rowell as commanding officer, the company numbered just under one hundred men. Kearney had told him that there were ten companies in total, so that meant that the 1st Boston comprised just about a thousand men.

They were back in the main hall now, and he looked around him. The temporary barracks smelled just as he remembered. The stale odour of sweat and too many bodies living in a confined space lingered, even with the men gone. Underscoring the aroma was the residual stink of boot blacking, damp clothing and gun oil.

'The men are at drill,' Robert explained.

'Where do you do that?'

'There's enough space in Dock Square. We drill there every morning. We draw a fair crowd too.'

'You must be good.'

'We're getting there.' Robert looked at Jack warily. 'You want to see?'

'Absolutely.' Jack smiled at the polite question. He was a sergeant talking to an officer, yet anyone listening to the conversation would be hard pressed to believe the slight young man was superior to the taller, leaner one with stripes on his sleeve.

It was cold outside. The morning air was damp and the

heavy grey skies promised only more rain. Jack could smell the faraway aroma of baking bread, and from all around him came the sounds of a busy city at the start of another day.

He noticed the looks sent his way as he followed Robert out of Faneuil Hall. It was the way in which civilians regarded soldiers, a mix of admiration and distaste. It had been a while since he had felt such a gaze, and he could not help but straighten his spine and return the stares with the calm, knowing expression only a fighting man could possess.

It was a short walk, and he could hear the sounds of commands being shouted long before he caught sight of the men. He saw immediately that Robert's claim that the company drew a fair number of spectators was false. No more than half a dozen young boys were standing watching. They formed a loud group as they mimicked the soldiers, and to Jack's eyes were making a fair fist of showing up the company of blue-coated troops attempting to comply with the orders that were being shouted their way.

He could not recall seeing a body of men as poor at their drill. Not even raw redcoats made such a mess of the simple commands the company's other lieutenant was reading from a manual. A few of the men had resorted to shoving a scrap of paper into one boot, an attempt, Jack guessed, to help them tell their left from their right.

It was not just the drill that failed to inspire. At least half a dozen of the men looked old enough to have fought in the war of 1812, if not the one fought for independence from Britain. Many of the others looked so young that they would not have stood out had they been playing with the group of boys aping the soldiers' movements. A couple of the men were obviously struggling to move with anything approaching a military demeanour, and at least one looked to be on his last legs.

Jack stopped Robert by tugging on his arm. 'You sure this lot are one of the two best-trained companies in the regiment?'

'Oh, yes.' Robert's eyes narrowed as he acknowledged Jack's scornful tone. 'We may not look like much to a grand old soldier like you, but I bet Johnny Reb will turn tail once he sees what he is up against.'

Jack searched Robert's face for some sign of irony. He saw nothing but the complacent gaze of a bullock waiting to be led to the army's butchers. 'You really believe that?'

'Sure I do.'

Jack let it go. He knew he would only be wasting his breath. He turned his attention to his new company. The officer with the manual had just ordered them to form a column. Judging by the confused melee in front of him, it was not a manoeuvre A Company had perfected. Jack searched the ranks and saw that neither O'Connell nor Rowell was present, nor were any of his fellow sergeants. He wondered if that could be the reason why the men were performing so poorly.

He left Robert and strode closer to the men, who were barging each other out of the way as they fought to form up. The performance was accompanied by shouts and bellowed curses. It took nearly a minute for any sort of cohesion to emerge from the chaos.

'Forward, march!'

The command was called out with little conviction. It was all Jack could do not to snort as the men started to shuffle forward in what he could only describe as a half-arsed amble.

He approached the lieutenant commanding the drill. The bespectacled officer glanced up from the page he was following.

'Are you one of mine?'

Jack could only smile. It could not have been more than an hour since he had sat in the same briefing as the junior officer. 'Yes. I'm the new man.'

'Ah, yes, of course. Kearney's Englishman.'

Jack frowned at the title. He was no one's man, but this was not the time to pick an argument with one of his new commanders. 'We weren't introduced properly.' He held out a hand. 'Jack Lark.'

The lieutenant took a moment to balance his textbook in one hand, then shook Jack's with a limp and unenthusiastic grip. 'Francis Clancy.'

Jack did his best not to react to the man's damp paw. Instead he turned his attention to the manual. 'What book is that?'

The lieutenant turned it so that Jack could read the title: *Rifle and Light Infantry Tactics*, written by a brevet lieutenant colonel called Hardee. He had never heard of it. He could not imagine any of his former sergeants relying on a book. They had known every facet of the drill they taught, every detail imprinted deep in their souls. He wondered what they would make of A Company.

He looked back towards the men. They were strolling quite happily down the street that he reckoned led towards the docks. He turned back to look at Clancy, who he supposed would give the order for them to halt before they disappeared. The lieutenant, however, was deep in thought, his finger tracing the lines on the next page of the manual.

'Lieutenant?'

'Hmm.' The officer did not look up.

'Say something to the men, sir, even if it's just goodbye.'

'What's that?' Clancy finally looked up and spotted his men moving down the slope. 'Oh, hell and damnation. Stop, you fools! You there, stop!'

The men came to a shuffling halt, those in the rear ranks turning to stare balefully at their officer, who was now gesticulating furiously at his fellow lieutenant. 'For goodness' sake, Robert, could you not have stopped them?'

Robert was leaning against a lamp post as he watched his company with an amused eye. 'I thought you had them under control, Frannie.'

'Why the devil would you think that?' Clancy squawked.

'About-face.' Jack muttered the command quietly.

'What's that, Lark?' Clancy matched Jack's quiet tone.

'Tell the men to about-face, Lieutenant.' Jack tried not to smile.

The officer looked at him, his brow furrowed as he caught a whiff of Jack's amusement. 'We are learning, Sergeant Lark. We do not claim to know it all; that is why we are practising, why we are *all* practising.' He looked away. 'Company, about-face!' he called, then smiled at Jack. 'But I thank you for the advice. I rather like what you said just now. I think I shall make a note of it. It will work very well in my journal.' He dug into a pocket and fished out a notebook and pencil, which he laid on his open drill manual before scribbling a quick note.

'Heh, Lieutenant, are we done?' The voice came from the rearmost rank.

Jack located the man who had called out. It was O'Dowd, the tall Irishman with blackened lips courtesy of Jack's fist.

'Give me a moment longer.' The officer slipped his notebook away and resumed scanning the pages of his manual.

The men were clearly not of a mind to wait. O'Dowd and a couple of others fell out and started to walk back to their starting point.

'You men there.' Clancy spotted the movement. 'Stay in the ranks.'

'For the love of Christ, sir.' O'Dowd ignored the command. 'We've been marching back and forth for bleeding ages. Can we not have a rest now?'

Jack watched the exchange, fighting to hold his tongue. The instinct to snap at the soldier was almost irresistible. But these were not yet his men and so he kept quiet.

'I have not dismissed you. The manual is very clear on that point.' Clancy peered back at the text. 'I must give you the command to break ranks.'

'Well, sir,' O'Dowd did not bother to look at his officer as he walked past, 'you shout out the command when you're good and ready, and you'll find me and the boys have obeyed it already.'

The Irishman found himself a spot, then sat down, his equipment and musket dumped unceremoniously on the ground. The rest of the company took it upon themselves to follow suit.

'Do you always just let the men do what they want?' Jack asked the pair of young lieutenants.

'Not always.' Robert seemed blithely unconcerned by the men's actions.

'And you don't feel the need to tell them not to sit down whenever it pleases them?'

'Not as a rule.' Robert smiled at something he saw in Jack's expression. Jack was saved from saying anything more as First Sergeant O'Connell appeared, walking towards them with two large paper bags in his arms.

'What have you got there, First Sergeant?' One of the men had spotted O'Connell's arrival.

The first sergeant walked past his two officers without acknowledging their presence and made for the men lounging on the ground, his face creased into a smile. 'A little gift from O'Donahue's bakery.' He handed the two sacks to a couple of the men who had got to their feet as he approached. 'Something for the boys.'

With his treat delivered, O'Connell finally turned his attention to the officers. 'What's the matter with you pair?'

'The drill did not go well, First Sergeant.' Clancy peered over the top of his spectacles as he answered, before pushing them higher up his nose with his forefinger. 'Not well at all.'

'Well, never mind. Let the boys have their buns, then try again.'

'Would you care to stay and assist?' Clancy could not hide a trace of nervousness at making the request.

'I'm sure you'll do just fine without me.' O'Connell barely looked at his lieutenant. He clapped his hands. 'I'll let you get back to work.'

'First Sergeant O'Connell.' Jack spoke only after O'Connell had started to walk away.

'Sergeant Lark.' O'Connell gritted his teeth as he replied.

'The men are in dire need of instruction.'

'The men are doing just fine.'

'How would you know if you are not here?'

O'Connell shook his head. 'You still don't get it, do you?'

'Get what?'

'What we are. What we are about.'

'What *are* you about?' Jack could not help the snap in his tone.

'My boys are volunteers. They're not forced to fight. They're not here out of desperation. They're here because they love this country. They're here because they believe in this cause.'

'That's not enough. Belief won't help you on a battlefield.'

'Won't it now?' O'Connell raised an eyebrow as he questioned Jack's statement. 'It helped us beat you damn Limeys back in the day. We hadn't had much training then either.'

'Your men need to be trained if they are going to fight.' Jack spoke with conviction. He did not agree with O'Connell's argument.

'Oh, they'll fight. We'll just blunt their edge if we train them too hard.'

'Blunt their edge!' Jack could not help his voice rising as he reacted to the first sergeant's complacency. To his eyes, A Company had as much edge as a sloppy shit. 'How are they going to fight if they don't know what they're doing? This won't be some brawl on a street corner.'

'They know what to do. They don't need us telling them how to stand up to those Southron bastards.' O'Connell took a few steps so that he stood nose to nose with Jack. 'Let us get something straight, Sergeant Lark. This is my company. We're not some child-murdering machine like the fecking English. We're Americans and we're damn proud of that. You might not like the way we do things, but—'

Jack stopped O'Connell in full flow. 'It's not about liking.' He was shorter than his superior, but he did not flinch from the challenge and glared at the man, his words coming out as hard as iron. 'When the enemy marches against you, and your men are shitting themselves in fear, it's discipline that'll hold them in the ranks and keep them doing their job. They need to know what to do without thinking, so that when half of them are stretched out on the ground, the rest of them will keep on fighting.'

'Oh, my boys'll stand. They won't turn tail and run like your lot did back in the day.' O'Connell glanced across at the troops. Every man in the company was watching the exchange, eyes riveted on the two sergeants, who looked just about ready to brawl. 'So you keep your advice to yourself from now on. Do what you're told and keep your fecking nose out of running my company. Is that clear, Sergeant Lark?'

Jack said nothing, even as O'Connell glared at him for several long moments before turning and marching away. He could almost hear the two lieutenants give a sigh of relief as their uncompromising non-commissioned officer left them. O'Connell was a man sure of his own mind and secure in his ability to dominate anyone who confronted him. It made him dangerous. For Jack knew him to be wrong. Courage and belief in a cause only went so far, and the men would need more than that when they fought. Much more.

Despite O'Connell's words, Jack would not hide from what he saw had to be done. He would do his damnedest to get A Company ready, even if that meant going toe to toe with the first sergeant.

He turned and looked over the men sitting on the ground taking a barely earned rest. If they were amongst the Union's best-trained troops, then God alone knew what Lincoln's new army of seventy thousand volunteers would be like.

He could not help sighing as he turned to address the two lieutenants. 'Mr Clancy. Mr Kearney. Shall we get the men back to their feet?'

It was time to start making his mark.

Chapter Nine

Jack sat in the quiet storeroom, savouring a moment's peace. It was hard to believe he had been in Boston for less than two full days. Yet here he was, in the midst of a volunteer army about to go to war for reasons he still didn't fully understand.

The rest of the morning, and much of the afternoon, had been spent drilling the men. They had not enjoyed it, and he was pretty sure he was already hated by at least half of them, but he had begun to see some improvement, the first sight of what they could be emerging from the lacklustre, lazy performance he had witnessed that morning. Despite their quickness to disobey their superiors, he was certain the men could be as good as those in any of the other companies in which he had served. They just needed to have some discipline instilled. When they had that, they would take some beating.

He was also beginning to understand O'Connell's fierce affection for his men. They had a spirit he could not recall having seen before, elan that even the hard-bitten legionnaires he had fought alongside at Solferino would be hard pressed to match. O'Connell had defined it as belief, and Jack was starting to see just what he had meant. The men truly believed in what they would be fighting for. Not one of them was there out of desperation, one of the prime motivations that led many a new redcoat into the ranks of the British army. They were there because they wanted to protect the Union, a cause they served with obvious devotion. If they could just learn *how* to fight, they would be one hell of a unit.

The men had eaten a good dinner at the end of the day; the company was well supplied by local tradesmen keen to be seen to be doing their bit to support their soldiers. They were now at leisure, but Jack had been dispatched to the warehouse in a side street not far from Faneuil Hall where much of A Company's equipment was housed. He had been ordered to check through the latest deliveries and tally them back to the company's books.

It was a task he remembered well from his time as a company captain, and one he had done all he could to avoid back then. He could read and write passably well, a legacy of his mother's rudimentary instructions and the generosity of the colonel of his first regiment, but it was not something that came easily, and he knew he was lamentably slow, even all these years later. But he was pleased to be given the task. It would give him a chance to go through the muster records and begin to learn the names of the men in his new company, something that would be of paramount importance if he were ever to be effective in his new rank.

Now that he had arrived in the company store, it appeared that he had a Herculean task ahead of him. A bewildering array of equipment had been delivered and the storeroom was crammed full of cases, crates, sacks and barrels. He was surrounded by new uniforms, ammunition, bayonets, scabbards, overcoats, pouches, cooking pans, haversacks, canteens, mess plates, blankets, boot polish, rope, leather belts, brushes and the first deliveries of field rations, all of which needed sorting and checking. It was a huge task, but not one that he would be left to complete alone.

'Ah, there you are.' Robert Kearney opened the door and came inside.

'Here I am.' Jack was pleased to see his officer. He had been told to wait for Robert, but a part of him had been dubious that the lieutenant would turn up now that evening had arrived, and with it a good number of invitations to dine or attend functions organised by the good citizens of Boston to fete the men who now found themselves in uniform. 'Did you not have somewhere else to be?' He half remembered a comment about an event at some respectable house that evening.

'I decided not to go. I cannot bear to see Frannie mooning over the Sinclair girl. It's like watching a starving man looking at a hog roast he is not allowed to eat.' Robert laughed at his own joke as he walked to join Jack at a table pushed into one corner of the room. He sat down heavily, then stretched out his legs and placed his feet on a conveniently located chest. 'Besides, Ethan wants me to look at the new rifle muskets and make sure we got what my father paid for.'

'Your father paid to equip the company?'

'No, but he put money in the right places and spoke a few words of encouragement into the right ears. He's good at that sort of thing.'

Jack heard something in Robert's tone that made him believe the son did not necessarily approve of the father's ways. 'What does your father do?'

Robert chuckled. 'Only the devil knows. Or at least I'm sure he has a better idea than I damned well do.' He shook his head. 'Father is a merchant. That much I know. But quite what he buys and sells is a mystery to me.'

'Come on, you can do better than that,' Jack pressed. He wanted to know what manner of man he had agreed to serve.

'Very well. I told you he buys and sells . . . Well, let's just say he trades in more than simple cargos. Secrets are his thing. Rumour and hearsay can often cost as much as a whole ship-load of cotton if you know the right people. Have you heard of this Pinkerton fellow that Lincoln is so keen on?'

'No.'

'Pity. But then few people know the man. Father is a correspondent of his. Men like that are the true power behind the throne here. Not that we have thrones, of course, but you get my meaning.' Robert chuckled at his own dry humour.

'So he has influence?' Jack was not bought by such easy charm.

'Oh, he has that. Even the Governor listens to him. He's got himself appointed to so many goddam committees that if you ask anyone in Boston, they'll tell you he pretty much runs things around these parts. That gives him power.' Robert smirked. 'He had enough influence to get you your stripes.'

Jack glanced at the chevrons on his sleeve. 'You don't approve?'

Robert laughed off the question. 'I neither approve nor dis-approve, my friend. I couldn't care less who is in the company.'

'You should.'

'Should I?' Robert raised an eyebrow at Jack's certainty. 'I'm not a soldier and I've no intention of being one for any longer than I need to be. I'm only doing it at all to keep Father happy. He thinks it'll harm my future if I'm not seen to join the great cause, if I'm not a hero. But if you ask me, the sooner this is over, the better.' He paused and his expression changed. 'I'm not my brother.' The words were spoken softly, so that Jack only just heard them.

'Your brother was a good man. He was my friend.'

'Well, he wasn't mine.' The confession was given through gritted teeth, and Robert looked at Jack with eyes that blazed with barely contained passion. 'He was a hero, my brother. He could do anything and everything. My father and sister doted on him, as did my mother before she passed. Can you imagine what that's like, to be the younger son, to have to live up to your brother's standards and spend your whole goddam life in his shadow?' Jack heard the pain of a lifetime's worth of angst in Robert's voice.

'You're not in it any longer,' he said.

'Oh no, I'm not now.' Something of the former charming smile returned to Robert's face. 'And you know what, I reckon that's a whole lot worse.'

'You're right. Now you cannot hide.'

Robert puffed out his cheeks and exhaled as if absorbing a blow to the gut. 'You're not pulling your damn punches.'

'I don't have to.' Jack offered a half-smile. 'I am no one's brother, nor am I anyone's son. I'm just me.'

'I envy you.'

'Well, don't.'

'Is that why you're here? Because you've no place else to go?'

Jack inclined his head to acknowledge the truth in Robert's words. 'Partly. And partly because you buggers need me.'

'Do we indeed?' Robert laughed off the seriousness in Jack's words. 'Well, don't let Scanlon hear you say that. He thinks we can win the whole damn war all by ourselves.'

'You won't. If Scanlon believes that, he's a fool.'

Robert made a face of mock surprise. 'If you'll allow me to give you a word of advice, keep that opinion to yourself. Scanlon does not take kindly to hearing anything but praise for his precious regiment.'

'Maybe he needs to hear the truth.'

'Maybe he does.' Robert looked at Jack as if he were crazy. 'But it won't come from my lips.'

'Sometimes you have to stand up and be counted.'

'Not me, Jack, I leave that to fellows like you and my poor departed brother. Show me the shadows and leave me to skulk in them; that's what works best for me.'

'You hold a very low opinion of yourself.' Jack could not help smiling. He was taking a liking to Robert Kearney. Many of the young men he had known would have been proclaiming their bravery and their desire to bring the enemy to heel. Robert clearly didn't give a hoot. It was a refreshingly honest view, and Jack found he rather enjoyed it.

'Everyone else does and I see no reason to dissuade them of it. I shall always be a disappointment, especially now poor Thomas is gone. What's the point in trying to prove everyone wrong? Especially when you can have so much more fun when you stop trying.'

'With girls? And drink?'

'Amongst other things.' Robert guffawed at his own answer.

'What about when they run out?'

'Oh, they won't do that. Father may be disappointed in me, but he's never anything but generous. So long as I have money, I shall have my comforts.'

'And that's all there is?'

Robert got to his feet with a sudden bound of energy. 'What else would a fellow want? Give me a whisky and a pretty girl and I'll want for nothing.'

Jack was finding it hard to come up with a good counter. 'What about duty?'

'Duty? Goodness me, are you truly that dull, Jack? To hell with duty! We are not on this good earth for long; Thomas proved that pretty damn well. If we don't enjoy ourselves now, then when will we?'

'There's more to life than drinking and whoring.'

'If there is, I have yet to find it.' Robert seemed invigorated by the conversation. He moved away from the table and pushed open the uppermost crate in a stack not far away. 'Although I suppose war could be fun.' He reached inside the crate and pulled out a rifle.

Jack caught a whiff of the oil that had protected the firearm on its journey from the factory. He did not recognise the weapon in Robert's hand so he got to his feet and came to have a closer look.

'War is not fun,' he spoke as he walked, 'and if you think that, you're going to be sorely disappointed.'

Robert pulled the rifle into his shoulder and sighted down the barrel. 'Are you always so goddam dour?' He spoke out of the corner of his mouth as he tracked an imaginary target.

'Yes.' Jack reached into the crate and pulled out another rifle. 'What are these?'

'Springfields. Brand new, too. Only the very best for us, thanks to my father.'

Jack hefted the weapon in his hand. It was heavy, but no

more so than the Enfield rifle musket he had used in India, or the French Minié version used by the Foreign Legion.

'We had some of these before. They came with a tape instead of percussion caps. Maynard tape or some such.' Robert seemed thoroughly uninterested and tossed the rifle back into the crate. 'The damn stuff didn't work, so we sent them back. These are fired with standard caps.'

'Where are they made?'

'Why, here in good old Massachusetts.' Robert injected false enthusiasm into his voice. 'And they are the reason we'll win this war.'

'How so?'

'They are proof of all that we have here in the North. We have more people, we have two thirds of the factories, hell, we even have all the goddam money. Those Southrons have nothing. They won't be equipped like us and they won't have our numbers.' Robert laughed. 'It's why I let Father sign me up to this nonsense. The South doesn't stand a cat's chance in hell.'

For the first time, Jack saw something else in Robert's behaviour. For all his attempts to play the rake, he was an articulate young man who explained the North's advantages over the South clearly and concisely.

'So what has the South got?' Jack tried to draw Robert into conversation. He needed to find out more about the man he was being paid to keep safe. This was as good an opportunity as he would likely get, and he wanted to keep him talking.

'Slaves and cotton, that's about it.'

'What happens to the slaves?' A thought was forming in Jack's head. Robert's father had made it clear that he considered the war with the South to be some sort of righteous crusade to free the slaves, at least in part.

'What do you mean?'

'Afterwards. After you win.'

'You? Don't you mean *we*, Jack, after *we* win?' Robert teased, his face sporting a good-natured grin.

'Yes, all right, after *we* win.' Jack could not help smiling back.

'They'll be set free, of course. That's one of the things we are fighting for.' The answer was instant. 'The Underground Railroad has been running for years. Father, bless him, has helped with that. With money, of course; he would never get his own hands dirty. Thousands of slaves have escaped and come to the North. Hell, Father seems to employ half of them. This war will just complete the job and set the whole damn lot of them free.'

'And what about their owners?'

For the first time, Robert scowled. 'What do you mean by that?'

'Well, I presume these devils in the South actually buy the slaves. That makes them valuable. I suppose you could even call them capital. Are the owners going to get reparations if they suddenly lose them all?'

'That's not the point.' Robert's scowl deepened. 'I don't think anyone will lose any sleep if those rich Southern boys lose everything. Serves them right.'

'Why? They were likely born into it. Just the same as you were born into your family.' Jack was watching Robert closely. He was challenging him, testing his beliefs.

'It's just plain wrong and it needs to be stopped.'

'And you're going to help do that?'

Robert laughed. It was a rich sound and it filled the quiet storeroom. 'You twisting my tail to see if I bite, Jack?'

'Maybe. It sounds to me like you care more for this war than you let on.'

'Does it? Hell, that's no good.' Robert was still laughing. 'I'll have to try harder.'

'No, you'll have to drop the image you seem so keen to maintain and be the man you can be.' The words felt odd as they came out of Jack's mouth, and he realised he was lecturing the younger man.

'And where would the fun be in that?' Robert reached out and clapped Jack on the shoulder. But his smile had faded.

'You might enjoy it.' Jack did not back away. He had started down this road and would not turn back. Somehow he had allowed Robert to become his responsibility. 'You might even make your father proud. Your sister too.'

'My sister?' Robert's smile returned. 'I reckon she is proud of me already.'

'Why's that?'

Robert shrugged. 'I'm her younger brother. It pretty much comes naturally. She looks out for me, keeps Father off my back.'

'That might change when she marries Rowell.'

'Only if she wants it to. Rowell will just be taken along for the ride. He'll do what she says, just as he does what O'Connell says now.'

Jack made a note of the comment. Rowell looked the part, that much was certain, but Robert's words revealed something about the man behind the immaculate facade. Yet it was not either Captain Rowell or First Sergeant O'Connell that he wanted to talk about. Elizabeth Kearney was the most beautiful woman he had ever seen, and her image was emblazoned across his thoughts in glorious detail.

'You think she and Rowell are not well matched then?'

'Hell, no! My dear sister's a goddam challenge. People think that because she's so pretty, she cannot think for herself. Well, I tell you, Elizabeth is the cleverest, shrewdest person I ever met. She got through governesses like you or I get through new shirts, one a season almost. None of them could keep up with her. She fair taught herself by the end. She works with Father now, and she probably knows his business even better than he does.'

Jack smiled. Once again Robert spoke with passion. He wanted to ask more questions but was prevented from doing so by the sound of someone else arriving at the store.

'Mr Kearney?' The main door of the warehouse opened and a voice called timidly through the opening.

'Over here,' Robert answered immediately. 'Is that you, Amos?'

'Yes, sir, it's me.' A fresh-faced soldier looked anxiously around the door before creeping inside. 'I hope I ain't bothering you none, sir.'

'Not at all. Sergeant Lark and I were just checking the new rifles.' Robert walked casually to the table and sat down again, his boots rising immediately to rest on the nearby crate. 'What do you want?' The casual manner was back.

Amos walked forward nervously, snatching his forage cap from his head then clutching it across his belly, his fingers screwing it into a tight ball as he approached. 'I'm afraid there's some trouble, sir.'

'Trouble? What sort of trouble?' Robert rested his hands in his lap as if settling for a nap.

'A fight. Down on North Street.'

'There's a fight there every damn night, Amos. Half those damned cribs exist only for such vicious forms of entertainment.'

The young soldier's eyes widened at his officer's language and tone. 'Begging your pardon, Mr Kearney, sir, but it's our boys that started it. My brother and me, well, we only went along cos they made us. When the trouble started, we knew we had to get someone. It could turn real bad.'

'Real bad.' Robert mocked the soldier's tone. 'Well, I suggest you go back to Faneuil Hall and rouse up someone from there. Sergeant Lark and I are busy.'

Amos's fatigue cap was screwed tighter. 'Begging your pardon, Mr Kearney, sir, but it was First Sergeant O'Connell that sent me here.'

'Hell, is that so?' For the first time Robert took real interest.

'Yes, sir.'

'And I don't suppose you would be content to say you could not find me?'

Amos opened his mouth but no words came out.

'Stop torturing the lad.' Jack decided to intervene. He looked at Amos, who appeared to be about twelve years old and was wearing a uniform at least two sizes too big for his slender frame. 'We will come directly, Amos.'

'You can go, Jack. I have no intention of getting caught up in a ruckus. Least, not one not of my own making.' Robert made a show of relaxing into his seat.

'These are your men.'

'They are O'Connell's men. If he did not see fit to attend to them, then I see no reason why I should.'

Jack was of no mind to argue. Instead of wasting any more

breath, he took a pace forward, then kicked Robert's boots off the crate. 'Get up.'

Robert's eyes widened as he was forced to sit upright. 'I'm not going.'

'Yes, you are.' Jack reached forward and took a firm grip of Robert's upper arm, hauling him to his feet. 'These are your men and they need you.' He started to frogmarch the lieutenant towards the door.

'All right!' Robert shook off Jack's grip. 'I thought I out-ranked you. Do sergeants normally order their officers around?'

'Only the good ones.' Jack placed a hand between Robert's shoulder blades and shoved him forward, ignoring the lieutenant's bleat of protest. He glanced across at the young soldier, who was looking on aghast as the newly arrived Englishman manhandled one of his officers.

'Well, lead on, Amos. You can show us the way.' He gave the order with a half-smile that he hoped would reassure the young man.

Amos looked anything but reassured, but Robert spared him from summoning an answer. 'There's no need. I know the way. I've spent enough time there after all. Amos, head back to the hall and tell First Sergeant O'Connell that I was only too happy to see to our men. And make sure you tell him that Sergeant Lark is assisting me.' He flashed a devilish smile at Jack. 'That should grab his attention. He won't like you interfering, but then that serves him right for having me dragged out. At least we can have a drink whilst we're there, so it won't be a total waste of our goddam time.'

He took a moment to straighten his uniform before he made for the door, with Jack trailing dutifully in his wake.

Chapter Ten

The Fiddling Sailor had little to recommend it. It lurked in a dank alley a few streets away from Faneuil Hall, and the sign advertising its presence was so faded that the establishment's name could barely be discerned. Jack was not impressed. Robert had called it a crib, a new name to Jack. Whatever it was called, it was clearly a seedy dive, the type of place where back in London he would have expected to find bear baiting and whores.

The alley stank to high heaven, but it was not the ripe stench that concerned him. What worried him more was Robert Kearney showing no sign of hesitation as he proceeded down the steep flight of stone steps that led to the crib's cellar.

Jack followed him. If anything, the smell inside was worse than the stench of the alleyway. As soon as he walked in, the pungent whiff of piss and sweat mixed with the heady aroma of fresh vomit and stale bodies to create a stink of debauchery so fetid that he nearly choked on it.

The crib itself appeared to consist of little more than a single wide room with a great slab of wood forming a bar at one end and a bench that extended around the walls. Jack saw three dishevelled barkeeps working the crowd that thronged the bar. Nearly every customer was competing to be served. Their demanding cries added to the general hubbub. Men shouted and bawled at one another, every conversation carried out at full volume. There were no tables and many of the patrons simply thronged together in closely packed clumps that left little space for anyone to move around.

'You come here a lot?' Jack was forced to shout the question directly into Robert's ear.

'It's not my favourite, but it's cheap and it offers an interesting form of entertainment. Just don't talk to the whores. A finer set of jilt girls cannot be found between here and New York.'

'Jilt girls?' Jack asked as he scanned the room. He saw nothing to tempt him to stay there a moment longer than was necessary. Even the rookeries of his youth could not compare to the Fiddling Sailor.

'They'll lead you a merry dance and promise you an array of delights, but they'll be off with your money before delivering on any of them.'

Jack grunted. He had known girls who played the same trick. Jilt girls, B-girls, teasers or just lazy whores, the game was the same.

The crowd in the crib was mixed. Coloured men and women mingled with the sailors, soldiers and longshoremen who made up the majority of the customers. Seated on the benches were a number of provocatively dressed women of all ages and colour, whilst at the side of the room a couple of Negro musicians played a jaunty quadrille on a fiddle and base viol.

'Look over there.' Robert threw out an arm and pointed to a far corner, nearly catching a heavily bearded fellow in the face as he did so.

Jack followed the pointing finger. Seated at the room's only table was perhaps the fattest woman he had ever seen. She was wearing a scrap of a dress that left her half naked, and a throng of admirers were competing with one another for her attention. As Jack watched, one of them, a skinny old man with barely a scrap of hair left on his head, dived across the table and grabbed one of the woman's enormous breasts with both hands. The crowd bayed with laughter at the attempt, their cries and yells doubling in volume as the woman slapped the old fool away with a hand as big as a dinner plate.

Jack had seen enough. 'Let's find our boys and get out of here.'

'You don't want to stay?' Robert laughed at Jack's expression.

'No.'

'You really should. Watching Fat Sally at play is great sport.'

'I'm sure it is.' Jack had seen his fair share of freaks in London. He had no desire to see any more.

'They're over there if you must speak with them. Although from what I can see, there is no sign of any damn trouble.' Robert pointed to a group of half a dozen blue-coated soldiers huddled together a short distance from one end of the bar.

Jack recognised three of them immediately. It was the same Irish lads who had greeted him so violently on his first day in the city. The other three also belonged to A Company.

'I'm going to get a drink.' Robert made to go to the bar. Jack grabbed his arm, steering him instead towards the men from their company. The lieutenant was spotted almost immediately.

'Why, hello, sir! I said you might be joining us again.' The tall Irishman with the blackened lips greeted his officer warmly, raising a tankard of ale in his direction.

'Good evening, O'Dowd.' Robert slid past another group of men and joined the soldiers' circle. 'Good evening, all.' He beamed at each of the men in turn. 'We heard there was trouble.'

'Trouble!' O'Dowd feigned surprise. He was a poor actor. 'Only trouble here is getting served!'

His cronies laughed on cue. The merriment was cut short as Jack finally pushed his way close enough to be seen.

'What the feck are you doing here, maggot?' O'Dowd greeted him with a sneer.

'We were told there was a fight,' Jack replied evenly.

'Was that little Amos? Why, the poor wee fella, he must have been quite worried. We had a little discussion with some boys from the 6th that came by.' O'Dowd clearly enjoyed being the centre of attention, and he preened as he saw everyone in the small group looking his way. 'I think they know not to come here again.' He made a show of looking at his knuckles. They were bruised and bloodied.

'Well done.' Jack could not hold back the sarcastic reply. 'Now drink up and go back to your barracks.'

'Now why would we be doing that?' O'Dowd's reply was sharp.

'Because you are under orders to parade first thing in the morning.' Jack would not be cowed, even with six hostile stares sent his way.

'Aye, we know that. That's why we're having ourselves a little drink before we go to war.'

'And now you've done that. Finish those and leave.'

'Are you giving us orders now?'

'Yes.'

'And why would you think we would be needing those?' O'Dowd lifted his tankard to his lips and drained the last of the dark liquid it contained, then handed it to one of the other men in the group. 'It's your round, McSweeney. Make sure you get the lieutenant a drink while you are about it. But don't worry yourself about Sergeant Lark. I don't reckon he'll be staying.'

'Stay where you are.' Jack snapped the command at the man now being handed tankards by the rest of the group. 'You have a lot to say for yourself, O'Dowd. How about you and I take our discussion someplace else?'

'We can talk just fine here.' O'Dowd was unconcerned by Jack's suggestion.

'You need to learn to do as you are bloody told.' Jack was forced to bellow as a nearby group of sailors suddenly roared with laughter.

'Are you going to teach me, maggot?' Spittle flecked O'Dowd's lips as he snarled at Jack.

'I'll teach you the hard way if you're too stupid to learn by any other.' Jack kept a weather eye on the group of sailors, who were starting to take a growing interest in the blue-clad Irishmen.

'Too stupid, is it!' O'Dowd cackled. 'It's not me making threats in a place like this. You want to get your throat slit, maggot, then you're going the right way about it.'

'I'll take my chances. Now, since you've finished your drink, it's time to leave.' Jack saw two or three of the sailors whispering and nodding in the soldiers' direction. He did not need to have visited this particular bar before to know what was brewing, the brawl the Union soldiers claimed to have already won making it clear what kind of entertainment much of the crowd had come for.

'I'm not taking orders from you, maggot.' O'Dowd was oblivious to the sailors' attention. 'None of us joined up for that.' He spat out the words so quickly, they slurred together. 'We had enough of that sort of thing back in Kilkenny. You just leave us here and we'll be seeing you in the morning.' He smirked at Jack, then looked around his friends for support. 'Isn't that right, fellas?'

Jack took a deep breath. It was fast becoming time to stop talking and take action. But still he hesitated. He did not want to fight men he would one day have to stand alongside in battle, especially not with a group of sailors looking at them with obvious distaste.

He opened his mouth to give the order one more time, but before he could speak, someone barged into his back, throwing him forward and into the arms of the soldier carrying the group's empty tankards. With his hands full, the man could do nothing to steady himself, and the two of them went down together, the tankards and their dregs of ale sent flying as they hit the floor.

'Heh!' O'Dowd reacted instantly. 'What the feck do you think you're doing?' He shoved the man who had barged into Jack, throwing him back against his own group.

'You lot need to keep your voices down. We're trying to drink over here,' said one of the sailors. Jack recognised his accent. The man hailed from Merseyside. He likely worked on the same line that had brought Jack to Boston. No matter where he came from, though, it was clear that he was spoiling for a fight.

'Feck you and your friends.' O'Dowd turned and balled his hands into fists.

Jack saw the reaction. He had landed on top of the unfortunate soldier he had collided with, but the contact with the ground had still sent a flash of pain coursing through him as the point of his elbow hit the floorboards, and he was slow to get up.

'Shut your mouth!' the sailor roared back.

Jack scrabbled back to his feet, but he was up too late to stop O'Dowd. The rangy Irishman had both hands free and he used them to unleash a series of punches at the sailor. His fellow Irishmen needed no further urging to join the fight, and they piled in, fists flying.

'Shit.' There was time for Jack to spit out the single word before he was caught up in the melee. A stout man with a dark beard grabbed one of O'Dowd's cronies and swung him violently to one side. It left him open to attack, and Jack did not need a second invitation. His fist rose sharply, catching the sailor directly on the nose. The man reeled backwards, hands covering his face, blood already starting to flow freely through his grasping fingers.

'Fecking come on, then.' O'Dowd reeled past Jack, his hands clasped around a sailor's chest in an odd embrace. He had clearly seen Jack land his first blow and he cackled with delight at witnessing the Englishman join the scrap.

Jack had no idea what O'Dowd planned, but the man he clutched was hammering his fists down on top of O'Dowd's head to stop whatever it might be. The blows sent the Irishman spinning away, his feet doing a merry dance.

'You fool.' Jack snarled the words, then punched hard. O'Dowd's opponent never saw the blows coming. Jack's right fist caught him on the side of the head with enough force to snap it to one side. The left followed a heartbeat later. It landed true on the sailor's temple and knocked him from his feet as if someone had pulled his legs from under him.

'Get up, you dolt.' Jack hauled O'Dowd upright.

'Good on you, maggot.' The words came out as little more than gasps, then O'Dowd danced away again, his fists bunched as he threw himself back into the fight that now swirled around them both.

Jack turned on his heel and tried to make some sense of the confusing brawl. He looked for Robert and spotted him almost immediately. The young officer was doing his best to stay behind one of O'Dowd's stouter companions. Two of the Irishmen had succumbed to the sailors' fists. One lay flat on his back, his nose pouring blood. The second was bent double and crabbing away from the fight, sobbing as he fought for breath.

'For fuck's sake.' Jack tried to get across to Robert, but the wide back of a fat man wearing a brown overcoat blocked his way. He had no idea on which side the man was fighting, but he did not care. He simply reached forward and grabbed the man's collar before hauling backwards with enough of a jolt to topple him over. He stepped into the gap he had created in time to see O'Dowd batter a sailor to the ground with a series of well-placed punches to the gut.

Jack moved into the open space, making it to Robert's side just before a tall sailor with close-cropped blonde hair. There was time to grab Robert's shoulder and push him out of harm's way before the sailor slammed into Jack, sending him reeling. This time, Jack kept his footing and twisted to one side before coming back at the man. The sailor was a head taller than Jack, and his body was lean and well muscled. Jack took one look at his new opponent, then punched hard, catching the man in the very centre of his midriff.

'Fucking hell.' He could not help the oath escaping his lips. It was like hitting teak.

The sailor grunted as he took the blow, then punched back. His giant fist slammed into Jack's shoulder, half spinning him around. A second followed hard on the heels of the first, but this time Jack was aware of it coming, and twisted past the blow that would have caught him high in the ribs.

'Fuck you.' He unleashed a quick series of strikes, stepping into the blows that he aimed at the man's gut. Each landed true, but he was rewarded with nothing more than a series of loud grunts. With his punches having no effect, he swayed instinctively to one side, expecting the man to lash out in retaliation. But instead, the blonde sailor grabbed him around the waist and prepared to throw him to one side. Jack felt the man's hard fingers digging into his flesh as he took a firm hold. They hurt like the devil, but he ignored the pain and did the only thing he could think of.

He slammed his head forward. His forehead connected with the very centre of his opponent's face. Blood erupted from the man's nose in a spectacular fountain, much of it splattering across Jack's face. He felt its heat on his cheeks, and his head rang from the vicious contact. Neither stopped him from driving his head forward for a second time, smashing it into the very same spot, the remains of his opponent's nose crushed to pulp. This time he kept his head in place and pumped his legs, driving his weight forward so that he pushed his bleeding foe backwards. The taller man was hurting badly and could do nothing as Jack drove him from his feet. He fell away, his arms windmilling before he hit the ground on his back.

Jack staggered after him, head swimming and vision greying. He was only saved from a second ignominious fall by a pair of hands that hauled on his upper arms and pulled him backwards. He turned on the spot, panting, his opponent's blood hot and salty on his lips, and found himself staring directly into the pugnacious face of First Sergeant O'Connell.

He was given no time to think on the appearance of the company's most senior non-commissioned officer. O'Connell pushed him to one side, then stepped into the melee, fists raised. Jack let him go. He bent double, sucking down a few lungfuls of air before smearing a hand across his face.

There were few men left for O'Connell to fight. Jack watched him knock one sailor to the floor before grabbing another in a vicious headlock. Two sharp raps to the fellow's crown ended his fighting for the evening, and O'Connell dropped the half-senseless man face down onto the floorboards.

The Irishmen cheered then. All were bloodied and a couple were finding it hard to get to their feet. Yet still they shouted out in victory as the group of sailors picked up their fallen friends before slipping away. Jack finally managed to straighten up, just as O'Connell pushed his way through the huddle of battered Irishmen and came to stand directly in front of him.

'What the hell do you think you were doing?' O'Connell's face was flushed from his brief participation in the fight.

Jack's shoulder and his head were hurting badly, and his elbow was throbbing painfully, but he would not show weakness in front of the first sergeant. 'I was looking after the men.'

'Looking after them, is it? Is that what you call this?'

Jack tried to read O'Connell's expression, but failed. Life in the Fiddling Sailor was quickly returning to normal and the noise was already at its former level. The men from the 1st Boston were standing around their sergeants. Each man was grinning widely, and although all bore some reminder of the

fight, with bloodied noses or bruised bodies, none were injured badly enough to stop them joining in the celebration of their second victory of the evening.

Jack focused his attention on his superior. O'Connell was staring at him, his chin thrust out and his eyes narrowed. 'It's my fault, First Sergeant, I should've tried harder to stop them.'

'Stop them!' O'Connell was incredulous. 'These are Irish boys, Lark. Irish boys don't duck from a scrap.'

'They fight well,' Jack agreed.

'Of course they fight well!' O'Connell reached out and clapped Jack on the shoulder. 'Didn't I tell you that?'

Jack shook his head gingerly, his skull pounding after the pair of head butts he had delivered. 'This isn't the same as a bloody battle.'

O'Connell had left his hand on Jack's shoulder, and now he squeezed. 'We'll learn what we have to learn.' He paused. 'Then we'll kick the living shite out of those Southron feckers.'

Jack realised that something had changed in the first sergeant's stare. He no longer saw disdain and dislike. Instead he saw approval. 'They've a lot to learn.' He was forced to shout.

'Maybe.' O'Connell gave the ground grudgingly. 'You fought for my men, Lark.' His fingers squeezed tighter. 'I appreciate that, so I do.'

Jack glanced at Robert and remembered how the lieutenant had corrected him earlier that night. '*Our* men, First Sergeant, I fought for our men.'

O'Connell barked out a short laugh, then nodded. 'Aye. They're our men now.' His face split into something that might have been a smile. 'You're still an English fecker, but maybe you'll do.'

He turned on his heel and snatched the tankard from O'Dowd's hand.

'Here's to the First!' he bellowed, loud enough to make heads turn in their direction. 'The first and the best!'

Jack had no tankard to lift, but he joined in the cheer that followed. It might have cost him a half-broken elbow and a cracked skull, but the fight had cemented his place in the company, or at least had started the process. It was enough for now. There was plenty of time.

But tomorrow they would take the first steps on the journey that would end on the battlefield. He could not help looking at the faces of the men standing around him and wonder which of them would return to their homes in the city, and which would end their days on the field of battle, their bodies broken and torn.

Chapter Eleven

Faneuil Hall, Boston, Thursday 18 April 1861

Jack awoke to the beat of the drum. The rhythm matched the thumping in his head and left his skull ringing. It hurt. A lot.

'On your feet, you pathetic worms!' First Sergeant O'Connell was walking around the lower floor of Faneuil Hall. 'Get yourself up, boys!' His thunderous voice was easily louder than the single drum sounding reveille. Jack was glad not to be close to either.

He swung his legs out of his cot in a corner of the upper landing and reached for his trousers. The hall was still dark, but the men had to be up early if they were to be ready for the grand parade that would mark their departure from Boston.

Loud footsteps thumped on the stairs and O'Connell's leering face loomed large in front of Jack. 'How's your noggin?' A short cackle of amusement burst from the man's mouth as he caught sight of Jack's forehead. 'That's a rare bump you got yourself.'

Jack's fingers lifted to press against the swelling. He could feel the tender flesh and he knew he would be bruised for days.

'Goddam webfoots. They think they own the fecking city.' O'Connell glanced around him, making sure his company's sergeants were getting themselves together. 'They needed a good pasting, so they did. You did well to give it to them.'

He addressed all four sergeants. 'Now there's a long day ahead, fellas. Make sure the boys look grand for the Governor and all. We wouldn't want anything to spoil the celebrations.'

'Celebrations?' Jack could not help snorting as he repeated the word. It left a bitter taste on his tongue.

'You don't think we should be celebrating going to war?' O'Connell watched him carefully.

'No.' Jack did not withhold the honest reply. 'Do you?'

'I don't see the sense in it, no.' O'Connell shook his head.

'Have you fought before?'

'Aye. Out west. It wasn't pleasant.'

'Mexico?' Jack tried to remember what Scanlon had said of his men's experience. He knew next to nothing of the country's history.

'No. Against those Navajo feckers.'

Jack nodded as if the name meant something to him. He guessed it had to be one of the indigenous tribes, the fabled redskins who occasionally featured in a story in the London papers. 'This'll be different.' He felt safe making the comment. He doubted the local tribesmen had fought in a traditional style. Men like O'Connell knew war, but they knew nothing of the battles where tens of thousands of men fought one another on a front miles wide.

'Maybe.' O'Connell shook his head. 'Maybe not. It'll still be man against man. I reckon they all fight just as hard to stay alive, no matter the colour of their skin.'

'You think we're ready?'

'No.' O'Connell plucked a tiny scrap of cotton from the front of his uniform jacket. 'But don't let that worry you none. Those boys down south won't be ready either. I reckon we'll both just have to make the best of it with what we got, and have this battle that everyone wants. Then we'll see what happens next.'

'You don't think one battle will solve everything?' Jack finished buttoning his jacket, then sat to pull on his boots.

'I've never heard of one battle solving anything much at all. But the eejits in Washington are spoiling for a scrap, just like the gombeens down in Richmond. So I reckon we'll give it to 'em. Then they'll see that this ain't going to be the three-month bullshit they've been talking about.'

'Then what happens?'

'Then we get ready for a proper war.' O'Connell smiled wolfishly at the notion. 'This ain't nothing but the start of the damn show.'

He nodded at Jack then turned his back on the sergeants and thumped noisily back down the stairs. Jack turned to finish getting ready. He was sure O'Connell was right. The 1st Boston were marching to war, but the battle they longed for was just the first act in a play that would go on for far longer than anyone contemplated.

He forced the uncomfortable thought from his head and thought like a soldier. He would worry about what he could see ahead and leave the future to fate.

A Company of the 1st Boston Volunteer Militia paraded outside Faneuil Hall just as the sky started to show the first sign of the approach of dawn.

Jack stood to one side with his fellow sergeants whilst

Lieutenant Clancy went through the roll. They should have taken their places in the ranks, but the company's non-commissioned officers had their own way of doing things. For his part, Jack used the time to watch as the names were called. He wanted to be able to put a name to every face in the company.

'Beckett,' Clancy called out, then paused, waiting for a reply. No one answered. He was only a short way through the company's names, yet already he was faced with a missing man. 'Beckett!' he repeated, louder this time.

'He's not here.' A laconic voice from somewhere in the middle ranks answered the officer.

'Not here?' Clancy peered at the men through spectacles misted by the damp in the air. 'Then where in the name of all that is holy is he?'

'He went home last night. His sister started courting a lad from over Cambridge way. He had to go sort that out, but he said he'll be back before we march.'

'Well, that is good of him!' Clancy made a note in his book, then peered down at the roll again. 'Clooney?'

'Here, sir.'

'Thank goodness for that.' The lieutenant greeted the reply with icy humour. 'Your sister is quite well, I hope, Clooney?'

'I ain't got a sister.'

'Praise be to God. Who knows how many men we would have lost if you all had sisters.' Clancy seemed well pleased with the remark, but if he expected some reaction from his men, he was to be disappointed.

'Good morning, Sergeant Lark.'

Jack's name-learning was interrupted by Major Bridges, who had come to stand beside A Company's sergeants.

'Good morning, sir.' Jack was pleased to see the major. He would be joining them for the journey to Washington, and Jack had a hundred questions that he thought Bridges would be able to answer.

'That does not appear to be a regulation revolver, Sergeant Lark.' Bridges nodded towards the holstered handgun on Jack's hip.

'It's not.'

'Will you remove it if I ask you?'

'No.' He made the refusal with a smile. He would not march without his revolver. He had been an officer for too long. As a sergeant he would be expected to fight with a rifle in battle, but a revolver had saved him too many times for him to consider going without one. 'Do you really want me to get rid of it?'

Bridges chewed his moustache for a moment before replying. 'No. I suppose that doesn't seem like a wise thing to do. I expect it will prove useful.'

'It will.'

Bridges let the matter lie. He stood next to Jack in silence for a moment or two, his hands clasped behind his back, his eyes watching over his men as Clancy carried on with roll call. 'So you have experience of this sort of thing. Do you think the men are ready?'

'No.'

'You are a man of few words this morning.'

Jack grunted in acknowledgement of the observation. His head still pounded and his back was aching like a bugger. Still, he resolved to be more fulsome in his remarks. 'What would you have me say? You've been playing at soldiers. Well, now you have to *be* them. I reckon you'll find that a damn sight harder than swanning around the city feeling important.'

'Is that what we have been doing?' Bridges kept his eyes on the men. 'Swanning around.' He repeated the phrase carefully, as if it might bite him.

'You haven't been doing what you should've been doing. You should've been drilling, or practising loading your lovely bloody rifles, or out on a route march.'

'You think we have been remiss in our preparations?'

'I do. You need to decide if you're making toy soldiers or real fighters.'

Bridges gnawed on his moustache in silence. In front of them, Clancy progressed with the roll. Another two men were missing.

'I think you are right.' Bridges spoke thoughtfully. 'We need more training.'

Jack had used the pause in the conversation to study the major. Robert's father had declared him to be dull, but Jack saw something else. Bridges was calm and steady, and he thought before he spoke. Men needed that steadying influence in battle. If he could maintain his thoughtfulness when thousands of men were trying to kill him, he could be a fine officer indeed.

'What happened between you and Kearney?' Jack decided the blunt question was as good as any. He had learned a little about Kearney from Robert, but he wanted to know more. Kearney had been enigmatic when it came to Major Bridges. There was clearly a past between the two men.

Bridges scowled momentarily. 'I thought Englishmen had a reputation for being circumspect.'

'Not me. But then I don't come from the best part of England. We tend to be a bit blunt where I'm from.' He watched Bridges carefully, checking the major was not too vexed. 'So what happened?'

'I dared to speak my mind.' Bridges' chin lifted as he replied. 'That is all I shall say. I am not one to gossip, Sergeant Lark.'

'This isn't gossip.' Jack thought for a moment before he spoke again. 'I find myself beholden to a man I barely know. That worries me. If there is something I should be aware of, I'd like to hear it.'

This time Bridges sighed. 'Perhaps it was not wise to attach yourself to a man you do not truly know.'

'Perhaps.' Jack acknowledged the barbed comment. 'But I didn't have much choice.'

'I understand you knew Thomas.'

'Yes. He was my friend. He's the reason I am here.'

Bridges nodded. 'Do you know why he left?'

'Yes.'

'Then you will know it was not a happy circumstance.' Bridges fixed his gaze on Jack. 'I dared to interfere. For my sins, I tried to mediate between father and son.' He sounded weary. 'We attend the same church. I even taught Thomas in Sunday school when he was younger. He was a fine boy and an even better man. I could not stand by and say nothing.'

'What happened?'

'I was told to hold my tongue. As you will know, the situation did not mend itself and it did not end well.'

Jack knew Kearney just about well enough to know that he would likely not take well to interference in his private affairs. But it spoke well of Bridges' character that he had tried.

Lieutenant Clancy's roll call had stalled as the men discussed whether one of the missing soldiers would indeed be returning. Many thought he would not, something that vexed Clancy no end.

'What did you do before all this?' Jack enquired with

genuine interest. It was not a question often asked of a British soldier. Usually a man's past was something to be forgotten. He was learning that this new army was different. These were not professional soldiers. They were a civilian force made up of men with real lives. Lives they had put to one side so that they could fight for a cause they believed in.

'I am a senior clerk, up at State House. In the Governor's office.'

The answer made complete sense. Bridges didn't look like a soldier. He was stout, and his habit of gnawing on his moustache could be taken as a sign of nervousness. Yet he possessed the quiet confidence of a man who was sure of who he was.

'So will you tell me why you are all going to war?' asked Jack. The roll call looked set to go on for a while longer.

Bridges inevitably chewed on his moustache for several long moments before he replied. 'What have you heard?'

'That it's about protecting the Union and putting an end to slavery.'

'Those are good reasons, aren't they?'

'Good enough for war?'

Bridges returned his gaze to the roll call, which had finally restarted. 'Are there ever good enough reasons to start a civil war?'

'I reckon the slaves would think so.' Jack aimed the barb.

Bridges grunted. 'Freeing the slaves is a laudable ambition. We should have free men in this country. The South, well, they want to own slaves, that is for sure, and it should not be allowed to happen. We are all God's creatures.' He paused, then glanced at Jack again. 'You know the North had slaves?'

'No, I didn't. I thought all the slaves were in the South.'

'They are now.' Bridges pursed his lips, as if tasting something sour. 'The practice died out in most of the Northern states before it was forbidden or there were laws passed making it illegal. It was simple business, the forces of supply and demand. We have enough people here, immigrants mostly. They provide an ample and cheap source of labour. I am sure there are some here who would welcome the return of slavery. Not all in the North agree with this war.'

'So why are you fighting about slaves?'

'I don't think we are, not really. It goes deeper than that. North and South want this country to be different things. We want tariff barriers against imports to protect industries that are just emerging, whilst they want free trade to export their cotton and tobacco to Europe. Even our societies are poles apart. Every ship coming across the Atlantic brings hundreds more immigrants from the Old World; young, ambitious people hoping to make their fortune. And they stay here, in the North, building up our industry and making lives for themselves and their families. That does not happen in the South. Theirs is a different world. There are great plantations, but all are family-owned. I suppose it is more like the world you knew, back in England. Their society is already becoming static and they are setting down all these conventions as to how that society should behave. They want to rebuild the nation as if we are still part of the Old World. And we are not that, not that at all. Perhaps, one day, everywhere will be like we are. Perhaps all countries will one day be made in our image. But it started *here*. We must preserve that, even when the going gets hard.' He shook his head and looked ruefully at Jack. 'I expect that is a longer answer than you may have wanted.'

'No.' Jack was fascinated by everything he had heard. He

had never wondered at the reasons for the wars in which he had fought. He was a soldier. He went wherever he was told to go; killed whoever he was told to kill. This war was different. Men were choosing to fight for a cause they believed in, one they would die to protect. He did not doubt it was the same on both sides, the armies of both North and South filled with men prepared to kill, and be killed, to preserve their ideals. It was quite unnerving to be surrounded by such passion when he did not share in it. He was there for very different reasons. He was there for money and for a place in the world. What did he believe in? What would he be prepared to die for?

'I see you are wrestling with this matter.' Bridges had been watching Jack carefully, and he was an astute enough man to understand something of what was going on in his mind. 'As you should. A man must understand what he is fighting for, what he may end up dying for.'

Jack smiled at the observation. 'Perhaps it's best for you to go your separate ways.' He tried to steer the conversation away from himself. 'Isn't that what the South has done by declaring their independence? Why not let them be who they want to be? Must you go to war to stop them doing so?'

'Yes.' Again Bridges gave a slow and measured reply. 'We cannot allow them to seek to be independent of the Union. It is our destiny to make this land a great nation.' He looked at Jack for a reaction. 'It was the vision our founding fathers had, and I think it's a good one. We are unique and we cannot give that up. We must not give that up. I agree with President Lincoln, on that at least. The preservation of the Union is everything.'

This time Jack nodded. He had heard a similar argument from Kearney. The two men might have had their disagreements, but it was clear they shared a political ideal. 'And that's worth fighting for?'

Again there was the now-familiar pause. 'Yes. Yes, I think it is.' Bridges gave the answer firmly.

'You may think differently when you have been shot at.' Jack wanted to test the strength of the major's opinion. 'Ideals, ambition, values; they all tend to disappear when the bullets are flying and another man is coming at you with a bayonet. Do you think you can hang on to those ideals then?' He heard some bitterness in his own words. He had lost much of the man he had once been along the way. He had set out to better himself, to prove that a boy from the foulest rookeries of London could do just as well as anyone born with a silver spoon in their mouth. Such youthful ideals had been washed away in the sea of blood that he had seen spilled. The conversation with Bridges was making him wonder what was left. Was he just a soulless husk of a man? A man trained to kill?

'I don't know the answer to that, Jack.'

'But these values of yours are worth dying for?'

This time the pause was longer. To their front, Clancy had completed the roll and was running through the day's orders to make sure the men knew what was ahead.

'Yes. Yes, I think they are.' Bridges inclined his body so that he faced Jack. 'We have something here; a meritocracy I guess you would call it. We welcome everyone to join in with that ideal. We are not French or German,' he smiled at Jack before he named his next country, 'or English. We are Americans. We are equal; whites, blacks, all of us. I don't want to die. I know that much for certain. But I will lay down my life for this Union, for this United States.' He fixed his eyes on Jack. 'So in answer to your question, yes, I would die for this cause of ours.

If it requires it, I shall lay down my life to preserve the Union and the way of living that we have built here.' He paused, his stare boring into Jack's skull. 'Would you?'

'I'm a soldier. Dying comes with the job.' The glib reply fell flat, even to Jack's own ears.

'And that's it? You would lay down your life for employment?'

Jack held Bridges' intense gaze. 'Yes.' This time he answered seriously. He did not shirk the question he saw in the other man's eyes. He lifted his chin. 'I'm a redcoat, or at least I was once, and I'm still a soldier. I made that choice a long time ago.' He offered Bridges a thin-lipped smile. 'It's all I know.'

Bridges shook his head, as if the reply saddened him. 'Then I rather think I pity you.'

'No. For God's sake don't pity me.' Jack's smile faded.

In front of them the men were dismissed. Immediately they started to chatter, the quiet of early morning broken by the sound of the company's building excitement.

Jack nodded farewell to Bridges and went to do his job.

Chapter Twelve

———◆———

'God bless you, sir.'

Jack did his best not to wince as a thickset man dressed in a black frock coat stepped forward to shake his hand. Faneuil Hall was packed to the rafters as the well-to-do citizens of Boston crammed inside to bid farewell to the first soldiers being sent to war. The men had spent the early hours of the morning in preparations for their departure. Now the first well-wishers had been allowed in ahead of the company's formal farewell from the Governor.

The man who had shaken Jack's hand with such enthusiasm moved on to clap another soldier on the back. Jack had a moment's respite and so turned to check that his equipment was still where he had left it. The sergeants had vacated their living space now that the men had cleared the lower level in preparation for their departure, and the regiment's band had installed themselves up in the gallery. They had struck up a tune the moment the first of the day's guests had arrived, the bandmaster choosing 'Hail, Columbia'. They played well, to Jack's ear at least.

The music helped to fill the hall with a carnival atmosphere, and the men's wives, sweethearts and families filed inside to say the first of many farewells to their menfolk. Their voices competed with the band and the noise levels were growing with every new arrival.

Jack stood remote from it all. Many of the visitors gave him a wide berth, only a few willing to approach the stranger with the scarred face and hard eyes. Those who did moved on quickly, not one of them lingering for conversation, something that pleased Jack no end.

A grey-haired woman brushed past him as she pushed through the crowd. He followed her passage, wondering whom she sought so eagerly. He heard her cry of delight as she spotted two young soldiers standing shoulder to shoulder. He recognised them at once: the pair of identical twins known to every man in the regiment. He could not help but smile as she dived forward and embraced both at the same time, one under each arm, her face turning quickly from side to side to smother them with kisses. He was close enough to see the tears streaming down her face. His smile faded as she spotted his scrutiny and immediately grabbed her boys' hands and frogmarched them towards him.

'Are you in charge here?' She had to shout to be heard over the music and the general hubbub.

'No, ma'am.' Jack tried to sound polite.

The woman scowled at the answer. Her face was puffy and blotchy from her tears, but her eyes blazed. 'My boys ain't old enough for this. They need to be excused.'

'I'm sorry, but you'll need to take that up with one of the officers.' Jack tried to deflect the woman. Her boys, Amos and James, would not meet his gaze; both looked at the floorboards, their embarrassment obvious.

'I told them not to join up.' The twins' mother kept talking, his words clearly not registering. 'But they defied me, the little devils, and now here they are, about to go to war when they should be home with me doing their lessons.'

'I'm sorry,' Jack bent forward so that his mouth was closer to the woman's ear, 'but you'll have to speak to—'

'You should all be ashamed of yourselves, taking boys like this.' The woman continued without drawing a breath. 'Why, my lads are barely sixteen! That's too young, you all know that, but you keep turning a blind eye. You know they're meant to be eighteen.'

Jack tried to feign interest. 'I am sure the recruiting officers would have checked their age, ma'am.'

'Oh, you think that, do you?' The woman's round cheeks were colouring. She shook both her hands, geeing her boys up. 'You tell the man, you tell the man what you did.'

The twins glanced at one another before one of them spoke, his words barely audible. 'We put a slip of paper in our shoes.'

'You speak up now, so that the man can hear you.'

The first twin grimaced, then lifted his gaze to Jack's face. 'We both wrote on a scrap of paper and put it in our shoes.'

Jack was starting to find the conversation rather amusing. 'Why would you do that?' He spoke slowly and carefully.

'We wrote the number eighteen on it.' This time the second twin replied. It was often the way. Jack had only had a few conversations with the twins, and he still could not tell them apart, but he had found that they had the habit of speaking as if they were one person.

'Why?'

'So we could say we were *over* eighteen,' the first twin replied.

Jack could not help the guffaw that escaped his lips. There was something in the intensely earnest way that the lad made the confession that he found amusing.

The twins' mother did not. 'My boys are good Christian lads. They couldn't lie, they ain't capable of it.'

'Did no one question this ruse?' Jack tried to sound serious.

'I vouched for him.' One spoke first.

'And I vouched for him.' The second chimed in almost immediately.

'They need to be excused.' Their mother spoke before Jack could say anything further. 'They're clever boys, with keen minds. They ain't cut out to be soldiers. Why, Mr Spratt at the schoolhouse says they could both be lawyers one day.'

'Well, they're soldiers now.' Jack sensed someone else approaching. To his relief, it was Rowell. 'But here is the man you need to be speaking with, Mrs Thatcher.' He waved for his captain's attention. 'Captain Rowell, have you a moment?'

Rowell came over, smile in place on his face. As the company's commander, he was a busy man, not least because all the worthy people allowed in to see the troops wanted a moment with the hero of the hour.

'Mrs Thatcher would like to speak with you, sir. About Amos and James. She believes there is a problem with their attestation.' Jack gave the introduction smoothly, then stepped back to take himself out of the conversation. But he had no intention of slipping away. He wanted to see how Rowell handled the situation.

'Good morning, Mrs Thatcher.' Rowell came close and beamed at the twins' mother. 'How may I assist you this morning?'

'Well, sir, Captain Rowell, it's about my boys.'

Jack could not help but notice the change that came over Mrs Thatcher. She was a much older woman, yet she could not hide her salacious appraisal of the company's captain.

'They are fine boys, and fine soldiers. You must be very proud of them both.'

Rowell was all oily charm, to Jack's eyes at least. It was enough to make the twins' mother turn coy and flutter her eyelids as she looked up at the handsome officer. Rowell looked particularly fine that morning. His uniform was immaculate and his skin glowed as if it had been buffed. Jack did not think he had ever seen anyone quite as heroic. Even the fabled General Nicolson, the commander of the army that had attacked Delhi, had never looked as valiant as the magnificent Captain Ethan Rowell.

'Oh, I am, Captain, I am indeed. But, Captain Rowell, you know they ain't old enough to be soldiers. They're still just boys. They've had their fun, but enough is enough. They've got a bright future ahead of them; one that means they should stay home with me.'

'They do indeed have a bright future, Mrs Thatcher.' Rowell's lips curled into an even more expansive smile as he reached out to take her hand, which he held carefully, as if frightened he would break it. 'As soldiers.'

'But they're just boys.' The twins' mother fought against Rowell's charm. From the flush on both cheeks, it seemed she was losing the battle.

'The colonel won't have it, Mrs Thatcher, and nor will I.' Rowell still held the woman's hand, which he raised as if about to kiss it. 'They'll be back in three months, perhaps sooner, and they shall return to you as men. This adventure will be the making of them, and I'll warrant they'll study harder once they've seen the elephant.'

'The elephant?' Mrs Thatcher fairly breathed the words, her eyes locked on Rowell's handsome face.

'It's what we soldiers call battle, Mrs Thatcher.' Rowell adopted a tone that implied he was sharing some great secret with her and her alone. 'Your boys will tell you all about it when they get home.'

Mrs Thatcher tried to reply. Her words, whatever they might have been, came out as little more than a whimper, and the tears started to flow. The twins buried their heads against her shoulders.

'They've got to go?' She tried one last time, but there was no force in her words; her defeat was almost complete.

'Do not upset yourself, Mrs Thatcher.' Rowell, unmoved by the emotion, was all charm. 'Your brave lads are doing something that will live long in the memory of this country. You'll make your mother proud, won't you, boys?'

The two young soldiers looked up at their officer and nodded forcefully. 'Yes, sir!' they chimed in unison.

Their mother looked back at Rowell with eyes full of pain before finally nodding and embracing her two boys as if she could hold on to them for ever.

His victory complete, Rowell finally let go of Mrs Thatcher's hand. 'Sergeant Lark.'

'Sir?' Jack's amusement had faded. He saw a mother's love for her children on open display, and it shamed him.

'The Kearneys have arrived to say goodbye. They have asked to see you before we leave.'

'That is kind of them.' Jack looked around him. Elsewhere there was as much laughing and joking as sadness. The men were loud and confident, and were having a ball as their relatives fussed around them. He had thought it would all pass him by, his lot to stand and watch. But the arrival of the Kearney family had changed that. He might be a stranger in the great city of Boston, but someone had still come to bid him farewell.

'Ethan!'

Jack was slightly behind Rowell when Elizabeth Kearney spied her fiancé emerging from the crowd of well-wishers and soldiers.

'Elizabeth!' Rowell's reaction was enthusiastic, and he swept forward to take her hand and hold it to his lips. 'I am so glad you are here, my love. I cannot tell you what it means to see you one last time before I embark on this great endeavour.'

Jack hung back, awkward in front of the pair's meeting. Elizabeth glowed. A delicate covering of rouge and powder adorned her face, and her lips had been tinted the colour of winter berries. She looked radiant, and Jack could see every man in the vicinity glancing in her direction.

'I have something for you.' Elizabeth was very aware of the attention directed her way, but to her credit she did not seem to dwell on it, instead focusing on Ethan. She handed him the pale linen sack she was carrying. Ethan made a play of nearly dropping it, as if surprised by its weight.

'Why, it is so heavy!' he exclaimed, then looked around him to check that everyone was watching his display. 'Whatever can it be?'

'Why don't you open it, my love?'

Jack was watching Elizabeth as closely as any other man in the vicinity. Did he detect a moment's iciness in her reply? It was delivered with the same beaming smile, but he thought he saw a flash of something in her eyes, as if she was far from impressed by her intended's display.

'Indeed I shall!' Ethan spoke overly loudly, like an actor on a stage. He turned and looked around him. To Jack's dismay, his eyes alighted on him. 'Sergeant Lark, a moment's assistance, if you please.'

Jack did his best not to grimace, and walked forward dutifully. He glanced at Elizabeth as he came closer, but her eyes were focused solely on Rowell, who was fishing inside the linen sack.

'My love, what have you given me here?' Rowell was playing to the crowd, many of whom were bobbing their heads as they tried to see what was going on. He succeeded in freeing a large dark-wood box from within the sack and placed it in Jack's hands, then opened the lid with excruciating slowness, drawing the big reveal out for as long as he could. He need not have bothered. The gift was so splendid that it needed no such preamble. The crowd gave a loud moan of delight as he finally pulled out a revolver.

Jack was only just able to hold back a sigh of his own. The metal of the revolver had been buffed and polished so that it glowed like silver, whilst the handle was inlaid with ivory. It was a magnificent example of the gunsmith's art, and in a room full of soldiers it was sure to draw almost as much attention as the beautiful young woman who had presented it.

'Do you like it?' Elizabeth asked as Rowell stood with the gun held carefully across his palms.

'Like it?' he breathed as he turned, his eyes alive with pleasure. 'It is beautiful.' He stepped towards her, his back now turned to Jack. 'Thank you.'

Jack did his best to hide his jealousy. At least Rowell now blocked his view of Elizabeth's face. Seeing her pleasure at her fiancé's reaction would likely make him want to spit.

He glanced down at his own revolver. Rowell's gift bore little comparison to the scratched and scuffed weapon he carried. It was hard not to see the two firearms as being made in the image of their owners. One was a hand-crafted jewel of a weapon, a thing of beauty that would inspire jealousy and envy. The other was mass-produced, battered and scarred from long use; a tool to be used in battle then hidden from sight once the fighting was done. It was not a flattering comparison.

Rowell and Elizabeth were now speaking quietly to one another. The onlookers had mainly turned away, giving the couple less attention now that the ceremony of the gift-giving had passed. Jack was content to merge back into the crowd, but not before he dumped the revolver's case and the linen sack on a pile of haversacks resting against one of the room's many pillars. Arms free, he looked around for Robert.

'You finished mooning over her now?'

Jack started as someone addressed him. It was the young maid who had disturbed his bath. He had not seen her amongst the crowd.

'Is it that obvious?' He felt the burn of embarrassment on his cheeks.

'Oh yes. But don't you worry none. You aren't exactly alone.' The maid stepped closer. 'Half the room is looking at milady over there.' She turned to stare at Elizabeth.

Jack used the moment to look more closely at the girl in front of him. He was struck by quite how pretty she was. There was a flush on her cheeks from the heat in the room that accentuated her high cheekbones. The crimson tinge sat well on her dark skin, but it was her eyes that demanded attention. They were too widely spaced to be considered classically beautiful, yet the whites were bright and the irises were a brown so dark they appeared to be almost black. There was beauty in her finely defined features, but it was marred by the thin scars he had noticed the first time they had met. Now that he stood close to her, he could see that they were made up of a number of thin welts that stretched across the lower part of her right cheek and underneath her jaw. Each scar was razor thin, the raised flesh pinker than the darker skin surrounding it. His scrutiny had to come to an abrupt end as she turned back to face him once again, but he was left wondering how she had been injured.

'What's your name? You didn't tell me when we last met,' he asked as soon as he had her attention. She was a good foot shorter than he was and so was forced to crane her neck far back so that she could look him in the eyes.

'Is that how you Englishmen introduce yourselves?' She was clearly not impressed. 'Well, my name's Rose, for whatever that's worth to you. I know yours, so don't worry none about telling me.'

'Have I made you jealous, Rose?' Jack teased. Everything she had said to him up to that point had been peppery. He wanted to see if he could draw out another emotion.

'No.' The denial was sharp. 'Don't you have no one of your own to moon over?'

'No.'

'Never?'

'Maybe once.' Jack scowled. He had been immediately put on the back foot by this slip of a girl half his size.

Rose's mouth twitched as if a smile was being hidden. 'Figures.'

'Why's that?'

'You're too old to never have had someone.'

'Too old!' Jack could not help the exclamation.

'Just saying.' Rose glanced away, hiding her expression. When she looked back at him once again, her face was serious. 'So why have you signed up for this?'

'I needed employment.' He shrugged as he replied. He felt comfortable talking to Rose. He sensed they were equals. They had very different types of master, but they both served.

'That all this is to you?'

'I'm a soldier.'

Rose shook her head, clearly not impressed with his statement. 'So you're a mercenary.'

'No.' His answer was immediate.

'You sure 'bout that?' The rejoinder was just as quick. 'You look like one to me.'

He laughed. 'The way I see it, there are a lot of us doing what we are told for money. Soldiering. Fighting.' He looked pointedly at Rose. 'Serving.'

'I had no choice.'

'Why?'

'I was a slave. We don't get to choose.'

'You were a slave?' Her answer caught him unprepared.

'I was born into it. My mother and father were both slaves, so that meant I became one.'

'Where are they now?'

'My mother died of sickness after I was born. My father is still down Charleston way, as far as I know.'

'In the South?'

Rose looked at him in disapproval, like a mother regarding a child who had repeatedly failed to spell his own name correctly.

'How did you leave?' Jack tried a different question.

Again Rose did not answer. Her hand strayed to the series of scars on her face and she looked away, as if staring at an object on the far side of the room. His own hand twitched, moving just a fraction as he felt a burning desire to reach out and touch the scars for himself. He wondered what it would be like to feel them, to run his fingertips along their length.

Rose focused back on his face and her hand dropped to her side. She saw where his gaze was directed and scowled. 'I escaped. People, *good* people, helped me to come here to Boston. I went to the black school. They educated me and got me a place with Mr Kearney.' She was glaring at him now. 'You should think about what you're doing here.'

'What do you mean?'

'You need to think about what you're fighting for.' Her scowl deepened. 'There ain't no future in being a mercenary. You need more than that.'

Jack opened his mouth to reply, but before he could speak, a voice called his name.

'Jack! I've been looking all over for you.'

He saw Kearney approaching and lifted a hand in greeting. When he looked back to say something to Rose, she was gone.

'What do you think of the troops?' Kearney asked as he made his way to stand with Jack. Many heads turned their way, the soldiers and their families all clearly aware of the man's importance in the city.

'We're not ready. We've not had enough time to train them.' Jack did not shirk from offering the criticism.

'Well, that doesn't matter, at least not for the moment.' Kearney brushed off the remark. 'Washington is exposed and needs protection. There will be time for more drill when you are there.'

'It might not be enough,' Jack answered quickly. He could not help looking away to search the room for Rose.

'You are still better than those Southrons. The Confederates are never going to put up much of a fight. They might shout and yell, but they do not have the discipline to be soldiers. They are just a damn rabble.' Kearney made sure to speak loudly enough so that all in the vicinity could hear his opinion.

'Let's hope so.' Jack could see there was no point in gainsaying his sponsor.

'Good fellow.' Kearney clapped his hand on Jack's shoulder, then bent forward so that he could speak more candidly, the words for Jack alone. 'You will not forget why you are here, will you?'

'No, sir.' Jack matched the older man's tone.

'Protect my son. Whatever it takes.' The words were fierce, as was the glare sent Jack's way. 'You must protect him.' The instruction was hissed for a second time before Kearney pulled away. He beamed at Jack, the smile warm. None of it reached his eyes.

'Ah! Here comes Elizabeth. I shall let you speak with her for a moment. I need to talk to Scanlon before the parade.'

His message delivered, Kearney was clearly keen to move on, and was already easing his way through the crowd before Jack could say anything in way of reply.

'So there you are, Jack. I was wondering where you had been hiding.' Elizabeth closed in on him before he could gather his thoughts. 'I thought you might be avoiding me.'

'Why would I do that?' Jack forgot all about Elizabeth's father and his orders. He was pleased she had addressed him by his given name. He hoped it meant she had forgiven him for failing to fully answer her enquiries about her brother's death.

'I was afraid I had annoyed you with my questions. Besides, men do it all the time. Us womenfolk are not important.'

Jack could not help a short bark of laughter. He could not imagine there was a man alive who would ignore Elizabeth.

'Now you are laughing at me.'

'I apologise.' He searched Elizabeth's eyes. They sparkled with life and were looking into his with what he read as amusement and pleasure. She gave every impression of liking him, yet there was something guarded in her gaze. He had the feeling that nothing was as it seemed with her. She was beautiful, that was obvious, but he was certain that the real person was very carefully hidden from view.

She angled her body, hiding her hand then slipping it forward, taking his into a warm grip. Instinctively he tried to pull it away, but she held fast and he could not act more forcefully without drawing attention to them both. He saw her frown as she squeezed his fingers. One was crooked, a gift from a London villain, and he felt her hand slide over it.

'I broke it.' He spoke quietly, letting none of the emotions she stirred reveal themselves. 'In London.' He remembered how he had stood powerless, a seventeen-inch steel bayonet pressed hard against his kidneys.

'It must have hurt.'

'Like you wouldn't believe.'

'Rose told me you had been in the wars.'

Jack laughed. 'You've been talking about me?'

'Of course. What are ladies to do if not talk about menfolk?'

Again Jack saw something else in her stare. The notion of Rose and Elizabeth talking about him was at once both uncomfortable and flattering.

'She told me about your scars.' Elizabeth's mouth moved in a smile. 'She said you have a lot.'

'Enough.'

Elizabeth's hand retreated. He wondered if it was due to the coldness in his response.

'I do believe I have made you cross, and that is not fair, not on such a day as this. You must think badly of me.'

'I don't know what to think of you, Elizabeth.'

For the first time he saw some of her smile appear in her gaze. 'I think that is a good thing.' She looked away and ran her eyes around the room. A group of soldiers on the far side chose that moment to erupt in a series of cheers. 'At least you are all in high spirits.'

'The men are.'

'Do you think it really will be over soon?'

'It's possible.'

'I hope so. And then we can go back to being normal, although I hope Ethan stays in uniform. I rather like it.'

Jack smiled at the remark. The world loved a soldier when the enemy was close. He reckoned their attitude would change if the much-longed-for battle turned out to be just the first in a long, protracted war.

'Ladies and gentlemen!' Rowell himself spared him from finding a reply. The captain had clambered onto an ammunition crate and now addressed the room. He was forced to shout to be heard. 'Ladies and gentlemen, please.'

Slowly the noise subsided and all eyes turned to the splendid young officer.

'Thank you.' He gazed around the room, his habitual smile plastered across his face. 'I am afraid that it falls to me to put an end to these happy moments. There is a schedule that we must adhere to, and so I must ask you to step aside so that my men can move outside and form up. We cannot keep the Governor waiting!'

The crowd laughed on cue. Jack did not join in. He was trying not to stare at the revolver Rowell now wore holstered at his hip. He wanted it more than he could ever remember wanting anything. It would mark its owner out, the finely crafted firearm a bewitching mix of beauty and power. It was the weapon of a warrior. In battle men would see it and know that they fought against a man who was something special.

Once Jack had owned a fabulous curved sabre called a talwar. It had been a beautiful thing, created by the finest swordsmith for an Indian maharajah. He had carried it into battle with pride, knowing that the men he fought would see it and wonder quite how and why a British officer carried it. He had lost the weapon in the desperate struggle to stay alive the day the mutineers rode into Delhi. At the time he had not given it much thought, the horror of that bitter day leaving no room for regret at losing a simple possession. Now he felt its absence keenly. Such a weapon would mark him out as a warrior, or at least as something other than a lowly mercenary. And he wanted that distinction; craved it even. He wanted the world to know what he was.

Elizabeth rapped him on the forearm to regain his attention. 'You do not have much conversation.'

'I'm sorry.' Jack forced his attention back to the woman in front of him.

'You will have to improve by the next time I come to visit.'

'The next time?' Jack did not understand the comment.

'We shall be moving to our house in Washington. Father wants to be closer to the main affairs.' There was a moment's pause as Elizabeth tried to read his expression. 'You will not get rid of me so very easily.'

'I would never want to be rid of you.' Jack gave the gallant reply. It was easily said.

Elizabeth laughed at something she saw in his expression. She would not be given time to say more. The men were streaming past them now, bustling and jostling as they went to obey Rowell's instructions. It was time to end the goodbyes and prepare for the parade that would finish with the 1st Boston leaving the city and heading for war.

'I shall see you soon, Jack Lark.' Elizabeth's hand reached out to brush against his arm before she turned and slipped into the crowd that was following the soldiers out of the door.

Jack watched her for as long as he could. It was only when she was hidden from view that he caught a glimpse of Rose. She was looking directly at him, slowly shaking her head.

Chapter Thirteen

The company marched through streets lined with people. Jack imagined that every single citizen of Boston had come out to see the celebration. The pavements, and much of the streets themselves, were packed with men, women and children. All cheered or clapped as the troops marched by, their enthusiasm infectious. Many of the women were wearing small Stars and Stripes on their bosoms, or rosettes of red, white and blue, whilst the younger girls sported small flower bouquets. Many waved flags, the miniature Stars and Stripes matching the bright bunting strung from one side of the street to the other. It was a gay display, a riot of noise and colour, and the men of A Company paraded through it all with their heads held high.

Although the men marched smartly, to Jack's eye they still looked ragged, the spaces between the ranks and files uneven and more than one man marching completely out of time with his fellows. His former colour sergeants would have had a fit, but by the standards he had seen already, the troops were rising to the occasion.

K Company did not appear to have reached any higher

standard of drill. The other men from the 1st Boston ordered to Washington had arrived outside Faneuil Hall behind Gilmore's Band and Mooney's Juvenile Drum Corps, the musicians charged with adding still more noise to the day's cacophony. Shortly afterwards, the ten companies of the 6th Massachusetts Militia joined them, their long column filling most of Dock Square.

The Drum Corps now led the way, with the twelve militia companies following in column, the men marching to the mesmeric beat, or at least trying their best to do so. It did not take long for the procession to reach the State House on Beacon Street. There its progress was stopped, the crowd so dense that the men could simply not march through it. The roars of the onlookers seemed to double in intensity as the men stood and waited for the city officials to clear the way. Men and boys ran forward to shake the soldiers' hands, and in the span of no more than a couple of minutes nearly every one had been given a rosette or a miniature flag with which to adorn their uniform.

So it was a much jollier-looking column that finally resumed the march. Not one man minded the delay, the time well spent in cheering or waving at pretty girls in the crowd. Even Jack smiled when one girl in a green and cream dress braved the catcalls and good-natured jeering, and darted forward to plant a kiss on James Thatcher's cheek, much to the delight of Amos, who stood at his side and whooped with joy as his brother's face turned bright scarlet.

The column pressed on along Beacon Street, the full ranks of each company filling it from kerb to kerb. They wheeled at Charles Street then marched onto Boston Common. The crowds were no thinner here, but there was a good amount of open space kept clear in front of a small stage erected for the morning's events. The men re-formed, and it did not take long for the column to turn into several long ranks that faced the stage.

Jack stood in his allotted place and waited for the first of the day's speeches. He was warm in his new uniform, the march long enough to start him sweating. He was out of condition, his body soft after so long away from campaigning. He wondered how long it would take for him to get fitter, and how painful a process it would be. He was most certainly no longer the lean young redcoat who had first impersonated an officer at the Battle of the Alma.

The great crowd had used the pause in events to throng around the twelve companies. They now formed one great mass that encircled the blue-clad soldiers, the younger members of the crowd pushing and jostling their way to the front to be able to see. To a great cheer, a group of dignitaries took their place on the stage. Jack watched them arrive with interest. Two men were dressed in uniform, whilst the rest wore formal frock coats and hats. All were old and walked with the air of statesmen.

'Who's that leading the way?' he whispered to Robert, whose place in the company required him to stand close to Jack behind the two lines of men.

'Why, that's the Governor, John Andrew, a fine fellow. He came to dinner with us last month. Ate like a trencherman.'

'And that fellow in uniform?'

'That's General Butler. He commands all the Massachusetts militia.'

The man who had ordered the 1st Boston to Washington was not much to look at. He was bald on the top of his head, but still had rich, flowing hair on both the back and sides, with a small, neat moustache on his top lip.

Jack was not given time to ask any more questions. The first sergeants called their men to order, the loud barks of command enough to quell much of the crowd's noise save for a low murmur of whispered conversation. The Governor moved forward to take his place at the front of the small stage. There he paused to look around his audience, giving them time to settle. Only when the last of the conversations had died away did he begin to speak.

'I thank you all for coming this day. I must start by congratulating you on your splendid achievements to this date. In just a few days we have men ready and equipped for the campaign, and I think we can all rightly be proud of that effort.'

As if reacting to a cue, the audience clapped the opening words, a few hearty cheers and hear-hears thrown in for good measure. The Governor was clearly comfortable in front of such a large audience. He spoke loudly and clearly, his voice carrying easily over the body of troops, although Jack was sure that much of the vast crowd would struggle to hear a single word.

His first lines delivered, the Governor paused and focused his attention on the soldiers standing in front of him. He looked suitably sombre, but he clearly relished the attention he was getting. 'Yesterday you were citizens; today you are heroes. Your country has called on you to join this great endeavour, and you have responded most courageously to that call. On behalf of the people of Massachusetts, and of this most wonderful city of Boston, I thank you.'

More cheers came then. The large crowd knew their role in the proceedings well enough and they responded to their Governor's words with gusto. Jack felt no urge to join in. The crowd's passion was something new to him, and he could only wonder at such fervour in a nation state that was still so young. He wished he could return in a few months, or even years, to see if the good men and women of Boston could maintain their enthusiasm for the cause. The city had done wonderfully to have so many regiments ready for the start of the campaign. But how many more would be needed before the war was done? How many more times would the crowd assemble in this same place to send more of their young men off to the battlefield? Would they do so with the same passion? Or would the flags and bunting be replaced by black banners and posters protesting for the war's end?

'It would have been wrong of us not to mark your parting for the seat of war, and I thank you for giving us this opportunity to do so.' The Governor spoke only when most of the cheers had died away. 'This land of ours owes you a debt that will take a long time to discharge, and you will be remembered for generations to come as the brave men who stood up against those who would see this great nation of ours torn asunder. I understand that many of you derive your origin, either by birth or descent, from another country than this. For this is the great unifying design at the very heart of our nation.'

He paused and pumped one fist into the palm of his other hand, his passion rising with every word. 'The United States of America knows no distinction between its native-born citizens and those born in other countries. We do not discriminate against those who hold religious views different to our own and we shall not tolerate those who seek to divide us simply by the colour of the skin with which we are born. In all of us flows the blood of a common humanity, and into our hearts, by the inspiration of the Almighty, has been breathed a common understanding. We are one people. We are one nation under God.'

There were huge cheers now, enough to make the Governor

step back, as if he were astonished by the power of his own words. After several long moments, he lifted his hands for silence. He was roundly ignored and the cheers continued unabated, the crowd revelling in their role. It was enough to make the Governor laugh before he tried for a second time to quieten them down. Eventually he hushed them enough to continue.

'There is a difference, I will say, between our Southern brothers and ourselves, in that while we love our state with the true love of a son, we love the Union, and the country, with equal devotion. We place no state rights above or beyond the Union. To us our country is first, because it is our country, and our state is next and second. Our oath of allegiance to our country and that to our state are intertwined harmoniously, and never come into conflict. He who does his duty to the Union does his duty to the state, and he who does his duty to the state does his duty to the Union, one inseparable, now and for ever. The Union shall and must be preserved.'

With this the crowd went wild. Their shouts and cries had built steadily as the Governor spoke, and now they were released. It went on for several minutes, the noise washing over the men of the 1st Boston. The Governor again stepped back from his place at the front of the stage, and stood there laughing and even wagging a finger at the crowd as if it were a misbehaving child. The cheers doubled in intensity then, the crowd playing along, until eventually the Governor managed to calm them once again and returned to his spot at the very front of the stage.

'Now this day I shall put into your hands the ensign of this commonwealth. I would have you recognised wherever you go as coming from this great state of ours. When you look upon this venerable flag, you will think of your homes and your families here in Massachusetts. Take it as a pledge from the state of the affectionate care of your kindred and homes, and of the sincere and undying interest its people feel for you. In the utmost confidence in your patriotism and valour, we send you forth as citizens of Massachusetts, assured that her honour will never be disgraced by any one of you.'

This time the inevitable cheers were almost drowned out as the Drum Corp rattled into life. Yet the crowd kept going as three sergeants approached to collect the flag that was being brought to the front of the stage, ready to be passed into the hands of the Governor. The men, all of whom came from the ranks of the 6th, marched smartly towards a series of steps set into one corner of the stage. They clearly knew their drill, and they kept their backs straight and their faces impassive even as the crowd grew louder and more raucous.

Suddenly the leftmost of the three men stumbled. His toe caught the lip of the second step and he lurched forward, grabbing at his companion to avoid a fall. For one single heart-beat the crowd was silenced, the moment marked by every person who saw it. Then, as if goaded by their own negative reaction, the cheering returned louder than before, the crowd making up for their own slip by redoubling their efforts to drown out the Drum Corp.

If the Governor saw the stumble, there was no trace of reaction in his expression as he collected the flag then presented it to the men now charged with its care.

For the first time that day, Jack felt the stirring of emotion. He knew what it was to go into battle following the colours, and the sight of the new flag awoke something hidden deep inside him. There was splendour in the gaudy square of silk.

To the men who would follow it into battle, it represented the pride of the regiment. Men would fight for their colours, would die to prevent them falling into the hands of the enemy.

He doubted if any of those around him felt the same. These new soldiers did not yet understand the power of the flag. They might recognise its splendour, or see it as a fitting decoration for their regiment. But they could not yet know what it would be like to see the same colours ravaged by gunfire, dulled by powder smoke and stained with the blood of the men who had died carrying them. They could not envisage the desperation with which men would fight to keep those colours flying.

Jack shivered. He was surrounded by a great carnival, the celebration of a city proud of its endeavour and certain of its future. Yet whilst others cheered, he smelled the bitter tang of battle, his mind replaying the full horror of war, and saw again the faces of the men he had killed.

The Governor once again took his place at the front of the stage. This time the sergeant carrying the flag and his two escorts formed up behind him.

'Soldiers, go forth bearing that flag; and as our fathers fought, so, if need be, strike you the blow. We stay to guard the hearthstones you have left behind. I speak to you as citizens and soldiers alike, not of Massachusetts, but of the American Confederate Union. While we live, that Union shall last, and until these countless thousands, and all their posterity, have tasted death, the Union of the American people, the heritage of Washington, shall be eternal. Soldiers, go forth with stout hearts and stalwart frames, bearing with you the blessings of your country and the confidence of your fellow citizens. On your shields be returned, or bring them with you. Yours it is to be among the advance guard of Massachusetts's soldiers. As such, I bid you God speed and fare you well.'

The Governor stepped back. It was the signal to the multitude that his speech was done. The crowd cheered with every last breath in their bodies, the noise pounding across the heads of the soldiers and completely drowning out the Drum Corp, which continued to play valiantly in competition.

To the front of A Company, First Sergeant O'Connell turned and bellowed an order. It was lost in the storm of sound, but the men knew what was needed and they moved into a column with Gilmore's Band at their head. This time the march would be short, the orders for the day calling for the men to parade around the edge of the great common, after which they would be allowed to fall out, stack arms and enjoy some refreshments. Later they would march to the station and board the locomotive that waited to take them away from their families and their homes.

As they marched, Jack did his best to shake off the feeling of foreboding that had filled his mind since the presentation of the state flag. He felt as if he alone knew what was to come and what the good citizens of Boston were asking of the men in blue uniforms. The city, and even many of the men themselves, expected an easy war. There would be a single campaign that would force the rebel Southern states to come to heel; one battle to enforce the will of the North. The men would be back in just a few months. And they would return as heroes.

But Jack knew different. There was nothing easy about war. One battle would decide nothing. The people of Boston lived with false hopes, hopes that would likely be shattered when the two armies met for the first time.

Chapter Fourteen

Philadelphia, Wilmington & Baltimore Railroad,
Friday 19 April 1861

The locomotive clattered over a set of points at speed, sending enough of a shudder along its length to wake Jack from his sleep. He had been resting his head against the train car's window, and now it bounced up far enough to crack painfully back against the glass, sending a jolt of pain lancing through the tender spot on the centre of his forehead.

He wiped a hand across his face and sat up straighter, then looked out of the window, but the countryside flashing past meant nothing to him. He turned and nudged the man sitting next to him, who was wide awake and staring into space.

'Where are we?' Jack's voice cracked as he spoke, so he coughed, clearing his throat. The smell of woodsmoke, soot, oil and sweat was thick in his nostrils, the stink of the railroad car the men had been in for many hours now ripe and fermented.

'Nearly at Baltimore.' The reply was given without much enthusiasm.

Jack would not have been able to find Baltimore on a map,

but he did know it was the point in their journey when they would have to detrain and cross the city before boarding another train to Washington. Yet such activity was still in the future, so he rested his head back again against the window and did his best to ignore the clanking and hissing as the locomotive thundered along.

He kept his eyes open, staring through glass that was streaked with rain and dirt, and watched the countryside. It had been a long journey already. They had left Boston the day before, arriving in New York late that same day. They had marched through great cheering crowds, their parade down Broadway a spectacle that would live long in the memory of all who had witnessed it. From there, they had proceeded to board the train for Philadelphia, and the citizens of New York had come in their thousands to wave them off. The fanfare had been enough to reduce many of the men to tears, the New Yorkers giving three great cheers for the boys of the Old Bay State.

They had left Philadelphia at midnight, changing trains in the darkness. By the time the sun had risen, they were well on their way to Baltimore, the next destination on their long journey to Washington.

Their reception at the towns along the way had hardly been any less joyous. At every stop the men were treated like heroes. Great patriotic crowds greeted their arrival, the stations decked out with banners and miles of red, white and blue bunting. Inevitably there were bands, and the men had disembarked to every patriotic tune ever composed before the crowd swarmed over them, the women and children handing over glasses of lemonade and thick slices of cake wrapped in paper napkins.

The men had loved every minute of every stop.

'Do you think there'll be another parade in Baltimore, First Sergeant?' asked James Thatcher from the other side of the train car to where the sergeants from A Company sat together.

'You never know your luck.' First Sergeant O'Connell, sitting opposite Jack, answered without enthusiasm.

'Why, I sure hope there is.' James clearly relished the idea.

'That's because you want another kiss.' His brother was quick to poke him in the ribs.

'You're just jealous.' James's reply was just as quick.

'Enough, boys.' O'Connell put an end to the squabble. The twins could fight like cat and dog when the mood took them. 'This isn't the time for your nonsense.'

'But none of us mind getting ourselves kissed!' O'Dowd was sitting close enough to pick up on the conversation. 'You saw the girl in the yellow dress back in New York, Sergeant Lark? I know young Amos did! Why, he was blushing like a virgin in a fecking whorehouse!'

The men around them whooped with laughter, the sound building as Amos blushed on cue.

'I don't think Amos would know what to do with a girl like that, would you now, son?' O'Dowd was not done teasing the younger man. 'You know what goes where, boy?'

Amos did not reply, his face now crimson.

'When we get to Washington, I think it'll be high time I took you to find out what's what when it comes to women.' O'Dowd was enjoying himself. 'I'm sure there'll be plenty of girls happy to send a soldier on his way with a smile on his face. Why, I reckon they'll see it as their duty! When they see you two, feck me, I think they'll all want to take you home. We'll be following you around just hoping to get ourselves a bit of attention!'

The men around O'Dowd hooted and clapped in agreement.

'You think the rebels know we're coming, First Sergeant?' Amos asked tentatively.

'How the hell am I supposed to know that?' O'Connell's answer was sharp.

'I ain't worried about the damn sechers.' O'Dowd was quick to fill the silence that followed the bad-tempered reply. 'If they turn up looking for trouble, I reckon we'll make them turn tail quick enough.' He looked around him to make sure enough of the men were paying attention. 'It's those langers in the 6th that worry me. If those dirty feckers get to Washington before us, there won't be a clean girl left in the city!'

The men laughed at the remark, and even Jack found a smile. The troops of the 6th Massachusetts Volunteer Militia were in the cars ahead of them.

The train slowed. Immediately the men pressed themselves to the windows, expecting to see another crowd come to wave and cheer as the locomotive took on wood or water. To their disappointment, there was no sign of anyone as they came to a complete halt, and the car fell quiet as the men peered outside and wondered why they had stopped in what appeared to be the middle of nowhere.

They would not have long to wait to find out the reason. The door at the front of the car opened and Major Bridges entered. The officers from both regiments were travelling at the front of the train in their own, more private space. His appearance got the attention of the whole company at once.

'What's going on, sir?' Inevitably, O'Dowd was the first to call out.

'Nothing to worry about.' Bridges walked carefully down the aisle. He nodded a greeting as he saw the sergeants sitting together. 'Good morning, gentlemen.'

'Good morning, sir.' O'Connell got up from his seat. 'What's occurring?'

'We have received dispatches from the railroad officials warning that there's going to be trouble ahead in Baltimore.' Bridges made the announcement softly. The car had fallen silent, and now every ear strained to hear what was happening.

'Trouble, is it?' O'Connell scowled at the notion. 'Who's causing trouble all the way up here?'

'The Pennsylvania Militia were handled roughly by a crowd there yesterday. Rocks were thrown.' Bridges shook his head as he delivered the news. 'It's possible that the same troublemakers will know we are passing through this morning.'

'Fecking slave-loving bastards.' O'Connell's verdict was given quickly. 'Don't they know which side of the line they're on?'

'I am sure they know, First Sergeant.' Bridges still spoke in an even tone. 'But it is clear that the city of Baltimore is in favour of secession, and so that makes it unfriendly ground for us.'

'Feck 'em. If they want trouble, I'm sure the boys will give it to 'em.' The men greeted O'Connell's fiery reply with a soft growl of agreement.

'No one will be fighting anyone.' Bridges was firm. 'But the colonel is worried. He has agreed with the commander of the 6th that both regiments will be loaded when we travel through the city. He has asked the quartermaster to issue twenty rounds per man.'

'That's madness.' Jack spoke for the first time. 'It just takes some idiot to fire and a bad situation will be made much worse.'

'That's as maybe.' Bridges held Jack's gaze. 'But the colonel has ordered it and so that is how it will be. You will hold your men in check. No one will fire unless the order is given. Is that clear, gentlemen?'

Jack did not join in the murmur of assent that followed. He had read Bridges' expression well enough. It was obvious that the regiment's second in command did not agree with the order.

'That is all for the moment.' Bridges nodded firmly to the sergeants before easing past O'Connell as he headed for the car containing K Company.

Jack stayed silent as the men immediately started to chatter. It did not take long for the first shouts of bravado to follow, the troops reacting in a similar fashion to their first sergeant.

If the people of Baltimore wanted to start a fight, the boys of A Company would be ready to give it to them.

The locomotive was moving slowly again when Colonel Scanlon entered the train car, his thin-lipped smile unaltered by the tension in the air.

'Listen up,' he called as he made his way through the car, his voice loud and steady. 'We are about to pass through Baltimore. There will be trouble. I'm sorry to say that, but it's the truth and there's no getting round it. You will be insulted, and maybe some of the sons of bitches will attack you, or throw stones, or any other such projectiles as they see fit. You will not respond. I repeat, you will not respond, no matter the provocation. You all understand me?'

'Yes, sir.' The men chanted their response in unison. They stared at their colonel, hanging on his every word.

'Good.' Scanlon kept moving down the car, swaying from side to side as it jolted along, his hands holding each seat top as he passed. 'But hear this, boys. If they fire on you, and one of you is hit, then your officers will order you to fire back. If that happens, you will pick your target and you will drop the son of a bitch right where he stands.'

At this, the men cheered. It came from deep in their bellies, a feral sound, the roar inspired as much by fear as bravado. Jack stayed silent. The men were not trained marksmen. If they opened fire, it would be indiscriminate. At close range, their Springfield rifles would be dreadfully effective. A single volley would likely kill dozens of bystanders, with little chance for the men to make sure they only hit those firing on them. It would be bloody murder.

He felt someone's gaze on him so turned his head, seeking them out. It was Major Bridges. It was easy enough to read the other man's thoughts. Jack was not alone in finding Scanlon's orders horrifying.

The troop train approached Baltimore with excruciating slowness. Yet not one man complained about the slow progress as they peered through the muck-streaked windows and wondered just what was ahead.

'There's Fort McHenry.' One of the men called out in recognition as he spotted the outline of ramparts on the skyline.

Jack looked out of the window and saw the fort easily enough. The Stars and Stripes flew from a flagpole high on the ramparts, flapping gently in the breeze, a bright flash of colour against the dark grey clouds that filled the skyline. He looked around the car. The company's officers had joined them just outside the city. Their presence had done little to reassure the men, who had been quiet since receiving Scanlon's orders. Yet he sensed their determination and thought it boded well. They were reacting like proper soldiers encountering an unpleasant task. They did not shirk the challenge, but faced up to it, ready to get it done.

'Listen up!' O'Connell had paced to the front of the car and now he turned to address the company. 'Prepare to load!'

The men sat up straighter. The quartermaster had passed through the carriage a little while before, handing out twenty cartridges per man and a full packet of percussion caps. Now the men dipped into their pouches and made ready for the next command.

'Load!'

The car was soon filled with the rattle of ramrods. It was awkward to load the long rifle whilst seated, but the men got on with it with little enough fuss. Jack took his time. He had not had the chance to practise with the Springfield, but the drill was familiar enough. Even the cartridge itself was similar to the Minié bullet he had used before.

The cartridge was cleverly designed. It was conical in shape and just narrower than the barrel of the rifle so as to make it easy to load. The genius in its design made itself known when the charge it rested on was fired. Then the hollow bottom section of the bullet would deform and expand so that it fully gripped the rifling inside the barrel, spinning the bullet to make it more accurate whilst also trapping the full power of the exploding charge. It made the bullet wickedly effective, and Jack had seen dreadful damage done to the enemy's ranks.

A loud clatter brought his attention back to the present. Amos Thatcher had dropped his ramrod and then kicked it under the seat in front of him. Jack did not need to look at the boy's pale face and wide eyes to know what was affecting him. He got to his feet and moved across the car, bending forward as he did so to retrieve the fallen ramrod.

'Here.' He handed the whey-faced lad his own Springfield, then took the half-loaded rifle from the boy's hands. It did not take him long to finish loading it, using the ramrod to give the bullet two good taps to make sure it was well seated against the charge at the bottom of the barrel. 'Here you go. Put on your percussion cap, but for God's sake don't cock it.'

Jack handed the loaded rifle over, then took his own back, noting the sweaty marks Amos's damp hand had left on the barrel. He turned to the boy's brother, making sure that he was loaded too. The other sergeants started to move through the car, checking their men's weapons.

The locomotive jolted then slowed as it advanced further into the outskirts of Baltimore. It was almost noon. The men of the 1st Boston were ready for their first fight of the campaign; a fight that would likely take place on Northern soil.

Chapter Fifteen

The streets were eerily quiet as the locomotive approached the President Street depot. The men were doing their best to sit calmly, but every set of eyes was riveted on the scene outside the windows. The troops were as primed and ready for trouble as their rifles. Now they had arrived and it appeared that no one was there to so much as shout a single insult their way.

'Where is everyone?' Major Bridges had chosen to stand next to Jack's seat. Now he voiced the remark that was on everyone's lips.

Jack shrugged. 'Maybe it's a fuss about nothing.'

'It doesn't feel like nothing.' Bridges replied without taking his eyes off the window.

'So what's next?' Jack craned his neck to try to see along one of the passing streets. He spotted nothing more dangerous than a butcher's wagon parked outside a shop.

'We have to switch locomotives.' Bridges glanced at Jack. 'The line going south leaves from Camden station, about a mile and a half west of here. The city officials have forbidden locomotives from crossing the city, so the railroad will uncouple us from the locomotive here, then use horses to haul each carriage through the streets to the other depot, where we will be reattached to another locomotive.' Bridges was forced to hold tight to Jack's seat as the train shuddered and bumped to a halt. Outside, a large number of railroad workers were coming forward to start the task of uncoupling the cars.

'How long will all that take?'

'Not long.'

As if on cue, the car jolted backwards. The railroad workers were nothing if not efficient. As the men from A Company watched, the depot was filled with activity. Some of the workers were swarming around the carriages, whilst others brought forward teams of horses. It did not take long for them to have the first cars ready to leave. They looked cumbersome now they had been detached from the locomotive. As Jack watched, the first one trundled out of the depot on tracks that he presumed led all the way through the city to the station where the other locomotive waited for them. The car moved slowly and Jack could see dozens of faces pressed against its windows as the men from the 6th Massachusetts looked out anxiously. He followed their gaze and understood their unease immediately.

Outside the depot, the streets were no longer quiet. A growing number of bystanders had arrived to observe the first cars leave for their odd journey through the city.

'Trust us to be last.' Robert Kearney had come to stand next to Jack when Bridges had left to join Colonel Scanlon outside.

'Someone has to be.' Jack could think of nothing else to say. He could see the tension beginning to affect the men. Their hands gripped their rifles tightly enough for the whites of their knuckles to show. They were quiet, too. He could not recall a time when they had been so hushed, the relaxed discipline of their sergeants and officers usually allowing them to chatter in the ranks in a way that would have got a redcoat flogged. But this time, not one man was speaking.

Outside the depot, the crowd of bystanders was getting bigger and louder. There was a low growl coming from them. It was as if the few hundred people had somehow formed into a single beast that was watching the Union infantry with growing anger.

The second section of train cars pulled out from the depot, causing an immediate reaction from the crowd, its low growl replaced by angry shouts. Jack could not make out what insults were being hurled at the men inside the cars, but it was clear that they were not the same cries and cheers of adulation that had greeted them at every stage of their journey to date.

Despite the crowd's ugly reaction, the cars pulled steadily forward. There was no sign that the men inside them would respond to the provocation, and it did not take long for them to be lost from sight. A large part of the crowd moved away after them, but enough stayed behind, and now they turned their attention to the other sections of the train still waiting to leave the security of the depot.

'This is madness,' Robert muttered. 'We are waiting here like so many damn fools.'

'We should all be going together.' Jack agreed with his officer. 'Why the hell are we waiting here to leave on our own?'

'The streets are too narrow, or at least that's what the railroad officials told Scanlon. If we all travelled together, it would take twice as long. This way we can move at full speed. It'll be quicker.'

'Not if those bastards get in the way.' Jack was watching

the crowd. Another section of the train pulled out of the depot, the last companies of the 6th Massachusetts beginning their uncomfortable journey across the city. Again, a large portion of the crowd peeled off to follow them, but hundreds stayed in place. The crowd was smaller, but it still outnumbered the men from the 1st Boston by dozens to their every one. More were arriving every minute, and already there were angry chants directed towards the Union soldiers still waiting in the depot.

'Here we go.' Robert had spotted movement around the car.

Major Bridges was still outside with Colonel Scanlon. The two officers held a final conference, then Bridges moved to the car containing A Company whilst Scanlon went to join K Company.

'We're off. I want everyone away from the windows. Sit on the floor if you have to.' Bridges fired off the orders as he entered the car.

The men did as they were told. Only the sergeants and the officers stayed at the windows, the right to see out a privilege of their rank. Within a minute the car had jerked into motion, the team of horses now attached to its front hauling it forward.

The crowd saw the movement and instantly its jeers grew louder. Jack could see the rage on the faces of the men at the front of the mob as they bayed at the soldiers, their shouts and insults growing in intensity. The first missile came flying towards the car, hurtling through the air before slamming into a window near the front. It hit the glass above Amos Thatcher's head with enough force to make him flinch.

'Don't shit your pants, Amos.' O'Connell saw the young

soldier's reaction. 'It's just a lump of horse dung. It won't hurt you.'

The men laughed, just as they were meant to. Jack knew the laughter was louder than it needed to be for such a poor jest, the troops using it to calm their fears.

A thunderous roar came from somewhere further away in the city. It echoed through the streets, the sound immediately goading the crowd around the depot to increase their own abuse. Their cries intensified further, their anger building quickly, directed at the last two cars pulling out of the President Street depot.

As if at some hidden signal, a fresh flurry of missiles came flying out of the crowd. More shit rained against the windows, but a few of the projectiles hit with more force, the crack of rocks loud against the car's sides.

'Hell fire!' A man to Jack's right cursed as a choice morsel of horseshit splattered across the window by his head. 'Why, those dirty sons of bitches.'

The men around the unfortunate soldier laughed at his choice of words. The sound died away quickly as another salvo of missiles clattered into the car, and the soldiers looked at one another, their faces betraying the same mix of shock and fear.

'What have we done to deserve this?' Robert fired the question at Jack.

Jack heard the younger man's fear, but he was given no time to answer. Something cracked the glass a foot or so away from both their heads.

'What the hell was that?' Robert gasped. Around him the men were turning their heads this way and that, their alarm building quickly.

Another of the missiles hit the glass towards the rear,

followed quickly by a further one that smacked into the other side of the car. Jack recognised the sound immediately.

'Some bastard is shooting at us.'

'They're what?' Robert was incredulous.

'They're firing at us!' This time Jack shouted the answer.

Already the car was slowing. It was under constant fire now, all manner of bricks, stones and rocks beating against it. They all heard the scream of one of the horses as it was hit, the animal's shriek of pain clearly audible above the roars of the mob.

'Lie down!' Jack shouted the order. Another bullet smashed a window at the rear of the car, showering the men nearby with a vicious storm of broken glass.

'That ain't manly!' a soldier near Jack complained.

'I don't care!' Jack ducked and peered out of the window. The mob was surrounding the car as it slowed, the shower of stones and rocks constant now. There were mercifully few shots being fired, most of the mob content to hurl insults and less deadly missiles at the Union soldiers incarcerated in the cars. But it was still only a matter of time before someone was hurt, and Jack was determined to minimise that risk.

The car crawled onwards. It was making slow progress, the animals charged with dragging it across the city struggling to force a passage through the crowd. Yet they were still moving, and as they passed under a bridge, the sound of missiles hitting the car's sides suddenly cut off.

The respite was short. The moment they emerged from underneath the bridge, the storm intensified, the rioters hurling everything they could lay their hands on. This was followed by two great thumps as the rioters pushed something heavy off the bridge and onto the car's roof. Every man glanced up in terror.

'Shit.' Jack grabbed at a seat back. It was clear that they were stuck where they were. The attack continued without pause, the stationary car an easy target.

Jack was not the only one to see it. Bridges was moving from window to window, stepping around the men lying on the floor. He turned to see Jack looking at him.

'We have to disembark, cross the city on foot.' The major looked grim as he made the decision.

Jack nodded. It was the only course of action.

'We going out there, Sergeant?' asked a quivering Irish voice.

'Yes.' Jack's reply was curt.

'It's a goddam riot!' Another man's voice rose in protest. 'We can't do that.'

'We'll do whatever we're damn well told.' Jack's reply was fierce. 'Now shut your mouths and get ready to move.'

His command did little to quell the dozens of conversations going on throughout the company. The men still lay on the floor, but the hum of low conversation was constant, only broken by the crack and thump as the car was hit by a steady flow of missiles still coming from the crowd.

Jack was about to shout again when he noticed people leaving the crowd. Large numbers were peeling away from the rear of the mob. Some were running. He had no idea if they were escaping from the building threat of violence or rushing to join another ruckus somewhere else. Either way, the flurry of missiles lessened as the crowd thinned.

'Sergeant! Can we get up—'

'Shut your mouth!' Jack snapped the command, stopping the question. He was watching the crowd. Over half had gone, with still more leaving every second.

'Now's the time.' He turned to Robert, who was bent low

near one of the car's windows. 'We need to get out now.'

Robert's mouth opened as if to reply, but no sound came out. Jack shook his head and turned to look where Captain Rowell was standing with Major Bridges at the front of the car. He was not the only one to have seen what had to be done. First Sergeant O'Connell had already moved across to the two officers, and the three men were having an urgent conversation that came to an abrupt end as Jack reached them.

O'Connell turned to face the company. 'We're going to move out,' he shouted, silencing the anxious murmurs that still rippled through the ranks.

'Wait!' Rowell countermanded the order almost immediately. He had spotted a man in uniform running through a side street. For a moment the man was lost from sight as he ducked through the crowd of rioters, then he emerged once again and came sprinting towards the car.

The crowd saw the runner. At least a dozen missiles were thrown. They struck the ground around him, the sound of their impact just about audible over the roar of anger.

'Shit.' O'Connell caught Jack's eye as he gave his verdict.

The two sergeants watched the courier as he ran to the train car containing Colonel Scanlon and K Company. He was gone from sight for no more than a couple of minutes before he emerged again and dashed for the one holding A Company. Every man was silent as he vaulted into the car and looked at Major Bridges.

'Sir, the tracks are blocked.' The courier was gasping for air, and his face was flushed and streaked with sweat.

'What the hell?' O'Connell took it upon himself to answer for his officers. 'What the feck are those langers in the 6th doing about it?'

Bridges chose to ignore O'Connell's choice words. 'What are the colonel's orders?'

'Both companies are to disembark and proceed on foot.' The courier gulped down a mouthful of air before he continued. 'You're to be advised that there is fighting ahead. Major Watson of the 6th ordered his men to return fire.'

'They fired on the crowd?' Bridges sounded appalled.

'Yes, sir.'

Bridges asked no further questions. He gnawed on his moustache for a moment before turning to Rowell. 'Captain. Let's get the men outside.'

Rowell looked appalled, but the order had been given. The men of the two companies from Boston would have to complete their journey across Baltimore on foot.

Chapter Sixteen

---◆---

'Kill the white niggers!'

The foul invective spewed from the mob as the men from the 1st Boston formed up by the side of the tracks. The jeers and insults vomited forth, the torrent of abuse unrelenting.

'Face front!' Jack had been one of the first out. Now he stalked around the men as they started to form into a column. The two companies of the 1st Boston would march one after the other, with A Company in the lead. Bridges and Scanlon would be in the middle of the compact formation, leaving Rowell to lead the way with First Sergeant O'Connell at his side.

It was hard for the men to hear orders over the howls of the mob. Now that the soldiers were out of the car, the crowd pressed closer. They were making noises more like wild beasts than human beings, baying for blood.

'Forward, march!' O'Connell bellowed the order as soon as the column was ready.

The tight streets left little room and the men were forced to march through a narrow corridor of hate lined with red-faced rioters intent on making every step a torment of misery and abuse.

'Eyes front!' Jack shouted. He knew he would be ignored, but he wanted the men to hear his voice. A little way behind him he could hear the other sergeants doing the same, while at the head of the column O'Connell was spending as much time looking back and hollering at his men as he was watching the path ahead.

Every so often the noise of another mob could be heard. Jack had no idea what was happening elsewhere in the city. From the distant roars and cheers, he could only suppose other rioters were tormenting the men from the 6th.

'Amos! Keep your fucking spacings,' Jack snarled at the nearer of the two twins. Amos had been looking left and right instead of concentrating on his marching. His dereliction caused him to catch the arm of the man at his side, making him and three other men stumble.

Jack glanced at Robert. The lieutenant's face was as white as a sheet. He had said nothing since they had abandoned the train car. Less than three or four yards separated them both from the densely packed mob.

A sudden flurry of missiles thumped into the tight company column. Half a dozen soldiers were hit, their curses barely loud enough to be heard above the hoots and catcalls that followed hot on the heels of the barrage.

'March!' Jack shouted the order. Two of his men now had bloodied faces, whilst another was limping after a brick had hit his thigh. 'Keep fucking going!'

A rioter burst from the crowd and dodged his way to the front of the column, a few dozen paces ahead of Rowell and O'Connell. The mob cheered him, the feral roar doubling in intensity as the rioter unfurled a palmetto flag that he had attached to a piece of lumber. With his makeshift colours flying, he made a parody of marching like a soldier. The crowd bayed and roared as the man mocked the Union troops. It was a fine entertainment and it inspired the mob to let loose another flurry of missiles.

'Keep it steady!' Jack called out in encouragement. His men's faces betrayed their horror. They were on home soil and yet they marched as if through the heart of an enemy's domain. He doubted if any of them had ever experienced anything like it. He knew he had not. The hatred on display that day was far beyond his experience. He had fought in the bitterest battles, against foes desperate to kill him. Yet he had never faced an enemy that displayed such loathing as the mob through which they now marched.

He looked at Robert. 'Stay close to the men.'

For a moment Robert stared at him in incomprehension. Then he managed to nod, his tongue flickering out of his mouth to lick nervously across his lips.

Jack moved away immediately, double-timing along the side of the column. Hands reached out from the crowd, fists shaking in his direction, and more than one man tried to grab at him. He kept going, forcing his way and ignoring the invective aimed at him. He kept his eyes focused on the man marching with the makeshift flag.

As he burst around the leading corner of the column, he could see both Rowell and O'Connell turning to stare at him. He cared nothing for their thoughts. It was time to show his men that they still controlled their own destiny.

It did not take him long to reach the man marching with the enemy's flag.

The rioter turned in mid-stride as he sensed Jack's arrival. Jack gave him no time to speak. The man was young, perhaps no more than twenty years old. His bravado had brought him to this place. He had danced to the roars of the crowd, revelling in his mockery of the hated Union soldiers. Now a grim-faced Northern sergeant confronted him and he stumbled to a halt, uncertain how to react.

Jack had planned the punch with care, and it landed exactly where he had intended. His right fist connected perfectly with the rioter's mouth. Anything he wanted to say was rammed back down his throat as his lips were mashed against his teeth. Jack reached forward and snatched the brightly coloured flag from the pole.

'You damned Yankee bastard.' The rioter was not done, even with the blood now streaming over his chin. His flag gone, he twisted the long piece of lumber around in his hands, turning the splintered pole into a weapon.

'Shut your muzzle.' Jack saw what the man intended. It was easy enough to sway back and let him lash the lumber past his front. The rioter stumbled as his blow failed to connect. It gave Jack an opening, and he stepped forward, slamming his fist into the man's throat. The rioter fell on his arse, his hands clutched to his crushed windpipe, his angry cries shut off as he choked and spluttered in the dirt.

'Face front and keep marching.' Jack tossed the man's flag at a soldier in the front rank, then roared the order. He did not bother to drag the rioter out of the way. Instead he double-timed to one side, leaving the company to flow around the man's prostrate body. More than one blue-coated soldier lashed out with his boots at the man who had taunted them.

'Double time!' O'Connell was quick to grasp the opportunity

Jack had given them. The men responded immediately. The shouts of the crowd were drowned out as the column increased its pace, the insults and cries of derision hidden beneath the sound of army boots pounding onto cobbles and the noise of the soldiers' equipment thumping and clattering against their bodies.

The men pressed on, moving more quickly now. Their breath started to rasp in their throats as the faster pace tested their strength, but Jack doubted any would complain. He had moved to one side as the column came past, and now he jogged alongside it once again, back in his place in front of Robert. More than one man flashed him a smile, their approval of his actions clear. He had given them heart, just when they had needed it.

The mob was still following the men through the streets, but no more missiles flew towards the fast-moving soldiers. Jack began to dare to hope that the worst was behind them. The howling mob had tested the company's mettle, but they had come through the ordeal with nothing more than a couple of bloodied scalps and a few bruises. If they could just get to Camden station without having to deal with another confrontation, then the day would serve to temper them and help prepare them for the harder fights ahead.

'Company! March!' O'Connell shouted the order that slowed the pace.

Jack felt an icy rush flush through his veins. He looked ahead to see what had made the first sergeant reduce the men's speed.

The street was blocked. A makeshift barricade had been thrown across the path the soldiers would have to take. It was made of mounds of sand reinforced with heavy anchors, and

the train tracks used by the cars as they passed through the
city had been ripped up and used to strength it further. Behind
the barricade was another mob. They were armed with
crowbars and picks and they were waiting for the soldiers to
arrive.

Jack's hopes died. There would be no easy passage to the
other station. The Union soldiers would have to fight their way
through.

'Company, halt!' O'Connell gave the only order he could.

The men came to a noisy standstill. Most gasped for air, the
fast pace stretching their lungs and draining the strength from
legs not yet used to such exertion.

'Stand fast.' Jack had just enough breath for the command.
His own lungs burned from the strain of moving at double
time, but neither he nor any of the men in the two companies
would be given respite.

With a great roar, the mob unleashed a fresh salvo of
missiles. The Union soldiers were hit from every direction as
the crowd that followed the column surged forward to surround
them once again.

It was chaos. Stones and rocks rained down on the troops.
Dozens were hit, their cries of pain lost against the storm of
noise coming from the mob. A man in the rank to Jack's left
went down. Jack had no idea what had hit the unfortunate
fellow, but he was given no time to render any aid. Suddenly a
volley of gunshots snapped past. He could not help flinching as
he heard the dreadful whip-crack sound. It was as if the air was
alive with a plague of snapping, biting insects, and more than
one man ducked or waved his hands around his head as if he
could somehow shoo the deadly missiles away.

'They're shooting at us!' Amos cried out in a dreadful mix of fear and shock.

'Shut up!' Jack placed himself between Robert and the rioters. They still hung back, but the closest could not be more than five yards away. He could see the snarls on their faces as they bellowed insults at the soldiers. A few still had missiles to throw, and Jack could only watch as they hurled them at the stationary soldiers.

'We need to get moving,' he bellowed. 'We can't stay here.' As if to emphasise the fact, a brick smashed violently on the cobbles a couple of inches from Robert's boots.

'Jesus Christ!' The lieutenant cried out as fragments hit his legs. 'We need to go back!'

'No!' Jack knew there was no way to retreat. The company could only press on and hope to God that none of them were killed.

He turned on his heel, thinking to run to Rowell and tell him what had to be done. As he did so, another volley of gunfire spat out from the mob. Once again the air was alive with the bowel-churning hum of bullets cracking through the air. And this time the mob had aimed lower.

A man screamed. 'They hit the lieutenant!'

Jack heard the horrified shouts from the far side of the company. He pushed his way through the ranks, careless of hurting the men he barged past, emerging from the last files to see Clancy sprawled on the ground. A bullet had hit him in the throat. He lay on his back, staring at the sky, his broken spectacles beside him. Blood pulsed from the dreadful wound, flowing down his neck and onto the cobbles. The young officer's mouth opened and closed as he tried to speak, the blood that poured down his throat drowning his dying words.

'Give it to them!' Jack heard the crowd baying for more blood. 'Kill the white niggers!'

The news was spreading fast through the company that one of their lieutenants had been killed. The men looked around them, their pale, drawn expressions betraying their shock and fear.

'Can I shoot!' O'Dowd stood in the ranks near Clancy. Now he shouted at Jack, his rifle held ready to open fire. 'Can I fecking shoot!'

Jack saw the madness in the Irishman's eyes. He moved fast, stepping past Clancy's corpse and using his own rifle to batter O'Dowd's upwards so that it pointed at the sky. 'Wait for your fucking orders.'

'They're killing us!' O'Dowd bellowed back. 'They're fecking killing us!'

Other soldiers started to shout out. Many held their rifles ready to pull them into their shoulders, and some were already preparing to fire.

'Hold fast!' Jack stalked up and down the flank of the column, daring the men to disobey him. 'Hold fast, damn your eyes.'

His shoulders twitched as he turned his back on the mob. He expected to be struck at any moment, but he forced himself to ignore the fear.

'Advance!' The order rang out. Jack thought it was Scanlon, the command coming from the rear of the company's ranks.

'Pick up the lieutenant!' he bellowed. He would not leave Clancy behind. Two soldiers obeyed him, quickly handing their rifles to a comrade before bending down to retrieve the body.

The company started to move, the men pressing on towards

the barricade that blocked their path. There was nothing else to be done. The barrier would have to be cleared.

Through a gap in the ranks Jack caught a glimpse of Scanlon and Bridges. A man he did not recognise was with them. He could only presume a city official had somehow found his way to the beleaguered men of the 1st Boston. He had no idea what message had been delivered, but whatever it was, it had led to the correct command being given. The men could not stay where they were.

'Come on!' He shouted encouragement to the men around him. They were moving more quickly now. From his position on the left flank he could not see what Rowell or O'Connell were doing. He could only run alongside the troops and hope that the mob would not stand their ground.

'Forward!'

The men increased their pace. They stormed onwards now, their ranks disordered. The mob behind the barricade saw them coming. Many stepped back, ceding the obstacle to the soldiers, but enough stayed to contest their passage.

'Come on!' Jack could see enough to know that the barricade was not going to be given up without a fight. His boots thumped on the cobbles as he began to run. He could feel his equipment bouncing off his body and his ears were filled with the roar of his own breathing.

His boots scrabbled on the barricade, slipping on the mounds of sand before he managed to find purchase on one of the heavy anchors that formed the bulk of the wall. He scrambled up the front, holding his rifle awkwardly in one hand whilst using the other to haul himself up. For a moment, his boots slipped, then he felt them grip and he swung himself up and over the top, his backside scraping across a torn-up rail.

A rioter armed with a crowbar stood behind the barricade. He braced his feet and lunged the moment Jack's boots hit the ground. The crowbar came at Jack fast, but he had fought a hundred battles like this and he swatted it aside with the butt of his rifle before he had even found his balance. He saw a look of fear flicker across his opponent's face as the man realised he had missed. It was almost too easy. Jack stepped forward, his arms still jangling from the contact with the crowbar. He kept the rifle swinging, bringing the barrel around then slamming it into the side of the rioter's head.

The contact was brutal. The rioter staggered to one side. Jack gave him no time to recover. He lunged with the rifle, driving the barrel into the pit of the man's stomach. The rioter could do nothing and he bent forward, the air rushing from his body in a single great gasp. He was defenceless and hurting, but Jack would not leave him standing. He brought the rifle butt down on the man's head, bludgeoning him into the dirt without mercy.

'Come on!' He roared encouragement at his troops. He need not have bothered. The men of the company had not hesitated. They came over the barricade together and drove the rioters backwards. Any who tried to stand were dealt with without pity. Half a dozen were knocked down. It was enough to send the rest packing, and now they streamed away from the wall.

For the first time that day, the Union soldiers cheered. They had seen one of their officers killed and they had endured everything the mob had thrown at them. Now they roared in defiance, daring the rioters to come back and fight like men.

'Form up!' O'Connell came striding through the company's broken ranks. If he was impressed by his command's achievement, he was not showing it. 'Lark. Get the men formed up. Now!' He marched on, repeating his message.

'You heard the first sergeant!' Jack stepped past the man he had struck down. 'Form up! Look lively now!' He grabbed the closest man and shoved him forward.

The men moved quickly, obediently filling out the ranks. Jack left them to it and went to find Robert. He had abandoned his charge, and now he needed to make sure the man he was being paid to protect was still in one piece.

Chapter Seventeen

---◆◆◆---

Robert had perched himself on the rear of the barricade whilst the company reformed. To Jack's relief, he was unscathed save for a great stain over one side of his uniform jacket.

'You look knackered,' Jack said by way of greeting.

Robert looked up. 'Where were you?'

'Helping with Clancy.'

'I cannot believe he is dead.' Robert appeared ready to vomit.

'Well, he is.' Jack spoke harshly. There would be a time to mourn the young officer. That time would only come when the rest of the company were safe. 'You'd better deal with it pretty damn fast.'

'You're cruel.' Robert looked at Jack as if seeing him for the first time. He was clearly appalled at such callousness.

'It's just how it is.' Jack ignored the look on his officer's face. 'Are you hurt?' He gestured to the side of Robert's chest that was stained brown.

'No.' Robert plucked ruefully at his jacket. 'I was hit by shit.'

'Well, aren't you the lucky one.' Jack did not give him time to say anything further. The company was nearly re-formed and he had seen Major Bridges arrive with Scanlon.

'Get moving, goddam it.' Scanlon bustled through the last of the re-forming ranks. 'Captain Rowell, get your damn company moving.'

'Sir, the roads are blocked!' Rowell protested. 'We must turn back.'

Scanlon moved fast. He got into Rowell's face, thrusting his chin upwards. 'We ain't turning back, Captain Rowell. We don't run from lily-livered pieces of filth.'

'Sir, it's—'

'Shut your goddam mouth.' Scanlon snarled the words into Rowell's face, flecks of spittle splattering across the younger man's cheeks. 'Major Bridges and I will take Captain Thompson's company south and try to get to Camden station that way. I want your company to go straight ahead. These merry fuckers cannot be everywhere.'

'You are splitting us up?' Rowell was aghast.

'Those are my orders, Captain Rowell,' Scanlon snapped back, then he turned away, giving Rowell no chance to say anything further.

Jack had noticed Rowell stiffen with anger as he was shouted down. His uniform was still immaculate. He also noticed that the captain had drawn his revolver. The sight of the beautiful ivory-handled Colt sent a jolt of pure jealousy running through him.

'Get to your feet.' He snapped the command at Robert, who had made no attempt to stand.

'We're not ready to go.'

'Get to your fucking feet now.' Jack was in no mood to be

ignored. He reached forward and hauled the lieutenant upright.

'Who the hell do you think you are?' Robert was angry at being manhandled in such a way.

Jack growled in lieu of an answer. He shoved the lieutenant forward, forcing him to walk. It was time to stop thinking. It was time to march.

It had not taken long for the rioters to regather their courage. They might have fled from the barricade without much of a fight, but they had regrouped and now they came back looking for revenge.

The two infantry companies had not hung around waiting for them. K Company had already marched south with Scanlon at their head, whilst A Company had stayed on the road they were already on. They had resumed the march without interference, the swift taking of the barricade buying them some time.

'Here they come again,' Amos Thatcher cried out in warning.

Jack stared ahead. The company had covered no more than four city blocks and were at the corner of Gay and Pratt streets. The mob filled the width of Pratt Street. There were thousands of them, and they were heading straight for the column.

'Holy mother of God,' breathed Robert as he too saw what was approaching.

The first rocks and stones came flying from the depths of the crowd. The range was long and they skittered across the cobbles in front of the now stationary infantrymen. The sight was still enough to elicit a great roar from the mob, which now stormed forward.

'What are we going to do?' Robert pressed close behind Jack's back.

'We fight.' Jack fired back the reply. He knew that most of those nearby were listening.

'We cannot fight that many!'

'We have no choice.'

Ahead, the mob continued to advance, an almost constant barrage of missiles hurled at the soldiers. The range was closing quickly, and already stones and rocks were crashing into the front ranks. Soldiers cursed as they were hit. The impacts were painful but not dangerous. Yet that would surely change as the mob got closer.

'Stand your ground.' Jack looked only at his men. He was forced to shout to be heard over the roar of the mob. 'You're soldiers, not a damn rabble. Stand your ground and if one of those bastards comes close, hit the bugger hard. Knock them down so they won't get up again.'

He saw the men grip and regrip their firearms, the tension of waiting stretching every man's nerves.

'Use your rifles. Beat the fuckers with them if you have to. But you will not open fire. No matter what happens, do not fire on them.' Jack shouted his instructions. It would be a desperate affair. The mob outnumbered the soldiers. Most of the rioters were armed with some sort of weapon: crowbars, shovels or just lumps of lumber. But the soldiers had their rifles and he reckoned they could use them well enough.

And they had him.

The mob slowed as it closed the distance, coming to a halt a few dozen yards in front of the soldiers. The noise was dreadful. The mob jeered the troops, insults and oaths thrown with as much heart as the missiles that still rained down without pause.

'Stand firm!' Jack saw the ranks moving. The men were fidgeting. Fear was taking hold.

A soldier was hit on the head by a rock, gashing him above the eye. He fell, the strike of sufficient force to knock him from his feet.

'They got Carter!' The cry went up almost immediately. The sight of the bloodied man on the ground convinced those around him that he was dead, even though he was already trying to get back to his feet.

The words rippled through the company like wildfire. Men who had been facing front now turned to look at their mates. Those who had been standing still twisted on the spot, their heads turning left and right as they sought a way out.

Jack saw the fear take hold. Another flurry of missiles slammed into the ranks. One caught him a glancing blow on the upper arm, but he barely felt it.

'Stand firm!' he shouted at the men.

The mob might have stopped surging forward, but it still came on a pace or two at a time, the men at the front trying to summon enough courage to lead the final rush towards the infantry. The shouts and jeers continued unabated, those further back urging those at the front to attack whilst they hurled anything they could find at the hated soldiers who refused to retreat.

One rock hit Rowell.

It was the size of a closed fist. It came from deep in the mob and it struck him on the right cheek with enough force to knock him backwards. The blood came fast, surging from the deep crevice gouged in his skin, spilling down his face and running into the collar of his shirt.

'They got the captain!' The agonised cry echoed through the company.

Jack heard the panic in the shouts. Men shuffled backwards,

a movement that could turn into a panicked rout in a heartbeat.

Rowell turned to look at his men, his face covered in a mask of blood. He stared at them in horror, as if he were unable to believe what was happening.

Jack saw the mob begin to move. It was as if the rioters had become one being, and they came forward together, the movement slow and hesitant at first, but gathering momentum with every passing second.

'Kill the Yankees!' The cry sounded clearly over the wild chants. 'Kill them!'

A musket fired. Jack had heard the noise too many times not to be able to pick it out, even over the roar of the mob. Another gunshot followed, then another.

'Kill them!' The feral roar was picked up by the mob, the words shouted in unison, repeated again and again, coming from a thousand mouths as they moved forward. 'Kill them! Kill them! Kill them!'

Another flurry of gunfire rang out.

Jack was standing in front of Amos Thatcher when the musket ball hit the boy just below the left eye. It smashed through his face, showering those around him with blood and broken bone. Amos fell without making a sound.

'They killed Amos!' screamed the man behind the young soldier. 'They killed Amos!'

Every man present looked at Amos's twin. James Thatcher was standing in the file next to his brother. Now he stared at Amos, his mouth hanging open in a silent scream that went on and on, his eyes wide with horror.

'They killed Amos!'

The cry reached Rowell. Jack saw the news register on the captain's bloodied face. He glanced back at the men before turning to look at the mob. It was horribly close now, the pace of its advance increasing as those leading, goaded by their fellow rioters, found the courage to rush the infantrymen.

'Prepare to fire!' Rowell screamed the command, his voice rising in pitch so that he shrieked like a girl.

'No!' Jack knew what was about to happen. Rowell was about to make a dreadful mistake, one that would likely kill dozens of civilians. There was no knowing what would happen afterwards.

The men in the front ranks hesitated. They looked at one another, their whey-coloured faces betraying their fear.

'Prepare to fire!' repeated Rowell.

Half a dozen men lifted their rifles. The rest just stood and stared at one another, or at the mob that was surging towards them.

'A Company!' This time O'Connell bellowed the order. 'Ready!'

The troops obeyed their first sergeant. Any man who could see the mob pulled his rifle into his shoulder.

'Don't fire!' Jack shouted the futile command.

He was ignored.

'Aim! . . . Fire!'

O'Connell's order was drowned out as rifles fired in unison. The volley unleashed a great thunderclap of sound, the roar echoing off the buildings. The viciously spinning bullets tore deep into the crowd. Dozens fell, the head of the mob ripped apart in a storm of blood.

'Company! Double time!' O'Connell's voice was the first to be heard in the aftermath of the volley. The wild cries of the mob had been silenced by the slaughter.

The company obeyed. They moved forward as one, the

ranks easing into an awkward run. They brought the bodies of Lieutenant Clancy and Amos Thatcher with them.

The mob had been thrown into confusion by the volley. Some were tending to the dead and the dying, but most lost heart and fled from the advancing soldiers, any threat of violence forgotten.

The company ran through the dispersing mob, the men doing their best to pick their way past those they had shot down. A few cried out in horror as they saw the damage their Springfields were capable of inflicting. Limbs had been ripped from bodies, the heavy bullets tearing through flesh to leave what remained looking like little more than offal. The ground was swathed in gore, gobbets of flesh and scraps of bone strewn across the cobbles so that it was as if the company ran through a butcher's yard. It stank like hell; the bitter stench of powder smoke mixed with the acrid smell of blood and opened bowels.

'Sweet mother of God.' Jack heard Robert mutter under his breath as they both stepped over the body of a rioter. A bullet had struck him in the centre of the face. What was left was barely recognisable as human, the man's head all but destroyed. Robert gagged and stumbled, his legs turning to jelly as he choked on the dreadful sight.

'Come on!' Jack hauled his charge on, forcing him to keep moving. The lieutenant's face was the colour of ash.

The company pressed on. They moved more slowly now. Some were wounded, whilst others lugged the bodies of the two men who had been killed. Yet they kept moving towards the distant station that would offer them sanctuary.

A sanctuary they would have to fight to reach.

Jack heard the roar of another mob before he saw them. A

wave of sound battered into the company. The pace of the advance slowed immediately, a barely audible groan rippling through the ranks as the men realised they were still far from safety.

'Oh no!' Robert greeted the fresh crowd with a moan of horror. 'We can't get through.'

'We can and we will.' Jack's lungs were hurting, but he still found the breath to refute Robert's doomsaying.

The roar of the mob intensified as the company came closer. The inevitable flurry of missiles smashed into the ranks, the violent storm no less powerful than the ones that had gone before.

'Halt!' O'Connell shouted. 'Prepare to fire.'

This time the men did not hesitate. Those still with loaded rifles pushed forward. The company had crossed the line.

'Ready!' O'Connell's voice was calm. 'Aim! . . . Fire!'

The volley spat out death and vengeance. It tore into the mob blocking the road. The killing had begun again.

'Load!' O'Connell was commanding the company now. Rowell stood at his side, his fabulous revolver pointing at the ground, the officer taking no part in the slaughter.

The men behind him reloaded with a will. Their faces were blackened with powder. Their eyes were hard.

'Aim! . . . Fire!'

A second volley crashed into the mob. Men died as the heavy bullets smashed their flesh into ruin.

'Double time!'

A Company knew the drill now. They advanced through the cloud of powder smoke their two volleys had thrown out, emerging into a scene straight from the bowels of hell.

'Keep moving!' Jack did not look at the grotesque sight of

men lying in the awkward poses of death. He kept his eyes on his men, Robert trailing in his wake like a beaten puppy.

The company doubled past the men they had killed. They were still abused, the mob still dogging their every step, stones and bricks still clattering into their tired, aching bodies. But the jeers and even the filthiest of abuse counted for little now against the sight of broken bodies and torn flesh.

Jack continued to encourage his men. They were tired. Their faces ran with sweat, their breath came in laboured gasps and their chests heaved with exertion. They were hard yards now, cruel yards, the men pushing the limits of their endurance.

'Barricade!' The warning cry came from the men at the front. Those around Jack let out a moan. They had nothing left.

'Come on!' Jack forced authority into his voice. His own body protested and his lungs burned as he sucked down another laboured breath. But he would not give in.

He angled his path so that he could see ahead. The barricade stretched across the road. But this time it was manned by men in uniform. He looked behind him. The rioters were pulling back, the sight of the armed policemen of Baltimore enough of a deterrent to keep them at bay.

Behind the barricade was a building that could only be Camden station.

A Company had crossed the city. The journey between the two stations had taken less than one hour.

Chapter Eighteen

The men of A Company staggered into Camden station. Their faces were streaked with sweat and powder. Most bore wounds or had uniforms stained or scarred by the missiles that had pounded them from the moment they had abandoned their train car.

Exhausted and drained, they laid the corpses of their two comrades on the concourse. Those with wounds flopped to the ground. Those left on their feet walked like men half dead. Most sucked on their canteens, gulping down the water they contained with as much relish as if it were the most valuable liquor.

The troops of K Company were already there. No one shouted across in greeting. Their own passage through the city had been just as hard, and those that had survived were in no mood to compare stories with their comrades. The tired men from A Company made their way to an area free of the wounded, then slumped to the ground, their equipment dumped around them.

Jack picked his way across the concourse. There was blood everywhere. The bodies of Lieutenant Clancy and Private Amos

Thatcher were now being tended to by dour-faced railroad workers. K Company had lost one man of their own, with two others more seriously wounded than any of the men in A Company. The men from the 6th Massachusetts were far away on the other side of the concourse. From what he could see, they had fared little better; there were a number of bodies laid out in a line, their faces hidden beneath newly issued blankets.

'O'Dowd, Malloy.' Jack called out two names as he made his way amongst the company. 'Take some of your mates and go see to our boys. We don't want strangers looking after them.'

O'Dowd looked up. He held Jack's gaze for a moment, then simply nodded and pushed himself to his feet. Malloy did the same, as did four other men from the company.

'Come on, boys.' The Irishman gave the encouragement softly. 'Let's do what the sergeant says.'

Jack noted the change in tone. Even O'Dowd had been affected by the bitter struggle to cross the city. It was not the way he had intended to win the men over, but he could sense that he had gone some way to gaining their approval.

'Who's going to tell his ma?' O'Dowd asked Jack as he turned to help another man to his feet.

'Oh my.' It was Robert who spoke first. He had followed Jack and now he reached out to clasp a hand on O'Dowd's shoulder. 'The poor woman, she doted on those boys.'

'She's still got one.' O'Dowd turned his head and nodded towards James. The surviving twin sat alone, staring into space, as if looking at an object only he could see. 'He ain't said a fecking thing.' The Irishman shook his head as he contemplated the boy. 'Not a single word.'

Jack looked at the faces of the troops sitting around him.

Their expressions told all. These were not redcoats like the soldiers he had once known. They were ordinary men fighting alongside friends and neighbours. Every man in the company had known Amos Thatcher and Francis Clancy. Some had grown up with them, attending the same church and walking the same streets. Their deaths had not been contemplated. Not one man had marched out of Boston carrying the notion that within just a few hours, citizens of a Northern city would have killed some of them. Their shock was complete.

'I want you all to take a look.' Jack walked amongst his men. 'You go over there and take a good hard look at those two men we lost today.' He spoke slowly and carefully. He wanted to be understood. 'That's what war looks like, and you had better get used to it. This is what you are preparing for, not some brawl in a fucking tavern.'

Few of the men were able to meet his gaze. Most looked at the floor, or stared into the distance.

'So you think on today. This isn't some game. There are no winners or losers. You're not going to whip Johnny Reb's arse just by turning up.' He used the soldiers' favourite name for the rebels for the first time. It was enough to make some of the men look up at him. 'He's going to fight just as hard as you, maybe even harder. So you have to be ready. You have to stop fucking about and start listening. Because if you don't, then it's going to be you lying on your bloody back staring up at the stars.'

More of the tired soldiers lifted their gaze. He had their full attention now.

'But it doesn't have to be that way. If you listen, and if you do your damned drill, then we can be the best bloody soldiers in this army. We can be so damn good that the rebels really will shit in their breeches when they see that it's us coming for them.

We can be good. We can be very good. We can beat Johnny Reb's arse so hard the fucker will run screaming back to his ma begging for us to leave him be. But only if you stop all this horseshit about knowing better. Only if you learn how to fight, and I mean fight like soldiers, not drunken bullies in an alley. Learn to fight like soldiers and you stand a chance of being the best.' He paused and looked around him, meeting the stares of the men looking up at him. 'And you stand a chance of going home.'

He stopped. He had said enough. The urge to find fresh air was suddenly overwhelming, so he left his men sitting in silent misery and went to find it.

'You did well today.'

Jack started. He had not heard anybody approach. He had walked to the main doors and found a quiet spot where he could look outside, watching the crowd that still milled around in the streets that led towards Camden station. The threat of violence no longer hung in the air. The devil had been fed, the souls of those killed that day enough to satiate the mob's lust for blood.

He turned to see First Sergeant O'Connell standing behind him.

'I did precious little.' He heard the bitterness in his own words. It was the truth. He had done his job, keeping the men moving, and he had helped clear the mob from their barricade. But it was not like being an officer. He had not led the men. He had been led. The notion bothered him.

'You kept the men together. And you fought. I saw you take down that gombeen at the barricade. You did it easy, like it was nothing.'

'It *was* nothing.' Jack thought about the man he had struck down. He did not think he had killed him, but he could not be sure. Perhaps even now the man's corpse was being dragged to his home, where his family would weep for their loss and damn the blue-coated Yankee who had taken one of their own.

'Feck me, you don't take praise easy.' O'Connell chuckled. 'Fecking Englishman.'

Something in the first sergeant's tone made Jack smile. The expression cracked the crust of sweat and dirt plastered to his skin. 'I suppose I should say thank you.'

'Yes, you fecking should.' O'Connell shook his head at Jack's foolishness. He moved forward, coming to stand at Jack's shoulder. Together they watched the rioters still on the street.

'What a fecking day.' O'Connell muttered the words under his breath, as much to himself as to anyone else.

'We didn't have to fire.' Jack kept his tone even as he offered the criticism. 'We could've fixed bayonets. They wouldn't have stood against us.'

'You sure of that now?' A trace of anger crept into O'Connell's voice. Both men still stared ahead.

Jack grunted. 'No. But we should've tried. How many men did we kill? Half a dozen? A dozen?' He shook his head as he contemplated the slaughter the well-armed soldiers had inflicted. 'We didn't have to open fire.'

'No, maybe not.' O'Connell gave the admission grudgingly. 'But the captain ordered it and Colonel Scanlon made it clear we could return fire if the feckers fired first. Which they did.'

Jack said nothing as he wrestled with the rights and wrongs of what they had done. No matter what orders they had been given, they had still fired on civilians.

O'Connell glanced at him. 'This ain't the kind of war you're used to. I didn't get it myself. Not till today. It's not about two armies finding a great big field and slugging it out until one fecks off. It's brother against brother; countryman against countryman. It's not going to be soldiers dressed up nice and neat for one grand old battle. It's going to be hard and dirty. We aren't fighting another country, or some foreign enemy. We're fighting ourselves.'

Jack understood. O'Connell was right. This was not war as he knew it. Even the bitter struggle during the mutiny in India had been different. The violence then had been terrible to behold as the native troops rebelled against their white masters. Both sides had committed all manner of atrocities as they waged an all-out war without any trace of compassion. But there had been two clear sides, two foes fighting each other for the right to run the country as they saw fit.

This war was different. Here the two sides were not so neatly divided. Men would have to decide which cause they would fight for, and it would split the country in two, not just by lines on a map that demarcated the North and the South. It would split every town, every city and every family into those that wanted to preserve the Union and those that believed in a state's right to govern itself.

'It's going to tear this country apart.'

O'Connell nodded slowly. 'I reckon it will. We're still in the North, for feck's sake, still in the United States. We're marching to fight to preserve this fecking Union, yet people here wanted to kill us to stop us doing it.' He shook his head, as if it were all beyond him. 'But that's not why I told the men to fire.'

'Then why did you?'

'To protect my boys. Those feckers had killed Clancy, and

Amos too. I weren't going to sit by and let any more of my lads die.'

This Jack understood. He remembered serving alongside men he would have killed to protect. It was the creed of the soldier. They might have fought any enemy they were told to, obeying orders as if they were machines rather than men. But when the bullets started to fly, they did not fight for lofty strategic aims, or glory, or their generals, or even for their country. They fought for their mates; for the other poor bastards sent to do their country's dirty work. O'Connell was voicing the same thought. He had killed civilians to protect his men.

'I get it,' Jack breathed. He looked O'Connell in the eye. 'You did what had to be done.'

For a moment the Irishman said nothing. Then he offered a tight-lipped smile. 'Thank you.'

Jack barked a short laugh. 'You don't need my damn approval.' He paused. A single rioter was looking at them. As Jack watched, the man pointed in their direction. Whatever invective he threw their way was lost in the breeze that blew across the approach to the station. Jack had to admire the man's stamina. Despite all that had happened, he had enough hatred to still be standing there hurling insults at men who no longer cared what they heard.

'You know it's going to take more than one battle.' Jack nodded towards the rioter. 'Hatred like that doesn't just go away.'

'I reckon you're right.' O'Connell was watching the same man. 'You think I could shoot the fecker from here?'

Jack made a play of considering the notion. 'No. No chance.'

'Then I had best go find the captain.' O'Connell stretched

his spine, then turned his head from side to side to make his neck crack. 'Bridges has something for you.'

Jack frowned. 'What's that then?'

'I'll let him give it to you. I didn't want it, but I reckon you might. I reckon you'll do better with it than I ever could.' O'Connell finished his stretching then walked away, leaving Jack to ponder his cryptic remark.

The single rioter shouted a barely audible series of insults. Then he turned and walked away. Jack watched him go. He wondered what inspired men with ordinary lives to take to the streets in an attempt to kill those being sent to do their own country's bidding.

He heard the sound of more footsteps. He glanced over his shoulder and saw that he would not have to wait long to discover what Major Bridges had for him. The major was coming to join him, his face creased into a frown as he picked his way through the discarded equipment that was scattered across the station concourse.

'A bad business.' Bridges spoke as he came to stand at Jack's side.

'It's only going to get worse.'

Bridges grunted as he acknowledged the gloomy rejoinder. 'I know that now.' He twitched his moustache before he continued. 'I think you always knew it would be like this.'

Jack shrugged. 'Maybe, but I guess you had to understand it for yourselves. No one believes in an elephant until they see one.'

'An elephant?' Bridges contemplated the word. 'I fancy we have all seen the damned elephant now.' He looked down at his boots before continuing. 'Perhaps we will listen better next time.'

'Perhaps you will.' Jack offered a thin-lipped smile. 'But it's not your fault. I've been in this situation more times than I care to remember. I should've done more to prepare the men.'

'You were not here long enough. But we are glad you are here now. I think we need you.'

Jack shook his head at the notion. 'You don't need me. You just need to get the men trained, one way or another. You need to stop them thinking they know how to fight, because they don't. They don't know shit. Even after today.'

'You're a harsh judge.'

'Harsh? Maybe.' Jack did not shirk the intensity in Bridges' eyes. 'When I went to the Crimea, I thought I'd be good at leading men in battle and I wanted to do it. Can you believe that? I wanted to go into battle. I wanted to prove myself.'

'And did you?'

'No. I simply went along with my men.'

'And afterwards?'

'I just kept going. Some people, they think it's all about luck. If you're lucky, you live. If you aren't, you die.'

Jack smiled as he remembered the man who had told him he was not good, just lucky. That man was worm food now, his body left lying on a battlefield the day his own ration of luck had run out. But Jack thought he had been wrong. Luck played a part; there was no denying that. But some men had a talent for battle. Just like some men could turn wood, or draw, or write, he could fight. And he could fight hard.

'I think that means I'm a fool.' He made the admission ruefully.

'No,' Bridges replied firmly. 'You are most certainly not a fool, Jack Lark.' He fished in a pocket, then held out his hand. 'We want you to have these.'

Jack could not see what he was being offered. He held out his own hand and let Bridges place the items he had retrieved into his open palm.

They were a pair of plain, pale blue rank slides of a second lieutenant in the Union army.

'We need you to replace poor Clancy.'

'You want me to be a lieutenant?'

'Yes.'

Jack now understood O'Connell's earlier enigmatic remark. 'You already offered them to O'Connell.'

'I did. He refused. Offering them to you was his idea.' A hint of a smile played across Bridges' lips.

'What about the other sergeants?'

'They don't have experience. It appears you do.'

Still Jack hesitated. He kept his palm open, not yet taking the rank insignia for his own. He thought on why he was there. He had been employed as a bodyguard. His place in the company had been created at Kearney's request so that he could protect his only surviving son. Would that task be made easier if he were an officer? Or would it be harder? Then there was Rowell to consider. The company's commander clearly needed all the help he could get, his performance that day all the proof Jack required that the company needed better officers than it had currently.

He watched Bridges. The major was staring back at him, his eyes narrowing as he waited for his answer. Jack wondered if he could see his desire. For he wanted the rank. He wanted it almost as much as he wanted Rowell's fabulous revolver. As a sergeant, he did not command the company, but just followed his officer's lead. It was a vital role. Without the best non-commissioned officers the company was surely doomed, but he wanted more. Ever since the first moment he had taken another man's uniform for his own, he had always been an officer. He had led men in battle. And he was damn good at it.

He laughed at his own arrogance, then laughed some more as he saw Bridges' expression change at hearing the man he wanted to be the company's second lieutenant cackling like a madman.

He did not care. He no longer knew quite what he was. Was he a mercenary? A bodyguard? A soldier? None of the titles seemed to fit. But he knew what he wanted.

His hand closed over the rank slides. He would be what he was meant to be.

Chapter Nineteen

Emmart's Farm, Washington, Wednesday 3 July 1861

Jack awoke to the fife and drum sounding the reveille. It may have been different to the call to wake used by the British army, but the meaning was clear.

'Good morning to you, Mr Lark.' Private O'Dowd pulled back the flaps of the tent that housed the company's two lieutenants and bustled in carrying a large enamel jug full of steaming water. Like all orderlies, O'Dowd was up and ready to face the day long before the two officers he had elected to serve. As lieutenants, they were too junior to be officially allowed their own orderly, and neither Robert nor Jack had requested that O'Dowd serve them, but the Irishman had been insistent and had ignored all their attempts to put him off.

Jack sat up on his camp bed and rubbed his face vigorously to bring it to life. 'Good morning, O'Dowd.'

'Major Bridges asks if you'll take surgeon's call this morning, sir.'

'Very well.' Jack agreed readily enough. He pushed himself to his feet, stretching to ease out the kinks in his spine. His back ached as normal, but he had no complaints about his living conditions. He shared a large wall-sided ridge tent with Robert. It was well furnished with a full groundsheet, a pair of camp beds, a couple of folding stools and a matching table. There were white bowls and jugs for washing and two chests for their belongings.

'A Company, fall in for roll call.' Jack heard First Sergeant O'Connell bellowing for the company to assemble ready for the first parade of the day. O'Connell would take the roll, making sure that none of the men had slipped away in the night, either to abscond or to enjoy a night in the city.

'Does he have to be so goddam loud?' Robert's voice came from underneath his blanket. Jack's fellow lieutenant had not yet bothered to move.

'Yes,' Jack replied with force.

Robert had only been in his pit for a couple of hours. The young officer never failed to find entertainment, and his choice of nocturnal activity meant that he was not good in the mornings, something that Jack found highly amusing. His exploits did make him popular amongst the men, though, and the soldiers of A Company had taken it upon themselves to look out for their wastrel of an officer, especially when Colonel Scanlon was around. Robert's drinking and almost perpetual good humour might have endeared him to his men, but Jack was worried that his charge would kill himself long before he had a chance to face the enemy.

O'Dowd had busied himself getting Jack's things ready for his morning ablutions. He had spread a sheet on the ground and filled a bowl with the warm water he had brought with him.

'Shaving this morning, sir?'

Jack frowned at the question. O'Dowd's attentions felt

awkward; overly intimate. He had had an orderly once. Tommy Smith had been an ally in Jack's first attempt at impersonating an officer, but he had died on the ground by the Alma river. Since then, Jack had always fended for himself.

Still, O'Dowd was trying his best, so Jack resisted the urge to growl and instead ran a hand across his face. His fingers brushed over stubble, but he did not much fancy shaving. He generally only did it once or perhaps twice a week, and his fingertips told him that he could last a day or too longer before submitting to the painful process that would inevitably leave his skin raw and sore.

'No, not today.'

'Very good.' O'Dowd immediately turned and bundled up the roll of cloth that contained Jack's shaving things. 'Would either of you two fine gentlemen be wanting anything for your breakfast?'

'Is there anything other than hardtack and coffee?' Jack sighed and dropped his drawers. There was no being shy, not in an army encampment.

'I doubt it, sir.' O'Dowd did not so much as glance as a naked Jack took his place on the sheet in front of the bowl of now tepid water and began to wash. He did turn away to pull out fresh drawers and a clean shirt from Jack's trunk, which he then laid out on the bed before gathering up Jack's uniform trousers and jacket and laying them next to the first two items.

'Then I think I'll pass on breakfast.' Jack continued to wash.

'You're probably wise, sir, so you are.' O'Dowd stood back as Jack brushed away the worst of the water and began to dress. 'I've seen cattle that's fed better than us.'

'That's because cattle are valuable.'

O'Dowd smiled at the reply. The men were comfortably

housed in well-equipped tents, but they were not well fed, the army struggling to provide for the thousands of troops now encamped around Washington.

Jack forced the last button through its buttonhole, then made to leave the tent. He did not bother to take any of his weapons with him. He had been issued with a regulation sword with the rest of his officer's uniform when they had arrived at Emmart's Farm, but he barely bothered to wear it. It was simply too hot to carry any unnecessary equipment.

He stopped near the entrance, then turned to face Robert's camp bed. The company's other lieutenant had not moved. 'You need to get up,' he snapped.

'And you need to remember that I am first lieutenant, whilst you are merely second.' There was little rancour in the reply from underneath the grey blanket.

Jack shook his head and left O'Dowd to try to get Robert out of his pit. He stepped outside, immediately blinking furiously as he walked into the bright morning sunshine. He felt the first beads of sweat break out across his forehead. It was already oppressively hot, the air close and sweaty. The men had been issued with havelocks, white cotton cap covers that were long enough to hang over the neck and protect it from the sun. They helped a little, but the sweltering heat was still a constant hardship that simply had to be endured.

The encampment stretched away before him. It appeared to grow every day as more and more men and equipment arrived. When the first two companies of the 1st Boston had arrived, they had claimed just a tiny corner of the massive open area. Now there was a great sea of canvas, the rows of tents stretching away in every direction.

The soldiers' constant marching through the encampment

had ground any grass there had once been into so much dust. Every uniform, every tent, every weapon was thick with the stuff. The men had quickly grown sick of its constant abrasive presence, and more than one longed for the orders to march on the enemy simply to escape the dust bowl in which they now lived.

Jack walked towards the open area the regiment had been allocated for their parades. The rest of the 1st Boston had arrived in mid-June. The route through Baltimore was still the only practical way of moving troops into Washington, and President Lincoln had taken the dramatic step of declaring martial law to ensure the free and unfettered transit of troops through the city. Such drastic action had allowed the rest of the regiment to travel without calamity. Their only moment of excitement had come when Lieutenant Colonel Murphy had slipped on some fallen bunting and twisted his ankle severely enough for him to have to return to Boston. He had not been replaced.

Now reunited, the regiment was close to being at full strength, with just fewer than one thousand officers and other ranks living under canvas a few miles downstream from the centre of Washington. They had lost a few men to sickness or injury, and a handful had been sent home simply for being physically unsuitable for life as a soldier. The rest rubbed along pretty well, their days spent mainly at drill or on fatigue duty, their sergeants and corporals becoming adept at keeping the men busy.

It did not take Jack long to round up that day's sick and deliver them to the regimental surgeon. Duty done, he returned to his tent and was pleased to see the flaps tied open, a sign that Robert had managed to get up. He ducked and went inside, his nose twitching as he walked into the now-familiar stink of sweat and sun-warmed canvas.

'I see you're up. If not quite dressed.' He smiled at the sight of Robert sitting at the camp table in nothing more than open shirt and drawers.

'It's too damn hot to wear uniform.' Robert looked up from the heavy ledger he was working on, then tossed his steel pen to one side. 'You must be baking.'

'No.' Jack denied the assertion as he slipped his uniform jacket from his shoulders. 'I am broiled, perhaps, but not baked.' He tossed the jacket onto his bed, then undid his cuffs. It felt like he had walked into an oven. But there was no sense in taking the table outside and working there. They had tried it before. The heat was almost as bad outside the tent as in, and once away from its protective walls, they would have to contend with the wind that whistled down the lines of tents, blowing dust into their faces with all the force of a cannon firing a case of canister.

'I cannot wait to leave this place.' Robert spoke with genuine feeling.

'I thought you were having a fine time. Where did you go last night?'

'No place special.' Robert was evasive. 'And nowhere I am in a hurry to return to.'

Jack raised an eyebrow at the remark. Robert had a habit of finding the lowest dives and the foulest dens of iniquity. Somehow, though, he always managed to come away intact, even the denizens of such loathsome places succumbing to his charm.

With his clothing loosened as much as possible, Jack drew up another chair and placed it next to Robert's. He sat down and took up a pen, then pulled the heavy ledger towards him. As much as he hated writing, he hated sitting around doing nothing even more.

He dipped the pen into ink then started to fill out the day's record. 'Any more trouble from D Company?' he asked as he worked.

'Nothing. I think the boys have seen sense at last.'

'It's about time. But I don't know what Scanlon expected would happen. I cannot imagine any company would take well to the officers they had chosen being replaced with Scanlon's favourites.'

Jack shook his head at the folly of the regiment's decision to allow the men to elect their own officers, only to subsequently replace them with men of the colonel's choosing. The men of D Company had not taken the change well, and had even refused to muster the first day under the new regime. It had taken much parleying and persuasion to get them back to work, but the problem had resolved itself when the men discovered that the replacement officers were in fact much better than the ones they had chosen for themselves.

'Just so long as Scanlon doesn't try the same trick again,' he added.

'You think he might?'

'I wouldn't put anything past the old man.' Jack used the company's nickname for their colonel. Scanlon had proved himself to be a fierce and uncompromising leader whom the troops viewed with a mixture of fear and respect. Jack had yet to form a firm opinion on the man who would take the regiment into battle. Scanlon was no martinet, but he did insist on high standards, something that Jack admired, even if he did not agree with some of the colonel's ideas as to the areas in which the men should concentrate their efforts. However, Scanlon was also a firebrand who was keen to get his troops into battle so that they could whip the Confederates into line. In that respect, Jack had disagreed more vocally. The men had been training hard in the weeks they had been at Emmart's Farm, but they were still a long way short of being the finished article.

'You nearly done?' Robert had rocked his chair back onto its rear legs and now tottered precariously at Jack's side.

Jack wrote his last words, then laid the pen down on the table next to the bottle of ink. 'Yes.'

'About time.' Robert reached over to pull the ledger towards him. He peered at Jack's script as if unable to read it before snapping the book shut and getting to his feet. 'I'll have James take it to the adjutant,' he said as he walked to the tent's open flaps.

'Good idea.' Jack agreed readily. James Thatcher had not said a word in all the weeks that had followed his twin brother's death. The entire company fretted about the young lad. 'We need to keep him busy.'

'We need to send him home.' Robert shook his head, then looked back at Jack. 'What will happen to his mother if the same fate befalls James?'

Jack got to his feet and walked to Robert's side. The two officers looked out, both men picking out the figure of James Thatcher. The soldiers were engaged in their morning fatigue duties. The company lines had to be cleaned and swept, tents tidied and brushed down, wood found and split ready to be used to cook the day's rations, and picket details attended to.

'You want to tell the lad that he has to go home?' Jack asked.

Robert sighed. 'No. No, I don't. The poor fellow has more right to be here than any of us.'

Jack grunted by way of acknowledgement. It was a sad business. The company had lost men before the campaign proper had even started, but at least it had galvanised the rest into taking their drill more seriously than they had back in Boston.

There had been weeks of it: company drill, regimental drill and even a few days when they had marched to a large series of open fields further from the city and joined with other regiments to practise brigade drill. On another occasion the regiment's two flank companies had been detached from the rest to learn their role as skirmishers. It had proved to be an interesting diversion from manoeuvring as part of a cumbersome formation, the looser skirmish order allowing the men a greater degree of freedom.

The role of skirmishers was vital. A Company and K Company would be ordered to leave the main battle line and fight on their own in front of the regiment. Their primary task would be to screen the main line from any of the enemy's own skirmishers. If they got the opportunity, they would fire on the opposing battle line, the men trained to shoot down the enemy officers and sergeants, eroding their ability to command and control their men whilst picking at their morale. They had taken to it well, the distinction of being skirmishers marking them out as being the best men in the regiment, but quite how adept they would prove in the role was anyone's guess, their scant training certain to be tested once they engaged the Confederate forces.

The regiment could now form line or column with some degree of proficiency, and they could form a square ready to repel cavalry. The formations, and the drill itself, were all so familiar to Jack, the training of the Union soldiers very close to the training he had been given a decade before. And it was horribly out of date.

'Are you taking firing drill again?' Robert seemed content to stand in the sun. He looked incongruous in his drawers and unbuttoned shirt, but even the smirks of the passing soldiers did not encourage him to dress properly.

'No. The colonel is insisting on more bayonet drill.' Jack spoke through gritted teeth.

'You need to mind your tone. Hell, if Scanlon hears you complain again . . .' Robert left the sentence unfinished.

'I know.' Jack could not help sighing. He had argued with the colonel on more than one occasion. In the world of modern weaponry, the drill the army's generals insisted upon was a throwback to a bygone era. Moving men around in large, densely packed formations was tantamount to suicide given that rifle muskets like the 1st Boston's own Springfields were so much more powerful than the smoothbore muskets that had been the mainstay of all armies for so many decades.

Jack had seen at first hand how the new design of rifle and its deforming bullets could destroy a tightly packed column. There was a need for the men to learn about fighting in extended skirmish order; a more loosely formed line that would make them less of a target for the enemy's rifles. Scanlon disagreed, insisting that the men follow the rulebook handed down from the general staff. Above all, he wanted them to practise with the bayonet.

'So do the bayonet drill.' Robert had read Jack's expression well enough. 'You won't get your way.'

'It's not about getting my way.' Jack could not resist the

lure. 'It's about making sure the men stand a chance when we eventually leave this bloody place and face the enemy. They have to still be alive in order to bayonet anyone.'

'You need to take a deep breath.' Robert chuckled at Jack's passion. 'In this heat, getting yourself all worked up will be the death of you.'

Jack scowled, but he did pause and take a breath. 'I'm not getting worked up.'

'Well, it sure looks that way to me.'

Jack's mood was not improved by the smile he saw on Robert's face. 'Perhaps you should try getting worked up yourself. You need to take this more seriously.'

'Now where would be the fun in that?' Robert laughed off the advice, then laughed twice as hard as he saw Jack's scowl deepen. 'Come on, Jack, you need to lighten up.'

'You need to stop pissing around and do some work.'

'Why? You seem perfectly happy to do everything. I reckon I'd just get in your way. If things aren't done as you like them, you only get angry, and I've no desire to be shouted at for half the goddam day.'

Jack heard the truth in Robert's words, but it did nothing to mollify him. His frustration was overwhelming. It felt like he alone knew what was coming. The men had had a taste, their bitter experience in Baltimore enough to make them work harder than they had before. But they still had no idea what battle would be like. They were lambs being led to the slaughterhouse, and not one of them could see what awaited them.

'I'll see you at dinner.' Robert nudged Jack's arm.

'I'll be there.'

'I shall try to find us something more palatable to eat.'

Robert was trying to put a smile on Jack's face. 'I may even track down some of that bacon you like so much.'

Jack understood what the younger man was trying to do. He did not remember when he had become so dour, and tried to smile in return. 'Do you think you can find some more tea? I've run out again.'

'I'm not surprised. You drink enough of the goddam stuff.'

'I've had my fill of bloody coffee,' Jack answered with feeling. He needed tea. Starting the day with coffee was just not the same. He was not alone in feeling unhappy with the rations the army fed them. When the regiment had been in Boston, they had lived well on the generosity of the locals, with businesses even competing to feed the troops as a display of their commitment to the cause. Now a part of the Army of Northeastern Virginia based in Washington, they lived on army rations alone and every man in the regiment deemed them insufficient. There was simply not enough food to feed them properly.

Major Bridges had come up with a partial solution. The army-issue soup was made with more water, the meat carved smaller and the bread sliced thinner. Even the rice and beans were soaked in water to make them expand, and the coffee that Jack so despised was made weaker. Bridges had been unable to conjure more rations, but somehow they now felt larger, which went a little way towards mollifying the men's complaints.

Like many things, though, the solution merely papered over the cracks. To Jack's mind, the same philosophy permeated the thinking of the whole army. He just hoped that the Confederates would not force those cracks wide open.

Chapter Twenty

'**G**ood morning, gentlemen.'

Jack tried not to bristle as his company commander sauntered towards them. It was rare to see Captain Rowell so early in the morning, especially as the company's day promised nothing more than the same dreary routine of parades, fatigues and drill.

'Good morning, sir,' Robert replied cheerfully enough, saving Jack the effort.

'Why, Lieutenant Kearney, could you not be bothered to put on your clothes this morning?' Rowell's handsome face creased into a frown as he took in the appearance of his first lieutenant.

Robert looked down at his bare knees as if noticing his lack of uniform for the first time. 'I suppose I should get dressed.'

'Yes, Lieutenant, I think you should.' Rowell's reply was laced with scorn. 'Otherwise the men will think they're commanded by a goddam scarecrow rather than an officer.' He turned his attention to Jack. 'Lieutenant Lark.' The greeting was spoken warily, Rowell treating Jack very differently to his familiar handling of Robert.

'It's nice to see you this morning, sir. You haven't been around for a few days.' Jack fired his first barb and smiled as he saw Rowell scowl, the captain understanding the tone well enough. He noticed the hint of a scar on Rowell's cheek, the legacy of the rioter's missile. It had almost faded, but Jack had to admit it added a rakish air to the captain's features. He just wished the thick weal on his own face did the same to his.

'I have been busy at general headquarters.' Rowell brushed off Jack's sarcasm. 'Some of us must look to more than just one company's drill.'

'Ah, I see, sir.' Jack deliberately kept his expression neutral. 'Well, it's nice to be busy and I expect it's a little more comfortable at headquarters. Less dusty, for a start.'

'I am not there for the comfort, Lieutenant,' Rowell snapped. 'I am bound to go where my duty calls me.'

'Of course, sir, I never doubted that for a moment.' Jack stared at Rowell but the captain would not meet his gaze. 'I expect it's nice to be near Elizabeth and her father. Their Washington house is rather fabulous, I hear. Lieutenant Kearney was telling me all about it. It's so considerate of them to put you up there. Saves the army paying for your keep.'

Rowell glared at Jack. 'Do you disapprove, Lieutenant?'

'It's not my place to disapprove.' Jack looked back at his officer calmly enough.

'Then perhaps you should keep your comments to yourself.'

'Perhaps you should spend more time with your men.'

'Are you saying that I am shirking my duties?' Rowell's face was colouring with more than just the heat.

'Your duties, sir? I was not aware you knew what those were.'

'What the hell do you mean by that?'

'Your place is here, with the company. You need to learn how to lead your troops just as much as they need to learn how to be led.' Jack could not contain his frustration.

'Are you suggesting I don't know what to do?'

'*Do* you know what to do?'

'I have read the manual.' Rowell bristled.

Jack raised his eyes to the heavens. 'It takes more than that.'

'What *does* it take? What do you think I am lacking?' Rowell took a step forward.

'Where do I start?' Jack's reply was biting. 'You need to lead the men. That means being here, sharing their lives and enduring the same hardships as they do. One day they'll have to follow you into battle. They won't do that just because you shout the right bloody orders. There'll come a time when they won't want to go forward. They'll hunker down and refuse to move. That's when you'll have to stand up and lead them. It'll be up to you to get them moving, to get them to follow you even though their every instinct will be to stay where they are. There will come a time when you will have to earn that lovely gold braid and the fancy damn buttons, and being called "sir". When that day comes, you'll have to know more than the bloody words in the bloody manual.'

Jack paused and met Rowell's gaze. 'That's what you have to learn, *sir*. That's why you have to be here. Because as sure as eggs is eggs, that day is coming, and when it arrives, you had better bloody well be ready for it.'

'I *am* ready.' Rowell looked away, treating Jack's words with disdain.

'No.' Jack reached forward and turned the captain back round so that he was forced to look at him. 'You're not bloody ready. And that means men will die. They'll die because you couldn't be bothered to get off your pampered bloody arse and get yourself into the field with your troops.'

'You know an awful lot, Lieutenant,' Rowell's voice shook as he replied, 'for a man who is only here because Mr Kearney felt he owed you. And for what, exactly? For bringing over some goddam letters and coming up with some horseshit fairy tale about Thomas dying in your arms?' Rowell was speaking more quickly now. The two men were of an equal height and were standing eyeball to eyeball. 'Why, for all we know, you could be nothing more than a fraud; just some goddam trickster who happened to find a dead man's letters and sniffed out an opportunity to get something for nothing. We don't know a thing about you, yet here you are, lording it over us poor damn colonists like you know better than all of us.' Rowell was in full flow now. 'Well, I tell you this, Lieutenant, we managed pretty well when we threw you British out of here, and we'll manage pretty well right here and now without your goddam interference. If you don't like the way we do things, I suggest you pack up and leave us to it.'

'You'd like that, wouldn't you just?' Jack would not back down. The men deserved better than an officer who thought he was learning his trade by sitting reading a book in a fine drawing room miles from his command. 'Because I make you uncomfortable. I'm a reminder that you don't know shit about this great battle you're so keen to have. I've been in battle. I know what'll happen. I look at you and at the men, and I wonder which of you will die. I wonder which of you will be blown to smithereens; which of you will be lying on the ground with your guts spilling out into your own bloody hands.'

'You still don't get it, do you, Lieutenant?' Rowell's mouth twisted as if he were sucking on something sour. 'You think you can frighten us with your tales. Well, you know what, I think you're scared of fighting this battle because you'll be revealed as the great fraud you really are. You're so goddam certain that we're marching to some great slaughter. But what if we're right and you're wrong? What if Johnny Reb skedaddles at the sight of us? Where will you be then? What'll you do? *We* all have lives. *We* have futures. What do you have?'

He paused, his expression mocking Jack's silence. 'That's right. You cannot answer, because you have nothing. You need this war. You need it to go on and on, because without it no one will listen to you. No one will heed your wise goddam counsel or listen to your stories of how you have suffered.'

'You two need to quieten down.' Robert spoke for the first time. The half-dressed lieutenant was looking from one man to the other.

'Lieutenant Lark needs to learn to hold his damn peace.'

'And the good captain here needs to learn to do his fucking job,' Jack growled. He was not bothered by Rowell's opinion of him. He knew what he was. He did not need some jumped-up prick to tell him.

'And you both need to know that my sister is walking right this way.' Robert spoke quietly. 'So you will now smile and try to pretend you've been having a lovely conversation about the weather.'

Robert's warning grabbed Jack's attention in a way that Rowell's words had failed to do. He had seen Elizabeth Kearney only twice, when she had come to visit her brother, and he had not been able to engage her in conversation on either occasion. The thought that she was approaching was enough to send a jolt through him. It also explained why Rowell was there. Clearly the Kearneys had chosen to visit the regiment and so A Company's captain had been forced to join his men.

'Smile, you bastard.' Jack hissed the words softly so that only Rowell could hear them.

Rowell glared, then stepped backwards, a fake smile plastered hastily across his face. 'I think you and I will have to finish this discussion at some other time.'

'I'll look forward to it.' Jack's smile was just as insincere.

Rowell's eyes narrowed a fraction before he turned as if sensing Elizabeth's approach. 'Why there you are, my dear.' He greeted her warmly. 'I thought you would've stayed with your father.'

'I wanted to see my brother.' Elizabeth walked towards the three officers. She was dressed in a soft pink linen cambric dress and carried a gaily painted parasol that she had balanced on her shoulder. 'But now I find all my favourite people already gathered together.'

'And Lieutenant Lark is here also.' Rowell thought the remark funny and he smirked at Jack.

If Elizabeth heard something untoward in her fiancé's tone, she did not show it. She walked close enough to link her arm through Rowell's, then laid her head on his upper arm. 'Father will be lunching with the colonel, so I said you would take me home.' She lifted her head and looked up at him. 'You don't mind, do you?'

'Not at all.' Rowell reached down and patted her hand. 'We can go to Spotswood House.'

'That would be enchanting.' Elizabeth smiled at the suggestion, then finally turned her attention to her brother. 'Why aren't you dressed?'

Robert grinned at her. 'It's the new fashion. Do you not approve?'

'It does not seem to be suitable attire for war.' Elizabeth could not help laughing.

'Is it not?' Robert made a play of inspecting himself. 'I thought it quite the thing.'

'You might need boots.'

'Ah, yes.' He looked ruefully at his bare feet. 'Perhaps you have something there.' He laughed. 'I'll just go and get dressed.'

'You should.' Elizabeth glanced past her brother's shoulder. 'You do seem to have made yourselves nice and cosy in there.' For the first time, she looked at Jack. 'I trust my brother's snoring doesn't disturb you too badly.'

Jack's throat suddenly felt constricted. He cleared it rather noisily before replying. 'No. It's fine.' He tried not to stare. Elizabeth's cheeks bore a tiny smudge of pink. She looked radiant.

'Well, I hear you will be marching soon enough.' The corners of her mouth turned up as she sensed how awkward he was.

'Is that so?' Jack found himself watching her lips as she spoke. They captivated him.

'The newspapers are full of it. You are off to Richmond, or at least that is what they say.'

'Let us hope that is the case.' Jack heard the stiffness in his reply.

'You sound like you do not approve.'

Jack frowned. Elizabeth's tone had changed. When she had spoken to Rowell, her voice had been dripping with sweetness. Now it hardened as she challenged him.

'No, it's not that.' Jack glanced at Rowell. He seemed

perfectly happy now that Elizabeth was on his arm. Jack did not blame him. A man could go a long way with someone as beautiful as Elizabeth at his side.

'Ethan does not like to talk of the war.' Elizabeth glanced up at Rowell and gave him a reassuring smile.

'And you do?' Jack did not bother to look at the captain and focused all his attention on Elizabeth.

'I confess I find it interesting.' Again she glanced at her fiancé.

'Elizabeth wants us to fight.' Rowell could not keep the condescending tone from his reply. 'But of course she does not know what that will be like. Not like you, Lark.' He slipped the barbed comment in with a smile.

'The battle needs to happen. There can be no peace or compromise, no union or secession, until war has determined which one it will be.' Elizabeth spoke firmly and with certainty. 'We are blockading the Confederate coast, but that can only go so far in forcing them to come to heel. We have already beaten a Confederate force in West Virginia. The secessionist forces retreated so fast that the papers called it the Philippi Races. That shows that the enemy will not stand. Now there is just a river between them and us. It is time to take the fight to them and bring this to a conclusion.'

'Why must we attack?' Jack was fascinated by the change that had come over the woman in front of him. Any simpering sweetness was gone.

'If we don't, then perhaps they will attack us here.'

'I don't think you have to worry about that.'

'Don't patronise me, Jack.' Elizabeth's reply was sharp.

'I was not patronising you.' Jack's face burned. He looked at Rowell and saw the smirk back on his face.

'You think we women cannot hear the truth, that it might damage our ears?'

'No, I don't think that at all.' Jack was firmly on the back foot.

'We are not just here to adorn your world. So you don't think they will attack?'

'No, I don't.' Jack was finding it hard to keep up.

'Why not?'

'I don't imagine they're any more ready than we are, and it's harder to launch an attack into enemy territory than it is to sit on the defensive. You need more men, for a start, not to mention a better supply chain. It's much easier to defend, and a well-entrenched enemy is nearly impossible to shift.' He answered her seriously.

'And being on the defensive plays to their cause.' Elizabeth considered Jack's opinion. 'They already see us as the aggressor. It is our telling them how to live their lives that has caused this war, at least in their eyes. They want to self-govern. After all, isn't that what our forebears fought for when they beat off the British? The South want to be free, not of the Old World this time, but of Washington. It will be so much better for them if we invade. For then they will be standing up for their liberty; the injured party forced to defend their homes. Yes, I think if we attack, it will suit them very nicely indeed.'

She turned her attention back to her fiancé. 'Why does Jack say we are not ready? Do you think he is correct?' She asked the question in the sweetest tone.

'Lieutenant Lark is not aware of the full situation, my love. The junior ranks are not generally made aware of all that is going on.'

'So we *are* ready?'

'We're getting there.' Rowell patted the hand that was still resting on his arm.

'But you think differently?' Elizabeth fired the question at Jack.

'I do. The men are too slow. We need to be doing more rifle drill.'

'Why is that important?' Elizabeth looked deep into his eyes.

'It's how we kill the enemy. It's what we are here for. We need to kill more of them than they kill of us.' Jack heard the coldness creep into his tone. He wanted to make her shiver. She was so composed and so knowledgeable. She was well informed and understood many of the reasons for the war that was coming, yet she did not know everything. She might know why they would be going to fight, and she might wish for the battle that could end the dispute between the two halves of the country, but she did not know what she was asking for.

For a moment, Elizabeth did not reply. She just looked at Jack as if she was gazing into his very soul.

'Such talk is not for a lady's ears, Lieutenant,' Rowell objected.

Jack paid his captain no heed. He was watching Elizabeth. His skin was on fire and his body thrilled to a pressure building in the air.

'I think it's time to take you home.' Rowell would have had to be blind to miss the look Jack was giving his beautiful bride-to-be.

'Yes, of course.' Elizabeth blinked twice, then looked up at her fiancé and smiled. 'You take such good care of me, Ethan. I am so lucky to have you.'

Rowell beamed at the praise. He was still smiling as he

turned to lead Elizabeth away. He completely missed the final look she sent Jack's way.

Jack felt the weight of her gaze for no more than the span of a single heartbeat, but he was sure she had felt something of the same sensations he had. He did not know what it meant, but he was sure of one thing.

There would be a storm that summer, one that would engulf the whole country. He sensed there would also be a thunderstorm closer to home, the tension between him and Rowell certain to explode into something more violent. Then there was Elizabeth. There was a very different type of pressure between them, but when it erupted it would likely be no less spectacular.

He looked up at the sky. A thick band of grey cloud was smothering the blue, and already the sun was being shrouded in darkness.

The storm was coming.

Chapter Twenty-one

Emmart's Farm, Washington, Thursday 4 July 1861

Independence Day had arrived bright and hot, with blue sky stretching from one horizon to the other. The men had been up early; there was a lot to be done to have them looking their best for the long day ahead. Uniforms had been scrubbed and brushed. Leather had been buffed so that it glistened in the morning sunlight. Rifles had been oiled and bayonets polished again and again so that they would catch the sun.

The parade was timed to commence at noon. Now the men stood in their ranks and sweated as they waited to march across the great open space kept clear for this day. For once they were silent, waiting stoically even as they boiled in their own sweat. Every man looked across the open ground to the great throng of men, women and children who had been arriving since early that morning.

The day was to be one of celebration, the large dusty space on one side of Emmart's Farm where the men had learned to manoeuvre in larger formations now given over to a great fair. The crowd had grown throughout the morning. Now thousands of relations and well-wishers had gathered to celebrate the day with men about to fight in the great climactic battle that would decide the fate of their nation once and for all.

'A Company! Prepare to march!' First Sergeant O'Connell shouted the order that had every man in the company straighten his spine.

Jack thought the men had never looked better. Even the scallywags in D Company had made sure that their turnout was first rate. The 1st Boston Volunteer Militia looked like soldiers.

'Forward! March!'

The instruction was repeated all the way down the regiment's column of companies. On cue, the band began to play. The strains of 'The Star-Spangled Banner' washed over the troops as they began to march. Straight away a number of men turned and grinned at Jack, the song's lyrics a defiant reminder of the colonists' defence of Fort McHenry, the same fort the 1st Boston had glimpsed on their approach to Baltimore. The song was a favourite of the regiment and Jack heard it most nights. The men never tired of teasing the Englishman in their midst for his country's role in the history of their young nation.

The troops marched from their allotted place on the far side of the open ground. Scanlon led the way mounted on a fine black charger. The colour party, eight corporals and one colour sergeant, followed close behind him bearing the national colours along with the Massachusetts state flag. The regiment's bandsmen followed the colour party, with Major Bridges, the only other officer mounted, leading the second half of the regiment.

Jack marched on the right of A Company. It felt decidedly odd to follow the flag of a foreign power, one that had once been Britain's enemy, but he could see what it meant to the men around him. They marched with pride. Their ranks had become a little ragged by the time they reached the reviewing platform set up for the great and good of Washington society who had been invited to join the celebrations, but they still marched past with swagger.

There were cheers and applause as the men wheeled left. The sound washed over the marching soldiers and was loud enough to drown out the band. To their credit, they kept their heads facing front, even as the crowd waved banners and flags, all the while roaring their delight at the sight of such a fine body of men. It took several long minutes for the rest of the regiment to pass the reviewing stand. The noise of the crowd did not diminish, even as the very last company in the column marched past.

With the short parade completed, the men formed up in long ranks facing the stand. They stood to attention, their arms shouldered. To Jack's surprise, it was his paymaster who stepped forward to make the first of the day's speeches.

'We stand here together on this our Independence Day to give thanks to the great men who forged this wondrous country.' Kearney's voice was loud and clear, any frailty hidden. There was no stick being used this day. 'And we give thanks to you, our soldiers, for your unswerving loyalty to the flag that flies over us all.'

He paused as more cheers surged from the crowd. He held the moment, smiling beneficently as he waited for the noise to subside. 'We have never been prouder than we are today. Thanks to you, the Union will be preserved. Through your efforts we will show the world what we are about.'

Again he was forced to pause, as the cheers grew more

raucous. It took the best part of a minute for the crowd to calm enough for him to continue.

'Today we must remember the founding fathers of this great nation of ours. What they set up cannot be undone. It is our duty to preserve this most precious Union. We are one nation under God and we cannot let the work of our founding fathers be undermined. The Southerners are not evil. They are just misguided. They are stubborn, and like a stubborn child they need a lesson. One short, sharp shock and they will see the error of their ways. We must smack them into line.'

The crowd erupted. The cheers were interspersed with cries to smite the secessionists, Kearney's words resonating with a large number of the more belligerent onlookers. If he planned to say more, he would not get the chance. The crowd had seized control of the moment and now they held on to it, cheering and shouting for all they were worth. The soldiers stood in their long ranks and let the noise roll around them.

Jack watched the spectacle without feeling. It was as if he were observing the parade from afar. He felt detached, somehow not a part of the proceedings, which were growing more passionate by the moment.

'Three cheers for the Union!' Even O'Connell had been captured by the surging tide of emotion. He shouted the order from his place at the front of the company.

The men needed little urging to obey. As one they roared, their deep voices thunderous enough to drown out the crowd. Only when the third cheer died away did the crowd redouble its efforts to shout themselves hoarse.

'Company! Company, dismiss.'

All along the line, first sergeants bellowed the order. It was time to let discipline fall by the wayside. It was Independence

Day; a day to celebrate the birth of the nation and to give the men a rousing send-off, even though they had yet to be given any orders to march.

'Jack!' Robert plucked at Jack's sleeve, shouting to make himself heard. Around them the men were rushing to stack the weapons before disappearing to enjoy the fair that was waiting for them to arrive. 'I think I'm going to get drunk.' Robert cackled with delight as he told Jack of his plans.

'Go! Go!' Jack had no desire to hold the lieutenant back. There was no stopping any of them today.

Robert bounded away, leaving Jack standing alone. He did not follow the rest of the regiment as they swarmed towards the fair. There was a shooting range for those wishing to display their newly acquired martial talents. For those less well trained, there was archery, the usual target butts replaced with straw figures dressed as Confederate soldiers. There were skittles and shies for the younger members of the crowd, and apples ready to be ducked from barrels of water. There were pony rides for the children, and the officers would compete in a steeplechase later in the afternoon, when the heat of the day had lessened.

For the hungry and thirsty there were stalls selling lemonade and dozens of tables smothered with a feast laid on in the men's honour. There was even a photographer's stand for those wishing to capture a memento of the day. The temporary studio had been set up in the shade of one of the few trees in the vicinity. To Jack's eye it appeared to be little more than an accumulation of scientific equipment and uncomfortable-looking braces to keep the subjects still for the many seconds it took for the image to be fixed onto the photographic plate. Already dozens were forming a queue there, the demand for the fashionable *cartes de visite* certain to outstrip the small team's ability to supply them.

The only thing missing was beer or any form of spirit, the good citizens of Washington preferring to celebrate the day in more temperate fashion. But they had other bounty for the boys about to wage war on the secessionist foes. There were woollen scarves, caped overcoats, mufflers and patchwork blankets to keep the men warm and comfortable when the campaign started. There were sacks of coffee, tins of biscuits, loaves of bread and jars of preserves to keep them sustained. Finally, there was a bewildering array of knives, revolvers and machetes to arm them so that none would be lacking when they eventually faced the foe on the field of battle.

Nearly every man was overwhelmed with gifts. Jack doubted much would be kept beyond the first day of marching. He knew from experience how soldiers quickly tired of carrying anything they did not truly need. The generosity of the crowd would be wasted, the carefully prepared jars of preserves and hand-stitched patchwork blankets destined to be dumped by the roadside by soldiers unwilling to carry them another yard.

'Are you not taking part in the day's festivities then, Lieutenant Lark?'

Jack started. He had chosen a vantage point near a wagon park from where he could observe the day's events without being easily seen. He had not heard anyone approach, but he smiled when he saw it was Elizabeth Kearney who had managed to find him. 'I don't think it's my place to join in. These are not my people.'

'Not your people?' Elizabeth came to stand beside him so that she too could study the great throng. 'What an odd thing to say. Are you not fighting for these very people? If that does not make them yours, then I cannot see what would.'

'I'm not from here.' Jack could not help looking at Elizabeth and wondering which part of her character he was speaking to. He had seen two very different sides to her personality. He did not much like the one that fawned and played up to Captain Rowell. But the other one, the one that had spoken so intently about the war, fascinated him.

'Tell me about your home.' Elizabeth did not look at him, preferring instead to watch the soldiers as they moved through the crowd. She smiled as she saw one young soldier stagger away from a pair of middle-aged women completely smothered by a patchwork quilt that must have taken them weeks to create.

'There's not a lot to tell.'

'Do try.' There was a touch of pepper in the demand. 'Tell me what it is called. That should not be so hard, and it would surely be a good place to start.'

'It's called Whitechapel.'

'And that is in London?'

'Yes. In the eastern part of the city.'

'So you come from the city itself.'

'Yes.' Jack did not try to hide his discomfort. He did not like to think of the place he had come from.

'My goodness, but this is as hard as having a tooth pulled.' Elizabeth shook her head. 'So you were born there?'

'Yes.' Jack sighed. He sensed he would not escape without telling her something of his former life. 'I grew up in a gin palace. It was a good one, not like the dives near Spitalfields. It was my mother's place. I worked there until I joined the army.' He kept the details brief. He made no mention of John

Lampkin, the man his mother had taken into her bed after Jack's father had left and who had made much of Jack's early years a relentless misery. Nor did he mention the fight that had seen Lampkin left half dead and Jack banished from his mother's home.

'How old were you then? When you joined the army?'

Jack had to make a rough tally in his head. 'Nineteen, I suppose.'

'So that makes you . . .' Elizabeth still did not look at him. He heard something change in her tone. She was trying hard not to sound too interested, but he sensed she was waiting for the next answer.

'I'm thirty-one. I'm an old man.'

'Thirty-one is not so old.' Elizabeth laughed.

'I'm sure you're just being kind. How old are you? Twenty?'

'I'll be twenty-two in the fall.'

'My goodness, twenty-two! Why, aren't you the old maid.' Jack could not help scoffing. He had been a redcoat at her age. A few years later and he had led men into battle. It seemed a lifetime ago.

'Do not mock me, Jack.' For the first time, Elizabeth turned to look up at him.

'I'm not mocking you.' Jack adopted a more serious tone. 'But you do not come across as being just twenty-two. You're well informed about the world around you and you're clearly intelligent. Neither of those are traits people would normally associate with a young woman.'

'Am I only supposed to be interested in what petticoats I should be wearing this season then?' It was Elizabeth's turn to mock. 'There is more to me than what you see.'

'What do you think I see?'

'You see what everyone sees.' Elizabeth sighed. 'Look at me, Jack. Tell me what you see.'

'I see you.' Jack was uncomfortable. He did not understand the rules of this new game.

'But what did you see the first time you saw me?'

'I saw that you were beautiful.'

'Exactly. Men look at me like I am a creature from a dream. Can you understand how frustrating that is?'

'I imagine there are plenty of women who would happily trade places with you.'

'Perhaps.' Elizabeth pouted. 'Yet I cannot stand being treated like a china doll. When men meet me, they become gallant and noble, as if I am incapable of tolerating a normal conversation. When women meet me . . .' She looked down, then sighed again. 'When women meet me, they tend to be a little bit mean.' She lifted her eyes back to Jack's face. 'No one takes me seriously. Even you.'

'I take you very seriously.'

'Only because you want to take me to your bed.'

Jack swallowed his desire with difficulty. 'It is not just that.' He tried to be glib.

'Rubbish. I know what men want. I just don't think anyone knows what *I* want.'

'So tell me.'

Elizabeth laughed. It came from deep in her throat, the sound warm and genuine. 'Will you find it for me then, Jack, like a knight from a fairy tale? If I tell you my heart's desire, will you journey to the ends of the earth to steal it away just so that you can bring it back to me?'

'The ends of the earth might be a little too far. If it's in Baltimore, then maybe.'

Again she laughed. 'You're a rogue, Jack. I think that is why I like you so much.'

'I'm pleased to hear you like me at all. I was wondering.'

'I like you perhaps too much. You don't moon at me, at least not quite as badly as most men, and certainly not like Ethan.'

'You behave very differently around him.'

'It's how I have to behave. If I behaved any other way, he would not know what to do. I have tried. From his reaction, you would think I had asked him to run naked through the streets.'

'So why do it? Why behave like that?' Jack could not hide his disgruntled tone.

'Father wants me to marry him. So I have to make him happy. Make him feel good about himself. And he is very handsome, even you must see that.'

'Is that what you want? Somebody handsome?' Jack did not even try to hide his jealousy.

'Perhaps.' Elizabeth was evasive. 'Isn't that what I am supposed to want? Somebody handsome. Somebody rich. Do I need to look for anything more? Must I also expect wit? Intelligence? An interest in the world around us?'

'Ethan is a good man.' Jack tried to sound sincere.

'How valiant of you to be so magnanimous. Ethan *is* a good man . . .' she paused, 'but sometimes he reminds me of a tailor's dummy. He looks so dashing, but underneath I fancy there is nothing but so much stuffing.'

'I'm sure there's more to him than that.' Jack felt odd as he stood up for his rival for Elizabeth's affection.

'Perhaps. But I know he will do anything I say, no matter what it is, so long as I ask it in a certain way. I do not think you would be so malleable. If I ordered you to do something you did not want to do, you would just growl at me and give me one of your scowls.'

Jack snorted as Elizabeth made a face that he supposed was meant to represent his own. He could not hold back a peal of laughter as she then growled at him, the noise reverberating deep in her throat.

'I sound like I have cold, then?'

Elizabeth beamed as she saw her impression have the desired effect. 'You have a mongrel spirit in you, Jack. Ha!' She pointed as he scowled on cue. 'There, the perfect example.'

'Am I not allowed to scowl when you pick on me so pitilessly?'

'I'm not mocking you.' Elizabeth looked at him with a serious expression. 'I think it is perhaps your finest trait. Do not be ashamed of who you are, Jack.'

Jack shivered as if a feather had traced down the back of his neck. 'I am what I am.' He wanted to sound light-hearted, but it came out with a hint of a growl.

It was enough to make Elizabeth smile. It was the expression that had captivated him since the very first moment he had seen her walk into Kearney's study. She was right to say that few people could see the person behind the beautiful facade. For at that moment, Jack did not think there was a woman walking on the face of the earth that could hold a candle to her.

'My goodness.' Elizabeth was watching him closely. 'If it were not you, Jack, I would swear you were mooning at me.' She did not give him a chance to reply. 'I noticed that Mr Brady has brought his photography studio into the field.' She fixed him with eyes that sparkled with devilment. 'I think we should get our photographs taken.'

'Why would you want to do that?' Jack saw the look on her face. He knew he would not escape easily.

'It will be fun.'

'Fun?'

'It would please me,' Elizabeth dipped her chin, 'and it is just over there. It is not even as far as Baltimore.'

Jack could not help smiling. Elizabeth was as beautiful as an angel, but she had a mind as quick and as agile as any person he had ever met.

'Very well.' He gave the agreement with good grace. 'Shall we?'

'Thank you, Jack.' Elizabeth was clearly pleased he had agreed. She slipped her arm into his as they began to walk through the wagon park, pressing her side against him. He could smell her now that she was so close. She smelled expensive.

'Do you think they'll suppose we are sweethearts?' Elizabeth had to crane her neck back so that she could whisper into his ear as they walked.

'I very much doubt it.'

'I do not agree.'

She came closer, the warmth of her breath washing over the skin below his ear.

'In one hundred years' time, someone will look at this photograph and think we were lovers.'

The word slipped into his ear on a rush of air. His desire for her surged through him and he gasped.

Elizabeth heard it and stopped. For a moment she looked up at him, her eyes locked onto his. Then she lifted onto her tiptoes and kissed him.

Jack's breath stuck in his throat. The kiss lasted for no more than the span of a single heartbeat, then they were walking on as if nothing had happened.

It was only then that he spotted Rose standing near a wagon no more than twenty yards away, a wicker hamper held in front of her, her eyes locked onto the couple walking along arm in arm as if they did not have a care in the world.

He did not have to be close to her to see the amused expression on her face.

Chapter Twenty-two

———◆———

Jack walked through the encampment having left the celebrations early. He had lost interest in the day when Rowell had intercepted Elizabeth shortly after they had had their photograph taken. If he were honest with himself, he felt relieved to have left her behind. As he walked along the long line of tents, he felt a little heady. Elizabeth's company was intoxicating.

He did not understand why she had kissed him and he had even less of an idea what it meant. He did know that it was a complication to his life he could well do without. He had a fair idea how Rowell would react if he discovered that his beloved had kissed another man. The fact that Rose had seen them made a wider audience's discovery possible. The thought made Jack sigh.

It had also been a relief to walk away from the clutches of the photographer and his assistants. Mr Brady had been delighted to see Elizabeth approach his makeshift studio and they had been ushered past the queue as the photographer's assistant fussed around them as if they were royalty. Elizabeth had been seated in a high-backed chair, her head held in a metal frame, its bars slipped into her hair to hold her still. Jack had been posed awkwardly to one side, his hand clasped to the back of Elizabeth's chair, where it had been secured by a cuff. A metal frame had been placed around his spine to hold his posture, the contraption digging into his flesh so that the first pain had arrived within a minute of his being in its iron embrace. Both of them had been told not to speak or move.

Brady's assistant did all the work whilst Mr Brady himself stood to one side and peered at Elizabeth through thick spectacles. He was an odd little man and Jack had spent his time in the uncomfortable posture wondering how someone who appeared to be almost blind could become one of Washington's pre-eminent photographers.

Despite the pain of the sitting, Elizabeth had enjoyed the whole experience. As Rowell had dragged her away, she had promised to send Jack one of the images. Jack had paid the promise little heed, his attention focused on his commanding officer, who had only just been able to keep a lid on his anger at finding his fiancée on the arm of another man.

A loud English voice interrupted his thoughts. It was the first English accent he had heard for a long time, so he paused as a short, heavily bearded man stomped his way along the line of tents, heading in the opposite direction to Jack, followed by a major and a pair of red-faced captains. The Englishman was berating his escort loudly as he walked, his hectoring tone making it clear he was not happy.

'Excuse me, sir,' he snapped as he saw Jack standing in his way. He clearly expected him to stand aside.

'Where do you think you are, Pall Mall?' Jack could not resist the retort.

It was enough to bring the Englishman up short. He stopped so abruptly that his escort nearly clattered into his back.

'I say. Are you English?'

'I am.' Jack took in the odd-looking man who now peered up at him. He was dressed strangely in a pair of Indian boots, cord trousers and jacket and an old felt hat. A flask and a revolver hung from his belt.

'William Russell of the *Times*.' The introduction was curt and was followed by a hand.

Jack's eyes widened. Russell was the most famous journalist in the world. He had been the man who had first brought to the attention of the British public the dreadful conditions the wounded soldiers were enduring at the hospital at Scutari. Jack had himself been wounded in the Crimea. He had survived the appalling filth and squalor of Scutari. Hundreds of other wounded soldiers had not been so fortunate.

'Jack Lark.' He just about managed to say his own name.

'What is an Englishman doing here?' Russell fired the question as he shook Jack's hand.

Jack's tongue felt twice its normal size. 'I'm serving in the 1st Boston Volunteer Militia.'

'I have never heard of them.' Russell's reply was abrupt. 'But are you not ashamed, sir, to be part of such an army? I have never seen such lax discipline. This whole place is filthy dirty. The general has no staff, and those he does have are completely inadequate to an army on campaign. The army has no cavalry, only a few scarecrow men who will dissolve partnership with their steeds at the first serious combined movement!'

Jack had not expected the tirade. He was saved finding an answer as Russell paused to rummage in a pocket.

'I like that, indeed I do.' The journalist was clearly well pleased with his own description and he quickly scribbled it down in a notebook before looking back at Jack. 'Are you an army man, sir?'

'Yes, sir, I served in the Crimea and then in India and Persia.'

'Then you will understand of what I speak. There is no carriage for reserve ammunition and the commissariat drivers are civilians, under little or no control. The officers are the most unsoldierly-looking men, whilst the troops themselves are dressed in all sorts of uniforms. From what I hear, I doubt if any of these regiments have ever performed a brigade evolution together, or if any of the officers know what it is to deploy a brigade from column into line. That is if they have any men to deploy, since most of them are about to go home now that their three months' service is up!'

'But they can fight.' Jack felt his temper rising. Russell's negative opinion grated. 'My company is as fine a body of men as I have ever had the privilege of serving alongside. They may do things differently, but when it comes to a fight—'

'Poof, fight!' Russell did not hesitate to interrupt. 'You think these men can fight? When I was in the Crimea—'

'I too was in the Crimea, sir.' Jack returned the compliment. 'I fought my way up the slope below the Great Redoubt alongside the bravest and the best men I have ever seen, and—'

'Then you should be ashamed to be in such company now!' Russell stuck out his chin and snapped back at Jack. 'They talk of these know-nothings; why, these generals are just the same! They've not got a decent map of Virginia between them. They have no idea of geography or knowledge of main roads or the surrounding countryside. How do you suppose McDowell can plan a campaign when he has no idea if the enemy are on the far side of a river or even halfway up a damn mountain?'

Jack could think of no defence. Brigadier General Irvin McDowell was the commander of the Army of Northeastern Virginia, of which the 1st Boston was a part. It would be McDowell who would take his army onto the field of battle when the war started in earnest. To hear that he had insufficient maps of the ground he was likely to fight on was indeed shameful.

'I see that has got your attention,' Russell piped up in triumph. 'I fancy you have allowed yourself to be caught up in an affair of amateurs, sir, an affair that will only end badly. You mark my words. This army of yours is a half-trained rabble. I warrant the Southerners will not lose any sleep over the prospect of an attack.'

'Then they would be mistaken.' Jack stuck to his resolute defence.

'Do not let your pride cloud your judgement.' Russell took a pace forward and lowered his tone. 'If you fought at the Alma then you know what this mob will face if they insist on attacking the secessionists.'

'I know what they face, sir. That does not mean I will abandon them.'

Russell studied Jack's face. 'Then you are either one of the bravest men I have ever met, or the greatest fool. Either way I shall wish you good fortune. At the end, you are an Englishman and a soldier at that. I shall look for you again, sir. I hope you will live long enough for us to continue this conversation at another juncture.'

'I hope so too.' Despite Russell's abrasive and disagreeable nature, Jack could not help having enjoyed being able to speak to a man he had long admired.

He thought on what Russell had said as the journalist and his posse of escorting officers walked away. The man from the *Times* had been quite correct. Jack was an Englishman and he was a soldier. He thought the two titles defined him pretty well.

'Lieutenant Lark, I apologise for disturbing you.'

Jack sat up quickly. He had been lying on his camp bed, his mind wandering from his encounter with William Russell to the more troublesome time spent with Elizabeth. He was almost relieved to be disturbed.

'Good afternoon, sir.' He had recognised the voice that had interrupted his rest immediately. He wondered why the regiment's second in command had sought him out. He got to his feet and quickly tucked his shirt back into his trousers. His uniform jacket lay on the foot of the bed.

'May I come in?' Bridges hovered on the tent's threshold.

'Of course.' Jack sensed the major was uncomfortable. He gestured towards the chairs pulled under the tent's camp table. 'Do sit down.'

'Thank you.' Bridges nodded firmly and took one of the two chairs. He removed his kepi and placed it on the table in front of him. Unlike Jack, he was wearing his full uniform. He was clearly hot, his neck and cheeks flushed, but he made no open display of discomfort as he waited for Jack to join him.

Jack walked across the tent and took the second chair. 'I'm afraid I cannot offer you tea.' He offered a smile as he attempted to be humorous.

'This is not a social call.' Bridges' reply was stiff and formal.

'I see.' Jack held back a sigh. 'How can I help?'

'I shall not dissemble.' Bridges gnawed the lower reaches of his moustache. 'I must ask you to desist in your pursuit of Miss Kearney.'

'My pursuit?'

'I have heard a rumour. If it has reached my ears, then I expect it is hardly new.' Bridges kept his gaze riveted on Jack's face.

Jack had to give the major credit. He clearly knew that he would not be the first to hear of any tittle-tattle. He was also acting true to his word. No one could accuse him of dissembling. 'I don't know what you've heard, sir. But I promise you, I'm not pursing any woman, Miss Kearney least of all.'

Bridges' eyes narrowed as he pondered on Jack's denial. 'You were seen.'

'Seen?'

'This very afternoon.' Bridges' stare was glacial.

'I suspect I'm seen most afternoons.'

'Do not make me spell it out, Lieutenant. You were seen with Miss Kearney at the fair. I understand that it was an intimate moment.'

'You mean some nosy, prying bastard saw her kiss me?'

Bridges scowled. 'I would ask you to moderate your language.'

Jack controlled his rising temper with difficulty. He had known this could happen. Elizabeth had chosen a very public arena for her gesture.

'I apologise, sir.' He spoke through gritted teeth. 'May I ask who dobbed us in?'

'If you mean who started the rumour, then I do not know and I do not care to find out. What does concern me is how Captain Rowell will react if the story reaches his ears.'

'If you've heard it, then I imagine he will too soon enough.'

'Perhaps. Perhaps not. Either way, you must desist in pursuing Miss Kearney's affection.'

'Is that what I was doing?' Jack could not help growling the reply. He knew he had encouraged Elizabeth, if only through the display of his obvious attraction to her. She was to be another man's bride and yet he had gone sniffing around her like a mongrel finding a bitch on heat.

'It appears so.' Bridges was not warming to the topic.

'Then I apologise.' This time Jack meant it. He was disappointed with himself. He had started to like Major Bridges. The man might not be everyone's cup of tea, but to Jack's mind he had the calm, composed nature that would serve his troops well in battle.

Bridges nodded in acceptance. 'Let us hope that Captain Rowell does not hear of it. Or if he does, that he turns the other cheek.'

'And if he doesn't?' Jack did not know Rowell that well, but he was pretty sure the captain was not the kind of man to let something like this lie.

Bridges agreed. 'Then he will fight you. I don't think he has a hope of winning, but he will still fight you if it becomes clear you have stolen his honour.'

'What do I do if he does?' Jack asked the question sincerely. He did not want to fight Rowell.

'You must refuse.' Bridges looked Jack directly in the eye. 'You must show forbearance.'

Jack grunted. He did not think he had an ounce of forbearance in him. If Rowell tried to fight him, Jack did not think he would be able to stand back.

'I trust you to do the right thing, Jack.' Bridges read his thoughts.

'You do?' Jack could not help sighing. 'You've more faith in me than I do.'

Bridges bristled his moustache, then stood up. 'I have every faith in you, Jack. You are a unique individual. I suspect the only person who doubts you is yourself.'

He said nothing more as he left the tent.

Jack stayed seated. He did not know if he could live up to Bridges' opinion of him. But he was sure that if Rowell came looking for a fight, it would take one hell of an effort not to give it to him.

The first salvo of fireworks sounded like a distant artillery barrage. They lit up the sky, the bright flashes of colour momentarily casting an eerie hue over the encampment.

Jack stood on the far side of the ground where the regiment had paraded earlier that day. He had not gone to join the great crowd of people that thronged behind the line of rope laid out to stop them coming too close to the men charged with setting off the display. From their viewing area, the spectators cooed and cheered each explosion, their delight at the spectacle laid on for them reaching across to where he stood and watched from a distance.

It was a vibrant end to the day of celebration. The crowd had enjoyed the entertainments, then feasted on a giant hog roast that would have fed at least double the number of people present. Jack had stayed clear of the whole thing, eating a lonely dinner of hardtack and coffee whilst thinking on how he would react if Rowell did demand they fight. He had no doubt in his mind that he could better his captain. Rowell might possess the physique of a fairy-tale hero, but Jack was a lad from Whitechapel. He had been fighting his whole life. Rowell would not stand a chance.

He heard someone approaching. He peered into the darkness, half expecting it to be Rowell come to demand a duel. He saw a shadowy figure walking towards him. He knew who it was immediately.

'What are you doing here, Rose?' he asked.

'Same as you, I'd say.' Rose walked closer so that he could just about make out her face in the light of the exploding fireworks.

'And what's that?'

'Hiding.'

'Why do you think I'm hiding?' He snapped back at her.

'Perhaps you're hiding from someone. From Mr Rowell, maybe? Or perhaps you're hiding from my mistress.'

'You know a lot about my business.'

Rose came closer. 'Maybe you shouldn't do your business in front of everyone. You should learn to be more discreet.'

'And you should learn to keep quiet.'

'Ahh,' Rose cooed as she heard his temper. 'I'm making you angry.'

'Yes, you bloody well are,' he growled back at her. 'You peached on me, didn't you?'

'Peached?' From her tone, it was clear Rose was not frightened of him.

'Dobbed me in.' He shook his head in exasperation as he was forced to translate. 'You told on me.'

'Yes. I did. And I'd do it again if I had to.'

'You need to keep your damn nose out of business that doesn't concern you.'

Rose laughed at his harsh tone. 'You don't scare me, Jack Lark. I've seen men who make you look like one of the little boys who sing in the church choir.'

'Is that so?' He loomed over her. She was small and fragile. He could reach out and throttle her without breaking sweat. Yet she looked up at him with eyes blazing with defiance.

'Oh yes. I've known bad men.' Her hand strayed to the thin scars on her face. The gesture was enough to make him take a deep breath and bring his temper under control. He was not a bully. Frightening young women was for other men. It was not who he was.

'You shouldn't have told on me.'

'Why not?' Rose glared up at him. 'It was better it came soon enough to put a stop to you mooning over that woman.'

'That woman? You mean Elizabeth?' He did not understand the disgust in Rose's tone as she referred to her mistress.

'Of course I mean her. She's the only set of petticoats you've been chasing, isn't she?'

'I haven't been chasing her.' He half turned away. He had had his fill of talking about Elizabeth Kearney.

'Of course you have. We all saw it.' Rose reached out and laid a hand on his arm as if she was worried he would move away before she could finish speaking. 'She's not what she seems. She uses men, plays with them. You're just another one of her games.'

He scowled. 'She's not like that.' He thought back to the conversation that had led to the kiss. 'You don't know her.'

'And you do?' Rose cackled at his claim. 'I've spent every day with her for three years now, yet you think you know her better because she kissed you.'

'It's more than that.'

'You're a fool.'

'No. You—'

Whatever he wanted to say was lost as Rose put her hands on his shoulders and pulled herself up high enough to smother his mouth with her lips. There was no passion in the kiss. It was fierce and it crushed his own lips back into his teeth. She looked at him the whole time, her eyes blazing. Then she pulled away, stumbling back a half-pace as she hit the ground.

She glared at him then. 'There. Now you know me as well as you know her.' She shook her head and placed her hands on her hips. 'You're a fool.'

He raised a hand to his lips, his fingertips running over the bruised flesh. 'If I'm a fool, then what are you?' he retorted. The fireworks still lit up the sky. The colours of the explosions played over Rose's face, casting it in odd shades whilst leaving much of it in shadow.

'Don't you worry none about me. Worry about yourself.' Rose took another half-step away, losing herself in the darkness, leaving Jack standing alone once more.

Chapter Twenty-three

Emmart's Farm, Washington, Monday 15 July 1861

'Good morning, gentlemen.' Colonel Scanlon brought the hum of conversation to an abrupt close. The officers of the 1st Boston had been gathered at the colonel's request. They stood in a group in front of a folding table outside the large bell tent that contained the regimental headquarters.

Jack was on the periphery of the group. He knew few of his fellow officers well enough to be comfortable in their company. He had looked for Robert, but A Company's other lieutenant was missing. Rowell stood on the far side with some of the other captains. He had seen Jack arrive, but he had not extended any sort of welcome other than a momentary scowl.

The air felt dreadfully close. Jack watched Scanlon patiently as the colonel waited for the expectant conversations to hush completely. He did his best not to fidget, despite the river of sweat running down his neck to soak the collar of his second shirt of the day. It was a small mercy that O'Dowd had become adept at getting his officers' shirts cleaned, otherwise Jack would have reeked to high heaven. Judging by the ripe aromas coming from some of the regiment's other officers, not all of them were fortunate enough to have an orderly looking after them.

It was nearly two weeks since the Independence Day celebrations. Each day had been more tiresome than the one before. The men were itching to leave the encampment behind and chafed at the delay, becoming worse-tempered by the hour. There had been at least half a dozen fist fights, as frustration boiled over into violence. But there had been no confrontation between Jack and Captain Rowell. If Rowell had heard of Elizabeth's kiss, he had not come to challenge Jack about it. He had kept away from the company almost completely, only turning up for the formal weekly parades in front of the colonel. On those occasions he had not spoken a single word to Jack.

Jack had found the silence something of a relief. He had resolved to steer clear of both Elizabeth and her maidservant. He understood neither of them and he had no desire to alter that state of mind. He had thrown himself into training the company and making sure they knew their drill as well as they could. It was not the most satisfying work, but it helped keep his mind clear of the two women who had taken it upon themselves to interfere in his life.

'I have the news we have all been waiting for.' Scanlon could not hide his excitement. The announcement sent a murmur of conversation running through the group of officers, which he immediately quelled by raising a hand. 'We have orders to march.'

One of the officers hurrahed. The others quickly picked it up and joined in. Jack looked around him and stayed silent. It was a relief to hear that they would be leaving Emmart's

Farm, but he would not cheer the order that would send the men on their way to battle.

'Quieten down, you damn rascals.' Scanlon was clearly in good humour, and he laughed as the cheers slowly died out. 'Now as you know, General McDowell is in command of the forces here around Washington. General Patterson's force is thirty miles to our north-west in the Shenandoah Valley, near Harper's Ferry.' He paused to ensure he had every officer's attention. 'We know the enemy has one army opposite us and another one opposite Patterson.' He scanned the eager faces looking back at him. 'It has been decided that we will be the army making the attack.'

Again there was a noisy reaction to the bold announcement, and again Scanlon stopped it quickly by waving his hand. 'Quieten down, goddam it,' he snapped with enough force to silence even the noisiest.

'Now listen up. McDowell will lead the attack on Manassas Junction, which we believe is held by some twenty thousand Confederate troops. It is crucial that General Patterson holds the enemy forces in place in the Shenandoah Valley to prevent them from reinforcing Manassas. Once our attack is successful, we will hold the rail junction and gain access to the rebel capital in Richmond. More importantly, we will have shown the South that they do not stand a hope in hell of opposing us. The goddam sechers will give up this nonsense and we can all go home!'

This time Scanlon let the cheers come. He stood straight and preened as the officers hurrahed and slapped each other on the back.

'We're not ready.'

The lone voice could barely be made out above the excited conversations.

'We're not ready.'

This time Jack shouted the comment loudly enough to be heard. The group of officers stopped cheering and turned to glare at the man who had dared to offer a contrary opinion. Jack stood straight-backed as he felt every face turn towards him. Even such hostility was not enough to stop him from continuing.

'The men are not ready.' He kept his voice firm. 'The army has not got enough support, and from what I hear, McDowell doesn't even have a decent map of the area he wants us to attack.' He paused and looked around the angry faces. 'This is not the right decision.'

The moment he stopped speaking, the other officers reacted with angry jeers and shouted denials.

'Quieten down, quieten down.' Scanlon hushed them calmly. 'Lieutenant Lark is right to question this. We're officers, not sheep.' He looked around the faces that had turned towards him. 'I want no man to be fearful of speaking out, even if they are a goddam Limey son of a bitch.' He chuckled at his own joke. It was enough to make some of the officers laugh, even though most still threw angry looks in Jack's direction.

'I thank you, Lieutenant, for your forthright opinion. I expect it will surprise you all to know that the general shares your concern.' Scanlon raised his eyebrows and stared at the more vocal officers. It was enough to quell the last of the disapproving murmurs. 'McDowell knows we are underprepared. That is why our orders tell us to proceed with caution and to make sure the men do not fire on one another.' Scanlon smiled. 'We're not marching off like fools, Lieutenant Lark. We will proceed slowly and carefully, and with all due care and attention. But I should also tell you that the President himself has approved this plan.' He spoke as if playing a trump card. 'There can be no doubting our purpose. We mean to engage the enemy. We march with the aim of seizing a decisive victory.'

Jack heard the murmur of approval echo through the group of officers. He knew there was no point in saying anything further. The die had been cast. Scanlon looked at him expectantly for several long moments. When it became clear that Jack was staying silent, the colonel looked away and beamed at his officers.

'We march in the morning. Make sure your men are ready.' He nodded firmly before walking away.

The officers began to disburse immediately, their conversations loud as they moved away to deliver the news to their own companies.

Jack had just begun the walk back to A Company's lines when Rowell barged past him. The captain had clearly aimed carefully and he hit Jack hard with his shoulder, causing him to stumble and almost lose his footing. When he caught his balance, he found himself standing face to face with his commanding officer.

'Do be careful, Lieutenant.' Rowell sneered as he saw Jack looking at him. 'You should watch where you're going. Why, you could get hurt if you don't pay more attention to your surroundings.' Before Jack could say anything by way of reply, the captain turned sharply on his heel and walked away.

The warning was clear.

The army was going to march. And Captain Rowell knew everything.

'You should be ready!' First Sergeant O'Connell howled in frustration as he stood over O'Dowd, who was feverishly stuffing food into the cotton sack that lined his haversack. 'That stinks!' O'Connell peered at the mess O'Dowd was making. The cotton sack contained a nauseating mix of hard-tack, raw pork, salt, sugar, coffee, desiccated vegetables and rice. The men had been issued with three days of rations, and it looked like O'Dowd had simply dumped the whole lot into his haversack.

'Well, he's the one who has to eat it.' Jack had walked over to see what the commotion was. The rest of the company was already formed up and ready to march. Only O'Dowd was missing from the ranks, and now the hapless private had the attention of both his first sergeant and the company's second lieutenant.

Jack had the same rations as the men in his own haversack. The food was just a fraction of their load. Each man also carried candles and candle holders, a razor, spare shoes, chewing tobacco or cigars according to preference, a block of lucifers, a housewife, a wash kit, handkerchiefs, spare clothes, a mess plate, a combined knife, fork and spoon implement, pen, ink and paper, a smooth-sided three-pint tin canteen covered with cloth and a tin cup. Most also carried a bible and any photographs they had of their loved ones.

Added to this were their Springfield rifle, scabbard with bayonet, caped overcoat, blanket, forty rounds of .58 calibre cartridges in a leather cartridge box, tools for their rifle and a pouch for the percussion caps used to fire their weapon. Then there was the myriad collection of gifts that had been given to the men on Independence Day. Most men had added patch-work blankets, machetes and every other type of weapon and comforter they could imagine would be useful on campaign.

O'Dowd finally straightened up, then nearly fell back

down on his backside as he tottered under the weight of his equipment.

'On your feet, you slovenly soldier.' O'Connell reached out and grabbed hold of the private's haversack.

'Feck me, sir. Are we mules or soldiers?' O'Dowd griped as he staggered.

'Shut your mouth and get in the fecking ranks,' O'Connell growled, shoving the hapless Irishman forward.

Jack laughed as O'Dowd stumbled his way towards the column. He hefted his own haversack on his back, trying to find the most comfortable spot. He was carrying nothing but the bare essentials, which meant his load was a great deal lighter than that carried by most of the men.

'Fecking eejits.' O'Connell stood at Jack's shoulder as the pair looked over the ranks. The first sergeant's equipment was as pared down as Jack's.

'Don't fret, First Sergeant. Half of that shit will be dumped by noon. The locals will have a field day with all the free booty.' Jack chuckled. 'Ah, Lieutenant Kearney has deigned to join us at last.' He had spotted Robert's slight figure wandering towards A Company's position at the head of the column.

'Good morning to you, sir,' O'Connell called out in greeting as Robert weaved his way closer.

'There's nothing good about it.' Robert staggered to a halt in front of the two men.

'You look a little green about the gills, sir, so you do.' O'Connell cracked a smile as he looked over his officer.

'Thank you for sharing that observation, First Sergeant.' Robert was finding standing still difficult. He shuffled from side to side as if being blown around by the morning's gentle breeze.

O'Connell glanced at Jack, then smiled. 'Shall I get him some coffee? There may just be time.'

'No.' Jack's reply was firm. 'You'll be all right, won't you, Lieutenant?'

'Oh God.' Robert retched as he tried to reply. 'I think I'm going to be sick.'

'Jesus Christ.' Jack skipped to one side, narrowly dodging the first spray of vomit that erupted from Robert's mouth. The lieutenant bent double, nearly falling onto his face as he did so under the weight of his haversack. Jack looked away, doing his best to swallow as the stink of fresh sick caught the back of his throat. The men were watching their officer with glee, Robert's misfortune greeted with good humour.

'My God.' Robert managed to pull himself upright. He noticed the men's reaction for the first time and a rueful grin spread across his face as he wiped his mouth on the cuff of his jacket. 'I think I feel better now.'

'Well, that's good to hear.' Jack reached out and steered his fellow lieutenant towards his allotted place in the column, sharing a smile with O'Connell as he did so. 'I'm sure a little stroll will do wonders to clear your head.'

It was time to put an end to Robert's nights of pleasure. It was time to march.

Jack drank some water, holding it for a few seconds to sluice it around his mouth before swallowing. It was brackish and warm, but it tasted divine. Lowering the canteen, he shook it gently from side to side, listening to the contents sloshing back and forth to gauge how much was left. It was still more than half full, so he took another careful sip.

'Oh God.' Robert retched for the tenth time in as many

minutes. The sound went on and on until the lieutenant spat twice then groaned.

'You're empty.' Jack could not help smiling at Robert's predicament. 'So give it up.'

'Oh God.' Another bout of retching prevented Robert from answering. It went on for some time. When he finally straightened up, he looked at Jack with watery eyes. 'I think I'm dying.'

'Not yet you're not.' Jack sighed at the foolish remark. Robert was clearly suffering. His eyes were red and the constant attempts to vomit had burst dozens of tiny blood vessels in his face. 'Have you any water left?'

Robert shook his head.

'Then you're a bloody idiot.' Jack could not help snapping at such foolishness. Robert was not alone. Jack reckoned half the company had emptied their canteens, and it was not yet noon. His fellow lieutenant would not be the only one suffering that day.

'Here.' He held out his own canteen. 'Just a mouthful, mind.'

Robert reached for it with eager hands. 'God bless you, Jack.'

Jack watched carefully. He was relieved to see Robert do as he had been told and take just a single mouthful. He took back the canteen, wiping the mouth carefully with his cuff.

They had halted on a low rise about five miles from Emmart's Farm, and the higher ground gave him the opportunity to look back over the great column of which the 1st Boston was just a part. It snaked back for at least a mile. Jack had seen his fair share of advancing armies. The Union force was not the largest he had witnessed – the French army at Solferino dwarfed it by comparison – but it made up for its lack of size by the sheer variety of the uniforms worn by its different regiments.

'Would you look at that?' he remarked to O'Connell, who had come to stand beside him.

'It's a fine sight,' the first sergeant replied.

Jack saw something very different. 'It's a recipe for trouble.'

'What do you mean?' O'Connell smiled wryly. He was getting used to Jack's gloomy opinions.

'How many different uniforms can you see?' Jack asked.

'Jesus, I don't know. Dozens.' O'Connell didn't even bother to hide his exasperation. 'What's your point exactly?'

'You know who they all are?'

'Some.'

'So who is that mob right behind us?' Jack pointed to a unit dressed as Highlanders, complete with kilts, sporrans and Glengarry caps.

'39th New York.' O'Connell answered quickly enough.

'And what about those boys in grey behind them?'

'7th New York maybe?' O'Connell screwed up his eyes as he made the guess.

'How about the ones behind them? The ones dressed as Italian Bersaglieri?' Jack was familiar with the stylish uniform from his time with the French Foreign Legion. Something in the distinctive hats with plumes took him back to another advancing army. Then he had been in Lombardy and the army had been French. Now he was just outside Washington, but you would have been hard pressed to tell from the European style of dress worn by this particular regiment.

'I've no idea.' O'Connell had seen where Jack was going.

'What about the boys in blue behind them, or those lads there? Hell, look over there. What are they, Zouaves?' Jack shook his head as he spotted a regiment wearing the baggy trousers and red fez that was the uniform of the French troops originating from North Africa. 'Do you have any idea how we will know who is who?'

'No.' O'Connell had no more to add.

'What about the other lot? The goddam sechers, as you're so fond of calling them. You reckon they'll all have a nice uniform for us to aim at?'

'No.'

'So it's likely they'll also be wearing every uniform under the goddam sun?'

'Yep.' O'Connell could only agree.

'So everyone wants this bloody battle, but no one stopped to think how the hell we are going to tell each other apart.' Jack fought the urge to spit as he considered such foolishness.

O'Connell was spared finding an answer. The order to resume the march echoed along the column.

'On your feet!' He turned away and started to bark at the men who had used the halt to sit down.

Jack took one last look at the kaleidoscope of colour that was the Union army, then went to help his first sergeant. He hoped he was wrong, that somehow in the chaos and confusion of a smoke-filled battlefield the two armies would be able to tell each other apart. Yet it was hard to shake off the feeling that they were marching to their doom.

Chapter Twenty-four

By mid-afternoon, the men were suffering badly. They had marched all day, only stopping for an hour's rest around noon. The weather continued hot and sultry. Few had any water left in their canteens. Those that did thought of nothing but drinking the last few precious drops; those that didn't just suffered.

The company had lost three men to sunstroke, the exhausted soldiers simply falling from the ranks as the column trudged its way south. No one had the energy to stop and help, the unfortunate souls left to the tender mercies of the regiment's bandsmen, who had stowed their instruments and now plied their secondary trade as stretcher bearers.

As Jack had predicted, the line of march was littered with the unwanted belongings the men had begun to shed before they had even covered the first mile. He did not care what they dropped so long as they kept hold of their rifles, bayonets and ammunition. Anything else was left for the locals who shadowed the Union host advancing across their land.

The column crawled along at a snail's pace. Ahead, the leading elements were forced to clear a path through the miles of woodland they were marching through. The enemy had long suspected that the Union army would have to advance over this ground, and the Confederates had taken every opportunity to slow their progress. Trees had been felled across every path, forcing the troops at the front of the column to waste their strength hacking a way through for the men coming behind them.

The route they followed was tortuous. The roads and paths, even when cleared of obstacles, were crooked and narrow. The column was halted every few hundred yards, the men constantly having to re-form so they could fit into the constricted spaces. All the while they sweated in their heavy uniforms, every step torture as the heat and humidity sapped their strength.

'Where the hell are you going, O'Dowd?' Jack snapped as his Irish orderly stepped off the path.

'I need a piss, sir, so I do.' O'Dowd's reply was terse.

'Tough shit. Wait until we stop.' Jack was hot and tired, and his temper was fraying.

'I need to go now, sir.' O'Dowd kept moving.

'I don't care if you piss in your fucking breeches,' Jack snarled back. He was in no mood to be argued with. He glanced across at the scrubby bushes they had just passed. He saw why O'Dowd was keen to leave the column. 'You don't want to piss, do you, O'Dowd? You want those damn blackberries.'

The Irishman did not bother to deny the accusation. 'Now, sir. I'll share 'em with you, so I will. Just let me go get them before some other langer spots them.'

'Stay where you are.' Jack bit back an angrier reply. The column was barely moving, the pace of the advance little faster than a child's crawl.

'Come on now, sir.' O'Dowd would not give up. 'Look

behind you. Half the boys are foraging about. Why should we miss out?'

'Because I bloody said so.' Jack was having none of it. He could do nothing about the rest of the regiment's discipline. But he could enforce it over his company.

'What's the problem here?'

Jack could not help sighing as Captain Rowell was drawn by the argument. A Company's captain had kept himself to himself for most of the morning. Now he had chosen to get involved in the petty dispute.

'O'Dowd was just getting back into the ranks, sir,' Jack replied in the tone of a man trying to end a conversation before it had begun.

'What's the matter, O'Dowd?' Rowell fired the question at the Irishman.

'Well, sir.' O'Dowd licked his lips nervously, glancing at Jack before he pressed on. 'I was just asking the lieutenant here if I could relieve myself.'

'Were you indeed?' Rowell turned to Jack. 'What's wrong with that? It's not like he'll be left behind.'

Jack glared at O'Dowd as he tried to keep hold of his fraying temper. He could see Rowell was spoiling for a fight. The captain's face was sheeted in sweat and his cheeks and neck were flushed with heat. Like all the men he was hot, tired and irritable. Jack was sure nothing good could come from whatever he said.

'I told Private O'Dowd to wait until the next halt.'

'Did you? Well, there's no place for a martinet in my company. If a man needs to relieve himself, we should damn well let him.'

'The men should stay in the ranks, sir.' Jack's tone was icy.

'Until given orders to fall out.'

'Goddam it, Lieutenant!' Rowell snapped. 'This is my company. I give the orders.'

'Then give the right ones.' Jack did not hold back.

Rowell's face was puce. 'Don't you dare tell me what to do.'

Jack was too tired to hold his tongue. 'The men can't just wander off whenever they bloody fancy.'

'Goddam you, Lark. This is my company, not yours.' Rowell's handsome face was contorted with rage. 'You seem to think that whatever I have is yours for the taking. I give you fair warning. Keep your damn distance, you hear me?'

Jack's heart was pumping now. He knew what Rowell was referring to, and it wasn't anything to do with O'Dowd taking a piss. 'The men need to be disciplined. If they walk off whenever they please, then they won't stay in line when the enemy starts shooting.' He tried to keep the topic on military matters.

'You know everything, don't you, Lark?' Rowell snarled back. 'It's all we hear from you. How we're not ready. How we should do things differently. How you know better.' He stepped forward so that his face was barely an inch from Jack's own. 'Well, I'm sick of your constant whining. You need to learn to hold your tongue.'

'And you need to listen.' Jack did not back away even as he felt Rowell's breath washing across his face. 'You need to learn.'

'Keep your mouth shut, you hear me?' Rowell paused and closed his eyes as if in sudden pain. When he opened them again, they blazed with fury. 'Keep away from my Elizabeth.' The words were spoken in a quieter tone, but his voice vibrated with passion. 'You understand that, you goddam son of a bitch. You stay away from her.'

Jack sensed every man listening avidly to the confrontation that most had seen coming. There were few secrets in a company.

'You need to get back to your place,' he fought to hold on to an even tone, 'and keep your mind on your fucking job.'

'Stop telling me what to do!' This time Rowell bellowed, his anger released.

Jack did not flinch. 'Then stop acting like a fuckwit.'

Rowell's mouth twisted, but whatever words it was forming were lost as another voice spoke first.

'Captain Rowell! Lieutenant Lark!'

Both men turned to see Major Bridges stomping his way up the side of the stalled column. 'What on earth is going on here?'

Rowell turned to look at Jack with loathing. 'Lark disobeyed my order.'

'Oh grow up,' Jack spat back. For a moment he thought Rowell would throw a punch, such was the hatred in his eyes.

'Get your company moving!' Bridges shouted before the captain could so much as twitch. 'For goodness' sake, Rowell, you're holding up the whole damn army.'

Rowell controlled himself with obvious difficulty. He stepped away from Jack. 'This isn't finished,' he hissed.

'Now, Captain!' roared Bridges.

It was the first time Jack had seen the major angry. The sight was enough to silence Rowell, who finally moved away and began to stalk up the side of the column. He did not look back.

'You should be fighting the Southrons, not each other.' Bridges glared at Jack as he came to stand at his side.

'Tell that prick.'

Bridges shot him a look. 'That is enough, Lieutenant. There

will be fighting aplenty soon enough.' He glanced over Jack's shoulder. The column was shuffling back into motion. 'I told you there would be trouble.' He spoke softly so that only Jack could hear him.

Jack sighed. His anger was spent. 'You were right.' He looked ruefully at the major. 'Well done.'

Bridges shook his head. 'I take no pleasure from this, believe me.' He turned to look at the column. The rear ranks of A Company were already filing past and the head of the next company was coming up. 'You had better get back to your place.' He reached out and clasped a hand to Jack's shoulder. 'I'll talk to Rowell when we stop for the day. See if I can calm him down.'

Jack bit back a retort. He hoped Bridges would be successful. Going into battle was daunting enough. Going into battle under the command of a man who hated him was a sure way to find a shallow grave, and he had no desire to die. He would not give Rowell that satisfaction.

Jack sat on the sun-baked ground and stretched his legs out in front of him before leaning forward and attempting to knead away the pain in his left calf. It hurt like a devil and he knew it would likely seize up overnight so that in the morning he would be limping like an old man.

The second day of marching had been even harder than the first. The company had lost another four men to sunstroke or sheer exhaustion, and although some had already returned to the ranks, it did not bode well that they were not strong enough to stand up to the easy pace. The day had finished with the bulk of McDowell's army around three miles away from the enemy. Or at least where Colonel Scanlon claimed the enemy would be. The men had not cared much either way. They had used up all their rations and faced a hungry day when they resumed the march in the morning. There was no sign of any resupply and Jack had heard them grumbling and grousing as they made camp for the night. His own supper had consisted of a lump of hardtack that he was dunking into a mug of watery coffee in the hope that it would soften enough for him to be able to eat it.

'You care to share some of that? It looks delicious.'

Jack looked up and smiled as Robert flopped to the ground at his side. 'You really want some?'

Robert pulled a face. 'No.' He removed his kepi and tossed it into the dust next to his hip. 'I think I'm a broken man.'

'You were that already.' Jack found some energy to tease.

'Lordy, listen to you. When will you give up being such a viperous son of a bitch?'

'The day they dig a hole and throw me in it.' Jack grimaced as Robert's words struck home. They echoed what Rowell had said the previous day. Jack did not know when he had become such a grumbling curmudgeon. Perhaps he was just getting old.

'This came for you today.' Robert fished into his jacket and pulled out an envelope that he tossed onto Jack's lap. 'From Elizabeth.'

Jack frowned. He opened the thick envelope and pulled out its contents. The sight of his own grimacing face greeted him. The photograph was a good one, as far as he could tell. It had captured Elizabeth brilliantly. Even in the grainy black-and-white image she looked like an angel. If he did not know better, he would say it showed a young officer and his beautiful girl. It had captured a life that was not his.

'What a handsome couple.' Robert eased onto one buttock

so he could peer at the photograph. 'I wouldn't let Rowell see it if I were you.'

'No.' Jack took one last look at the image, then slipped it into his jacket pocket. Yet it had set in motion a train of thought that he found disturbing, and he felt a sense of longing so profound that he shuddered.

'You all right?' Robert was astute enough for once to notice Jack's reaction.

'Yes. It's a good photograph.'

'My sister is a rare beauty.'

Jack looked up sharply. There was something being unsaid. 'But?'

Robert offered a half-smile at Jack's prompting. 'I don't understand her any more than you do, Jack. You'll get no revelations from me.'

Jack grunted. He could only agree with Robert. He didn't understand Elizabeth at all. There was more to her than just her beauty, but quite what that was, he didn't know. She was beguiling, fascinating even. But she was not straight-forward. Not like Rose. He could not help smiling as his thoughts turned to Elizabeth's maid. There were no shades of grey around Rose. He found that almost as appealing as Elizabeth's beauty.

'Have you heard the news?' Robert broke the silence.

'What's that then?' Jack shook away all thoughts of the women. Neither was his to worry about. That fact was some comfort.

'The President has called for five hundred thousand more men to be recruited.'

Jack raised an eyebrow. 'I'm not the only one who thinks this war will go on for a bit, then.'

'No. It would appear not.' Robert seemed unconcerned at the notion. 'So what does tomorrow hold in store for us? Another aimless ramble?'

Jack shook his head. 'You really should think about attending Scanlon's briefings.'

'I was busy.' Robert's reply was breezy.

'Doing what?' Jack's was sharp.

'Looking after my affairs.' He glanced at Jack to see how he was reacting. Whatever he saw reflected in Jack's stare was enough to make him lower his gaze. 'I was asleep.'

Jack was about to snap at such a lame excuse, but he managed to hold his tongue. The confrontation with Rowell was still fresh in his mind. He was not overburdened with companions. Driving Robert away would not help.

'Tomorrow we push on to some place called Centreville, then on to the Bull Run river. Our division is in the lead.'

'I expect old Tyler must be pleased. He hoped for this opportunity.'

Jack could not help smiling at the familiarity with which Robert spoke of the commander of their division. 'Let me guess. He's a friend of your father.'

Robert grinned back. 'Of course.'

'Who isn't?'

'No one worth knowing.' Robert laughed at his own pompous reply. 'But Tyler's a good man. Do you know what his orders are?'

'They're pretty clear, according to the colonel. We're to observe the roads to Bull Run and Warrenton. McDowell wants the enemy to think we are advancing on Manassas, but he really wants to turn their right flank.'

'That all sounds very military.' Robert was jocular as he

listened to the plan that had been sketched out at the officers' briefing he had not bothered to attend.

Jack could not help laughing at his friend's tone. 'I just hope McDowell knows what he is about.' The plan, as he had heard it, made sense. He had known generals whose only thought was to throw their troops at the heart of the enemy position and hope they won the day. The notion of a flank attack sounded as if McDowell was at least thinking strategically. If the Union troops could turn the enemy's right, it would open up the way to the vital train junction at Manassas.

'So battle really is coming?' Robert sounded anxious.

'This rail junction at Manassas is a strategic objective. The enemy are there in strength and I doubt they plan to give it up without a fight. Scanlon said the 3rd Division under Colonel Heintzelman is going to march to the east and turn the enemy line, then drive in behind the Orange and Alexandria Railroad. If that works, he'll be attacking from a direction the enemy does not expect. That gives him, and us, the advantage.' Jack paused and looked straight at Robert. 'So yes. That means there'll be a battle.'

Robert gazed back at him with eyes full of fear.

'Come on. Let's join the men.' Jack reached out and clapped the younger man on the shoulder before getting to his feet and brushing the dirt off his backside.

Robert hadn't moved. He sat and stared into space. Jack held out a hand and Robert glanced up. He tried to smile but just managed to look sickly. Still, he took Jack's hand and let himself be hauled to his feet, and together the two officers walked towards one of the large brushwood fires the men had got going to keep them warm through the night.

'Good evening, sirs.' First Sergeant O'Connell saw them

approach and greeted them warmly. 'Care to sit with us for a while?'

'Thank you.' Jack answered for them both. 'That would be kind.'

With Robert at his side, he found a space for them to sit. The heat of the fire felt unpleasant on his face after the day spent suffering in the humidity. But the smoke would keep the worst of the biting insects away, and for that alone, Jack was happy enough to sit in a pool of his own sweat.

'What are you doing there, Malloy?' He addressed one of O'Dowd's Irish cronies. The man was writing something on a scrap of paper, his tongue held tight between his teeth as he formed one deliberate letter after another.

'Writing my name, sir.'

'Why are you doing that?'

'The others all did it.' Malloy looked at his officer, then licked his lips with nervousness. 'I figured I should do it too.'

'Why?' Jack's patience was being stretched.

'We sew them in our jackets, so we do. So they know who we are, you know, if the worst happens.' Malloy's eyes flicked nervously over Jack's face, then returned to the piece of paper and the half-formed name.

Jack understood. It was a sobering way for the men to occupy their time. He looked around the campfire. He saw the men's fear as clearly as he saw their faces in the light of the fire.

'O'Connell, why don't you tell us one of your stories?' He looked to the first sergeant for a diversion. 'You're good at them, I've heard. I fancy we could all use the distraction.' The men clearly agreed with his suggestion, a murmur of encouragement rippling around the gathering.

O'Connell smiled as he became the centre of attention. 'I reckon I could tell you a tale or two. If you're sure and all?'

The murmurs grew louder and O'Connell did not bother to protest again.

'You all heard the one about the woman and the horse?'

A few of the men laughed as they recognised the tale. But enough shook their heads or called for it to be told.

'Well, one time there was this old girl that no one liked. She was a good cook and kept a good house, but her tongue was so damn sharp that no one would marry her.' O'Connell spoke softly and clearly. A circle of silence surrounded him as even the men who had heard it before listened intently.

'One man, though, he decided he'd give the old trollop a try. He knew she was still worth having around, in spite of her tongue. So he went and started courting her. Well, finally she said she'd marry him and they got hitched. Now, this fellow had gone to fetch her on a horse. It was a knackered old nag, but it was all he had. They'd bought themselves some rations and he'd bought her a whole heap of shite for their house and had all that tied on behind the saddle. The man got on and pulled his woman behind him and they set off. Well, the old horse didn't make it more than a mile before it threw 'em both in the dirt. That woman, she didn't complain. The man got the horse back on its feet, raised its head up by the bridle. He looked that old fecking horse straight in the eye and said, "That's once."'

A few of the men, those who knew the old tale, laughed, just as O'Connell intended. Jack knew they were using the story as a balm against their terror at the prospect of finally going to war. As he looked around, he saw that many of the soldiers were little more than boys. He remembered the night before the Alma. He had been a captain then, even if only a counterfeit one. His company would likely have looked no different to this one, yet now he saw the youth of the men about to go into battle. These were not men hardened to war. They were boys who had long dreamed of glory, but who trembled with barely contained fear now that the chance of finding it was near.

O'Connell had paused to let the laughter subside. The only sounds were the crackle of the fire and the murmur of other voices at other fires. He let the men enjoy the moment before he continued.

'Well, the pair of them got back on that poor old nag and on they went. But the horse gave out again after just another mile. This time they both landed hard. The woman, she got back up, brushed the dirt off her, didn't complain too much. That fellow, well, he pulled on the reins, got the horse up again and said, "That's twice!"' He delivered the line in a loud, stentorian tone that had the men rocking and hooting with glee. This time, even Jack laughed.

'Well, they'd done another mile when that horse fell again, and this time they all went down like so many sacks of shite. To be fair, that woman, well she didn't complain and just got to her feet.' O'Connell picked up the pace of his delivery. 'The man, he jerked on the bridle of that poor old fecking horse and got it to its feet, then looked right at it and said, "You useless fecker, that's three times." Then he pulled out his pistol and *bam*, shot it right between the eyes.'

The soldiers reacted to the cue. They were engrossed in the tale and they whooped and hollered as O'Connell shouted loudly enough to scare a few of the younger ones. Many of them called out, suggesting what was to happen next. Jack saw that they were diverted, the tale taking their minds off what was ahead. He caught O'Connell's eye and the first sergeant nodded, acknowledging Jack's understanding. O'Connell knew what he was doing.

'The horse fell, and that there woman, she was so surprised she just stood there gaping. Then she caught her breath and started in. "What the feck are you doing?"' O'Connell mimicked a high-pitched female voice. Even he had to pause to chuckle, whilst the men erupted with peals of laughter. '"You dumb gombeen. Now we got to carry all that stuff ourselves. What did you go and shoot him for?"' He was speaking quickly now, firing the words out. '"We could've walked and let him take all this stuff. I tell you right now, I'm not going to carry any of that there shite on my back! Shoot him, will you? You're a fecking eejit." And on she went, cussing and moaning like you wouldn't believe.

'That man, well, he just stood there, let her shake her finger in his face. When she finally shut up, he just looked at her, right straight in the eye.' O'Connell paused, holding back the last line. The men waited, hushed and expectant. 'And he said, "That's once."'

The men did not try to contain themselves. They clapped their hands and slapped each other on the back as they guffawed.

'So he shoved all that stuff in a sack he'd brought along, and feck me, didn't he just make her carry the saddle. She got to their house with a saddle on her back and the reins around her neck. Yeah, he had her saddled and bridled. He tamed her, all right.'

The men roared as O'Connell finished his tale in fine style, but Jack heard the desperation behind the merriment. He had seen it before. Men laughed the night before battle lest they weep with fear. The men of A Company were no different. They faked their delight as well as any.

'Why, we should do that with Johnny Reb!' shouted one of the soldiers.

'What say you to that, Lieutenant?' O'Connell asked Jack. 'You think we can tame the Confederates as easy as that fellow tamed that woman?'

Jack felt the attention shift onto him. Everyone went quiet. He could not help feeling uncomfortable as he became the centre of attention. O'Connell had done a fine job of distracting the men, but there were other things they needed to hear.

'In India, we all thought it would be easy. The native troops had mutinied against us. It was a nasty business, about as bad as things can get. Well, some said they couldn't fight without their officers. They said it would be easy to defeat them.' Jack looked around. Every face was turned his way. The firelight flickered across their features, their expressions hidden in the half-light. 'It wasn't so easy. Those native troops, they were brave men, just like us. They fought hard.'

He looked up at the night sky. He knew he was no good at telling tales, especially not ones that would assuage the men's fear. The stars twinkled down at him. They were serene and undisturbed by the struggles of man. They didn't care about states that wanted to self-govern, or the rights of black men and women to live free. He felt his determination harden. The men had to know.

'I reckon this Johnny Reb you all keep talking about isn't so different to any of us. If you ask me, I think he'll be sitting round a campfire just like this one, and him and his mates will be bragging about how us Union boys will skedaddle just as soon as we clap eyes on them.' He offered a thin-lipped smile as he used one of the men's favourite words.

He could feel their fear then. It was as if a cold breeze had just blown across the encampment. He sighed. 'But they won't have been trained like you've been trained.' He smiled. It was time to ease the men's fears, not add to them. 'Just do what you have been taught and you'll be fine. Shoot low, keep together and listen to your officers and your sergeants. Do what you are told without question. When we fight, give it everything. Don't dance with them. When the time comes, you put that man down. Kill him before he kills you.'

For the first time, he noticed that Major Bridges was standing on the far side of the campfire, watching as Jack imparted his final advice. He looked at Jack as he finished, and held his gaze. Then he nodded and turned to walk back into the darkness.

Jack fell silent. The men did not cheer him, or hoot with glee as he finished his own tale. But he saw something shift in their gaze as they confronted their fear.

Tomorrow they would likely go into battle. The time for bravado, for dreaming of glory, would be done. It would be time to fight.

Chapter Twenty-five

Centreville, Virginia, Thursday 18 July 1861

The men marched behind the regiment's colours for the first time. During the long march from Washington, the flags had been left encased in their leather sheaths, their splendour hidden until the enemy was close by. Now that the troops were advancing on that enemy, Scanlon had ordered that the colours be unfurled.

The column had marched early that morning. No great pace was set, the men allowed to rest frequently, as if the generals knew their strength had to be carefully husbanded lest it wither completely. They had covered the first few miles in good spirits, the bandsmen playing the men's favourite patriotic tunes to boost their morale. Now they marched in silence, the only sounds the thump of thousands of boots hitting the ground and the noise of equipment clattering and jangling.

Unlike an English regiment, the 1st Boston marched behind three colours: the national flag, the state ensign of Massachusetts and an Irish flag that had been given to them a few weeks before by the Governor, who had arrived at Emmart's Farm to present it to all of the Boston Irish regiments. The great silk square was green, with the American coat of arms of an eagle with shield in the centre, along with a phrase picked out in gold thread:

THY SONS BY ADOPTION
THE FIRM SUPPORTERS AND DEFENDERS
FROM
DUTY AFFECTION AND CHOICE

On the reverse, an Irish harp was surmounted by thirty-four stars and surrounded by a wreath of shamrocks. Over the harp was the legend:

As aliens and strangers thou didst us befriend
As sons and true patriots we do thee defend

Below the harp were two wolf dogs and another motto:

Gentle when stroked
Fierce when provoked

Underneath was the national motto: THE UNION MUST AND SHALL BE PRESERVED.

The Irishmen in the regiment had been moved by the presentation. Now the colour served to remind them why they were there; the solemn oath they had taken and against which they would now be judged.

'Company! Halt!'

The order rippled down the column as each company's first sergeant ordered the men to a stand. Jack could feel the anticipation in the air as if it were a physical thing.

'A Company! Company, fix bayonets!'

The air was filled with the scraping sound of bayonets being withdrawn from their scabbards, followed by a hundred resolute clicks as the men locked them in place on the barrels of their already loaded rifles.

The officers drew their swords. Jack hefted the weight of his own blade in his hand. It felt too light, cheap even. It was standard issue, the curved sabre made by the thousand. Most of the officers carried their own swords, gifts from proud family or friends. Jack's blade was inexpensive and lacked the decoration of many of the other swords, but he reckoned it would be enough to kill a man. It would do the job for which it was intended.

With the sun glinting off the steel of a thousand blades, the regiment resumed the march. They advanced through Centreville, the road rutted and littered with rocks and boulders. There were no crowds waiting to greet them this day, and the streets were not decked out with the bright red, white and blue of patriotic bunting. This was no parade. No grand celebration. The men marched through an empty town, the windows and doors of the stone buildings lining the street shuttered and barred, the streets themselves deserted.

They pushed on, advancing to the crest of a hill on the far side of town. The ground to their front opened out until the men looked across a well-wooded river valley. The river, the Bull Run, meandered through the centre of the valley, its pace gentle as it wound its way to a series of hills out to the west. It was no raging torrent, and in at least two places the water looked shallow enough for the men to ford it without too much difficulty.

The slopes leading down to the river were for the most part

clear and open terrain, the ground covered in long grass that washed back and forth in the gentle breeze. In places, patches of woodland broke up the pastoral scene. It was a beautiful sight, the kind that would have some reaching for a paintbrush and canvas.

But not on that day.

'There they are!' The shout came from the men in the leading ranks.

Jack was marching on the right of the company, and it took him a moment to see what had inspired the cry that had every man twisting and turning his head to get a glimpse of what lay ahead. He saw the river easily enough. Then he saw the enemy.

The Confederate army lined the far slope of the valley. It stretched for what had to be miles in either direction, the enemy standing in great long lines facing the river.

'There they are!' The call was repeated from man to man. This was the company's first sighting of those they would fight. Jack looked at the troops to his left. He saw a range of emotions displayed on their faces: curiosity, expectation, excitement and dread, the conflicting feelings of soldiers facing the enemy for the first time.

Scanlon gave the order for the 1st Boston to deploy into line, an instruction that was repeated by the regiment's drummers so that even the men at the far reaches of the column could be certain what they had been ordered to do. They obeyed readily enough. A Company wheeled to the right, then marched to take their place on the right flank of the regiment's line. The men knew the drill well, and the manoeuvre was completed with little fuss, even though most of the men stared at the enemy on the far side of the river the whole time.

Rowell moved to his place on the right of the front line,

whilst Jack, Robert and O'Connell formed a third rank behind the men. The regiment's colours took up their place front and centre, whilst Bridges took station behind the left half of the regiment and Scanlon behind the right half. The bandsmen formed up behind the centre.

Within the span of a few minutes, the regiment was re-formed and facing the river, the ten companies stretched out in a long two-man-deep line. Other regiments arrived, deploying on either side of the 1st Boston. The men in the grey uniforms of the 1st Massachusetts Volunteer Militia were on the regiment's left. There were a few jeers and insults thrown between the two flank companies ordered to stand next to one another, but the sight of the enemy was too thrilling to allow even the long-standing rivalry to spoil the atmosphere. Within the span of an hour, the bulk of Brigadier General Tyler's division had formed up on the gentle slopes of the river valley, the men primed and ready to start the battle that had been anticipated for so long.

And there they all stayed.

If the men had expected anything more dramatic, they were to be disappointed. With the manoeuvre complete, the regiment was left to stand in the sun, the men sweating freely under their heavy uniforms. The excitement of glimpsing the enemy palled, and any murmured conversation died away as the troops quickly tired of doing nothing. They stood in silence, fidgeting under their heavy knapsacks.

Jack could not help smiling as he saw the shift in the men's emotions. Excitement and a heady rush of fear quickly gave way to boredom. He spotted Major Bridges walking along the rear rank, chatting to the men, checking they were ready should any orders arrive. When the major reached A Company, he paused for a short conversation with O'Dowd and his cronies before moving towards Jack.

'Good morning, Lieutenant.' He greeted Jack warmly enough. They had not spoken much since Jack's altercation with Captain Rowell, and Jack had been concerned that Bridges would treat him coldly. He was relieved to hear a friendly tone.

'Good morning, sir.' He returned the greeting. 'Any new orders?'

Bridges came closer. He walked with his hands clasped behind his back, as if on a pleasant Sunday stroll rather than on ground that could soon be a battlefield. 'No. We will wait here for the rest of the army. Tyler has no orders for an advance. This is just a reconnaissance to see if there is a chance of turning the enemy's right flank.'

'I see.' Jack understood well enough. The Union army was strung out over miles of countryside. McDowell would need to concentrate his forces before he could launch a large-scale attack. The men might not like it, but they were in for a tiresome day.

'Have you made your peace with Rowell?' Bridges asked the question quietly so that the men in the ranks nearby could not hear it.

'No.' Jack saw a hint of disapproval flicker across Bridges' face. 'But I will.' He glanced across to Rowell's station on the right flank of the company. The captain had walked a short distance from the men and was now inspecting the enemy positions through a pair of field glasses.

'Ethan is a good man.' Bridges too looked across at A Company's captain. 'But he will need your help. He won't ask for it, but he will need it.'

Jack sighed. He had not treated Rowell well. The man

might be a difficult prig, but he was not an ogre, or a bully, just a mix of the bitter and the sweet, like any other. 'He can have it. For what it's worth.'

Bridges shook his head. 'Now you are being modest.'

Jack could not help smiling. 'Am I not always modest?'

'No, Jack, I do not think anyone could call you that. But you are honest, and you do not hold back. I think those are traits we will sorely need in the coming days. We will need *you*, Jack. More than any of us would ever dare admit.'

Jack heard the praise in the words. It meant a great deal. 'I won't let you down, sir.' He had to pause to clear his throat. 'I'll even shake Rowell's hand.'

Bridges nodded. 'Thank you, Jack.'

Jack said nothing more as Bridges moved back to his place behind the regiment. Yet he felt his determination harden. He was a soldier. He could not let petty disputes prevent him from doing what he did best.

It would soon be time to show the men of the 1st Boston what he was made of. It would be time to be the leader they so sorely needed.

'Now that's more like it.' First Sergeant O'Connell had seen something of interest. Jack turned. Two heavy cannon were being brought forward.

'Good grief!' Robert had wandered closer, the notion of staying in his allotted position anathema to him. 'What the devil are those things?'

Jack understood his reaction. The cannon were easily the largest field guns he had ever seen. 'Do you know what they are, O'Connell?'

The first sergeant shrugged. 'Twenty-pounders? Whatever

the feck they are, they should at least liven things up a little.'

The gun crews were very aware that they were now the centre of attention. The two teams of horses that had brought each of the guns forward were detached and taken to the rear. The gunners had dismounted and now fussed around each gun. They seemed to be in no great hurry. The day was warm and sunshine flooded the valley. The clement weather added a carnival feel to the proceedings, the two cannons and their teams the entertainment laid on to divert the thousands of soldiers from what lay ahead.

Eventually the gun teams were ready. Jack could just about make out the shouted orders that had the artillerymen scrambling to take up their positions.

'Fire!'

Thousands of Union soldiers drew breath as one. First one, then the other cannon fired, the dull boom echoing down the valley. Boredom was forgotten as every set of eyes turned to the far bank. Men held their breath, the expectation growing as they waited for the great explosions as those first two shots smashed into the enemy.

The groan of disappointment was clearly audible.

'Where did they go?' Robert was standing on tiptoe in an attempt to see over the heads of the men to his front.

Jack laughed at the expression on his fellow lieutenant's face. He himself was taller than most and could just about make out a smudge on the ground close to one of the enemy formations that he reckoned was a mound of churned-up earth.

'Did they miss?' Robert glanced across. 'What did they hit?'

'Nothing.'

'Nothing?' Robert's disappointment was clear.

The guns fired for a second time. The two dull thumps

echoed out, but this time no one cheered. The men still peered at the far bank, but again there was nothing to see, the heavy shells burying themselves deep in the soft ground.

The Union artillerymen did at least stir their Confederate brethren into action. A battery of enemy cannon returned fire. Jack saw the cloud of powder smoke a moment before he heard the dull crump of their firing. The enemy guns sounded different, the cannon of a lighter calibre than the monstrous guns the Union army had brought into play, but their effect was just the same.

For the next thirty minutes, both sides flung shells at one another. One of the Union shells hit the ground a dozen yards away from one of the Confederate units. It was close enough to shower a few of the men with clods of earth, something that drew a few ironic cheers from the watching Union troops. Otherwise the gunners of both sides had no effect, wasting their sweat in a futile bombardment.

'You think we are going to move any time soon?' Robert wandered close to Jack's station, swishing his sword at some nettles.

Jack had long since sheathed his own sabre. 'I think we are about to find out.' He nodded towards the centre of the regiment. A courier had arrived and dismounted before running towards Colonel Scanlon. There was urgency in his movements; a sudden injection of hustle to disturb what had been turning into a soporific morning.

'Come on.' Jack urged Robert to accompany him, and together the pair bounded towards Scanlon's position behind the right-hand half of the regiment. Other officers were doing the same. They came into earshot to hear Scanlon snapping at the young courier.

'Repeat my orders, if you please.'

'Colonel, you will send two companies forward. Two companies from the 1st Massachusetts will march on your left.'

Scanlon looked like he was being forced to chew on a turd. He looked down at the scrap of paper the courier had given him, scanning the words as if unable to believe what he was reading. 'Tyler has no orders to engage.' He looked up from the paper and thrust his red beard forward, his face colouring with building anger.

'Goddammit, Colonel, you are to advance on the enemy!' The courier, a lieutenant, threw his arm out and pointed at the army on the far side of the river.

For a moment, Jack thought Scanlon would strike the young officer. His mouth chewed furiously, then he turned on his heel, the precious scrap of paper pushed deep into a pocket.

Orders were being forgotten and carefully constructed plans ignored. Four infantry companies from Massachusetts were about to get the war started all by themselves.

The two flank companies from the 1st Boston advanced down the slope. There was a patch of woodland directly to their front, and it did not take long for the men to lose sight of the enemy on the far bank of the river.

Jack kept to his station behind the rear ranks. He had not bothered to draw his sword for a second time. He doubted there would be any hand-to-hand fighting that day. He had expected Rowell, or Captain Thompson, the commander of K Company, to order the men into a skirmish line, but the order never came and so they advanced down the slope in a regular two-man-deep line.

The companies pushed on. They entered the woods, the air

within cooler than the sunlit slopes behind. Their ranks broke up as the men moved through the trees. There was nothing to be done save press on, which they did with little direction from their officers. If they were fearful of what they would see on the far side of the wood, there was no showing it in the rapid pace of the advance.

It was pleasant under the trees, the damp, sweet aroma of a wood in summer enough to dull the smell of sweat. The canopy shaded Jack from the sun and the noise of the breeze rustling through the branches whispered calmly overhead. It was tempting to stay here, out of the sun and away from whatever lay ahead. But it was also tempting to push on, to find the enemy and fight. It was nearly time.

The blue-coated soldiers were moving more quickly now, their rifles held across their fronts and their equipment clattering and bouncing. They emerged into bright light and the heat of the sun. They were now a good few hundred yards down the slope, and the waters of the Bull Run river were ahead. As were the enemy.

Confederate skirmishers lined the slope above the river. They were spread thin, the ranks, if they could be called that, so dispersed that they looked more like bystanders than any fighting unit. Some kneeled and a few were even lying down. All held firearms aimed at the Union ranks emerging from the treeline.

At last Jack was able to get a good look at the enemy. They were dressed in a smart grey uniform, with white crossbelts and a tall, black shako topped with a stubby, white plume. To his eye it looked dreadfully similar to the uniform worn by 1st Massachusetts, the regiment on the 1st Boston's flank.

Even as he studied them, the confederate skirmishers opened fire.

It was a ragged effort. He saw the telltale puffs of smoke emerge from the enemy gun barrels a heartbeat before the roar of the volley reached his ears. He could not help flinching, the air suddenly full of the familiar whip-crack of bullets. Around him, most of the men threw themselves to the ground, their cries of alarm loud in the aftermath of the enemy volley.

'What the hell was that?' A man to Jack's front rolled onto his side as he called out, his expression betraying a mixture of shock and uncomprehending fear.

'Get to your bloody feet!' As Jack shouted his first order, he felt something stir deep in his gut. It had been an age since he had been under fire. The ragged volley had awoken a part of him that had lain dormant. It was not fear. It was not horror at what lay ahead. It was excitement.

'Hell fire! Over here!' A man lying on the ground to his left shouted for aid. Jack rushed forward, pushing through the men as they picked themselves up from the ground, expecting to find the first casualty of the day.

'Who's hit?' he snapped.

'It's O'Dowd!'

'Shit.' Jack elbowed his way through the disordered ranks. He knew where O'Dowd was positioned. Not that he was hard to pick out, the Irishman squawking loudly enough to wake the dead.

'Where are you hit?' Jack fired the question as he came close. It was only then that he realised the men were laughing.

'O'Dowd pissed hisself!' A buck-toothed lad from the file to O'Dowd's left bayed the comment. Jack looked down at the Irishman's front. Sure enough, his trousers were soaked.

'I did not!' O'Dowd shrieked in denial. 'The damn maggots hit my water bottle, so they did. Look here, you dopes.' He lifted his canteen, shaking it and spraying water into the faces turned towards him. His reaction just made the men around him laugh all the harder.

Jack turned away. He knew why the men were laughing so hard, the merriment a welcome balm to their fears. He looked ahead. The enemy skirmishers were already scrambling back up the slope on the far side of the river. He felt a flutter of anger at the sight. They had fired just one long-range volley, but it had lit the fire deep in his gut, and made him come alive in a way he had almost forgotten.

'Keep moving!' he roared, silencing the laughter. He needed to hide his emotions away, keep them under a tight rein. There would be a time to release them, to let the anger have its head. But that time had not yet arrived.

Chapter Twenty-six

The advance picked up its former pace. The ranks were ragged, but no one ordered a halt or a change in formation. With the two companies from the 1st Massachusetts to their left, the men from the 1st Boston raced down the slope, their hearts pounding and mouths dry.

'Where've they gone?' Robert was out of position and was close enough to call to Jack. He stumbled as he glanced across, almost losing his footing as the regiment streaked downhill.

'They were just skirmishers.' Jack kept his eyes on the ground to his front. At least half a dozen men had tripped or fallen. He would not be one of them.

'They didn't look like much.'

Jack did not waste his breath on an answer. He glanced up at the far slope. The enemy skirmishers had fallen back to the main battle line, which was starting to move down the slope. The Confederates advanced slowly, taking their time.

'Get back to your bloody position.' Jack would need to know where his fellow lieutenant was at all times, and that would be a damn sight easier if Robert stayed where he was supposed to. He had not forgotten why Robert's father had got him the place in the 1st Boston. At that moment, there was little danger to the young officer, but he knew that could change in a heartbeat. 'Go back to your station. Now!' He turned his head and snarled the instruction. He saw Robert blanch, but he did as he was told and jogged back behind the rear ranks on the left of the company.

The two companies from the 1st Boston were on the slope above what looked to be a ford. Jack could see that the river in front of them was shallow, with rocks and boulders standing proud of the flow. It would be easy for the men to splash across, the water likely to do little more than wet the bottoms of their trousers.

They would not get the chance to find out.

'Fucking hell.' Jack had stopped looking at the river. Instead he now stared at a unit of Confederate infantry that had marched calmly down the slope on the far side and now came to a halt facing the Union troops.

He was close enough to hear the enemy commanders shout their orders. He saw the hundreds of firearms rise as one. The Confederate soldiers aimed down the barrels of the guns, filling the sights with the image of the blue- and grey-coated infantry, who had stumbled to a halt well short of the river.

There was a moment of silence. Then all hell was let loose.

The Confederates fired as one, a great thunderclap of sound roaring out as hundreds of men pulled the trigger at the same moment.

Jack could not help flinching as the enemy volley crashed out. The storm of missiles ripped through the Union ranks. At least half a dozen men cried out as they were hit, the fast-moving bullets catching arms, legs and bodies as they zipped by. Many of the men threw themselves to the ground for a second time, any notion of discipline forgotten in the shock of coming under such heavy fire.

'On your bloody feet!' Jack screamed. 'They're only firing fucking muskets!' He had recognised the noise made by the Confederate's weapons, and he gave a moment's thanks that they lacked modern rifles. It gave the Union men a great advantage, but one they could only exploit if he got the men to stand and fight.

The men climbed sheepishly to their feet. Consternation and fear rippled through the ranks, even the calmer men reacting to the cries around them. Many shuffled backwards in confusion and uncertainty.

'Form line!' Jack's thunderous voice drowned out the chatter. 'Prepare to fire!' He scanned the company's ranks, looking for casualties. Not one man had fallen.

O'Connell stepped forward and picked up Jack's cry. To their front, the line was ragged as men who should have been preparing to fire simply stared into space or called out to their mates. Faces that should have been turned to the enemy glanced left and right, the frightened, shocked soldiers looking to their friends for support.

'Eyes front! Prepare to return fire!' Jack bawled, then glanced at Rowell. The captain was still standing in his allotted station on the right of the line. His mouth was open, but no sound was coming out. He was not alone. At least half the men hadn't moved. They just stood gaping at the enemy or at one another, faces ashen and panic in their eyes.

'Prepare to fucking fire!' Jack prowled along the rear rank, thumping the men not doing as they were told. He did not have to look at the enemy to know they were already reloading.

He glanced to his left and saw O'Connell mirroring his actions on the left of the company. The first sergeant was swearing and cursing at the men, his own fists working hard to force some sort of order into the ranks. Robert had not moved. Jack's fellow lieutenant stood like a man facing a gale, his arms pulled tight into his sides, shoulders raised as if he were trying to hide behind his collar.

'Stand fast!' A few men in the rear rank had taken steps backwards. Jack shoved them back into the line. 'Prepare to fire!' His voice was huge.

At last men were responding. The first few rifles were pulled into shoulders, barrels wavering but at least pointing at the enemy.

'That's it! Come on!' Jack urged others to follow. More men did as he ordered, at least half the company ready to fire. 'Aim!'

It would have to be enough. He had been counting the seconds in his head. The enemy would surely soon be ready to fire a second volley. He knew the men would not stand if he did not get them fighting.

'Fire!' He did not care that it was not his place to give the order. A quick glance at K Company confirmed that they too were struggling to return the enemy fire. The shock of the volley had been overwhelming.

The sound of A Company's ragged volley was like the tearing of a sheet of calico. It lasted longer than it should, the men firing one after another so that the sound blurred across several seconds. To their left, K Company opened fire too, their volley just as untidy, but at least the men from Boston were fighting back.

'That's the way!' Jack roared encouragement. 'Now load!

Look lively now.' He turned his head and spat as the familiar rotten-egg stink of spent powder caught the back of his throat, then strode along the ranks until he reached the right flank. Those men who had fired were already reloading, the drill coming instinctively. It was what they had trained for all summer. Now the hours of repetition were starting to pay off, the men going through the actions with little conscious thought.

Jack stepped around the right flank, shouting at the men the whole time. He was just behind Rowell when the enemy fired a second volley. Musket balls seared through the air, humming like bees in a beehive. A few men cried out as they were hit, but none fell.

Jack scanned the ground between the 1st Boston and the enemy. The distance had to be over a hundred yards, perhaps more. It was a fair way, even for the Union's powerful rifles. If the Confederates had older weapons, they were doing well to even hit the blue-coated ranks. At such long range they could never hope to deliver an effective volley. It explained why so few of A Company were being hit, and why those that were were not suffering anything more than minor flesh wounds and bruises. The Confederates could blast away for hours without ever delivering a decisive blow. But the Union troops had modern Springfield rifles. And they could.

'Rowell!' Jack reached out and clapped a hand on the captain's shoulder.

Rowell turned. His face was as grey as the uniforms of the regiment fighting on their flank. He blinked twice, as if unable to focus on Jack's face.

'You should be behind the company.' Jack leaned forward, trying to speak just loudly enough to be heard by Rowell alone. When the company fired, its captain should have moved from the right flank to the centre rear, from where he would direct its fire. 'Give the next order to fire from here, then move. You got that?'

Rowell managed to nod before turning back to face the enemy.

Jack looked to his left. Those men that had fired were reloaded. This time more of their comrades raised their rifles as they prepared for the company's second volley. He reached forward and thumped Rowell on the shoulder. 'Now.'

'Fire!' Rowell shrieked, his voice coming out tight and high-pitched. It did not matter. For the second time, A Company fired. The men on their left fired a moment later, so that the Union volley sounded like a child running a metal stick down a wooden fence.

Jack looked at the enemy ranks. Here and there a man had fallen, but the volley was having little effect, despite the power of the Springfields and their deforming bullets. The Union troops had better weaponry, yet they were wasting that advantage, their poor marksmanship letting them down.

'Off you go.' Jack pulled at Rowell's shoulder, encouraging him to move. He himself stayed on the right flank, from where he could see O'Connell prowling behind the rear rank. Robert had still not moved and Jack had no intention of summoning him. He figured he was just as safe where he was as he would be anywhere else.

'Aim lower!' Jack turned his attention to the company. 'Aim at their balls!' The two sides were on roughly the same level on either side of the river. It should have been a straightforward enough shot, but the 1st Boston were shooting like children at the fair. That needed to change if they were to stand a chance of pushing the enemy back with rifle fire alone.

The enemy fired again. Even as the men around him flinched and cursed, Jack ran along the front of the company, letting the men see him.

'Listen to me. You must aim low!' He slowed his pace and glared at the men, forcing them to watch him. 'Shoot the bastards in the balls! You hear me! Aim low!' He felt no fear, even with his back turned to the enemy. He was back in his element. Some men became master craftsmen, their skills turned to making objects of beauty. Others became artists, their talent entertaining and bewitching those who saw their work. His own skills had no use in any other place than on the field of battle. But there he was master.

Message delivered, he moved back to the right flank. He saw Rowell in his proper place behind the line and waved. It was time to fire again.

'Aim!' This time the captain's voice was louder and more certain. 'Fire!'

The company fired as one. It was a glorious sound, every trigger pulled in unison. The volley roared out, crisp, sharp and deadly. K Company fired a single heartbeat later. The heavy Minié bullets tore into the enemy ranks. This time dozens fell, the Union bullets spreading death with cruel abandon.

'Cheer!' Jack could not contain himself. 'Cheer!'

The men in blue uniforms roared. It was a feral sound, a deep-throated bellow that started way down in their boots. Jack threw back his head and bellowed with them, releasing the surge of emotion that powered through him.

'Now load!' He left the right flank and stalked along the rear of the company. 'Load, you bastards. You're beating them. You hear me? You're tearing the fuckers to shreds.'

He stopped as he came close to O'Connell, who was

patrolling behind the left half of the company. The two men grinned at one another, then both turned around and walked back the way they had come.

'Aim!' Rowell shouted the order. 'Fire!'

'That's the way! Pour it on! Kill the buggers!' Jack encouraged the men the moment the volley was away. He checked Robert had not moved, then resumed his fast pacing behind the rear rank. He did not have to look at the enemy to know they were hurting. The fact that they had not fired between the Union volleys told him all he needed to know.

The enemy volley, when it finally came, was ragged. Jack felt the air above his head punched by a dozen fast-moving musket balls, then it was over, the storm whistling past in the span of a single heartbeat.

A Union soldier staggered backwards, his face a mask of blood from where a Confederate bullet had scored across his temple.

'Get back in the ranks!' Jack pounced on the unfortunate soul.

'But I'm hit!'

'Get back in the fucking ranks,' Jack snarled. 'You can still stand so you can still fight.' He grabbed the man firmly around the shoulders and steered him back into his place.

'They're running!' The cry came from the front rank.

'Come back, you cowardly rebel sons of bitches!' A man at the rear stood up on his tiptoes and hurled the abuse at the enemy.

'Shut your faces and shoot the bastards!' Jack shouted at the men who had stopped reloading to jeer at the enemy.

A moment later, Rowell gave the orders, and another volley blasted out.

It would be their last.

'Cease firing!' Jack shouted as he reached the right flank. The closest enemy unit was rushing back up the slope. They were out of effective range and the men needed to save their powder for whatever came next. For the day was not yet done, and already he could see Confederate officers riding around the enemy's broken ranks, rallying the fleeing soldiers. They would be back.

Jack stood in front of A Company and looked at the smoke-blackened faces of his men. Some were bloodied, the Confederate musket balls having left at least a dozen men with flesh wounds. The rest were pale under the black smudges of spent powder, the shock of having fought for the first time only sinking in now that it was done. A good many had puked their guts into the grass, the stink of vomit mixing with the lingering smell of powder.

The four flank companies had been pulled back to the main battle line. They could not hope to press home the attack by themselves. The Union commanders would have to commit more men if they were to force a passage across the Bull Run. For now, both sides were drawing breath, the troops on both sides of the river waiting to discover if they would have to fight again that day.

'Lieutenant Lark.'

Jack looked up in surprise as he recognised who had come to speak with him.

'What do you want?' He had not meant to sound harsh, but he heard the bite in his own tone.

Rowell looked at the ground in front of his boots. 'I would like a moment of your time.'

'You have it.' Jack did his best to hold his anger in check. His doubts about Rowell's ability to lead had been proven correct, but there was no value in bawling the man out. The company needed them to be united. No matter how galling it would prove to be, he had to find a way to build a bridge between them.

'We are to hold our ground here and await further instructions.'

Jack was saved from replying immediately as a battery of guns deployed to the right of the men from Boston. The gunners filled the air with shouted orders as they detached the cannon from their gun teams and readied them for action.

'Colonel Scanlon has been summoned to join General Tyler. Bridges has the regiment.' Rowell spoke once the gunners had quietened down.

Jack did not reply. He sensed Rowell wanted to say more. He did not have to wait long.

'Do you think Bridges is up to it?'

Jack snorted. 'As much as Scanlon. Anyway, it doesn't much matter. We just need to look after our men.'

'Our men?' Rowell shook his head as he repeated the phrase. 'I thought they were yours more than they were mine.' The words were bitter.

'They did well.' Jack sucked down a breath. When forced to chew on a turd, it made sense to bite hard and quick. 'You did well.' He managed to offer the praise without the words sticking in his craw.

'I did?' Rowell finally looked at him, and Jack saw the need in the captain's eyes.

'It is no small thing, commanding men in battle. I was shit at it the first time I tried.' He thought back to a hillside far away in the Crimea, and to a desperate rally square surrounded by marauding Russian Cossacks. 'You did just fine.'

'If you had not been there . . .' Rowell did not finish the thought.

'If?' Jack chuckled as he repeated the single word. 'If ifs and buts were candied nuts then we'd all be fat bastards sitting on our arses back in Boston. Ifs don't matter. The men stood and fought. You gave the right orders. That's good enough for now.'

Rowell had to swallow hard before he was able to reply. 'I think I have treated you badly.'

'No worse than I have treated you.' Jack sighed, then addressed the real issue. 'Elizabeth is marrying you, not me. I'm not your rival for her affections.' He grunted as he heard what he was saying. They were the words of a fool.

Rowell shuffled from boot to boot. 'I thought I was losing her.'

'Not to me.' Jack could not help wincing at the awkwardness of the conversation.

'I could not bear the shame of that.' Rowell fixed his gaze on Jack. 'My reputation would be ruined if I was spurned.'

'That's it?' Jack laughed. He had nearly choked on the words of praise. He should not have bothered.

'What do you mean?' Rowell's eyes narrowed. Conciliation was replaced by icy distrust.

'That's what concerns you? Damage to your precious reputation?'

'Naturally.' Rowell shrugged. 'You know the Kearneys. You know the power of their influence; you're their man, after all.'

'I'm not their man.' The words came out as a growl.

'Please.' Rowell looked pained at Jack's denial. 'Everyone knows you're here to look after Kearney's son. You're a wet nurse with a gun, nothing more.' He laughed at his own remark. 'Why else would a man like you be allowed to serve with us?'

'A man like me?'

'A mercenary for hire.' There was steel in Rowell's words now. 'Oh, we know what you are, *Lieutenant* Lark.' He imbued the honorific with a healthy dose of scorn. 'When Kearney's precious boy goes safely home, he will discard you without a qualm, just as he would me if I lost Elizabeth's affection. You and I are quite alike, Lark. We are both beholden to the charity of the Kearney family, although it would appear only one of us knows what manner of man we are. We are pawns, Lark, pawns in Kearney's game. My place on the damn chessboard lasts as long as Elizabeth loves me. Yours as long as his worthless slug of a son serves in this army. So forgive me if I come across as rather heartless. Elizabeth is a means to an end, nothing more. Her beauty is a blessing, I admit, but if she were the ugliest sow in the brood, I would not pursue her with any less attention or diligence.'

'Captain Rowell!' A breathless courier shouted for the commander of A Company, ending the uncomfortable conversation. 'Compliments of the major. You're to prepare your men to advance as part of the main line.' The young soldier gabbled out the orders in between gasping for breath. 'The 12th New York Regiment will form on our right.'

'Very good. Tell the major we are ready.'

Jack noticed that Rowell was standing straighter. The captain's experience of combat had shaken his confidence, but now some of his customary bravado was back.

But Rowell was wrong about one thing. Jack did know

what manner of man he was, and he knew that the time for talking was done. He did not know if General Tyler's orders had changed. He did not care if they were about to turn the enemy's right flank or if they were simply advancing in a futile bid to further one man's ambition. He was a soldier on the field of battle. He had his orders. That was all he needed.

The 1st Boston was going back down the hill.

Chapter Twenty-seven

A Company reloaded their rifles then headed back down the slope. This time they marched on the right flank of the regiment. Ahead was the woodland they had walked through earlier, but for the moment they could see across the river to the enemy on the far bank. The Confederates had used the lull to bring forward more troops, but the sight did not deter the Union men, who advanced with a confident spring in their step.

'They won't stand, will they, Lieutenant?' a powder-blackened face called out to Jack.

'Shut your mouth,' First Sergeant O'Connell spared Jack from answering, 'and keep your eyes front.' The two men followed behind the line. 'Warm work,' O'Connell observed to Jack.

'It'll get warmer.' Jack glanced at the far slope. The enemy was forming up closer to the banks of the river. There were thousands of them.

'There sure are enough of the buggers.' O'Connell clearly saw what Jack was looking at. 'We'd better hope they feck off like the last lot did, or else we're going to be in a whole barrel-load of shite.'

'Come on now, Sergeant, we're going to whip them Southron sons of bitches and whip them good.' The same man turned his head. He was grinning from ear to ear even as he dared to contradict his first sergeant.

'If I have to tell you to shut your damn mouth again, then so help me I'll sew your fecking lips together myself,' O'Connell snarled, wiping the man's smile away in an instant.

O'Connell's threat silenced the ranks, but there was no hiding the men's confidence. They were fairly running down the slope now, and it did not take long to reach the wood. They moved into the shadow of the trees, the air immediately cooler, the sound of their boots deadened as they marched over the thick layer of soil, foliage and mulch that smothered the ground.

'They think it'll be easy,' Jack commented to O'Connell. He lifted his kepi and wiped the sweat away. It was a relief to be in the shade of the trees.

'Their dander is well and truly up, so it is,' O'Connell agreed. 'Let's hope they're right to be so fecking confident.'

'Let's hope.' Jack could not help being dour. The men of A Company had fought once. The enemy had run without inflicting a single casualty. Now the Union men thought they were veterans. To a man, they believed the enemy would flee at their first volley.

He could only hope they were right. He had seen the thick band of Confederate soldiers that waited patiently for the second Union advance. If they held their ground, the Union troops would have the devil's own job to shift them.

The 1st Boston emerged from the wood. Ahead, they could see the grass that had been crushed by their skirmishers' boots just a short time before. Further down the slope was the place where the men had stood and fired, their discarded cartridge tops littering the ground. The smell of spent powder lingered in the air.

'Mary mother of God, would you look at that now.' O'Connell still marched at Jack's side, and now he breathed the words as he saw what was waiting for them.

Jack said nothing.

The enemy had pushed a long way forward, the distance between the two bodies of men less than a hundred yards. They were close enough for him to see the whites of their eyes as they watched the Union troops emerging into the sunlight. Hundreds of them lined the far bank of the river and every single one of them had a raised musket aimed at the Union men.

'Mary mother of God,' O'Connell said again.

Then the enemy fired.

The volley roared out. Hundreds of musket balls seared across the river, tearing into the Union ranks. Dozens fell, their screams filling the air. The line shuddered as it absorbed the volley, then stumbled to a halt. Men who had been wounded shrieked and cried for aid. Those still whole shouted and called to one another. The dead lay silent.

'Form line.' Jack strode forward. The shock of the enemy volley seared through his veins. The fear was there. He could taste it, bitter and metallic on his tongue. He felt it too, deep in his belly, churning and twisting as it fought to be free. Yet it had to be ignored. He had work to do.

'They killed Adam.' A pale face turned to stare at Jack in anguish. The man in the file next to him now lay on the ground, his head turned to pulp.

'Eyes front.' Jack snapped the order. 'Leave him alone!' he

snarled at the man fussing over the fallen soldier. 'Prepare to fire, for fuck's sake! It's time to fight, you hear me. It's time to fight!'

The men heard him. Most obeyed, pulling rifles into shoulders, shaking fingers curling around triggers.

Jack looked for his captain. Rowell was hunched over a fallen man, his hands fluttering across the gaping chasm torn in the man's chest. He was useless.

'1st Boston! Aim! Fire!' Bridges gave the order from his place at the centre of the regiment.

'Fire!' Jack repeated the command. The men responded and the volley crashed out, flinging a storm of bullets at the thick band of enemy soldiers. There were so many Confederate soldiers that the Union troops simply could not miss. All along the enemy line, grey-coated men fell to the ground, the heavy Minié bullets tearing limbs from bodies or gouging huge holes in flesh and bone.

'Load!' Jack strode to the right of the line, shouting loudly enough for every man to hear him.

The enemy fired again. Jack could not help flinching as the air was torn apart by the heart-stopping whine of musket balls zipping past. Filled with sudden fear, he looked for Robert. To his relief, the younger man was standing in his allotted position, sword drawn and pistol in hand. Jack laughed at the sight. He had not bothered to draw his own weapons. The notion amused him. There was more than one way to fight in a battle. He was an officer, his weapons the hundred rifles that obeyed his command.

'Aim!' he bellowed. There was no trace of fear in his voice. 'Fire!'

The Union troops fired for a second time. The volley cut the enemy down by the dozen. Men screamed as they were hit, the dreadful, heart-rending shrieks coming hard on the heels of the sound of the rest of the 1st Boston firing. The Union soldiers were hitting their targets, but there were simply too many of them. They were outnumbered and outgunned. If they stayed, they would die.

'Pull back!' The order came from Jack's left. He was not the only one to see the danger. Major Bridges had come towards the right flank, shouting as he moved, making sure all the officers heard him. 'Pull back to the trees!'

Jack waved in acknowledgement as Bridges moved away. The far left of the regiment was already on the move, the men needing little urging to retreat from the enemy.

'That's enough!' Jack shouted his instructions. 'Pick up the wounded and go back to the trees.'

The men moved quickly, dragging the dead and the dying with them. The broken bodies left trails behind them in the grass, the smears of blood red and slick in the bright afternoon sunlight.

'Rowell! You need to get back to the treeline.' Jack pushed through the retreating soldiers and stalked to the company's right flank. 'Rowell!'

Rowell was still crouched over the fallen man. His hands were covered in blood. He looked ready to vomit.

'For God's sake, get on your damn feet.' Jack reached forward and pulled him up.

'Get your hands off me.' Rowell looked ready to lash out. 'Who the hell do you think you are?'

'The man saving your sorry hide.'

'Damn you!' Rowell's face twisted, mouth ugly as he spat words back at Jack. 'Why don't you just leave me alone?'

'Oh, shut the fuck up.' Jack pushed him towards the trees. 'Now get back.'

'Damn you, Lark!' Rowell's hands moved quickly as he turned, drawing his beautiful ivory-handled revolver in one smooth movement.

The enemy fired their third volley. It slashed through the Union troops, cutting down men all along the line even as they pulled back. Rowell flinched, the bullets zipping past his head.

Jack did not so much as twitch. He snapped his arm forward, snatching the gun from Rowell's grasp. It took him the span of a single heartbeat to turn the weapon around and aim it at the centre of Rowell's sweat-streaked face. His finger curled on the trigger and he held it there, the revolver as still as death. It would be easy to kill the creature in front of him. He had killed so many men. The notion of adding one more to the tally meant nothing. Rowell meant nothing.

'Pull back!'

Jack turned his head. It was Robert. The young officer called across to them, his voice wavering. He had stayed behind even as the rest of the company broke for cover.

'What the hell is going on? Come on!' Robert ran towards them, his gait awkward as he tried to move quickly yet still remain crouched.

Jack turned his gaze back on Rowell. The man had not moved. He stared at the gun held so steadily in Jack's hand, his eyes fixed on the gaping maw of the muzzle aimed squarely at his face.

'You want to kill me?' Jack did not bother to hide his disdain. He could feel the revolver's engraved ivory hilt under his hand. He wanted the weapon for his own. It was perfectly balanced, the weight snug in his hand. The temptation to keep it was strong.

'For God's sake.' Robert had stopped a few yards away and now waved to them. 'Pull back, you fools.'

Jack kept his eyes on Rowell. He could feel the hatred emanating from the man.

'Try that again, and so help me I'll blow your brains to kingdom come.' His words were like iron. He held Rowell's gaze for a moment more, then tossed the precious revolver to one side.

'Come on!' he shouted as he ran past Robert, grabbing the lieutenant by the elbow and hauling him on. They ran together, scabbards banging from their hips. Neither looked back to see if Rowell was following.

They staggered to a halt at the edge of the wood, and Jack let go of Robert's elbow. 'Form line! Quickly now,' he shouted at the men. He paused, taking a moment to make sure they had started to obey before turning to his friend. 'Back to your place behind the line.'

Robert's mouth opened, as if about to ask a question. Whatever it was was never uttered, and he nodded once then moved away to do as he was told.

Jack watched him go, holding him in sight until he was hidden behind the line that A Company was forming at the edge of the wood. The rest of the regiment was on the company's left, the other nine companies quick to re-form now that they were in the shelter of the trees.

'That's it. Now load!' Jack snapped the instruction, then stalked to Rowell's place at the rear of the line, not caring that he was usurping the man who rightly commanded the company. 'Aim!'

The men pulled rifles into shoulders. They had reloaded quickly.

But not quickly enough.

The enemy troops had advanced as the Union men retreated. Now they fired again. The musket balls struck the trees with a loud crack, showering the men with leaves and broken branches. A few found flesh, the sound like a butcher slamming a fresh carcass onto a chopping board.

'Eyes front!' Jack roared in the moment's silence after the wicked storm had passed.

The Union soldiers were wavering. Two men had fallen, crumpling to the ground in silence. Many of the rest had lowered their rifles or else pulled their heads away as they flinched from the Confederate fire.

'Look at the enemy!' Jack ordered. 'Now aim!'

Rifles were pulled back to fit snugly against shoulders, the men obedient even as they fought their fear.

'Fire!'

The volley roared out. It struck the enemy line, knocking men down all along its length.

'That's the way. Now load.' Jack watched the men closely.

Another enemy volley crashed into the wood, tearing bark from the trees and ripping away branches.

'Aim! . . . Fire!'

This time it was a crisper volley, the men pulling their triggers as one.

'Better! Load!' Jack turned his head and spat as the stink of spent powder caught in his throat.

Another enemy volley tore into the treeline. A man on the left flank of the company cursed as a musket ball seared through the flesh of his arm. Another, closer to Jack, screamed in a moment's horror as a ball ripped away two fingers of his left hand.

Jack wiped a hand across his face, clearing the sweat from his eyes. 'Aim at the officers.' He pushed through the ranks until he stood in the centre of the front rank. 'You hear me! Shoot at any of the bastards shouting orders.' He bellowed the instruction, watching the men to make sure they understood.

The thrill of commanding the company coursed through him. It was everything he remembered. He looked along the line, which was now wreathed in a cloud of smoke. The men's faces were streaked with sweat and smeared with black powder stains. Their eyes were wide and showed white as they stared at the enemy. He could feel their determination. They were beginning to understand what it meant to stand and fight.

Further to their left, the rest of the regiment stood at the edge of the woods. Each captain was controlling his own company, the distance too far and the wood too thick to allow the regiment to fight as one. It would be down to every officer to hold his men in place and keep them fighting.

Jack glanced at the enemy. They had closed the distance as the Union troops retreated and now lined the far bank of the river. Dozens had fallen, the Union volleys working a dreadful destruction on their ranks. Jack was pleased to see the bodies of at least two of the men who had been shouting orders on the ground, the men heeding his command and firing with enough accuracy to take down the Confederate officers.

As he watched them, so the enemy fired. The ordered volley fire was finished. Instead the Confederate troops were firing as soon as they were ready, each man fighting alone. It meant the Union men were subjected to a constant, withering barrage, but one that lacked the devastating power of the massed volley.

The Confederates were firing uphill and most were firing high.

'Come on!' He turned back to the men and encouraged them. They were doing well. 'Aim! . . . Fire!'

Another volley spat out. The men were finding the rhythm now. Their fear was mastered and they were fighting. And they were hurting the enemy.

'Jack!' O'Connell shouted for his attention. 'The 12th!'

Jack twisted on the spot and saw immediately what had caught the first sergeant's attention. The 12th New York Regiment were pulling back, their ranks disordered, leaving their dead behind. When he glanced across the river, he understood why.

The Confederates had the bit between their teeth. They were attacking.

The enemy came on fast. They splashed noisily across the ford, their boots flinging water high into the air. A strange ululating yell emanated from their ranks. It was an unearthly sound, the Confederates yipping and whooping as they advanced, the sound goading them on even as they advanced in the face of the Union fire.

'Stand fast!' Jack roared the order as he saw men starting to shuffle backwards. 'Load.'

Many looked at him as if he were mad. The enemy was already across the ford. They came on without pause, flooding the lower reaches of the slope with men, the strange yell now constant.

'We pulling back?' O'Connell reached Jack's side.

'Not until someone orders me to.' Jack looked at the enemy, gauging distances. Then he looked at O'Connell. 'Take post behind the line.'

O'Connell nodded. He did not seek to change Jack's mind.

Jack strode along the front rank, keeping his eyes on the enemy. The rebel yell was unsettling the men. It hardly seemed human, its high pitch making the enemy sound like some beast from another realm. He had never heard anything like it, not even in the wildest reaches of India.

'Aim!' He shouted the order as he moved back to the centre of the front rank. For the first time that day, he drew his revolver. It felt heavy and clumsy, the contrast with Rowell's beautifully crafted weapon stark. Yet it would do its job well enough.

He raised the firearm. The range was far too long for him to have any hope of hitting the enemy ranks. But a weapon could still have an effect, even if it did not strike a target.

'Fire!'

He pulled the revolver's trigger as he bellowed the order. The men obeyed, flinging another volley into the massive body of men coming towards them.

'Load!'

The enemy were closer now. The Union volley cut them down in droves, but the Confederates came on regardless, the discordant yell unaltered by the swathe of death cut into their ranks. Jack could only admire their bravery. They might have lacked the disciplined ranks of the Union army, but they were coming on in as fine a style as any troops he had ever seen.

'Aim! . . . Fire!' He fired his revolver again and then again, adding to the thunderous roar as yet another Union volley smashed into the Confederate ranks. At the shorter range, the heavy Minié bullets worked a wicked destruction on the bodies of the enemy, some passing through more than one man, the powerful Springfield rifles delivering a barrage that stopped the enemy advance in its tracks.

'That's the way. Load!' Jack had the men in hand. It took courage to stand when the enemy came on. Courage that the men from Boston had found they possessed.

The Confederate line had lost many men, the two Union volleys giving them a bloody nose. But they were not done fighting.

'Stand fast.' Jack straightened his spine as he saw the enemy raise their muskets. They were horribly close. 'Keep reloading.' He kept his voice calm.

Musket balls smashed into the Union line. Men screamed as they were hit, their bodies torn by the enemy bullets that cut through the ranks.

'Fire!'

Jack felt nothing. He had not flinched as the enemy bullets killed men just yards from where he stood. He shouted the order knowing they had to keep fighting if the enemy was to be turned.

The men obeyed. Even as their mates bled and died, those still standing pulled their triggers. Jack joined them, emptying the last barrels in his revolver, not caring that he was not likely to hit anything.

Their close-range volley gouged great gaps in the enemy line, knocking dozens off their feet. This time it would prove to be enough. The enemy started to edge backwards when they should have been reloading. The movement began slowly, the men backing away hesitantly at first. Then the first handful turned and ran. The rest followed.

As the enemy fled, the Union men cheered, their wild cries filled as much with relief as triumph. Jack did not join in, but he felt the same emotion deep in his gut. He had returned to where he belonged.

'They got O'Connell!'

The shout came from the right of the line. At first Jack could not fully hear it, the cheers drowning it out. Then it came again, the cry laced with horror.

'They killed O'Connell.'

Jack recognised the voice. It belonged to Robert. The young lieutenant pushed through the ranks, then grabbed Jack's arm, pulling him out of the line.

The cheers faltered. Men who had been shouting in the wild throes of victory stopped open-mouthed as the news rippled through the company.

Jack ran. He was still carrying his revolver, a thin trail of powder smoke snaking from the barrel. He followed Robert along the front rank. Every man was turning around, every face betraying the same mix of horror and shock as they absorbed the news.

He saw O'Connell's body immediately. The tall first sergeant lay on his back, staring up at the sky. He had been hit in the eye. All that was left was a gory hole. The bullet had passed straight through the Irishman's head, shattering his skull and killing him instantly.

Jack looked away. He did not need to see more. All that had been O'Connell was gone.

'Sir!' A courier called for his attention.

'What is it?' He answered calmly. He was no stranger to death.

'Compliments of Major Bridges. We're pulling back. To the top of the hill.'

'Very well,' Jack replied briskly.

'What?' Robert, still at Jack's side, reacted to the command angrily. 'We beat them back and now we're retreating?'

'That's the orders I was told to give you, sir.' The courier had to swallow hard as the officer berated him.

'That's enough.' Jack silenced Robert with a hand, then nodded to the runner. 'We heard you. Thank you.'

The courier did not wait to hear any more.

'Jesus Christ.' Robert wiped a hand across his face. 'What the hell is going on?'

Jack holstered his revolver. He did not care to listen to Robert. He was looking away to the right, where a lone officer was walking into the treeline. He carried an ivory-handled revolver.

O'Connell was dead, and Rowell was back.

Chapter Twenty-eight

Outside Centreville, Virginia, Friday 19 July 1861

Reveille awoke the men at first light. They forced their tired bodies into motion, ignoring the protests from their aching joints. They had slept on the ground. There had been no tents and no shelter, no comfort other than what they carried on their backs.

Scanlon had not returned. He was now permanently attached to the brigade staff. No one knew if it was reward for a job well done, or to add some experience to the men who had ordered the attack the previous day. Bridges had been given command of the regiment and he knew no more about the sudden appointment. If he was pleased, or daunted, by his promotion, he gave nothing away to his officers when he passed on the news.

He had been more informed when it came to what was to happen next. Tyler's division had pushed too hard the previous day. Tyler had exceeded his orders, but at least he had found out that the enemy held the river in force whilst also learning something of the ground McDowell had hoped to cross. The flanking attack that had been planned stood no chance of success. The Union army would have to find another way.

'What the hell is this supposed to be? This ain't food. It ain't fit for a sickly sow, let alone a man!'

Typically, O'Dowd's was the first voice Jack heard as he got to his feet. The night sleeping on the ground had awoken the pain in the small of his back and it was sending spasms running up and down his spine.

'What's wrong, O'Dowd?' Jack coughed as phlegm caught in his throat. He sorely needed tea, but he knew he would be lucky to even get some coffee.

'Have you seen this now, sir?' O'Dowd showed his mess plate so Jack could see the mush he was preparing to eat. 'I'm not an animal and there is surely more bloody dirt and goddam sand in this here muck than anything that ever grew on this bloody earth. Desiccated vegetables, my arse. More like desecrated fecking shite.'

'Is that all you have left?' Jack was too tired, and in too much pain, to deal with O'Dowd.

'It's this shite or hardtack.'

'Well then, make your bloody choice.'

O'Dowd took one look at Jack's face and decided not to press. But he did toss the contents of his dinner into the nearest fire whilst muttering under his breath.

'Heh, O'Dowd.' Robert was still lying where he had slept, but now he lifted his head to pull his haversack closer. He dug inside and pulled out a glass jar, which he tossed over to the muttering Irishman. 'You can have these.'

O'Dowd caught the jar then held it aloft as he peered at the contents. 'Mary mother of God, is that pickles you're giving me there, sir?'

'My sister sent them. She thinks they're good for my bowels.'

The men nearby laughed.

'Well, sir, you tell your sweet sister that she is the finest creature this side of Kilkenny. I thank you for these.'

Robert waved the thanks away and resumed his prostrate position, this time with his hands crossed comfortably behind his head.

Jack walked across and stood over his fellow lieutenant. 'You got any tea in there?'

'I'm afraid not. I have some blackberries, if you've a fancy for something sweet.'

'I need tea,' Jack grunted. He looked around. The men were making what breakfast they could. None had much left in the way of rations. Their day would start with desiccated vegetables, hardtack and coffee. If no fresh supplies were brought up, it would be how it finished too. Only O'Dowd was happy. He sat with Robert's jar of pickles between his legs, eating one after another with such relish it nearly made Jack smile.

He bent down and fished out a lump of broken hardtack from his own haversack, then sat on the ground next to Robert. He snapped off a chunk and held it out to his companion. 'You want to break your teeth on some of this?'

Robert grimaced as he glanced at the hardtack, then waved it away. 'I'm not hungry.' He sighed and forced himself to a sitting position. 'I don't know how any of you can eat after yesterday.' He spoke quietly so that only Jack could hear him.

'You have to eat something.'

'I cannot face it.' Robert rubbed both hands vigorously through his hair, then wiped his palms across his face. He looked warily at Jack. 'Have you spoken to the captain?' Every man in the company was aware of the spat between the two officers. They were also very aware which of the pair had stood and fought at their side, and which had been absent for most of the fighting.

'No.'

'Don't you think you should?'

It was Jack's turn to sigh. 'Probably.' He gave a thin-lipped smile. 'He pulled a gun on me.'

'What?' Robert looked aghast. 'When?'

'When we withdrew to the trees; just before you came and shouted at us.'

'I didn't see it.' Robert frowned. 'But I don't disbelieve you,' he added quickly when he saw the scowl on Jack's face deepen. 'Why would he do such a thing?'

'He wanted to kill me.'

'Kill you?' Robert was aghast. 'What the hell was he thinking?'

'I expect he was thinking how much he wanted me dead.'

'But why? I mean, I know he dislikes you; we all know that, but to want to kill you? Why, that would be murder.'

Jack snorted. 'Can you commit murder in a place where all men are trying to do is kill one another?'

Robert's lips twitched at the mention of killing. He looked down at the dust in front of him. He said nothing, but began to trace a pattern in the dirt.

Jack sat back and took a careful bite from his hardtack. It was as hard as rock and tasted little better. But he knew he needed something in his belly, so he ground his teeth then swallowed the gritty substance down.

'Do you think there will be another battle?'

Jack looked at Robert, his brow furrowed. 'That wasn't a battle.'

'It wasn't?'

'No. That was just a . . .' He struggled to find the right word. The previous day's fighting had been pointless. Men had died for nothing. 'It was just a skirmish.'

Robert lifted his gaze. His eyes were moist. 'So there is worse to come?'

'Yes.' Jack saw the fear in the younger man. He had seen it before, but now Robert had glimpsed the truth of war. Sometimes knowledge was worse than ignorance.

'How do you go back?' Robert paused. 'How do you go back to that?' His face had paled to the colour of old ash.

'You get used to it.' Jack prepared to take another cautious bite of hardtack, but found that he could no longer stomach it. He tossed it over so that it landed on his haversack.

'You get used to that?' Robert voiced his disbelief.

'You do.'

Robert shook his head. 'I truly do not believe I could ever get used to such a thing.' He paused, resuming his tracing in the dust. 'Does it go, then?' he asked without looking at Jack.

'Does what go?'

'The fear.' He whispered the words.

Jack sighed before he summoned the will to answer. 'No. It doesn't go. But you learn to master it. To control it.'

'But you could die.'

'You could. But you could die tomorrow choking on a lump of this bloody hardtack. Or you could get a fever and be dead in a day. Or you could be a stupid young idiot and drink yourself to death. There are a lot of dumb ways to die.'

Robert said nothing. He continued to trace a pattern in the dirt for a while, then crossly wiped it away with the heel of his palm. 'I don't want to die. When I think of what it means . . .' The words tailed away.

'So don't die.'

'How can I do that?' Robert scoffed. 'If they can kill O'Connell, they can sure as hell kill me.'

Jack reached out and took a firm hold on Robert's arm, forcing him to look up. 'You do exactly what I tell you.' He had to swallow hard to clear the knot that had formed in his throat. 'I'll do my best to keep you safe.'

Robert frowned as he searched Jack's face for something hidden. Then understanding dawned on him. 'My father.' He closed his eyes as if suddenly in acute pain. 'My father put you here to look after me.'

'He wants you to go back home in one piece.'

'So he pays for me to have protection.' Robert's eyes snapped open. 'You are nothing but a goddam mercenary.'

He held Jack's gaze, then the frown returned as he found a piece of the puzzle that he did not understand. 'But you fought yesterday. You *led* us yesterday. You didn't have to do that if you're here just to protect me.'

'That's because I'm a fool.'

'No.' Robert's voice was firmer. 'You are no man's fool, Jack Lark.'

'I must be a fool if I like a daft bugger like you.'

Robert found a wan smile. 'I quite like the idea that you're my bodyguard. Does that mean you'll do as I ask? Will you obey me?'

'No.'

'No.' Robert repeated Jack's answer. 'I think you have a problem doing what anybody tells you.' He sighed. 'I hope my father is paying you well.'

'Enough.'

'Enough? Is that all? He should be paying you a small fortune. I fancy I am worth that.'

'Don't get ideas above your station. I've been paid more for guarding a damn dog.' Jack could not help smiling. Despite his fear, Robert still had enough spirit left for mockery.

A rattle of drums came from near the centre of the regiment's line. It would soon be beating out the instruction for the men to assemble, which meant the time for idle discourse had come to an end.

Jack clambered to his feet, then stretched his spine, forcing away the worst of the stiffness. He looked down at Robert, who showed no sign of moving.

'Come on, you slovenly soldier.' He held out a hand, which Robert stared at for a moment, then accepted. With Jack's help, he hauled himself to his feet.

The two lieutenants were ready to face the day.

'Good morning, gentlemen.' Major Bridges paused as he waited for the assembled officers to quieten down. He stood under the shade of a large tree. The morning sun had risen and its heat was already making the men sweat. The new commander of the 1st Boston cradled a mug of coffee in his hands, a thin trail of steam emerging from within.

'The general's plan has changed.' Bridges spoke quietly, his delivery very different from Scanlon's. There was no fire and brimstone in it. Instead he told the officers what they needed to know in a calm, matter-of-fact manner, like a school teacher reading out the instructions for a task he knew would stretch even his brightest pupils. 'Yesterday's action at Blackburn Ford made it clear that there is no way around to the east of the enemy position. So the general is now looking to the west.'

Jack listened carefully. It was the first time he had heard the name of the ground they had fought over yesterday. He never normally gave much importance to such things. That could be left to those who would chronicle the actions; the men in warm, comfortable studies who would become armchair experts on the events others had endured.

'We do know that the enemy is on the defensive and that it will be up to us to shift him. These men are defending their homes.' Bridges paused and looked over his moustache at the officers. 'They have the advantage of the ground, they are well supplied and they have had all the time they need to reconnoitre the terrain. If they have any sense they'll sit tight and just let us come against them. That makes them hard to beat, and if any of you think otherwise then I am afraid you are deluded.'

'What about Patterson and the enemy army he faces in the Shenandoah?' asked Captain Joplin of B Company. 'If that Reb army slips away and comes over here, then we will surely be outnumbered.'

'The general has been told that Patterson is keeping them heavily engaged.' Bridges treated the question with respect. 'He believes there is no chance they will be able to play a part in the affair here. Even if they did succeed in moving away from Patterson, the distance is simply too great for them to arrive here before we bring the enemy to battle.'

'What about the railways?' Jack spoke up. He remembered the French flanking march before Solferino. The French army had used the railway line to move across the face of the enemy, a feat that would never have been possible had the men had to travel on foot; the distance too great and the manoeuvre carrying too much risk. The railway had allowed the French to steal the initiative from the static and slower-moving Austrian army. Warfare was changing. Commanders who grasped that fact, and used modern advances in technology to their advantage, were the ones who triumphed.

Bridges sipped at his coffee as he contemplated Jack's question. It gave another man the chance to answer.

'Lieutenant Lark doubts that our general knows what he is doing.' Rowell spoke in a much louder tone than Bridges had used when addressing the group. The commander of A Company stood on the fringe of the group. He looked exhausted, his eyes red and surrounded by puffy grey bags.

'There is a railroad,' Bridges answered. 'Mr Lark is right to think that could be a decisive factor.'

'For God's sake, Temperance.' Rowell used the major's first name in an arrogant, mocking tone. He did so deliberately. It reminded all present of the true pecking order in the regiment, one that was not necessarily delineated by rank. In the hierarchy of Boston society, Rowell's place as a future member of the Kearney family placed him well above a man like Bridges, a fact the captain would seize upon with relish. 'Do not listen to the fears of a whining goddam Englishman.'

Bridges did not utter a sound. He simply looked at Rowell, then took another sip of his coffee.

'Thank you, Captain Rowell.' When he did speak, his tone was unchanged. 'I appreciate your advice as always.' He turned to look at Jack. 'And I thank you, Lieutenant Lark, for your question. I shall present it to brigade.'

'For God's sake, man, if you are going to listen to a—'

'That is all, gentlemen.' Bridges cut Rowell dead. 'We have the day to gather our strength after the exertions of yesterday. I suggest you use the time wisely.'

Rowell's mouth was still open. He closed it with a visible effort, then turned sharply on his heel and walked briskly away. He did so alone, not one officer moving to his side.

Jack sat on a wooden packing case full of cartridges and cleaned his revolver with meticulous care, pulling a cloth through each chamber. He had learned the hard way never to take any weapon for granted.

'May I disturb you?'

He looked up sharply. He had been giving the weapon his full attention and so had not heard anyone approach.

'Of course.' He put down the cleaning rod, then rose to his feet and nodded an awkward greeting to Elizabeth Kearney.

She looked out of place. Her dress was made from a cool, dusky red satin accented with white lace. Amidst the greys and blues of the army camp, she stood out like a peacock in a dovecote. She also looked way more beautiful than he remembered.

He did not know what he was supposed to say. The silence between them was awkward and went on far too long. The last time they had met they had shared a kiss. He did not know what that meant, or whether he should mention it.

'Did my brother give you the package I sent?' Elizabeth lowered her eyes and smiled as she recognised his discomfort. It was an emotion she clearly did not share.

'Yes. Thank you.' He was doing his best not to stare. It was a temptation that was almost impossible to resist.

'Mr Brady took a fine portrait. I think we look quite the handsome couple.'

Jack tore his eyes from her and looked around him, noting the many faces turned their way. 'What are you doing here?' He could not keep the gruffness from his tone.

'Are you not pleased to see me?' Elizabeth stuck the tip of her tongue between her lips as she teased him.

'Have you see Rowell?'

'No, but I will.' The first hint of a frown appeared on Elizabeth's face.

'You should have stayed in Washington.'

'Why, half of Washington is here. It would look amiss if we did not come and visit, especially with my brother and husband-to-be here. Besides, we don't want to miss it.'

'Miss what?'

'The battle, of course. It has been the talk of the town for weeks now. Anyone who is anyone has come to see it.'

Jack scowled. 'A battle is not a spectacle to be watched as entertainment.'

Elizabeth's frown deepened. 'I wonder what has put you into such a black mood this morning, Jack. I thought you would be pleased to see me.'

'You shouldn't be here.'

'And why is that?' The first crack in the demure facade appeared.

'You should be with your intended.'

'I see.' The two words were glacial. 'I thought you would want a moment with me.'

'What I want has nothing to do with anything.'

Elizabeth took a pace closer towards him. 'What *do* you want, Jack?'

Jack could not help shaking his head at the question. 'I don't know.'

'I know what I want,' she whispered. 'But I don't have the courage to say it.'

Jack heard something in her tone then. He could not say

why, but he suddenly felt as if she were an actress on a stage. She was delivering her lines with perfection, yet they did not resonate with emotion. They were too schooled and bore a hint of premeditation. Every instinct told him that she was playing with him.

And he finally understood. Elizabeth could have anything she wanted. She could have any*one* she wanted. It gave her power, and like all such power it could only corrupt.

'Courage is a rare thing.' He looked at her, staring deep into the beautiful blue eyes that gazed at him as if he was the only man on earth. 'I saw courage yesterday. We lost men. Did you know that? Men from this company died. They died for a cause they believed in. It wasn't entertainment. It wasn't some bloody game.' He closed his eyes as he felt the emotion stir deep in his belly. 'Jesus Christ.'

When he opened them again, he no longer saw a beautiful creature standing in front of him, an angel given human form. He saw a silly girl playing games.

'I see I have made you angry.' Elizabeth stepped away, her eyes downcast. A single tear ran down her cheek, carving a narrow channel in the powder painted onto her face.

He looked away from the sight. Doubt flooded through his veins. He was being cruel. If he was wrong, then he was an utter bastard.

It was then that he caught sight of a mismatched pair approaching. One face was contorted with barely contained fury. The other displayed nothing but an amused smile. Captain Ethan Rowell stomped towards them, his legs working furiously to propel him across the ground, followed closely by Elizabeth's maid, Rose, who was forced into a jog to keep up.

Jack turned back to look at Elizabeth. He was quick enough to catch the tiniest flicker of a smile on her lips.

'What the hell is going on?' hissed Rowell as soon as he was close enough. His face was flushed with more than just the heat and the exertion of his fast pace.

'Miss Kearney came here looking for you.' Jack tried to hold onto his temper.

Rowell stepped forward so the two men were eyeball to eyeball. 'Horseshit. We all know the game you're playing.'

'Ethan!' Elizabeth gasped at Rowell's language. She turned to the maid. 'Rose, go away.' The command was snapped.

Jack thought he detected a hint of delight in her outrage. 'Mind your tongue,' he barked at Rowell. 'Before someone minds it for you.'

Rowell leered into Jack's face. 'That someone being you, I take it.' He shook his head slowly, but his eyes bored into Jack's skull. 'Why, you have dogged my every step since you got here. My every goddam step.'

Jack said nothing. There were no words that would mollify Rowell. Out of the corner of his eye he saw Rose walking away as she had been ordered.

'Now you stand here openly courting my girl in front of everybody.' Rowell's mouth twisted into something ugly. 'You are nothing more than a goddam Limey son of a bitch.'

Jack saw what was coming. Rowell was working himself up, the anger spewing out of him like vomit from a drunk. There was only one way it would finish.

Rowell's arm came up, the hand bunched into a fist. It moved no more than an inch before Jack snapped his own hand forward and seized it in a vice-like grip.

'Do not start something you cannot finish,' he snarled,

his voice low. He felt Rowell's arm vibrate under his grip.

'Why—'

'Enough.' Jack cut his officer off. 'You're wrong about me. I'm not here to interfere in your life.' He tightened his grip as he felt Rowell struggle to free himself. 'I'm not your bloody enemy.'

He threw Rowell's arm away, then tensed, waiting for a reaction.

Rowell was seething, his jaw clenched tight. Yet he kept his hands down. There was no sign of a second attempt at a punch. Jack kept his eyes locked on the captain's for a few moments more, then turned his back and ran after Rose.

She was a fair distance away, so it took him a while to catch her up. She turned as she heard the pounding of his boots on the sun-baked ground.

'You done mooning over that fancy woman now?' She raised a hand to shelter her eyes from the sun that was directly behind Jack's shoulder.

'She was never my fancy woman. And I never mooned.'

Rose's face split into a smile. 'You believe what you want to believe. I know what I saw, and you were mooning after that woman something bad.'

'I didn't think it was that obvious.' Jack managed to find a thin-lipped smile by way of return. He took a deep breath into his lungs. The short run had left him breathless, or at least he blamed the exertion for the tightness in his chest.

'Maybe a blind man might've missed it.' Rose teased him without mercy. 'But I wouldn't bet my life on that.'

Jack laughed. He did not mean to, but it escaped before he could hold it in. 'I think I've been a fool.'

'You have that about right.' She laughed back at him.

Jack liked the sound. He did not think Rose laughed often. A thought struck him. 'What were you doing with Rowell?'

'I was asked to fetch him.'

'By Elizabeth?'

'Who else.'

Jack felt a moment's relief. Any doubts he had left fell away. He was sure that Elizabeth had sent Rose to get Rowell simply to ensure the confrontation between the two men. 'Thank God for that.'

'Don't take the Lord's name in vain.' The rejoinder was given sharply.

'I apologise.' Jack could not help but smile. He looked at Rose and was struck again by how pretty she was. He had seen it before, but had not given it much thought. Now he did.

'Why are you grinning like a fool?'

'Because you were right.'

'Of course I was right.' Her reply was tart, but it was given with a smile.

Jack reached out to her then. There was a hint of colour high on her cheeks, and his fingers touched it.

Rose flinched, her head pulling away sharply.

'I'm sorry.' His hand dropped.

'No, don't be sorry.' Rose looked at him. 'I don't like being touched.'

'Because of those?' Jack nodded towards the thin tracery of scars on her cheek.

She nodded.

'How did you get them?'

'I was whipped.' Her chin lifted then. Defiance replaced timidity.

'Before you came to Boston?'

Her lips pressed tight together and she nodded.

Jack would not press her further. He knew what it was to bear scars. His body boasted a dozen of them. As did his soul.

'Rowell tried to kill me.' He spoke in an off-hand fashion, as if remarking on the weather. He did so intentionally.

'He did what?' Rose could not help the exclamation. The mood between them changed immediately.

Jack laughed. 'He pulled a gun on me. Just yesterday.'

'What did you do?'

'I stopped him.'

'You didn't think to kill him back?'

Jack snorted. 'No, I didn't think that.'

'I would have.' Rose's hand lifted to the scars on her face. 'I killed the man who did this to me.'

Jack's eyes widened. 'Well, he deserved it.' He deliberately kept the mood light. He had had his fill of darkness. He held out a crooked arm. 'Will you walk with me?'

He saw the shadow flicker across her face. Then she smiled. 'You sure you want to walk with a girl like me?'

Jack held her gaze, then simply nodded. 'I have never been more sure of anything.'

Chapter Twenty-nine

Outside Centreville, Virginia, Saturday 20 July 1861

Jack sat on the ground where he had spent a second night trying, and mainly failing, to sleep. Familiarity had not made the occasion any more pleasurable. His back ached abominably and he dreaded getting to his feet, knowing full well that he would be lucky not to fall back onto his arse. He cocked an ear as he heard a strange sound far off in the distance, one he thought he recognised.

'You hear that?' he asked Robert, who was lying at his side. He was ignored. 'Heh!' He reached over and jabbed a finger into his fellow lieutenant's side. It bounced off bone. There was more meat on a maggot.

'Can you not leave a man to rest?' The reply was muffled, Robert's head still buried beneath his blanket.

'Hush your noise. Now listen. Can you hear something?'

Robert groaned, but he pulled the blanket from his face and did as he was told. 'Sounds like a locomotive to me.'

Jack nodded. 'That's what I thought too. You think that's the enemy bringing in troops from the Shenandoah?'

'It can't be. It's too far away for that. Anyway, Bridges

said it wasn't possible. Patterson has the enemy well in hand.'

'You sure of that?'

'I'm sure that I'm damn near starved.' Robert threw back the blanket and forced himself to sit upright. 'I sincerely hope those fresh rations arrive this morning.'

'They'd better. Otherwise we've been sitting here on our bloody arses for nothing.' Jack shook his head at the folly. The army had wasted the previous day doing precious little. They had no orders to do anything but more of the same that day. McDowell was granting the Confederate generals one of the most valuable resources a commander of an army could wish for. Time.

'At least we're still here. I heard that the 4th Pennsylvania Regiment and the 8th New York are packing up to go home. Those boys only signed up for three months. Their time is done.' Robert spoke in an off-hand fashion.

'So they're just buggering off?'

'If you mean are they leaving, then yes, that's what I heard.' Robert smiled at Jack's choice of words. They had been together for many weeks now, but he still found the Englishman's turn of phrase at once both fascinating and incomprehensible. 'I wish I could go home.'

'Why? What is waiting for you there?' Jack asked.

'Life, Jack, life is waiting for me.' Robert looked at him to emphasise the meaning behind the words. 'A whole glorious life.'

Jack was saved from finding a reply as he spotted Major Bridges approaching. He was on his feet as quickly as his aching bones would allow, dragging Robert up at the same time.

'Good morning, sir. Have you got orders for us?' He fired off the question as soon as Bridges was near.

'Good morning to you both. In answer to your question, Lieutenant, no, I have no new orders.' Bridges did not bother to hide his impatience. Jack was not alone in finding the delay insufferable.

'What the hell is that lame-brained fool thinking of?' Jack let his frustration show.

Bridges' mouth was hidden behind his hefty moustache, but Jack saw his lips twitch in amusement. 'If the lame-brained fool you refer to is the general, then I am happy to say that I have been briefed on a new plan.'

'So let's hear it.'

'You sound dubious, Jack.'

'Dubious?' Jack gave a snort at the word. 'Too bloody right I'm dubious. I'm a downright doubting bloody Thomas, but if you've been told the general's latest scheme, then I'd like to hear it.'

Bridges shook his head. 'You are just a lieutenant, Jack, but I swear you think you should be commanding this entire army.'

'I reckon I could do a better job than this McDowell fellow. I wouldn't have left us sitting on our bloody arses for days on end. You think the men on the other side of the river are waiting around doing sod all, or do you think they'll be doing everything they can think of to prepare for our attack?'

Bridges looked at him carefully. 'I need you to mind your tongue, Jack. We might have failed to find a way around the Confederates' right, but the general believes he has found a way to turn their left. There is a ford over the Bull Run at a place called Sudley Springs that is good enough for wheeled vehicles. If the enemy's strength is to the east, where we ran into them the other day, then their left must be weaker.'

'Go on.' Jack wanted to hear more. He thought nothing of giving an order to a superior officer.

Bridges' moustache twitched, but he did as Jack asked. 'McDowell plans to send two full divisions to the west. They will fall on the enemy's flank with all their strength.'

'Which divisions?'

'The Second and Third. That's nigh on thirteen thousand men.'

'I see.' Jack knew the 1st Boston were in McDowell's First Division. 'What about us?'

'The First Division will make a feint here to the right of where we attacked the other day, where a stone bridge crosses the Bull Run. Richardson's brigade will advance against Mitchell's Ford. The Fifth Division will remain at Centreville in reserve.'

Jack considered the scheme for a moment. 'It's a sound plan.'

'I am sure the general will be pleased you approve.'

Jack ignored the barbed comment. 'It's a sound plan provided the enemy are where we think they are and that there are no reinforcements coming across from the west to bolster their left flank.'

Bridges nodded. 'That's about the size of it. We have been reassigned to strengthen one of the flanking brigades. We are to be attached to the Second Division under Brigadier General Hunter. We shall be in Burnside's brigade.'

Jack took the news in his stride. He reckoned the hardest fighting would be in the centre. The flanking march would likely be nothing more than a long, boring trudge through the Virginia countryside. He doubted McDowell had any idea where the enemy really was, let alone what ground he faced. If the reporter Russell was correct, the Union commander lacked even basic maps of the local area. Yet being reassigned to the flank march suited Jack well enough. Anything that kept Robert far from the fighting was a blessing.

'When are we marching? Is there time for the men to have breakfast?'

'We have a little longer than that. We march tomorrow.'

'Tomorrow!' Jack did not bother to hide his scorn.

'The general wants us to have a good rest.'

'We'll get all the damn rest we need when we're dead! We should be marching now.' Jack gritted his teeth and ground out his frustration.

'Those are our orders. We have no choice but to obey.'

Jack looked at Bridges sharply. The major would not offer any criticism, but Jack sensed his commander shared his own frustration. And he was right. There was nothing so close to a god as a general on a campaign. There was nothing for it but to idle the day away and prepare for what was to come in the morning.

Jack recognised the odd-looking wagon from the celebrations on Independence Day. The photographer, Brady, had ventured far from the capital, the long delay giving him ample time to record the faces of the men waiting for the battle that would finally settle the discord between the states.

Brady was not alone in visiting the troops. It was a bright, sunny afternoon and the temporary encampment was swarming with people who had no reason to be there. The army should have been marching on the enemy. Instead it was sitting idle, being visited by the great and the good of Washington.

Jack had left the company lines an hour earlier. He had

spent enough time sitting on his arse and a walk was preferable to languishing in the company lines with nothing to do.

The ground where the army had spent a second night was a hive of activity. McDowell might have been wasting time he did not have, but at least he had organised a delivery of fresh supplies. The train of wagons bringing up more salt pork, hardtack, desiccated vegetables and coffee stretched back for miles. Overworked supply officers were doing their best to distribute everything, but it was quickly descending into chaos.

Jack ducked past a blue-coated soldier shouldering a heavy crate of hardtack, then narrowly avoided an officer promenading with a young woman, nearly impaling himself on the spoke of the lady's parasol as he did so. He was in the wrong place for a quiet stroll, so he walked briskly through a queue of soldiers waiting patiently to be used as pack mules, then changed direction and headed up a short slope leading to an area that was mercifully free of anyone else.

On the higher ground, he paused. The Union army stretched away for miles in every direction. There was not a scrap of open land as far as he could see. Every square foot was filled with men and the materiel of war. The size of the endeavour of which he found himself a part was staggering. If the numbers Bridges had been given were correct, the Union army numbered some thirty-five thousand men. Jack had been in bigger armies, but it was rare to be given the opportunity to see so many at once.

'Jack? Jack, is that you?'

He heard his name being called and was tempted to ignore it. It would be easy enough to move away, to pretend not to have heard the voice. But he still needed Kearney's dollars, and so he turned on the spot and nodded in greeting.

'Good morning, sir, what a fine day it is.' He managed to summon a smile, even as he spied that Kearney was accompanied by both his daughter and his future son-in-law.

'A fine day indeed.' Kearney greeted him warmly. 'How go the preparations?' He leaned comfortably on his walking stick.

'We're ready, sir,' Jack answered pleasantly, whilst doing his best to ignore the two faces that glared at him from behind Kearney's shoulder.

'Good.' Kearney's expression turned grave. 'I hear the company lost men a few days ago.'

'Yes, sir. First Sergeant O'Connell was killed, as were three other men.'

'A terrible thing. I shall write to their families personally.'

'I'm sure they'd appreciate that, sir.'

Kearney's eyes narrowed a fraction. 'So Ethan tells me the battle will likely be tomorrow?'

'He's quite correct, sir. The enemy will not give up such strategic ground without a fight.'

Kearney nodded as if he had been seeking Jack's confirmation. 'Then we shall not miss out on the spectacle.' He turned to Elizabeth. 'You will get your wish, my dear. Jack agrees that tomorrow is the day. Your preparations will not be wasted.'

'Preparations, sir?' Jack asked warily.

'We shall be here to watch the events as they unfold. Elizabeth has organised a picnic. It will be quite the jolly affair. Half of Washington society plans to be here. Even Senator Ashby has voiced the intention to come along with us.'

'You can't do that.' Jack spoke without thinking.

Kearney frowned. 'I beg your pardon?'

'You cannot do such a thing.' Jack thought of curbing his tongue, but he was committed now.

'Explain yourself?' Kearney was not taking kindly to the Englishman's reaction.

'I have never heard such a ridiculous bloody idea.' Jack gave his master the whole barrel. 'This isn't some sort of entertainment laid on for your amusement.'

'Now listen to me—'

'No, you bloody well listen to me.' Jack cut Kearney short. 'Men will die tomorrow. They'll die screaming and crying with half their damn bodies ripped apart. You want to watch that?'

'I think you are getting ahead of yourself, Jack. Remember why you are here.' Kearney hissed the warning.

Jack shook his head forcefully. 'This has nothing to do with looking after your daft bugger of a son. It's about doing the right thing for the poor bastards who'll suffer when we finally stop pissing around and fight the damn enemy.'

'Jack, please mind your language in front of my daughter.'

'She's likely heard worse.' Jack's temper was firing. He looked at Rowell. 'You tell them. Tell them they are being bloody stupid.'

Rowell's lips curled as he looked at Jack. 'I shall do no such thing.'

'Why the hell not?'

'I'm sure Mr Kearney knows what is best.'

'No, he bloody doesn't. Stop being a damn lickspittle and tell them to keep the hell away.'

'It's not my place to—'

'Oh for God's sake.' Jack stopped Rowell in mid-flow. He looked back at Kearney. 'What if it all goes wrong?'

'What do you mean?' Kearney scowled.

'What if we lose? What happens to you then?'

'I do not think that is a possibility.'

'No? You think the Confederates are going to just take one look at us and bugger off? They'll fight to hold this ground. What if we cannot shift them off it? What if we lose?'

'That is hardly likely.'

Jack shook his head at such blind folly. 'Have you seen an army in retreat? Do you know what it's like when men are fleeing from the battlefield with enemy cavalry chasing them down?' For a moment he was back on the great plain to the south of Solferino, running for his life as rampaging Austrian cavalry cut down the French troops in droves.

He shook off the memory. Kearney was glaring at him. He swallowed with difficulty. His anger had been routed by the darkness.

'I would urge you to reconsider, sir.' He spoke in the flat tones of a man who knew he had lost.

'And I thank you for your advice.' Kearney's tone was glacial. 'But I hardly think we will be in any danger. We shall proceed as planned. I will not have it said that I cowered away in Washington whilst Senator Ashby was here. I shall not give the man such an advantage.'

Jack knew when he was beaten. He did not look at Rowell or Elizabeth. He could not bear to see the triumph in their eyes as his employer humbled him. 'If you will excuse me, I must see to the men.'

'Of course.'

He turned to leave. He would not do so in peace.

'Lieutenant Lark.'

It was Elizabeth who held him back. He thought about just walking on, but with Kearney present, he had no choice but to turn at her command.

'I'm told you have taken a fancy to my maid.'

'I'm sorry?' Jack feigned incomprehension.

'My maid, Rose. You were seen together.'

Jack felt a stirring of anger. 'I walked with her, yes.'

'I do not recommend it.'

He saw the anger burning in Elizabeth's eyes. It sat at odds with her beauty, like a turd placed centrally on a fine white porcelain plate.

'I rather think I shall walk with whoever I choose, ma'am. Now if you'll excuse me.' He made to leave again.

'It will not do, Jack.' This time it was Kearney who detained him.

'Why is that, sir?' Jack held the reins of his temper tight.

'She is a serving girl. You are a Union officer.'

'Temporarily.' Jack could not help snapping.

Kearney took a few steps forward. 'Must I speak plainly?' The words were fired in a hoarse whisper. 'She is an escaped slave, Jack. God alone knows how her former masters treated her. They whipped her; that much is clear to everyone who lays eyes on her. Who knows what other depredations she was subjected to? If that is not enough to make you reconsider, then there is the small matter of her colour.' He paused. 'She is not a suitable companion for a Union officer, especially not one in my employ.'

'I see.' Jack managed to force the words out. They came out as dead as a stillborn child. 'Is that all?'

'Yes.' Kearney stepped back. 'The maid will be sent back to Boston. You will not see her again.'

Jack said nothing. He nodded once, then turned on his heel and left the three of them to stare at his back, as much to hide the expression he knew was plastered across his own face as to avoid seeing the satisfaction on Rowell and Elizabeth's.

He was unconcerned by Kearney's warning. He had no intention of being told what to do. Not by Elizabeth and not even by his employer. He knew his own mind. If anyone tried to get between him and Rose, he would tell them to take a running jump and to hell with the consequences.

Two armies were fighting for the right to live as they thought best. Jack would not do any less for himself.

The evening sky was perfectly clear. It was still humid and muggy, but much of the day's heat had fled with the last of the light. The encampment was quiet now, calm after the day's hiatus. The visitors had left, returning to their temporary accommodation in the local area or making the longer journey back to Washington. The men were left to find what peace they could.

Jack stared up at the sky. There were enough stars there to form an army. The silent battalions stared back at him, serene and untroubled. He liked the stars. They were one of the few constants in his life. Their patterns had changed, the ones he now looked at arranged differently to those he had seen in India or the Crimea, yet they were still his companions.

The moon was bright. Its light cast the nearby woodlands into shadow but filled the open ground with a wondrous pale light. Only the glow of distant campfires spoiled the serenity of the scene. The enemy was close by, their presence casting a pall over the Union encampment. They reminded every Union soldier of what was to come. Two armies had been summoned to a single place. Only one would be allowed to remain.

Jack thought back to his youth. It was Saturday night, a day on which his mother's gin palace would have been busier than usual as the good men, women and children of Whitechapel celebrated the end of the working week and laid down a base of watered-down gin to help them endure another Sabbath. The queue would have stretched outside, the grey-faced customers standing in stoic silence as they waited for a pennyworth or two of liquor with a quart more taken home to see them through to Monday.

The street patterers would have been working the area outside the palace, the air full of ludicrous claims and devious blarney. They were as much entertainment as anything else, but still many in the crowd would part with a few pennies to buy whatever the industrious patterers had found to sell that day.

He wondered what was there now, what building, if any, had been erected on the burned-out husk of the palace. Did the locals miss the place and the mouthy bawd who had taken their pennies with a smile? Did they remember the soldier who had returned to bring such destruction?

A harmonica interrupted Jack's thoughts. Memories were replaced with the sights and sounds of an army encampment the night before battle. The song was 'Yankee Doodle'. It was played slowly and softly, the more usual rousing version replaced by the tone and rhythm of a mournful lament. The sound drifted through the campfires. This was the quiet time, when the stories had been told and the songs had been sung. It was the time for each man to wrestle with his demons and to wonder what the next day would bring.

Jack heard the soft scuffle of someone approaching. The noise annoyed him. He did not want to talk. He wanted to be left alone with his memories, the few that he would dare to release from their cages. There were not many he would allow out. Those he did, he wanted to be able to savour in peace.

He caught sight of a silhouette. It was shorter than most of the men.

'What do you want?' He stopped whoever it was in their tracks. It was the tired, ratty question of a man not wanting to be disturbed.

'Well, that's a fine welcome.' The figure kept walking.

'What the hell are you doing here?' Jack's annoyance fell away. He stepped forward quickly until Rose's face emerged from the darkness.

'I came to see you, although perhaps I should not have taken the trouble,' Rose mocked. 'I can go away if you prefer?'

'No, stay.' Jack felt absurdly pleased. Rose had taken a risk coming to see him.

'How did you get here?'

'I hitched a ride. There's plenty of wagons coming this way.'

'Wasn't it dangerous?'

Rose laughed. 'I made it all the way from Charleston to Massachusetts. I reckon I can get myself a couple a miles down the road.'

Jack could not argue. It reminded him how little he knew about Rose. 'You shouldn't have come. What if they find out?' He could not bring himself to name either of the Kearneys.

'What can they do to me?' Rose pulled a face at the idea. 'They ain't about to whip me. They don't hold with that.'

'Well, that's something good about them.' Jack stood awkwardly in front of her. He wanted to reach out, to pull her into his arms. But Rose was different to any girl he had met before. There was a reserve to her, and a toughness he had not known in any other. 'I thought they were sending you back to Boston?'

'They are. I go back next week. They need me till then.'

'For what?'

'For whatever they want. I don't get to ask.'

'So why did you come here?'

'To give you something.'

Rose took a half-step forward. She was smiling, mocking him again. She saw his awkwardness and hesitation, and it clearly amused her.

Jack was wary. 'What is it?'

'Me.' She whispered the single word and walked into his arms.

Jack lay on the ground and stared up at the stars. Rose was nestled against his side, her head resting on his chest. He let his hand wander to her hair, running the soft curls through his fingers. He wondered if he would look at the stars again the following night. Perhaps Rose was fate's parting gift, a last glimpse of the joy life could hold before his was taken from him.

For tomorrow, all the waiting would be over. It would be time for the much-longed-for battle, the opportunity for force to decide where diplomacy and negotiation had failed.

Tomorrow the Union would fight for its survival, whilst the South would fight for the right to govern itself as it saw fit.

Tomorrow the fates of hundreds of thousands of souls would be changed for ever.

Tomorrow.

Chapter Thirty

Outside Centreville, Virginia, Sunday 21 July 1861

Reveille sounded at two a.m. The men were roused in the darkness, the inky blackness of night wrapping around the encampment like a shroud. It was stiflingly hot and there was not a breath of wind.

Campfires were coaxed back into life. They cast an eerie light on the faces of the men as they packed up the last of their equipment, so that they resembled nothing so much as fairy-tale creatures summoned from the bowels of the earth.

'Leave your haversacks behind.' Jack gave the first of the day's orders. He spoke quietly, moving through the men as they prepared to assemble.

'Why do we have to do that now, sir?' An Irish voice asked the question. It was too dark for Jack to identify who it was.

'You don't want to carry them into battle.'

'And have someone pinch our stuff?'

'They'll be here when you get back.'

'When we get back, he says. Well, that's reassuring now, isn't it, fellas? I just hope that we gets to come back and find some damn maggot has pinched our stuff.'

'Be quiet, O'Dowd.' Jack finally recognised the voice. He had no time for the Irishman's mithering that morning. He had enough on his mind.

The night spent with Rose had complicated things. He had been alone for so long that he was not sure he could remember how to think of another. And he would go into battle hoping to see her again.

He felt anger then. He had not asked for his. He had no need for anyone in his life, the years spent alone the preparation he had needed to become the soldier he had always longed to be. Now he wanted to see her again, and that made him weak. It made him afraid. He finally had a future. The fear of losing it was more than he could bear.

'Get your bloody kit together and form up,' he growled at O'Dowd, who was busy ramming the last of his equipment into his haversack. The man was not alone. Half the company was fumbling in the darkness. Malloy had emptied the contents of his haversack onto the ground in front of him and was now searching frantically through the mess.

'I can't find my fecking cap pouch,' he muttered.

'For God's sake.' Jack crouched down. It was nearly impossible to see. He ran his hand around until it closed on the familiar shape. 'Here.' He thrust it into Malloy's chest. 'Now get your shit together.'

He rose to his feet. The company was struggling to be ready. The men were tired, their fears denying them sleep before the early reveille. Now the darkness was hampering their efforts to gather their equipment. It was an inauspicious start to the day.

'Jack, is that you?'

'Of course it's bloody me.' Jack recognised Robert's silhouette easily enough. 'Are you ready?'

The young lieutenant nodded.

Jack stepped closer and looked him up and down. 'You don't think you need your sword today then?'

'What's that?' Robert's right hand reached across his body, his fingers feeling for a blade that wasn't there. 'Confound it.' There was no need to say anything else, and he turned on his heel and stomped off to find the missing weapon.

Jack shook his head in exasperation. Officers were supposed to set an example. He reached down and patted the hilt of his own sword, just to make sure.

'Come on! Get yourselves together. This is the damn army, not a bloody Sunday school outing.' He strode back into the confusion. He would get the company ready even if he had to dress and arm each man himself.

'I wonder if this is what happens when you fight on the Sabbath,' mused Robert. He was standing with Jack near one of the last campfires left burning. In the distance, the first fingers of light were spreading across the horizon. Dawn was not far off and it would arrive to find the men of the 1st Boston formed up and ready to march.

'Don't be a fool.' The time spent getting the men ready had done little to improve Jack's temper. The hours that had followed had only added to his black mood, the men forced to stand idle whilst they waited for orders to move.

'It does not seem a wise decision to me, that's all.' Robert would not let the matter drop. 'We're both Christian armies. We should respect the Lord's day.'

'Sunday, Monday, Friday, Christ, what does it matter what day of the sodding week it is?' Jack ground his teeth in frustration. He needed a cup of tea badly.

'I'm just pointing out that this is the worst day to have to fight a battle.'

'Well, don't,' Jack snapped. His attention was diverted by the appearance of mounted men trotting along the road near where the troops were formed into a column. He moved towards them quickly, hoping they brought orders that would see the men of the 1st Boston finally get moving.

The riders arrived in a jangle of bridles and tack. Jack recognised one of them easily enough.

'Is that you, Lark?' Scanlon shortened his reins as Jack approached his stirrup.

'Good morning, sir.' Jack peered up at the colonel. He looked much more impressive on horseback than he did on foot. 'Have you got orders for us?'

Scanlon shook his head. 'We're waiting for the First Division to clear from our front. The bloody fools are taking an age. Only when they are clear can we march.' He ran his gaze over the company then glanced back at Jack. 'Look after my boys, Jack. It's going to be a hard day ahead.'

'I will, sir.'

'Good fellow.' Scanlon had no time for more. The other officers were kicking their mounts into motion. 'Good luck, boys! Teach those goddam sechers a lesson,' he called before spurring his own horse forward.

The men watched him go in silence. Their colonel's words were a reminder of why they had been roused long before dawn.

The waiting was over.

The day they had all been anticipating had arrived.

It had been getting steadily brighter for over an hour, the blackness of night turning to the pale greys and inky blues of early morning, before the order finally came to march.

The men could just about make out each other's faces in the pale light as they began to head west, following a cart track through a large expanse of dense wood. It was slow going, the column coming to a halt every few hundred yards. The air was damp, and it was muggy under the trees. It was not yet dawn, but already the men were sweating. Yet the sudorific air did little to dent their spirits. With the dark hours of fear left behind them, they marched along briskly, singing and laughing as they went. The high spirits and songs carried them over the first ten miles, their eagerness for the fight allowing them to deal with the continued delays with good humour.

Jack neither sang nor laughed. He did not stop the men from A Company participating, yet he could not find it in himself to join them. Instead he marched in silence, his foul temper only increasing as he was forced to listen to the men's jocularity.

He marched as a redcoat marched; his world reduced to the dusty track passing beneath his boots. He forced all thoughts from his mind. He did not think of Rose, or of Elizabeth. He did not think of the man he was there to protect or the man whose letters had started him on the journey that had led to this place so many thousands of miles from home. He thought of one thing and one thing alone.

He thought of battle.

His thoughts were interrupted as the air shook with the concussion of a massive blast. The ground vibrated underneath the boots of the marching infantry, who flinched as the explosion seared through the superheated air.

'What the hell was that?' Robert had left his station and had been ambling along with Jack in contented silence. Now he turned a pale face towards his fellow lieutenant.

'A cannon, and a bloody big one at that.' Jack was still wrestling with his black humour. The men had stopped singing as they ground out the miles, something that had improved his temper a little. But he was still in no mood to assuage his companion's fears.

'There's a thirty-pounder in Tyler's division. Must be that, I guess.'

'You're an officer. You don't guess, you know.' Jack delivered the sharp rebuke. 'If it's that big, then I'll bet you a thousand bloody dollars that it was a waste of bloody effort dragging the bloody thing all the way up here.'

'Do you have a thousand dollars, Jack?'

'Maybe I do. And I'd bet every single one of them on that bloody cannon doing as much bloody damage to the Confederate army as a sparrow's fart.'

Robert started to laugh, but he stopped quickly enough as he caught a glimpse of the expression on Jack's face.

The troops emerged from the woods and into the bright sunlight of early morning. After so long in the shade of the trees, the glare left the men blinking. To their front, the ground sloped gently down towards a river. Open fields stretched in all directions, the greenery broken up in places by clumps of woodland and a scattering of houses surrounded by split-rail fences.

The men followed the same cart track they had marched along all morning. There was a ford ahead, and the ground before it was covered with other Union troops, some resting, others forming up ready to march on.

Jack could hear a gentle rumble, like distant thunder. It

came in fits and spurts, the sound building to a crescendo then dying away for a few moments' silence before slowly building back up again.

'Cannon fire?' Robert raised an eyebrow in Jack's direction.

'What else could it be?' Jack could not help the waspish reply. There was nothing urgent in the sound of the distant cannon. It was not the roar of a massed bombardment, the kind that would leave the very earth shaking for miles around. Instead it sounded half-hearted, lazy even, as if the gunners were going through the motions rather than pouring on the fire in desperate haste.

'Is Tyler attacking, then?' Robert risked a second question. 'I confess I cannot tell.'

'If he is, then he's not exactly going for it.' Jack paused and cocked an ear. Much of the cannon fire had died away, so that he could hear the retort of individual guns firing. 'After yesterday, you'd think the man would be attacking hell for leather. Now it sounds to me like he is sitting on his back-side.'

'Maybe the general told him to hold back after yesterday.'

'Or maybe getting his arse handed to him on a platter taught him a bloody lesson.'

Robert shook his head at Jack's peppery judgement. 'Will this mood of yours last all day? I'm not sure I have the stomach to face both the enemy and you.' He paused and looked at Jack warily. 'I thought you would be happier today after your visitor last night.'

'What do you mean?' Jack snapped at the lure.

'I just thought Rose would've left you in a better humour.' Robert could not help teasing his fellow lieutenant.

'Were you spying on us?'

'Of course not.' Robert was genuinely affronted by the suggestion. He snorted. 'I saw her leave you late last night.'

'What's that if it's not bloody spying, then?'

'It was by happenchance. Nothing more.' Robert smiled. 'She's a pretty young lady.'

'You don't disapprove?'

'No, why should I?'

'Your bloody father and your bloody sister do. They warned me off her.'

'I see their words had a lasting effect.' Robert laughed away Jack's angry reply.

'I'm not one for doing what I'm told.' Jack could not maintain the anger. Robert was beaming like the cat that had got the cream. It was infectious.

'I think we've all learned that about you by now. If my father and sister haven't, well, more fool them.' Robert reached out and patted Jack's arm. 'I'm pleased for you, I really am. Rose is a fine girl. I know half the male servants tried it on with her. And I know that none of them got anything but a slap for their trouble.'

Jack could not help grinning at Robert's choice of words. 'She's different.'

'She *is* different, and she's damn pretty if you ignore those marks on her face. Did she tell you how she came by them?'

'She was whipped.'

'I thought as much. I cannot imagine what their lives are like. The slaves, I mean.'

'Well, aren't we fighting so they can all be free?' Jack felt his ill temper shift. He had Robert to thank for it.

'I suppose we are.' Robert looked pleased at the thought. 'Perhaps this does mean something after all.'

'So you're finally working out why you're here. It's about bloody time.'

Robert chuckled at the remark. But it lacked conviction. 'It's not as easy for me as it is for you.' His voice became more serious.

'Why's that?'

'You're here for money. I imagine that makes your choices easier.' He tipped his head back and looked around at the sky. 'I'm not really sure why I'm here.'

Jack opened his mouth to deny Robert's words, but the younger man was lost in his own thoughts, so he held his tongue. There was a hard truth in what Robert had said. Jack wasn't fighting for some lofty ideal, for some notion of setting the enslaved free. He was there simply to get paid. The fact scratched at his conscience. He had hesitated to promise Kearney that his son could be kept safe in the tempest of battle. Yet now he made the vow to himself. He would protect Robert, no matter what it took. It would give meaning to his being there. He reached out and clapped a hand to the younger man's shoulder, and they walked on together as the column wound its way down the sloping ground.

The track they followed improved in quality. It led towards a small church surrounded by a grove of trees. A few locals were out, dressed in their Sunday clothes, as they prepared for that morning's church service. The column came to a halt a few hundred yards from the church. An officer from brigade headquarters directed the troops off the road, then spoke quickly to Captain Rowell.

'Ten minutes' rest!' Rowell relayed the order he had been given.

The men did not need to be told twice. They fell out quickly, most making a dash for a dirty-looking pool. The water was brackish at best, but in the heat, no man would complain. With their canteens filled, they slumped to the ground in the shade of some trees near the church. They were hot, tired, their legs ached and they were already near exhausted. And the day had hardly begun.

'On your feet!' Rowell stirred his men. 'Fall in.'

Jack had been sitting with his back against a tree, eyes closed, savouring a moment's peace. It was cool in the shade. Reluctantly he stood, dusting himself down before bending to pick up his sword and revolver, which he had left on the ground. As he did so, he heard more cannon fire. This time it was no distant rumble. It came from much closer by and was much more intense.

'On your feet.' He echoed Rowell's order. The men obeyed slowly, but they were disinclined to leave the shade of the trees. He buckled on his weapons as he walked. 'Look lively now,' he urged them. 'Form up.'

He walked through the men to the head of the column. Thus far he had avoided conversation with Rowell. But the noise of the cannons meant that he could no longer do so. He was an officer and he would be helping to lead the company into battle. He could not do so if he refused to speak to its commander.

'Sir.' He nodded in greeting as he came to stand in front of Rowell.

'Lieutenant.' Rowell's own greeting was clipped.

'Do we know what is ahead?'

'The Rhode Island regiments are in the van. They must have run into the enemy.'

'Should the enemy be here?' Jack asked. 'I thought we were marching around their flank.'

'They must've seen us and redeployed. We kicked up a fair bit of dust.'

Jack heard the uncertainty in Rowell's voice, but the answer made sense. It would be nearly impossible to hide the movement of thirteen thousand men. If the enemy had seen them, they would now be frantically redeploying to counter the threat. It was time for the Union troops to press on and hit them before the flank was secured.

'Take your place, Lieutenant. Now is not the moment for idle chatter.' Rowell dismissed Jack with icy disdain.

Jack turned and looked at the troops. They were assembling into column with little enough fuss. There was time for him to say what he had to say. He looked back at Rowell, holding his gaze steadily and speaking quietly so that even the nearest men could not overhear them. 'We need to put what has happened behind us, for today at least. The men need us; it's our duty to work together and give them the leadership they deserve.'

'Do not tell me my duty, Lieutenant,' Rowell hissed. 'I fully intend to lead the men this day and I don't need your goddam help. Stay in your station and listen for my orders. Do your job and I shall do mine.'

He stepped away, leaving Jack standing alone. There would be no pact, no ceasefire between the two men. Jack would go into battle knowing that his own company commander hated his guts.

The men marched towards the sounds of battle. They had been on their feet for more than six hours. They were tired and footsore, and they advanced in nervous silence.

Major Bridges led them forward with his aide, Lieutenant Norris, at his side. Both were mounted on sorrel mares, the only officers in the regiment on horseback. The other officers would fight on foot alongside their men.

The sounds of rifle and cannon fire intensified as they splashed through the ford near the church. Not one man doubted that the day's marching was coming to an end.

'Mary mother of God, would you look at those poor bastards,' O'Dowd called out as a haphazard group of figures stumbled up the track towards them. Every one of them was wounded. A couple limped, their trousers soaked in blood. The rest staggered along, their uniforms ripped open or their torsos smothered in gore. One marched behind a mask of blood.

'Good luck, boys.' A man stumbling along by himself called out to A Company as they marched past the battered, bleeding men. 'You whip them sechers good now.'

A steady stream of wounded followed the first group. All wore the shocked expressions of men whose dreams of glory had been shattered in the very opening exchanges of the battle.

'Eyes front.' Jack attempted to divert the troops' attention from the sight, yet every head turned in unison as the company marched past the wounded soldiers, the sight a visceral reminder of what lay ahead.

A group of officers rushed past, dust kicked high by the fast-moving hooves of their horses. Bridges stopped his own horse and looked back over the column. Jack could not help but smile. The regiment's commander looked odd on horseback, his tall frame too big for the small mare. He reminded Jack of a gangly child he had seen being given a pony ride at the Independence Day fair.

Bridges gave the order to march in double time, and the men

forced their tired bodies into the faster pace. The air was filled
with the sound of boots thumping into the sun-baked ground
and the clatter of equipment as the regiment pushed on past the
last of the wounded stragglers. A man to the left rear of the
company collapsed from exhaustion, tripping half a dozen men
in the files behind. He was left behind on the verge of the road
without ceremony.

They pressed on through a scattering of trees, the momentary
shade a blessing that passed too quickly. A brigade courier
waited for them on the far side, the officer, a captain, holding a
piece of paper in his right hand whilst he pointed with his left.

'Deploy right. Form line!'

The men did as they were ordered, breaking off the road
and pounding across a grassy slope. The men from A Company
had furthest to go, as they would form the far right of the line.
Bridges rode at their side. He called no encouragement to the
sweaty, red-faced men in blue who stumbled and staggered
their way into place, but his presence reassured them nonetheless.

'Form here!' he shouted down at Captain Rowell. 'There
are enemy skirmishers across the way. Do nothing until I give
the order.' Once he had given his instructions, he turned his
horse around and trotted back along the regiment.

'Form line.' Rowell's chest was heaving, but he managed to
give the order loudly enough for the men to hear.

The men of A Company turned towards the enemy. To their
left, the 1st Rhode Island Regiment was doing the same, the
two Union regiments forming a two-man-deep battle line
across the face of what appeared to be a Confederate brigade.

Fire came against them almost at once. The enemy skirmishers did not fire in a volley like a regiment formed in line.

Instead they aimed shots as and when they were ready. The withering barrage snickered around the ears of the Union troops, the single shots snapping by with a strange fizzing sound. The range was long, but the enemy knew their trade.

The first man yelled as he was hit. He stood in the files near the middle of the company. Every eye turned to him as he keeled over, falling to the ground without another sound.

The day's dying had begun.

Chapter Thirty-one

⁂

Elizabeth Kearney laughed. She did not mean to. She sat on a seat opposite her father and his companion, Senator Ashby. The buggy they shared had been filled with the serious business of the Senate, the two men using the journey to tackle the pressing matter of what should be done with the freed slaves who would surely soon be looking to the government for aid. It was already stifling in the buggy and the two of them had done their best to add still more hot air.

But it was not affairs of state that amused Elizabeth. She was looking at the photograph that had been taken on Independence Day and she found it impossible not to laugh as she contemplated the expression on Jack's face that Mr Brady had captured for all time. The Englishman looked as if he was trying to hold in an especially significant bout of flatulence, and as soon as Elizabeth had that thought, she could not contain herself.

'Are you quite all right, my dear?' Her father could not help smiling as he heard his daughter burst into spontaneous laughter.

'I am, Father.' Elizabeth hid the photograph under her glove. 'It is a beautiful day, if a little hot, don't you think?'

'Let us hope it is hotter for the Confederates.' Kearney did not press his daughter on what had made her laugh. Senator Ashby was clearly besotted with Elizabeth; the man could not keep his eyes off her. It was exactly as he had planned. Ashby was a man of great influence and Kearney wanted him as an ally. If his daughter's beauty helped smooth the way, then Kearney would not hesitate to use it to his advantage.

The buggy eased to a halt on the crest of a ridge of high ground that was already thick with spectators.

'It looks like half of Washington has contrived to arrive before us.' Kearney glanced around. 'Henson, pull up over near those trees. I am sure those good people will not mind moving for the senator.'

The buggy lurched back into motion. Elizabeth was thrown forward, but she managed to avoid sliding off her seat by grabbing hold of Ashby's knee.

'Excuse me, sir.' She covered her mouth with a gloved hand as if horrified by the lack of propriety. 'I do apologise.'

'No apology needed, ma'am.' Ashby shifted in his seat and reached out a hand to his knee, as if the fleeting touch somehow lingered.

'Thank you, sir.' Elizabeth dipped her head and glanced up at the senator through her eyelashes. She did not have to look at her father to see the approval on his face. She knew the role he expected her to play well enough. It was not the first time.

'You must be worried about your fiancé.' Ashby leaned forward. 'I saw you looking at a daguerreotype just a moment ago. Was that your young man?'

'Yes, sir.' Elizabeth gave the lie easily. The buggy came to a halt and she heard Henson jump down and begin ordering those already situated there to move.

'It will be a testing day for us all.' Ashby spoke earnestly. 'Your fiancé will be in my prayers. May the good Lord keep him safe.'

Elizabeth repaid the comment with her most beaming smile. She did not think Ashby a handsome man. His face was thin, with a pair of beady eyes that darted quickly from side to side so that he looked like a continually alert weasel, a comparison not helped by the wispy salt-and-pepper beard and moustache that framed his small mouth. But despite his appearance, he did manage to exude a certain power, a sureness of his importance in the world and the notion that everyone else knew of it.

'Why, sir, that is most gracious of you.'

'It is my pleasure, ma'am. My absolute pleasure.' Ashby preened as the full weight of Elizabeth's smile was brought to bear on him.

'Sir, we're ready for you now.' Henson, a black man who stood easily over six feet tall, had opened the door of the buggy. The ground Kearney had chosen was now clear.

'Thank you, Henson.' Kearney got stiffly to his feet and the driver took his arm to help him disembark.

'Here, let me help you.' Ashby was quick to hold out a hand to Elizabeth. It made it harder for her to get out of the buggy, but she accepted it nonetheless, even as she was forced to stretch her arm awkwardly.

She did have to admit her father had chosen a splendid spot for them. They were on a hillside not far from Centreville. Flowers covered the ground, and with the scattering of trees the place had a pastoral, woodsy look that was quite enchanting. It did not match her imaginings of a battlefield.

A second buggy pulled up behind theirs, followed by a third.

Elizabeth did not look at them for long. One was filled with supplies for the day, whilst the other bore the servants they had brought with them. Instead, she turned and gazed away to the south and the rolling countryside that stretched for miles.

There was little for her to see. A single column of Union infantry marched along a cart track. Other than a scattering of wagons in one pasture, there was nothing she could see that suggested an impending battle.

'Ma'am. I think you'll be needing this.'

Elizabeth turned and saw Rose holding out a parasol ready to be opened.

'Thank you, Rose.' She took it, immediately opening it and balancing it artily on her shoulder before she was forced to step back quickly as a group of young children ran past in a rush of noisy excitement.

'Will there be anything else, ma'am?' Rose stood ready for instructions.

Elizabeth looked around her. The hillside was busy. Men strolled with their wives, or engaged each other in intense conversation. They were dressed as they would be for any outdoor social occasion, and the bright pastels of the ladies' dresses offered a wonderful mix of colour. The men's formal attire was utterly unsuitable for the heat, and most sported florid, sweaty faces. Moving amongst them all were liveried servants carrying trays filled with wine glasses containing the finest Bordeaux wines, or platters of Bologna sandwiches. Groups of young children intent on play ran about, and their laughter and shrieks added life to the murmur of conversation and the chink of crystal glasses.

'Do you not think this looks just like Mrs Singleton's last excursion to Salem?' she asked Rose.

Rose gave the scene a cursory glance. 'They all look the same to me, ma'am.'

'That was my point. You would not think we had come to see a war.'

'I don't think many people here know what a war is, ma'am.'

Elizabeth looked at the maid sharply, hearing something in her tone. 'What do you mean by that?'

Rose nodded her head in the direction of the ground to the south. 'Over thataways, men are dying.' She gestured around her. 'These people are laughing and drinking and eating like it's just another Sunday trip to the park.'

'What should they be doing?' Elizabeth asked the question without any hint of annoyance in her tone. She was good at hiding her emotions.

'Praying.'

'Praying!' Elizabeth exclaimed, then paused and gave the suggestion some thought. 'I rather think God will be inundated with prayers today.'

'Doesn't mean you shouldn't add one more, ma'am.'

Elizabeth heard the censure in Rose's tone. 'And who would you be praying for today, Rose? For a certain Englishman?'

Rose lifted her chin. 'Yes, ma'am, I'll pray for him. And for your brother and all those poor souls who won't see it through the day.'

'Do you like him? Jack, I mean, not my brother.' Elizabeth watched Rose closely.

'He is different, ma'am. He doesn't much care what people think of him. I like that.'

'And he is handsome; a little battered, of course, but handsome nonetheless.'

Rose said nothing. Whatever she felt about Jack's looks would stay in her own head.

The conversation, such as it had been, was brought to a close by a series of dull thumps from far in the distance. They were not overly loud, but they were enough to silence the hundred conversations on the hillside, and to start a hundred more.

'There!' Elizabeth turned, just as every other spectator did, towards the sound. She raised a gloved hand and pointed to the south, where a thin smear of smoke was drifting on the breeze several miles away from where the spectators watched with expectation. 'They came from over there.'

The dull booms sounded again. This time they were louder, and the crowd cooed as if being treated to a display of fireworks.

A lady dressed in purple silk arrived at Elizabeth's shoulder. She was staring southwards through a pair of gilded opera glasses.

'This is splendid. We shall be in Richmond this time tomorrow.' She lowered her glasses and smiled at Elizabeth. 'What say you to that, my dear?'

'It would be very fine, ma'am. Very fine indeed,' Elizabeth replied carefully. Her facade was firmly in place.

'You're Kearney's girl, are you not?'

'Yes, ma'am.' Elizabeth did not recognise the lady in purple, who had already turned to resume her scrutiny of the fields to the south.

'I thought as much.' The lady took one last look at the fields, then tutted loudly and removed her opera glasses from her face. 'We shall see nothing from here.' She smiled at Elizabeth. 'I knew your mother.'

'I hear she was a fine woman.' Elizabeth batted back the comment without a flicker. There were no cracks in her carapace, at least none that could be exploited by a stranger.

'Of course, you must have been very young when she died.'

'I was two years old, ma'am.'

The lady looked at Elizabeth as if tallying the years. Then she smiled again. It was the coldest smile Elizabeth thought she had ever seen.

'You must visit me in Richmond. We shall not lord it over the poor Southrons, at least not so much.'

'Thank you, ma'am, that is a most generous offer.'

'I shall have one of my footmen leave a card with your father's household when we are all settled.'

Elizabeth had to fight the urge to laugh. She was playing the role of a respectable young woman, just as she always did. She glanced around her. Rose was standing dutifully a yard or two behind her, her eyes averted, her poise just that expected of a maid waiting for her mistress's instructions. The rest of the crowd were engaged in animated conversation as they contemplated the hint of powder smoke, which had nearly drifted away.

She supposed she was not the only one playing her allotted role. Perhaps they were all just actors on some stage. Dutiful daughters acting with propriety. Respectful servants doing everything they were told, then complaining and mocking their masters behind their backs. Knowledgeable gentlemen claiming to understand the events that were about to unfold whilst being little more than know-nothings. Presumptuous old women plotting a social life in a city not yet forced from the secessionists' hands. Even the soldiers were acting quite as they should, marching willingly onto the field of battle even though many would end the day with their lives either taken from them or shattered by the events of the next few hours.

For a moment, the notion sickened her. She wanted to scream, the urge starting deep in her belly and rising with such speed and force that her mouth opened of its own accord ready to let the sound escape.

Hundreds, no thousands, of men and women were playing the roles life had assigned them without questioning why they were doing so. They were all sleepwalking to destruction while their country was about to be torn apart.

'The 1st will advance!'

Jack could only just hear the command from his position behind the company on the far right of the 1st Boston's line. The instruction was reinforced by the regiment's drummers, who beat out the rhythm on their heavy instruments so that no man was in doubt about what was expected.

There was nothing for him to do. Rowell was shouting instructions to the men from his place in the front rank on the extreme right of the line, and he needed no assistance. But at least Jack could see the enemy. They were lined across the brow of the hill to the regiment's front. There were not so many of them, but they had brought forward two cannon that were being readied to fire. The enemy skirmishers had pulled back, leaving the way clear, the open grassland inviting the advance that Major Bridges had just ordered.

The Union men would have to move ahead up the slope directly into the face of the enemy line, and Jack's mouth went dry at the thought. They would be under fire the whole time. Men were about to die.

'Skirmishers! Forward!' Bridges gave the order every soldier in the two flank companies had been waiting for.

'A Company!' Rowell shouted for the men's attention. 'As

skirmishers. On the left file, take intervals! Double quick! March!'

The rapid series of orders threw the company into motion. Everyone knew the drill, and the two flank companies ran forward, moving into a widely dispersed two-man-deep line across the front of the regiment.

Jack watched the men closely as they spread out. They worked in groups of four, with a spacing of twenty to forty paces between each of these comrades-in-battle, as the groups were known, and each man around five paces away from the next. The company was divided into four sections, each commanded by one of the four sergeants, with Jack and Robert taking responsibility for two platoons made up of two sections each. Rowell and the company's new first sergeant stayed in the centre with a small reserve, to act as a rallying point and to deliver fresh cartridges and replacements as needed by the rest of the company. Rowell also had a bugler at his side, the young soldier's job to relay his captain's orders with a series of calls that the men could hear far better than any shouted orders.

'Advance!'

Behind the skirmish line, the rest of the regiment started its advance. Immediately, the rhythm of the drums changed. There was no thought to marching in time. The men shuffled forward, uncertain at first, even the most unimaginative amongst them knowing what they faced. Then the pace picked up, the men increasing speed so that they moved at a brisk rate.

Ahead of the regiment, the skirmishers made their own advance, the men using any cover they could find and carrying their weapons in the way most suited to them. For the first time, Jack drew the sword he had been issued with his officer's uniform. It was no maharajah's talwar, but it felt good in his hand. Without breaking stride, he pulled his revolver from its holster. He would go into battle with the sword in his right hand and his revolver in his left. Deep inside, he detected the stirrings of an old madness, one that had been contained for so long it could barely move. The feel of the sword and the revolver had awakened it from its slumber.

The enemy opened fire.

The range was long, but Jack still heard the crack of Minié bullets as they zipped past. The sound made it clear that this time the 1st Boston faced an enemy armed with something of more modern manufacture than the out-of-date muskets they had encountered at Blackburn Ford.

Immediately the men increased their pace, the snap of the bullets goading them on.

'Steady!' Jack shouted his first order. The line was becoming ragged, the men beginning to move at different speeds. 'Watch your alignment.'

The men checked, heads turning from side to side as each group of comrades-in-battle looked to stay level with the ones next to them.

The enemy cannon opened fire for the first time.

Jack heard the guns quite clearly, one firing just before the other. Then there was a roar like an express train speeding down the line. Two fountains of earth were thrown into the sky, the enemy shot gouging great furrows in the ground ahead of the Union advance. The violent contact with the ground did little to slow the pace of the fast-moving shot, and they skipped back into the air, clearing the heads of the Union troops in one great bound.

'Cheer!' Jack urged the men. The company was silent. He could feel their fear. It was wrapping around them, slowing them down. 'Come on, you bastards! Cheer!'

A few men responded. It was enough, and the rest followed. The men of A Company jeered the enemy then, throwing insults at the Confederate line. The pace returned, hesitation forgotten.

'Forward!' Jack roared the encouragement. He looked to his left. Robert was in his allotted place, following his platoon; his sword was drawn and the steel blade glinted in the morning sunlight. There was nothing Jack could do to protect him during the advance. Robert would have to trust to fate, as would every man.

The enemy fired again. There was time for Jack to track a pencil-thin blur in the air before the two round shot slammed into the regiment.

He heard the screams. The shot had slashed through the line, knocking down men in companies near the centre. He paid them no heed. A Company was unscathed. That was enough.

They pressed on, the angle of the slope pulling at the muscles in their legs. The enemy was getting closer with every stride. From behind the regiment, the Union guns opened fire, their shells tearing through the air well over the heads of the advancing infantry. Jack watched them slam into the enemy line, each one gouging a great gap in the living wall of flesh. He heard the enemy screams.

'Halt!' To his credit, Rowell gave the order clearly. 'Commence firing!'

This was no organised volley. The men had crouched or lain down the moment Rowell called the halt. Now, working in pairs, they opened a harassing fire on the enemy skirmishers that protected the front of their battle line. The man in the front rank fired first. As soon as his shot was away, he began to reload whilst his partner in the rear rank aimed and fired. They would continue to work in tandem, firing and loading in sequence so that one of them was loaded at all times. They were also moving constantly. They had been trained not to remain in the same place as they reloaded, unless they were in cover, and so the loose chain of skirmishers looked to be in perpetual motion as they moved left and right as part of a tightly choreographed routine.

Jack watched the sections in his platoon carefully, looking for men who stayed in place for too long, or for those who moved too far. Ahead, the enemy skirmishers were following an almost identical routine, an indication that both armies had used the same infantry manual in the training of their light troops.

'Remember your drill!' he shouted as he saw men fumble with their cartridges. A man in a section to his front dropped his ramrod, whilst another tried and failed to seat a fresh percussion cap on its nipple.

The enemy fire came constantly, the Confederate skirmishers firing fast. Every few moments Jack would hear the high-pitched squeal as a bullet snapped past him. Then there would be several moments of relative peace before another angry shot buzzed close. Union soldiers were falling. He saw a man in Robert's platoon crumple as a rebel bullet found its mark in his flesh. Another man reeled back out of his own section, his right arm nearly torn from his shoulder. He staggered backwards, his rifle dropping to the ground. Jack reached him quickly, grabbing his good arm then pushing him away towards the rear.

'I'll take him!' His file partner was already lowering his rifle, his body half turned away from the fight.

'Stay where you are.' Jack stopped the man in his tracks.

'Goddam it, Lieutenant. He needs help,' the man pleaded.

'And I need you to bloody fight,' Jack snarled back. He could see the hope fade in the man's eyes as he was denied the chance to slip away.

'Sir—'

'Load your goddam rifle!' Jack reached out, his hand pushing the man back into his position. He glanced over his shoulder. The wounded man was lurching badly from side to side as he started to head for the rear. He made it no more than half a dozen steps before he fell.

The battery of six Union guns was still pouring on the fire in support of the regiment's advance. They pounded the rebel line, every shell smashing a hole in the enemy ranks.

'Keep firing!' Jack shouted at his men. The skirmishers were fighting their own private battle in the ground between the two main battle lines. It was getting harder to see the enemy troops, the smoke from the men's rifles drifting across the skirmish line. It gave the fight an unearthly feel, the feeling of isolation only enhanced by the roar of round shot and shell flying past over their heads.

The men in his platoon obeyed his order. He had no idea if they were hitting the enemy troops, but he kept them at their task. It was vital that they held their ground and kept the enemy skirmishers away from the main line.

'That's the way!' He roared the encouragement even as one of his men fell, a Confederate bullet buried in his brain. His comrades did not pause, carrying on firing as their neighbour died just a few paces away from where they stood.

The 1st Boston were learning what it was to fight.

Chapter Thirty-two

───────◆·❖·◆───────

'Rally on the battalion!'

Jack heard Rowell shout the order moments before the bugler sounded the retire. The skirmishers in the two flank companies had done their job. Now it was time to pull back and rejoin the rest of the regiment.

The men knew what to do. As soon as the bugle call finished, they moved at double time, clearing out of the regiment's path and running back to the right flank. They did so in as good order as possible, the men on the left of the company running hard as they had furthest to go. Once out of the regiment's way, they re-formed into line, retaking their place on the right of the regiment as it moved forward at a steady pace.

'Advance!'

It was time to press forward. Drums near the centre of the regiment beat out the pace of the advance. The rhythm was hypnotic, mesmerising even. The noise filled the ears of the men, the pounding matching the thump of their hearts and drowning out the roar of the breath in their ears.

The regiment's colours led the way, the colour party advancing six paces ahead of the centre of the regiment so that all the men could see them. Sergeants chosen for the honour carried the flags, guarded by the biggest and strongest corporals in the regiment. The colours were bright in the morning sunlight, the vibrant hues standing in stark contrast to the greenery of the fields and the blue of the men's uniforms.

The main enemy line opened fire. They didn't bother with ordered volleys. Instead they poured down the fire as fast as they could, a constant flurry of vicious missiles zipping down the slope and into the advancing troops. The Union soldiers hunched forward, walking into the teeth of the storm, the enemy fire snatching away a man here and there. They were ignored, their comrades callous and unfeeling even as men they had known their whole lives died. All that mattered was the advance, the need to carry on driving onwards.

'Keep moving!' Jack stalked behind A Company. It may have lacked the discipline of a British advance, but the Union troops were sticking to the task. Yet all along the line, men were falling. Many of the enemy bullets went harmlessly over-head, the inexperienced Confederate soldiers firing too high, but enough were finding their mark in the blue-coated ranks and every few paces saw another man crumple to the ground.

The pace of the advance slowed, the troops hesitating. Still the Confederates fired and fired. Men shrieked as they were hit, the cries coming constantly.

'Return fire!'

It was Rowell who gave the order. Jack did not know why he did it. It was a dreadful place to halt. The 1st Boston were halfway up the slope and the regiment was cruelly exposed.

'Aim!'

Jack wanted to scream in frustration. They had to keep going. If they stopped now, no one would be able to get them moving forward again. The rest of the regiment came to a halt as the order to return fire spread along the line.

'Fire!'

The Union soldiers did their best. They lifted their heavy rifles into their shoulders and returned the Confederate fire. Dozens of rebel soldiers were hit as the Minié bullets gored through their line.

But it would never be enough. The rolling fire from the Confederates came without pause, rippling out and striking down man after man from the Union ranks.

Jack saw a soldier on the left of the company take the first, hesitant step back.

'Stand fast!' he bellowed.

More of the men shuffled backwards. They were reloading and still faced the enemy, but they were inching away from the Confederate line.

'Load!' Rowell ran from his place on the right and now took station behind the centre of the company. 'Load, damn you! Load!' His voice was rising in panic. 'Stand fast! You hear me!'

Jack joined him, and the two officers shouted themselves hoarse as they tried to hold the men in place.

A man far on the right of the company turned first. He did not move far, no more than three or four paces, but it would be enough. The men in the files near him caught the movement in the corner of their eye, and they too turned and ran. It was like watching a dam break as the right flank melted away.

'Stand! Stand!' Jack spread his arms wide, holding his sword out to make himself the biggest obstacle possible. He was ignored.

A Company broke. One minute most of the line stood fast,

then they were moving backwards. The Confederates kept firing. More men were struck down even as they turned to run, their deaths adding impetus to the rout. The Confederates cheered then, jeering the Union troops as they turned tail and fled back down the slope, leaving dozens of their number in pathetic heaps on the ground.

Jack stood for a moment longer. The men ran past him, not one looking at him as they scuttled away. Then he was alone; just one man left facing the enemy line.

'Jack! Jack, we need to go!'

Robert had come across the line as it broke. Now he shouted at Jack, urging him to get away.

Jack ignored him. He stared at the enemy line. Their fire had died away. Instead of shooting at the routed Union troops, they were waving their hats and cheering as they celebrated their victory. The sight sickened him, and the failure of the attack stung his pride. The Union men, *his* men, had broken far short of the enemy line. They had not stayed to fight.

He stalked forward, first one pace and then another. He knew that the enemy had spotted him. Some stopped cheering and raised their rifles, aiming at the lone Union officer. Then they fired.

Jack felt the air around him stung by the enemy bullets. He did not flinch as they seared past. Instead he kept walking, closing the range, daring them to strike him down.

'Jack! Jack, come back, you fool!'

Jack heard Robert well enough. Other voices joined his cry. He glanced over his shoulder. The men from the company were turning around, their flight curtailed as they realised that one of their officers was still advancing.

More bullets zipped around him. Most went high, the enemy still shooting poorly. But enough came close enough that he felt the snap in the air as they flew past.

He felt no fear. He kept walking, each step slow and deliberate. He knew what he was doing. The men needed to see him. They needed to see that he did not fear the enemy. They needed an example to be set.

There was a fleeting moment of joy as he stalked forward; a touch of the madness that he knew was not far away. He stared at the enemy line as he walked, daring them to shoot him down. A few tried, but no bullets came close. The cheering had stopped. Not one Confederate soldier now jeered.

Finally satisfied, he turned and walked calmly back down the slope. He did not run, or duck away, even when a few more bullets were sent his way. One spat up a fountain of dirt as it hit the ground not more than an inch from his right boot; another whipped past his ear, so close that he thought for a moment it must have hit him.

'Form line!' he shouted. The tang of the spent powder caught in his throat, the stink lingering in his nostrils. He turned his head and spat out a wad of blackened phlegm, clearing the sour taste from his gullet. He could see A Company ahead. His lone advance had halted their retreat, the men turning to stare at the madness of his actions. Now they milled around at the foot of the slope, every man staring at the foolish Englishman who had gone on when they had turned tail and fled.

It was Major Bridges who halted the rest of the regiment. He rode through the retreating troops, daring the men to ignore him, his shouts preventing the retreat from turning into a rout.

Slowly order began to return to the ranks. They were not far from the ground where they had first formed up. The colours turned first, the sergeants carrying the regiment's pride providing a solid centre for the new line. The men re-formed around them. It was a ragged line, some of the companies hopelessly intertwined, but the retreat had been stopped.

A Company came in last. They had been the first to stop running, and they took their place on the right of the line with some vestige of order and an even smaller amount of regained pride.

Jack followed them, walking in alone. He paid no attention to the looks he sensed directed his way. He did not care what the men thought of him. He just cared that they had seen one man who refused to be cowed by the enemy fire. He had not set the example to prove his own courage. He had done it to show the frightened infantrymen what was possible.

'You're a goddam fool!' Robert left the re-forming ranks and strode towards him, grabbing him by the arms. 'What the hell were you thinking?'

'I was doing my job.' Jack fought the urge to laugh. The foolishness of his actions surged through him. He saw the look on Robert's face and gave up the struggle. He threw back his head and roared with laughter. When he looked at Robert again, the younger man had backed away.

'It's all right.' Jack thrust his revolver back into his holster then took hold of Robert's arm and steered him towards the line. 'I've not lost my wits. I was showing the men what could be done if they stopped being so damned fearful.'

Robert let himself be led. But it did not stop him shaking his head as he considered Jack's folly. 'But why? I mean, this isn't your fight. You're only here because my father is paying you to keep me alive. Yet here you are, trying to win the war by yourself.'

The words stopped Jack in his tracks. Robert was right. It was not his war. He was not there to fight for the Union.

He looked at the men watching him. James Thatcher was there, the surviving twin's face creased with anger. O'Dowd stood on the right of the line, surrounded by his gang of Irish cronies, who refused to leave his side even in battle. Then there were the rest of the now familiar faces; faces that he had first seen all those weeks before in Boston. All were now streaked with powder, their eyes red and sore from the smoke. A few were bloodied, the red bright against their pale skin. He did not know all their stories or even why they were there. Yet he looked at the men in his company and knew why he was with them.

He was there *for* them. He was there for the men.

'Come on.' He grabbed Robert's arm again and pulled him after him. He felt a clarity of mind that he had not experienced for as long as he could remember. He was a soldier on the field of battle. He would do what he had always done. He would fight for his men.

'Here they come!'

Jack was back in his place behind the line, but he saw the enemy almost immediately. They were streaming down the hillside, the counterattack coming hard on the heels of the Union retreat.

'Would you look at those beauties now?' Jack heard O'Dowd mutter the comment as he watched the enemy. It was easy to understand the Irishman's reaction. The troops coming down the hill were wearing a fabulous uniform of blue and white striped trousers, bright red shirts and jaunty red fezzes. 'What the feck do they think they look like?' O'Dowd was scathing.

'Well, at least you can't miss the bastards.' Jack clapped the Irishman on the shoulder.

The enemy were a fine sight, the bright uniforms gaudy against the green of the grass. Their colours led them forward, the Stars and Bars half folded, the lack of wind leaving the flag listless against its pole. As they came on, the Confederate soldiers began to yell. It was a strange sound, feral and unearthly, the mix of yips and yells undulating as they pounded towards the Union line.

'Aim!'

Bridges' voice came clearly. If he was disturbed by the eerie sound the rebel soldiers were making, there was no sign of it in his calm tone.

Rifles were pulled into shoulders. The 1st Boston's line was shorter now, but the regiment still numbered well over eight hundred men. They would greet the enemy rush with a single volley.

'Aim low, boys!' Jack drew his revolver from its holster as he called out to the men. 'Don't waste your powder.'

Bridges held them there. He was watching the enemy.

Rifles wavered, men struggling to hold them still. The enemy pounded down the slope, their line losing formation as they charged. The yell came without pause, the sound washing over the Union troops.

Bridges stood tall in his stirrups. The moment arrived in a rush.

'Fire!'

The regiment fired as one.

'Fix bayonets!'

The order was loud in the moment that followed the single, immense volley. The men obeyed instantly, their training making the action instinctive. Hundreds of clicks filled the air as the men locked the eighteen-inch-long blades in place on the ends of their rifles. It was the moment Colonel Scanlon had trained them for.

'1st Boston!' Bridges' voice was huge. 'Prepare to charge!'

The command was nearly lost in a great wave of sound that came surging over the Union men. Through the powder smoke they could see the Confederate troops advancing. They had lost a lot of men, the Union volley gutting the leading ranks. Still they came on, their wild, devilish cry increasing in intensity as they closed the gap on the soldiers standing in their way.

Jack felt the wild urge to fight. He looked ahead and hefted his weapons in his hands. It was the moment he had half forgotten, the pause before men would fight like animals in a dreadful battle to kill or be killed.

'Charge!'

The Union line cheered then. They went forward in a rush, roaring their defiance, teeth bared in animal snarls.

Jack cared nothing for holding a position. He left his post and ran behind the line so that he reached Robert in the moments before the two armies came together in a wild rush. He saw dozens fall from both sides, the impetus of the charge driving men onto bayonets thrust forward at the last moment. He pushed Robert behind him, then he was fighting. A man with a thick beard came at him, yelling as he thrust his bayonet at Jack's belly. There was time for him to see the man's yellow teeth before he twisted to one side and let the weapon slide past his hip. The bearded rebel's yell turned to a gasp of fear as he missed his target. It ended in a scream of terror as Jack sliced his sabre's leading edge through his eyes.

'Come on!' Jack encouraged the men around him. He held his rage at bay, needing to remain in control for a while longer.

'Stay behind me!' There was time to holler the command to Robert before another man dressed in one of the fabulous red shirts tried to slash his bayonet across Jack's face. It was a wild blow, driven by fear. Jack laughed as he swayed back, letting the steel whisper past his face before ramming his own blade forward and thrusting the sabre's point into the man's heart. He twisted the blade as he drove it home, then pulled back hard, fighting against the suction of the man's body that threatened to rip the weapon from his grip. He stepped forward and shouldered past the man, who had dropped his rifle and now clutched at the terrible hole rent in his breast, a soft sigh the last sound he would ever emit.

The two lines were hopelessly mixed in a vicious, swirling melee. Men from both sides died without even knowing who had struck them down. Jack held his ground, his only thought to screen Robert from the fight and to kill any man that came close.

The enemy's gaudy uniforms made picking them out easy, and he used his sword to batter away a rifle thrust at a defenceless blue-coated soldier's side. The man with the rifle turned in surprise, his eyes widening as Jack raised his revolver. He was still staring in shock when the first bullet took him right between the eyes.

'To me!' Jack called to the men in blue. 'To me!' He rallied them to his side, trying to bring order from chaos. He raised his left arm and gunned down another rebel, the bullet catching the man in the neck.

Men fought towards him. They formed a knot, fighting side by side, their bayonets driven at any of the red-shirted men who came close. Jack checked that Robert was still behind him, then snapped off another shot, narrowly missing a man with a sword whom he presumed was a rebel officer. His next shot killed the man, the bullet striking him full on the temple, his head blown apart. He felt the madness start to take hold and fought against it. It was not time to let the wildness have its head.

'They're running!' A breathless voice shouted in his ear. Jack saw the enemy start to break. He emptied the last barrels of his revolver, cutting down a man as he turned away, the heavy bullet catching him in the pit of his spine so that he fell forward, his body arching in sudden agony.

'Thank God.' Robert breathed the words in relief.

Jack looked at the men huddled around him. James Thatcher's chest heaved with exertion. The sleeves of his uniform were bloodied to the elbow so that he looked more like a slaughterman than a soldier.

'Form line.' Jack shoved his revolver back in its holster, then sucked down a deep draught of the heated air.

The rebels were breaking, but the 1st Boston was in no condition to go back on the offensive. The Union's flank attack had been stalled.

Chapter Thirty-three

---

*E*nemy reinforcements lined the top of the hill. Jack watched them file past the battered regiments that had held against the Union advance. He did not have to count the men in the bright shirts and striped trousers to know that they had suffered badly. The lower slopes were heaped with bodies, showing where the two sides had clashed. Some of the bodies still moved, the men wounded in the bitter melee struggling to find the strength to move away. Others just lay where they were and called for aid, for water, for their mother, or just for a bullet to end their misery. A great many lay completely still, twisted into the grotesque shapes of death.

As Jack watched, the Union gunners fired on the fresh Confederate troops. There were two batteries close to where the 1st Boston had re-formed well out of range of the enemy line, and the artillerymen were laying down well-directed fire, exacting a dreadful toll on the enemy. The infantry might have been unable to shift the Confederates from the crest of the hill, but at least the gunners were playing their part.

Jack gave up watching the enemy troops and turned to look at the men in A Company. Most sat on the ground. Those still with water drained their canteens. A few looked up at him, eyes white against powder-streaked faces. Their expressions were blank.

Robert stood at his side, holding his sword. It was clean, the steel still bright. Jack's own sword was in its scabbard, the blood and gore coating the blade hidden from view.

He heard Bridges before he saw him. The major had dismounted and was picking his way through the tired men under his command, offering what encouragement he could.

'Gentlemen.' The major saw Jack and Robert standing together.

'Sir.' Jack spoke for the two of them.

'The boys did well.' Bridges raised his voice to make sure the men of A Company heard him.

'They did,' Jack agreed with conviction. He did not have to force the praise. The men from Boston had fought hard.

'Hunter is down. Burnside has the division.'

Jack nodded as Bridges gave the news. The command of the division was not his concern. The command of the 1st Boston was.

'You did well too, sir.' He spoke softly. He wanted Bridges alone to hear him.

Bridges looked back at him, then pushed out his lips to bristle his moustache. 'That is good of you to say so, Jack. I confess I did not know what I was doing.' The words were said quietly.

'No. You don't at first.' Jack reached out and held Bridges' upper arm. 'But you did well, truly. You led the men. That's not an easy thing to do.'

Bridges grunted. Jack did not know whether it was in denial or if the words had reached the place he had intended. Either way, he had meant them. Bridges had done all a commander could do.

'You have a talent for this.' Jack let go of the major's arm.

'I hope not, Jack.' Bridges sighed. 'Where is Captain Rowell?'

Jack turned and looked over his shoulder. 'Just there, sir.' Rowell was sitting on the ground, sipping at his canteen.

'I need him to take command of the right wing. Poor Captain Thompson took a bullet to the shoulder and has gone back to the surgeons.'

'I'm sure he will be pleased.' Jack could not hold back the ungenerous remark.

'I am sure he will.' Bridges looked at Robert. 'It means you have the company, Mr Kearney.'

Robert turned at hearing his name. He had been staring at the enemy line. 'What's that you say, Temperance?' He spoke in an off-hand fashion, his attention still elsewhere.

'You are the senior lieutenant, so A Company is yours. Rowell has the right wing.'

Robert stood and stared at Bridges. Then he laughed.

'I'll take that as acceptance.' Bridges' expression did not alter, but he did look at Jack before clapping Robert on the shoulder. 'I must speak to Rowell. Good luck to you both.'

The two lieutenants watched the major walk over to Captain Rowell. They were too far away to hear anything that was said between the two men.

'Will you do it?' Robert plucked at Jack's sleeve as he asked the question.

'No.' Jack knew what Robert wanted. 'But I'll be here, don't you worry.'

'I cannot—'

'Stop it,' Jack interrupted. 'You will command this company.'

'But . . .' Robert's voice trailed off as he saw the look in Jack's eyes. He glanced down at the ground, then sucked in a deep draught of air before he looked back at Jack. 'You'll help me?'

'Of course.' Jack watched Robert closely.

'Oh Lord. I think I'm going to be sick.'

'Well, if you must, do it out of sight of the boys. It won't fill them with confidence if you puke in front of them.' Jack patted Robert on the back, but his attention was on Bridges and Rowell. Their conversation had just ended and Rowell had got to his feet. As the two senior officers passed the lieutenants, Bridges nodded but Rowell did not so much as glance their way. He walked away from his company without looking back.

'Come on.' Jack had kept his hand against Robert's back and now he used it to gently push him forward. 'Let's see to the men. Tell them to take off their bayonets, and I would suggest you have every man load. We won't be left in peace for long.'

Robert nodded, then shuffled forward. The new commander of A Company still looked ready to vomit, but he did what he was told.

'Jack!'

Jack had been sitting on the ground, loading his revolver as swiftly as he could. Now he rose as he heard Robert call his name.

'They're moving forward.' The younger man was standing a few yards away, pointing at the enemy line.

'On your feet!' Jack shouted the order. 'Form line. Look lively now, boys.'

The men were slow to obey. They were tired. The long march followed by the advance up the hill and the fight with the gaudy Confederates had drained their strength. But it was still not yet noon. There was plenty of the day left and the 1st Boston would have to find the will to carry on.

'What the hell are they doing?' Robert was watching the Confederate line as it swept down the hill. 'I thought we were attacking them?'

'Perhaps no one thought to tell them that.' Jack reached out and pulled the younger man around. 'Centre rear, sir.'

'What?'

'You need to take your place. The company commander stands behind the centre of the rear rank. Now come on.' He dragged Robert to one side. Behind them, the two-man-deep line was now nearly fully formed.

Away to the company's left, the rest of the regiment was doing the same, as were the other battered Union regiments in the line. The men who had been committed to the attack on the Confederates' left flank now found themselves on the defensive.

'Hold your fire!' Bridges had remounted. Now he rode along the rear of the regiment. 'Hold your fire!'

Jack got Robert into position, then ran to the right flank of the company. It was only when he reached the end of the line that he looked again at the enemy advance.

Their whole line was sweeping down the hillside. There was little discipline to the ranks, yet they came on quickly, following their red, white and blue colours and giving their strange, unearthly yell.

The Union artillery fired without pause, the gunners knocking huge gaps in the enemy ranks. Yet the gunners could no more stem the tide of the advance than a child could hold back the sea with a wall of sand. Only the massed firepower of the infantry regiments could do that.

But it would have to be timed to perfection. Jack stood on

the right of the line. He did not look at the enemy or pay attention to the rebel yell. He was measuring distances in his mind. The regiment's first volley would have to be held back until the enemy were close. If Bridges gave the order too early, the power of the volley would be wasted. Too late, and the enemy would be on them in a heartbeat.

For a moment, Jack contemplated leaving his post so that he could run over to Bridges. His body jerked into motion of its own accord before he managed to hold it in check. He could not leave Robert as the only officer in charge of the company. He would have to bite his tongue and trust Bridges to judge the right time to fire.

The enemy came on quickly. Dozens fell as the Union gunners fired and fired, yet still the line swarmed forward.

'Aim!'

The Confederates were close enough for individual faces to be picked out of the crowd. Jack could see the hatred in their expressions, the anger in their eyes. He hoped to hell that Bridges' instincts would be good. It was a huge responsibility, the weight of commanding a regiment in battle one of the heaviest burdens a man could carry. For an experienced officer, it was a trial. Major Bridges, like most officers that day, had no experience.

'Fire!'

Bridges gave the order early.

The Union line erupted in an explosion of violence. The heavy bullets fired by the Springfields spat from hundreds of rifles at the same moment. They ripped into the Confederate line, tearing men apart and spreading death with wanton cruelty.

'Load!' Bridges shouted the next order, his voice loud enough to carry over the rebels' yells and screams.

The enemy had been bludgeoned to a halt. They were in disarray, the dead and dying blocking the way forward, the broken, twisted bodies tripping those still trying to move forward. Yet although the Confederate line had been mauled, it had not been shattered. Now those still standing raised their own rifles to their shoulders and fired.

Jack could not help flinching as the storm of bullets stung the air around him. There was a moment of bowel-twisting fear that passed as quickly as the enemy bullets whistled by. Men in every company were hit. Some were killed outright, but most were left alive, great gouges ripped in their flesh or whole limbs ripped from their bodies.

'Close up!' he shouted. It was the same order he had heard on every battlefield he had fought on. The dead and the dying were ignored, their cries and pleas for aid falling on the callous ears of those left fighting.

'Aim! . . . Fire!'

The Union line blasted out a second volley, knocking more men down, bodies crumpling to the ground all along the Confederate line. But enough of the line still stood. Each man fired back as soon as he was loaded, the rolling fire picking at the Union line, snatching away a man here or sending another reeling back there.

'Fire by companies!' Bridges' voice rang out once more.

'Aim!' Robert shouted the command, his first order on the field of battle.

K Company fired first, the first company in the regiment line. As soon as he heard the crash of their volley, the young lieutenant sucked down a deep breath.

'Fire!'

A Company had lost at least a dozen men, but the rest stuck

to their task and obeyed their new commander's order. The volley crashed out crisply, the sound of the individual shots lost in the roar.

The company next to K Company on the left of the line fired moments after A Company. The fire then rippled down the regiment, each company firing in turn, whilst those that had already fired loaded as fast as they could. Each volley cut down men from the Confederate line.

Yet even now the enemy would not break. With the bodies of the fallen kicking and thrashing at their feet, the Confederates stood and returned fire.

'Load!' Robert's order was nearly lost in the now constant roar of rifle fire, but the men knew what was expected of them and they reloaded just as they had been trained.

'Close the ranks!' shouted Jack, then stepped to his left, watching the men closely. He had lost sight of the enemy, the regiment now completely covered in a thick cloud of powder smoke. All the men could do was load and fire as quickly as they were able.

'Aim!' Robert shouted, louder this time, warming to his task. 'Fire!'

Again the company fired. Men died even as they pulled their triggers, the barrage from the enemy line unceasing.

The routine of battle carried on without pause. Soldiers screamed as they were hit. Some staggered away from the line, blood pumping from their wounds. Others just slumped to the ground, their hands plucking at the arms and legs of those still standing as they begged for aid.

'Close up!' Jack dragged a blue-coated body out of the way, ignoring the pitiful screams of a man shot in the groin, then stepped left. 'Aim at the officers!' he yelled. He watched his men as they poured on the fire. O'Dowd was in the thick of it. The Irishman cursed as he reloaded, his mouth spewing forth a foul tirade at the enemy soldiers who refused to break. James Thatcher screamed as he fought, his need to kill insatiable.

The company was like a machine. Men fired and reloaded without pause. Few could see the enemy, a great cloud of foul powder smoke rolling across the line, but they could hear them, their screams and yells a constant undertone to the roar of rifle fire. And the Confederates fired back without pause, the air around the Union soldiers punched repeatedly as bullet after bullet seared through the smoke.

'Keep going!' Jack could only shout encouragement. It was a brutal fight quite unlike any he had ever known. The two sides were slugging it out in a vicious duel of rifle and musket fire. 'Aim low and kill the bastards!'

A man to his left spun around. A bullet had taken him plumb in the centre of his forehead. For a moment he stood there blinking, then he dropped like a stone. Jack hauled his body from the line. There was nothing to be done save endure.

'They're running!'

He did not know who had called out the words. He could no longer see the enemy, but it was immediately obvious that there were no more bullets directed against the Union line.

Not one man cheered.

Jack waited, listening for the order to pursue. None came.

Many of the exhausted men slumped to the ground, their bodies unable to hold them up any longer. Those still with the strength started to tend to the wounded. The rest simply stood and stared into the distance.

The men from Boston had held the line.

Chapter Thirty-four

Elizabeth Kearney sipped at a glass of Bordeaux. It was delicious, and she closed her eyes as she rolled the wine around her mouth and savoured the intense flavour before swallowing. She opened her eyes and gazed across the battlefield. There was more smoke now. The rolling clouds drifted peacefully across the grassy hills like individual patches of early-morning fog. She could smell the faintest taint of rotten egg caught on the breeze. The sound of cannons firing came without pause, but she felt it to be no more threatening than an orchestra's drums as they played an overture to an operetta. So far her first viewing of a battle was proving to be rather dull.

She turned away and strolled slowly back to the patch of shade her father had selected. It was hot even under her parasol, and she was beginning to feel rather dishevelled. She looked for Rose, thinking to ask for a damp cloth to wipe her face, but her maid was busy preparing an early luncheon and so the request would have to wait.

She sighed as she spotted another officer standing with her father and Senator Ashby. There had been a steady procession of enthusiastic young men riding up to the spectators' hillside, each keener than the one before to offer an update on the progress of the battle. She thought about turning to walk in the other direction, but her father had already spotted her and was waving her over to join them.

'My dear, this is Captain Osborne of the 29th New York.' He turned to the officer. 'Captain, please tell my daughter what you just told us.'

'Why, I'd be delighted, sir.' Osborne looked at Elizabeth. His face was flushed and he spoke with gusto. 'Ma'am, we've whipped them on all points. We've taken their batteries. They are retreating as fast as they can and we are after them!'

'That is fine news, Captain.' Elizabeth smiled. 'Thank you for taking the trouble to come all this way to tell us.'

'My pleasure, ma'am.'

'We must not detain you any longer. I am sure you are keen to return to your regiment.' She made sure to smile even more sweetly so that the officer would not hear the tartness in her words.

'Thank you kindly, ma'am.' Captain Osborne did a poor job of hiding his disappointment at being dismissed so quickly. But he did as he was told, nodding a farewell to Kearney then moving away towards his horse.

'You are cruel, Elizabeth.' Her father slipped to her side and offered the gentle criticism quietly so that Ashby would not hear it.

'Do you believe what he said?' Elizabeth ignored her father's remark.

'Do you not?'

'It's just the same nonsense as before.' Her attention was taken by a disturbance a few hundred yards away. Spectators were moving quickly away from one side of the hillside. She stood on tiptoes and craned her neck to see if that would allow her to make out what was causing such a reaction. 'What's happening over there?' she asked her father. 'I cannot see.' When he did not reply, she turned to look at him and saw that the colour had drained from his face. 'What is it?'

'It is the price we are paying for whipping the enemy.' Her father muttered the comment under his breath before turning to face her, grasping her arms firmly. 'I think it is time you left, Elizabeth. Henson can drive you back in the servants' buggy.'

Elizabeth shook off her father's grip and took several steps towards the commotion. A family moved away from in front of her, and she finally got her first glimpse of what had caused her father's face to turn the colour of ash.

A straggling line of soldiers were making their way slowly up the hillside. They looked nothing like the men she had seen marching from Washington. Their uniforms were filthy, but it was not their poor turnout that grabbed her attention and caused many of her fellow spectators to turn tail and run.

Every man was wounded. Some had limbs bound with bandages made from torn shirts, or else had stuffed neckerchiefs or torn havelocks into the tears in their flesh. A good many simply staunched the bleeding with their hands. They lurched and staggered towards the spectators, clearly exhausted, some tottering along alone, others supported by another man whose wounds were less severe.

'We must help them.' Elizabeth's reaction was immediate. She turned to her father. 'What can we do?'

Kearney was watching the men closely. 'The poor devils.' He turned to Senator Ashby. 'We must do what we can.'

Ashby's face was cast into a neutral expression. 'Of course.

I shall go to the general. There will be surgeons at his headquarters.'

'These men need aid now.' Kearney shot back the reply.

'What can we do? We have no talent for doctoring. You stay and supervise things here if you will. I shall go for assistance.' Ashby spoke firmly.

Elizabeth tried not to let any emotion show on her face as she watched the exchange. Ashby's tone might have been unaltered, but there was no doubting his keenness to be away.

'Very well.' Kearney did not waste breath arguing. 'Tell them we need wagons for the wounded.'

'I will not fail.' Ashby delivered the line with gusto, as if he were a great hero being dispatched on a quest.

Elizabeth turned away from him in disgust. The wounded men were closer now. She could see the strain on their faces, the pain and fear writ large in their expressions. She looked down at the glass she still held in her hand. The wine was the colour of blood.

'Ma'am?' Rose arrived unbidden at her side. She snatched the glass from Elizabeth's hand then tossed it to the ground. 'We must help these men.'

Elizabeth lowered her parasol and threw it aside. 'Do not presume to tell me what to do. Of course we will help them. Senator Ashby is going for assistance. You must give the men food and drink. Use our blankets too, tear them if you need to.'

'You can help too, ma'am. Go to the buggy and get your cloak and shawl. We can tear those into strips and use them as dressings.'

'Are you telling me what to do?' Elizabeth could not help being startled by Rose's tone.

'Yes, ma'am, yes I am.'

'Do not forget your place.'

'Oh hush now, missy. We don't have time for your airs and graces. And take off those fine gloves of yours. You won't want them getting all messed up.' Rose snapped out her instructions. 'Go on!' She pointed to the buggy.

Elizabeth was moving away before she knew what she was doing. It was a shock to see the change in her maid. Rose had never been obsequious, but not once had she ever revealed anything of this fierce young woman, the one who had just told Elizabeth in no uncertain terms what was to be done.

She had to move to one side as a mother ran past carrying a crying child, a grizzling toddler following in her wake. The sound of cannon fire was louder now, the guns surely closer than they had been before.

The first buggy raced away. She glanced at its occupants and saw the grey-haired lady in the fine purple dress who had been so keen to plan for life in Richmond. Delight at the thought of lording it over the Southrons had been replaced by fear.

'The men will prevail.' Her father had come to walk at her side. 'The fighting will be hard, but we shall be victorious.'

Elizabeth looked back at the soldiers with the broken bodies. She had no words to express what she felt.

Jack and Robert stood together watching a regiment march past their position. The men in the neat ranks looked wonderfully clean, their uniforms dusty but lacking the stains of powder and blood.

'Who the hell is that?' Robert found the energy to ask the question. 'Heintzelman's brigade?'

'No idea,' Jack answered honestly. He wanted to spit to

scour the taste of powder from his mouth, but his canteen was long since drained dry and he could not summon enough moisture.

'They look mighty fine.'

'As did we a few hours ago.' Jack turned away from the fresh troops and looked at the hill that he had been staring at for the past few hours. The slopes were no longer the pristine grassland they had been that morning. Artillery rounds had churned up great patches of mud so that it looked like an angry god had ripped and torn at the very fabric of the earth.

Then there were the bodies. Most lay in heaps, the grotesque piles showing where a line had stood and fought. A few were in smaller groups, broken by a fast-moving round shot or well-aimed shell. A rare few lay alone, the lonely corpses pathetic against the great heaps of the dead. Amongst them was all manner of abandoned equipment, the fields strewn with the detritus of combat, from broken rifles and muskets to forgotten ramrods and dropped ammunition pouches, swirling around them all the torn paper from a thousand opened cartridges.

The last of the reinforcements filed past the battered ranks of the 1st Boston. They went straight into the attack, their officers sending forward a skirmish line whilst the rest of the regiment advanced in formation behind them. Jack did not envy the Confederate troops who would have to stand against men fresh and ready for the fight.

'We did our bit, didn't we, Lieutenant?' a familiar Irish voice called across to Jack.

'We did that, O'Dowd. We did that.' Jack gave up watching the attack and turned his attention to his men. They still stood in line, just about managing to find the strength to stay on their feet. He didn't have to look at their hollow-eyed stares to know they were done in.

'Johnny Reb fought hard, didn't he just?' O'Dowd shook his head as he remembered the fight. 'But we licked 'em, we licked 'em good.'

'We certainly did.' Jack reached out and held O'Dowd's upper arm. 'You think you've got the strength to go find some water?'

The Irishman returned his stare for a good few seconds before he replied. 'I reckon I could.'

'I'm sure we would all appreciate it. Take a couple of others with you.'

O'Dowd nodded, then turned to organise a party. Jack had set them a hard task. Good water was as hard to find on a battlefield as mercy.

'I should've thought of that.' Robert sighed as he made the remark.

'It doesn't matter.' Jack looked at him closely. The young man had changed. Underneath the layer of dirt and sweat, he had grown up. 'You did well. Back then.'

'I did?' Robert raised an eyebrow.

'You did. The men fought at your command.'

'I just shouted some words.'

'You did your job. That's all any of us can do.' Jack caught Robert's eye and held it. 'It was bravely done.'

Robert pressed his lips tight together until they showed white. He said nothing, but turned to watch the fresh Union regiment as they drove home their assault on the Confederate troops on the hill.

The enemy forces did not stand. There was a brief flurry of rifle fire, then silence.

'Well, that's just fine.' Robert found his voice. 'We couldn't shift them, but now those dunderheads from New York wander up and they skedaddle as soon as look at them.'

'It was about time the stubborn bastards realised they were beat.' Jack was quite happy to see the enemy retreat. He was even happier that others would finish the attack. The Confederates had fought much harder than anyone would have believed possible. The men from Boston had done their bit, and had paid a high price to drain the enemy's will to stand and fight. But now, finally, the Union was winning the day. The South would lose, the Union would be preserved and they could all go home.

It was still before noon, but the day was almost won.

'Who the hell are they?' O'Dowd took a deep draught from his canteen then handed it to Jack.

'Sherman's brigade, or at least that's what the major said.' Jack drank a good slug of water. It tasted more like horse piss, but he was too thirsty to care. There had been a brief officers' meeting. Bridges had little information to share, but he had known that the men commanded by Colonel Sherman would be arriving to join the position the 1st Boston had held for the past hour.

'You sure they ain't the damn sechers?' O'Dowd looked askance at the grey-uniformed men forming to the regiment's right. He was one of the few in the company on his feet. The rest lounged or slumped on the ground, sharing what little water O'Dowd and his mates had been able to find.

'They're ours. And they've fought hard by the looks of them.' Jack could not fail to notice the state of the new arrivals. The soldiers looked just as dishevelled as the men from Boston.

'I fecking doubt that.' O'Dowd spat, then looked away from the men in grey. He tapped Jack on the shoulder. 'Major's coming.'

'Get the men on their feet.' Bridges sounded as weary as Jack felt.

'We moving?' Jack could not resist the question.

'In a while.'

'But sir!' It was O'Dowd. 'Now that ain't fair. We've done our bit. I reckon we earned the right to let someone else finish the fecking sechers.'

Bridges clasped his hands behind his back. 'We have done our bit, that much is true, O'Dowd. But the general has need of us and so we shall do as we are ordered.' He answered calmly, treating O'Dowd's complaint with the fullest respect.

'But sir—'

'That's enough, O'Dowd,' Jack interrupted. He could see Bridges was exhausted. He nodded once, then addressed the company. 'You heard the major. On your feet, boys. Look alive-o.' He turned back to Bridges. 'We'll be ready, sir.'

Bridges bristled his moustache. 'Thank you, Lieutenant.' He sounded oddly formal. 'We will form the right of the line. Sherman's men will form on our left, then Porter's brigade to the left of them.'

'Very well.' Jack looked for Robert. The company's commander was still sitting on the ground, his head hanging between his legs.

'Is he all right?' Bridges saw the direction of Jack's gaze.

'Yes, sir. He'll be fine.'

'You're still looking out for him, then?' A trace of amusement crept into Bridges' voice.

Jack found a thin-lipped smile. 'Of course.'

'You are a good fellow, Jack. I am heartily glad you are on our side.' Bridges paused to study the tired men of A Company. 'One last push and the day will be ours.'

Jack glanced at his men as they gritted their teeth and prepared to get on with it. He was saved from finding a reassuring reply by the sound of a group of horsemen riding hard. A posse of officers trotted into view, led by a man wearing more than his fair share of gold braid. He was a big man, with wide shoulders, a square jaw and a fine goatee and moustache.

'That's McDowell!' One of Jack's men identified the general. Jack was intrigued to see the man who commanded the army that day. Time would tell if he was looking at a hero or a villain. It would only be after the battle that some sense of the day would be made; only then would the watching country be able to judge if McDowell would go into the history books as one of America's finest generals, or one of its failures.

'Victory! Victory! The day is ours!' McDowell was shouting the words over and over. He did not linger, instead riding along the rear of the slowly forming line that was made up of the battered remains of three entire brigades.

The men were near the point of exhaustion but they still cheered as their general rode past. They heard McDowell's call of victory and it fed some vitality back into their tired limbs.

There would be one more advance. One more push to victory.

Chapter Thirty-five

'Forward!'

The line shuffled into motion. Jack marched behind them, where both lieutenants should be, and watched Robert as he advanced on the right of the line. He was starting to look like an officer; the change from wastrel to leader was nearly complete.

He glanced across to where Rowell marched in the position of the lieutenant colonel. Bridges had chosen to stay in the major's position on the left of the regiment. As second in command, there was little for Rowell to do. Bridges commanded the regiment, and the captains, or those now standing in their stead, commanded the companies. Rowell would not be called upon unless Bridges fell. If that should happen, he would assume command of the entire regiment. The thought made Jack shudder.

The regiment pressed on, just one of many in the advance. No skirmishers had been ordered forward this time; all the companies were needed in the main battle. They marched up the hill they had fought over for so long, the ground still littered with the rebel dead and soon-to-be-dead. As they crested the summit, they were given a glorious view over the rest of the battlefield. Ahead, the ground sloped gently down towards a stream before rising again. Another, slightly higher hill blocked the way ahead. It was dotted with trees, but was mainly just open grassland, the slope not steep until it neared the summit.

A turnpike wound its way along the bottom of the slope under the gaze of a cottage surrounded by split-rail fencing about one hundred yards above the road. A second, far grander, white-painted clapboard house stood near the summit of the hill. On another day it would have been a peaceful scene, a lovely example of rolling Virginia grassland. But not that day, for the grassland was swarming with troops.

Jack looked at the enemy, who stood in a large mass around the cottage overlooking the turnpike. He divided the group into quarters, then made a rough tally of their numbers. He reckoned there were around six to seven hundred. It was a strong force, but one vastly outnumbered by the three Union brigades now advancing down the slope towards them.

He looked beyond the enemy infantry. There were no more troops on the hillside or on the plateau at its top, and no sign of any artillery. It appeared that McDowell's confidence was well founded. Once they had pushed aside the small rebel force near the turnpike, the enemy flank would finally be forced open.

The enemy formed line, spreading themselves along the split-rail fencing around the cottage and facing the Union horde coming down the slope towards them. Jack could only admire their bravery. It was no small thing to stand when a vastly superior force was coming towards you. Some commanders would order a retreat, refusing to sacrifice their men in a futile fight where there was only one possible outcome. It was the pragmatic thing to do, but the Confederate force showed no sign of moving.

To Jack's mind, that meant two things: either their commander was a belligerent fool, with more fire in his belly than sense in his head, or else they were making a stand for a reason. And that reason could only be that they were buying time. He scanned the far hillside. He saw nothing but open grassland. If the enemy were hoping that reinforcements would arrive, there was no sign of them.

The enemy line opened fire. The range was long and there were thousands of men bearing down on the single Confederate unit. Barely a single shot came towards the men of A Company, the air around them wonderfully still. The Union brigades pressed on. The enemy kept firing, taking a man here and a man there, but they were like children flinging pebbles at the advancing tide.

'Halt!' Jack heard Bridges shout the command, then Rowell echo it. He saw Robert turn and slip through the line, taking position behind it as they prepared to fire. There was time for him to flash Jack a flicker of a smile before he turned and sucked down a deep draught of air.

'Ready!' Bridges' voice rang out. It was echoed all along the Union line by the other regimental commanders.

The men stilled. Hands gripped tight around rifles that had been reloaded for this moment.

'Aim!'

The Springfields were pulled into the shoulder. Thousands of rifles were brought to bear on the Confederate line.

'Fire!'

The roar was like nothing Jack had ever heard. The entire

Union line fired within moments of one another. When the explosion of sound had died away, there was a moment of almost complete silence.

'Advance!'

The Union line plunged through the cloud of powder smoke the single volley had created. Their heavy bullets had done dreadful damage, killing and maiming Confederate soldiers. Against such fearsome firepower, the enemy commander had no choice, and already his troops were pulling back, leaving behind the splintered and broken fence and the bodies of the men who had paid the price for delaying the Union advance.

A couple of Jack's men laughed as they charged forward. Their dander was up, confidence and success lending them strength.

'They're beat, sir! Johnny Reb won't stop us much longer.' Malloy turned to shout the comment at Robert as he retook his place on the right of the company.

'We have them now, boys!' Robert shouted encouragement. 'We sure have them now.'

The Union line pressed on. The enemy regiment they had mauled was streaming up the far slope, heading towards the larger house near the crest. The rest of the hill was still empty. There was no one there to prevent the Union brigades from taking the high ground.

The enemy's flank would be turned and McDowell would have his victory.

The Union line halted on the turnpike. There was no sense of urgency. Instead, the order to pause was passed down the line by a relay of couriers. The men sank gratefully to the ground. There was no sign of any water, but at least they could rest.

'What the hell are they playing at?' Jack had stomped over to join Robert.

'What do you mean?' Robert was leaning against a fence post.

'I mean, what are we waiting here for? We need to push on. Surely whoever is in charge can see that.' Jack took off his kepi and wiped the sweat from his face. He stank, the aroma rising from his body pungent enough to be smelled even over the stink of the powder deeply ingrained in his uniform.

'I wouldn't trust those hoopleheads to know what is to be done,' Robert replied. 'And speaking of hoopleheads, here comes the good captain.'

Jack turned and straightened his spine as he saw Rowell approaching. 'What's the hold-up, sir?'

'The enemy is running, Lieutenant.' Rowell came to stand in front of Jack then lifted his kepi so that he could slick down his sweat-dampened hair. 'The general has ordered us to hold our ground until he knows what is left of the Confederate force.'

'That is madness!' Jack was tired, hot and irritable. 'Has Bridges challenged the orders?'

'He has just left for brigade.'

'Thank God for that. At least someone has some bloody sense.' Jack felt the frustration burn.

'You know, the general might just know what he is about.' Rowell took the chance to nettle Jack. 'You look at everyone and see a fool.'

'Then perhaps they should stop acting so bloody foolishly.' Jack snapped at the lure, but before he could take it further, there was a loud blast of artillery fire. 'Jesus Christ.' He could not hold back the blasphemy.

'Where the hell has that come from?' Robert pushed himself upright and looked around anxiously.

'Over there, on the left.' Jack had spotted the telltale smudge of powder smoke. It came from the brow of the hill the men should have been marching up.

'Ours or theirs?' Robert raised a hand to shelter his eyes from the sun.

'Theirs!' Jack shook his head at the question. He turned to Rowell. 'We need to get off our bloody arses.'

'Our orders are to stay here.'

'Damn the bloody orders.' Jack pointed at the hill on the far side of the turnpike. 'We should take the high ground at least; surely even you can see that.'

'Don't be so damn impertinent.'

'Oh for God's sake. Take your head out of your arse for a bloody second. You're in charge with Bridges away. You can give us the bloody order. We need to move.'

'Do not tell me my job,' Rowell snarled.

'Then give the damn order.'

'Our orders are to stay here.'

'Look, this isn't about you and me. This is about doing what has to be done.' Jack took a step towards Rowell. 'That hill is defended by the damn Confederates. We need to shift them off it before they get there in numbers.'

'Our orders, Lieutenant, are to hold our ground.'

'Jesus Christ.' Jack grimaced at Rowell's refusal to listen. 'At least send someone after Bridges. Or let me take the company forward. Let me find out what's up there.'

'And how many men will be killed if you do that?' Rowell hissed. 'I will not allow my men to die to satisfy your damn ambition.'

'Ambition! It's not bloody ambition.' Jack thrust his face closer to Rowell's. 'It's about doing what has to be done.'

'But men will die.' Rowell spoke fiercely. 'I would be ordering them to their deaths.'

Jack heard the feeling behind the words. He could see the weight on Rowell's shoulders as if it were a physical thing. 'You're in command. You have to give the order.'

Rowell said nothing.

'I'll give the bloody order then.' Jack could see that indecision was paralysing Rowell. 'On my head be it.'

'No.' Rowell took a deep breath. The loathing returned to his eyes. 'I will not allow you to steal my authority.' He stepped back. 'We will hold our ground.'

The decision was made. The regiment was not going anywhere.

'Lieutenant! Sir!'

Jack was sitting on the verge of the turnpike when one of the men called out to him. The confrontation with Rowell had drained the last of his energy. He had had enough of fighting authority. He reminded himself of why he was there. He was doing it for money, nothing more.

'What?' He snapped the question at the soldier calling for his attention.

'Artillery on the move, sir.'

Jack sighed, then forced himself to his feet. His back was hurting like a bastard. 'Where?'

'There, sir!' The soldier was pointing towards where Jack believed the enemy to be.

He saw what had sparked the man's interest. An entire battery of Union artillery was trundling forward. And they were doing so without any support.

'What the hell are they doing?' Jack stood and stared. 'Robert!'

The two men watched as the artillery battery carried on up the slope. It was quite alone. The Union infantry could do nothing. They stood on the turnpike and watched as the gunners whipped their horses hard, forcing them to drag the heavy guns up the hillside.

Jack ground his teeth in frustration. Artillery had no business leading the advance. Their role on the battlefield was to support the infantry, not to try to win the affair all by themselves. He felt exhaustion seep into his bones. It was brutally hot and sweaty, and his thirst was terrible. Next to him, Robert was leaning on the split-rail fence, his head hanging down; sweat dripped from his forehead into the dusty soil at the edge of the turnpike.

The artillery battery was coming under fire, great fountains of earth gouged from the ground all around it. Its commander was a brave man. Even with Confederate round shot chewing up the grassland, he still ordered his men to deploy. As the 1st Boston watched on, the battery unlimbered, the gunners working fast. It did not take long for the teams of horses to ride away, leaving the cannons and their crews by themselves, and now without the means to move.

'Would you look at that?' Robert breathed. Then the battery opened fire.

The sound of the guns echoed down the hillside. They were firing at the house near the summit of the hill. The gunners knew their business, and the first volley riddled the building, smashing into the wooden timbers.

'At last!' Robert kept up his commentary. Jack turned to see that one of the infantry regiments waiting on the turnpike had been ordered to advance.

He watched them go. He did not envy them their task. The

men ran forward at the double, yet the slope slowed them and they ground forward with excruciating slowness. Jack chafed at standing idle, but at least someone somewhere had finally seen sense and ordered the foot soldiers to support the battery of guns.

'That's the 11th New York.' Robert was pointing at the men labouring up the slope. 'Look at them go!'

Watching the men from New York, Jack thought he could well be on a European battlefield. They were dressed as Zouaves, the same elaborate uniform that was worn by many of the regiments on both sides. Not for the first time, he wondered at the sanity of the army's generals. The lack of a common uniform was adding to the confusion on the battlefield, something that could only lead to disaster. But he had to admit that with their baggy trousers in a gaudy red, the men looked a fine sight as they advanced behind their colours. Yet they marched alone, the other men in the Union brigades staying where they were.

'This is fucking stupid.' Jack moved forward so that he stood next to Robert at the rail. His hands gripped the top spar, the wood coarse under his fingertips.

Robert was leaning forward, turning his head back and forth. 'Why is no one else moving?'

'Because someone has fucked up.' Jack did not mince his words.

The New Yorkers reached the guns. They stopped, then poured a thunderous volley at a target Jack could not see.

'What are they fucking shooting at? Angels?' Jack spat out his frustration. The New Yorkers were firing uphill. He doubted their volley had done anything more than frighten any birds foolish enough to still be loitering around the battlefield.

'Oh my.'

Robert spoke so softly that for a moment his words didn't register. When they finally did, Jack glanced up to see what had caused such a reaction. One moment the crest of the hill had been empty, the only troops on show the gunners and the regiment of gaudy New Yorkers. The next it was filled with thousands of Confederate troops.

They stretched for hundreds of yards in both directions. There were so many that Jack did not bother to try to count them, but he could see three separate colour parties, which surely meant there were at least that many regiments.

'Where the devil did they all come from?' Robert was staring at the enemy.

'Fuck alone knows.' Jack bit back the anger. The 1st Boston had fought hard that day and lost many men. Like fools, they had thought their work was done, the hard fighting they had endured clearing the way for other troops to take the enemy in the flank. Now the truth was revealed. Somehow the Confederates had found enough men to block the Union advance, men who would now have to be shifted if McDowell was to have his victory.

The enemy on the hill opened fire as one, each regiment pouring down a volley into the Zouaves. It ripped into their ranks, knocking men down like skittles at a fair. The New Yorkers held their ground. With stubborn bravery they returned fire, blasting out another volley at the men on the higher ground. It was a courageous display, but they were horribly outnumbered. Another Confederate volley seared into their ranks, and men fell all along the line.

Jack lost sight of the enemy. Powder smoke billowed down the hillside, hiding much of the fighting from view. Yet there was no hiding the sound of gunfire that rippled out constantly, the men from both sides pouring on the fire.

'What's happening?' Robert was watching the fight at Jack's side.

'We're losing this battle. That's what's happening.' Jack fought the urge to spit.

The New Yorkers were streaming back down the slope. Jack did not have to wait long to see what had driven them from the field. Enemy cavalry burst out from the smoke, charging after the badly mauled regiment of Zouaves, the men on the big horses cutting down any stragglers.

The sound of drums and fifes sounded far to Jack's left. Another Union regiment stirred into motion, emerging from the turnpike and heading up the slope well to the left of the route taken by the Zouaves. Like the Zouaves they marched forward in line, their colours flying proudly at their centre. Like the Zouaves they advanced alone.

'Where the hell is Bridges?' Jack turned and searched the ground behind the turnpike. He saw nothing but empty grassland. There were no couriers come to order the 1st Boston to join the advance, nor was there any sign of Bridges returning from brigade headquarters.

The fresh Union regiment made its way up the hillside. Mercifully the Confederate cavalry had withdrawn, yet the regiment still advanced against the entire enemy force, which had now realigned its ranks to face them.

Once again volleys of muskets and rifles roared out. Jack did not have to watch to see which side got the better of the exchange.

Another regiment moved forward. Men dressed in fine dark-blue uniforms started up the hill, following their colours into battle. Already the other regiment was pulling back, its ranks decimated by the Confederate volleys.

Jack turned his head away, unwilling to watch the slaughter. The slope was littered with bodies now. Hundreds of men had fallen. Most lay in great clumps, the high-tide mark of each regiment's advance denoted by a line of the fallen.

'We're feeding a monster.' Robert's eyes were wide with horror.

Jack had no words left. Smoke billowed across the battle-field, but it did only so much to screen the carnage. The Union regiments were being sent piecemeal to the slaughter, one juicy morsel after another. All the Confederates had to do was hold their ground and fight each one in turn.

A swathe of smoke twisted past the Union guns that had started the advance. Jack saw another blue-coated regiment coming towards the valiant gunners, who were still firing at the enemy line despite so many of their number now being stretched out on the ground.

'For God's sake, shoot the bastards!' he called out in a futile gesture as the regiment advanced from the southern flank of the hill.

'They're ours!' Robert was appalled at Jack's urgings.

'They're fucking not.' Jack already knew what was about to happen. Amidst the smoke and carnage, the Union gunners had no idea who the blue-coated regiment were. But only one side would come from that direction. 'They're the damn enemy.'

'No.' Robert shook his head forcefully enough to fling droplets of sweat. 'They can't be. They must be ours.'

Jack did not have to reply. The gunners had allowed the blue-coated regiment to get dreadfully close. Now they halted and raised their rifles.

'Oh, sweet mother of God.'

There was time for Robert to blaspheme, then the blue-coated regiment blasted out a single volley. It cut down the surviving gunners in droves. Their guns fell silent.

The action stirred another Union regiment into motion. The regiment to the left of the 1st Boston moved forward, the drummers beating out the rhythm of the march. The men, grim-faced and pale, obeyed without question, advancing stoically into the maelstrom ahead.

'They must know.' Robert breathed the words just loudly enough for Jack to hear.

'They must know what?' Jack felt sick to the stomach. The Union generals were gifting the enemy a victory when they should have had no chance of one. The whole Union line should have marched as one and swamped the Confederate troops with bullets before driving them from the field. Instead, men were dying in their hundreds as regiments were sent forward alone.

'They must know what's going to happen.' Robert turned to look at Jack, the horror writ large on his face. 'They don't stand a chance. They'll be cut down just like the others.'

Jack had no answer. The regiment moved forward at the double, heading towards the battery, determined to retake the Union guns. The enemy saw them coming and deployed into line, facing down the slope.

The Union men came on in fine style. Their colours led them, the red, white and blue bright against the grey smoke into which they marched. They did not hesitate even as the enemy opened fire, the volley slashing through the advancing ranks. Ignoring the fallen, they plunged into the smoke, their brave display hidden from the horrified spectators still on the turnpike.

The roar of a massed volley told of the Union regiment starting to fight. For Jack and the rest of the 1st Boston, there was little to see of the struggle going on just a few hundred yards away from where they stood in impotent silence. Rare glimpses through the powder smoke revealed the blue-coated Union regiment standing its ground, the men in its ranks loading and firing, their raw courage holding them in place.

'They're running!' Robert spotted the enemy first. A great rabble of men emerged from the clouds of smoke, their ranks broken, and ran back up the slope, leaving their dead and dying behind.

Not one man in the 1st Boston cheered the sight. Already another Confederate regiment was moving down the slope. They came at a run, charging towards the courageous Union soldiers who had fought so hard to retake the guns. Even from a distance, the men from Boston could hear the dreadful, unearthly yell coming from the charging Confederates as they tore down the slope and threw themselves into the rolling cloud of smoke around the guns, and into the Union regiment that had no choice but to stand and fight.

'Sir! Major Bridges!' One of Jack's men sang out as he spotted the return of their commander.

Jack was moving immediately, forcing his tired legs into a run. He was not alone; half the regiment's officers were racing to greet Bridges, desperate to know what fate they all faced.

Bridges dismounted, then strode towards the hastily assembled group. His expression was grim.

'Captain Rowell.' He addressed himself to the man who had taken command of the regiment in his absence. 'What is happening here?' The question was asked calmly enough, Bridges' tone clipped and businesslike.

'We have held our ground.' Rowell stood straight as he gave his report. 'As ordered.'

'What is happening ahead?' There was no trace of censure in Bridges' reply.

'It's a struggle. The Confederates hold the high ground. They are giving the rest of the division a hard fight.'

'Do they hold?'

'They do.'

'I see.' Bridges gnawed on his moustache. 'So it's a hard fight, you say?'

'It's a fucking slaughter.' Jack had had his fill of Rowell's dry delivery. Bridges needed the truth. 'The rest of the division is going up that bloody slope one regiment at a fucking time. The enemy can deal with them piecemeal and we are getting our bloody arses handed to us on a fucking plate.' He fought the anger that seethed in his belly. The futility of what was happening sickened him to the core.

Bridges looked at him for several seconds, betraying nothing. Finally he nodded, then turned to address the rest of his officers. 'Get the boys on their feet.'

'Where are we going?' It was Rowell who asked the question.

But Jack already knew the answer. He had known it the moment Bridges had returned. 'We're going up that hill, Captain Rowell.' He spoke formally, hiding his emotions.

Bridges grunted. 'Lieutenant Lark is correct. We have orders to take the hill.'

'By ourselves?' Rowell sounded appalled.

'Yes, Captain Rowell. Now fall the men in.' Bridges' tone remained mild, even as he gave the news that would condemn hundreds of his men to death.

It was the turn of the 1st Boston to advance.

Chapter Thirty-six

———◆———

'1st Boston!'

Hundreds of men heard the command that prepared them for the next order. As one they stiffened their backs, hundreds of hearts thumping in hundreds of chests.

'1st Boston, forward!'

The drums rattled into life, echoing the order and leaving no doubt what the regiment was being ordered to do. The line took the first pace forward, the men finally leaving the turnpike where they had waited whilst others fought and died just a short distance away.

It was now their turn.

Jack wiped the sweat from his face. He walked behind the line, his tired legs protesting at being forced back into use. He marched into the first cloud of lingering powder smoke, the familiar stink of rotten egg sticking in his gullet. The sickness he had felt still twisted deep in his gut. Once he had gone into battle fighting against the madness that took him so completely that he would drive into the bitterest, darkest moments without fear. Now he marched to what could be his last fight trying not to void his guts.

Like every man advancing up that bloodstained hillside, he knew what was to come. They had stood by and watched as every regiment the Union had sent forward was gutted, the stubborn Confederate soldiers refusing to yield their ground. Now the men from Boston had fixed their bayonets and were marching up the same ground, to the same beat of the drum and with the same glorious colours leading the way. Despite all they had seen, they plunged willingly into the drifting powder smoke and took the fight to the enemy.

Jack looked at the men to his front. Around half the number that had started the day were left on their feet. Dozens had died, or else been struck by the enemy's bullets and taken from the fight by their wounds. Yet still the men obeyed the order that would send many more of them to their deaths.

O'Dowd was still there. The tall Irishman marched in the rightmost file, his uniform bearing at least half a dozen rents or tears from where bullets had cut through the cloth. Still he marched on, his rifle held across his front, his knuckles showing white from where they clutched the barrel with a vice-like grip. He advanced in silence, his quick mouth hushed by fear.

The surviving Thatcher twin was in the centre of the front rank, his face twisted with barely contained hatred. He had not spoken a word of conversation that day, but every man had heard him cursing the enemy as he loaded and fired over and over again, his rage still bright no matter how many men he killed.

Robert marched in the captain's place on the front right of the company. He had drawn his sword, yet now balanced the weapon against his shoulder as if unable to bear its weight. To Jack's eyes, the face under the thick crust of dirt had changed. He was no longer a callow youth. There was steeliness where once there had been little more than a sarcastic sneer. There was also a similarity to another man, one that had been so noticeably lacking before. Amidst the powder smoke, Jack caught a glimpse of Robert's elder brother. A second member of the Kearney family had found his place on the battlefield.

Together they advanced up that fateful hill. Jack thought they must all be fools, to march so willingly into the bowels of hell. He wondered why not one man turned and ran. It would be the sane thing to do and he knew he would not stop anyone who made one last dash for salvation. Yet they all stayed in their long ranks, placing one foot after another, advancing alongside their mates without hesitation.

He forced the breath into his lungs and drew his weapons. It was almost time.

The air was choked with smoke. The 1st Boston ploughed on, every step taking them closer to the enemy they knew was waiting for them. It lurked in the distance like a monster from a nightmare. Every man in a blue coat who marched up that slope felt its presence, the knowledge of what was to come a burden to be carried by the tired bodies as they advanced.

'Forward!' It was Robert who encouraged the men now. Even as they slipped on spilt blood, or stumbled as they stepped over a corpse, he kept them moving, his voice carrying an authority that had been found amidst the violence and the horror.

The enemy opened fire. Men fell all along the line. Most just crumpled, their deaths no more dramatic than a child lying down to sleep. A few staggered back, arms spread wide, their despairing cries the last sound they would ever utter. However they died, their bodies were left where they fell.

'Close the ranks!' Jack shouted the bitter phrase. It was the litany of battle and he would repeat it a dozen more times in the next few minutes as the enemy fire tore the Union line apart.

The 1st Boston absorbed the casualties and advanced. Relentless. Silent. Marching into the meat grinder without pause.

Jack felt the familiar beast stir in his gut. Fear was forgotten. It was nearly time to let the wildness have its head. To forget who he was and why he was there and just fight.

'Come on!' he shouted then. The words released something deep in his gut. 'Come on!'

The line pressed forward. They were moving faster now, something unspoken urging them to increase the pace. Another enemy volley seared through their ranks. Dozens fell, bodies shattered by the fast-moving bullets. Those still standing barely registered their passing.

The regiment burst through a cloud of smoke. The enemy was to their front, no more than fifty yards away.

'Halt!'

As the line staggered to a stop, the orders came quickly. The men lifted heavy rifles into tired, bruised shoulders, then squinted down the barrels at the faces of the enemy that were close enough to see in the clearest detail.

'Fire!'

The volley blasted out. It gored the enemy line, striking men from their feet, the heavy bullets working a dreadful destruction at such close range.

'Load!' Bridges bellowed the order. His horse had been killed and now he stood with the colour party at the centre of the regiment.

The enemy returned fire.

Jack could no longer stand still. He prowled along the rear rank, his head always turned to face the enemy, stalking the ground like a caged animal. He cared nothing for the enemy bullets that buzzed past.

'Close the ranks!' he shouted, his voice harsh and without compromise. Men shuffled to their left even as they reloaded, stepping around the bodies of their friends. They worked fast, skinning knuckles on the bayonets fixed to the barrels of their rifles, sticking to their task even as friends and neighbours bled and died at their feet. They were fighting like veterans, standing and taking their casualties without flinching, their only thought to ram down another cartridge then fire at the enemy.

Another volley tore into the regiment. Everything was noise and confusion. Men screamed as they died. Others roared insults at the enemy, or simply cursed as they reloaded as fast as they could. Some just wept as their own flesh was twisted and torn by enemy bullets.

Jack saw one of the regiment's colours fall, the sergeant carrying it shot in the gut. It was picked up almost immediately by one of the colour guard, the brave corporal dying almost instantly as a bullet took him right between the eyes.

'Fire by companies!'

Jack could barely hear Bridges shouting the command over the dreadful clamour of battle. Through the smoke he glimpsed the major standing calmly beside the Stars and Stripes, his hands clasped behind his back. He had yet to draw a weapon.

'A Company!' Robert had moved behind the line and now took up the task of ordering the company to fire. 'Aim! . . . Fire!'

The men could no longer see the enemy, the powder smoke locking them inside a dreadful cloud. Yet still they poured on the fire, refusing to yield the ground they had taken.

'Load!' Robert bellowed the next command in the sequence. But the men would be given no time to obey as a new sound pierced the chaotic din of battle. It was the same unearthly yell they had heard earlier. It meant only one thing.

The enemy was charging.

There was time for the men to look up, to pause in their frantic reloading. Then the enemy burst from the smoke, a thousand faces twisted with rage screaming the dreadful rebel yell at the battered, bleeding Union line.

Jack saw them coming. He moved fast, covering the ground in great loping strides until he stood next to Robert.

'Charge!' he bellowed.

Other officers shouted the same order and the Union line surged forward, the remains of the ten companies throwing themselves at the enemy.

'Come on!' Jack shouted to Robert, then ran after his men, releasing the demons that lived deep inside him.

The two forces came together in a rush. Almost immediately the lines broke up, the men fighting and killing in a vicious swirling melee. Jack saw the soldiers in the files to his front charge into the enemy line. Two fell almost immediately, their bodies torn by rebel bayonets, creating a gap in what now passed for the Union line.

A Confederate with a thick, bushy brown beard rushed through the gap. He lunged at Jack with his bayonet. The momentum of his charge made the action clumsy, and Jack skipped past the blade without breaking stride. A moment later and the man fell, his throat slashed open by the edge of Jack's sabre.

'Stay close!' Jack checked that Robert had heard him, then raised his revolver. There was no time to pick a target, and he just pulled the trigger, firing into the mass of bodies rushing past.

A bowie knife slashed at his face. He twisted away, the blade whispering past his chin by no more than an inch. He glimpsed the man who had tried to kill him and fired without pausing. The bullet hit the man in the right eye, shattering his skull and showering those behind him with gore.

The fight swirled around him. The Confederates had charged, but the 1st Boston had stood their ground. The two lines were now hopelessly intermixed and the melee surged and twisted as men fought and killed.

A boy with a thin covering of wispy hair on his cheeks tried to bayonet Jack in the side. Jack battered the rifle away with his sabre, then lifted his revolver and shot the boy down. He fired again a moment later, taking another man in the side of his head so that he dropped like a stone without ever knowing who had killed him. He led Robert through the gap his bullets had created, then chopped hard with his sabre, bludgeoning a rebel to the ground with the finesse of a butcher and ramming down with the point, spearing the man through the chest.

He saw O'Dowd to his front. The Irishman was screaming like a maniac. As Jack watched, O'Dowd bayoneted a rebel soldier in the heart, his demented cries the last sound the South-erner would ever hear. A moment later and O'Dowd's shrieks of anger turned to a terrified yell of agony as a Confederate soldier drove a machete into his throat.

Jack whirled on the spot. A Confederate wearing a straw wide-awake hat came at him, his rifle lifted ready to fire. Jack snapped off his last shot, the bullet hitting the rebel in the gut moments before he would have gunned the Englishman down where he stood.

'Hold them! Hold them!' he roared at the men. He had no idea how many were left, or how many had died. He dared them to stand, to hold their ground a moment longer.

A Confederate officer emerged from the press of bodies. Men were hanging back now, the initial rush replaced by a slow, bitter struggle. 'Kill them Yankee sons of bitches!' he roared at his men, then he lunged at Jack, his straight sword driving at Jack's balls.

Jack saw the blow coming. He battered it aside, his own sword moving quicker than the eye could track. There was time to see the flash of terror in the officer's eyes before Jack backhanded his sword and smashed it into the man's skull. The blade chopped deep then bounced off bone, ripping the skin so that blood rushed to smother the officer's face in a grotesque mask.

Somehow the man still stood. He brought his sword back, cutting it at Jack's side. There was no force behind the blow and Jack swatted it away with disdain. He laughed then, mocking and cruel in the face of the enemy officer's death. Then he lunged with his notched and bloodstained blade, driving it through the man's throat.

'Come on!' He dared the nearest Southerners to face him. He feared no man. 'Fight, you mealy-mouthed bastards!' He stepped forward, sneering his challenge. 'Come on and fight! You hear me! Come on!'

The men nearest him backed away, not one of them willing to face the scarred Union officer with gore splattered across his uniform. The first turned and ran. Within moments the rest had followed. The survivors from the 1st Boston stood and stared as they fled, their expressions displaying the horror of the fight and the shock at having survived.

Jack watched the enemy go, then turned his back on their broken ranks. The rage that had sustained him fled in the span of a single heartbeat. It was time to return some sort of order to the regiment's battered ranks. The men had fought far past the point of exhaustion. They were bloodied and their faces were set grim, yet somehow they had held. Now they had to re-form and someone had to decide what the hell they should do next.

He looked back down the hillside, his gaze lingering on the dead and the dying, a dreadful reminder of the price that had been paid to get halfway up the benighted slope. Then he glanced to the rear. If he hoped to see fresh men coming to reinforce the decimated regiment, he was to be disappointed. He saw nothing save the corpses and the broken bodies of the wounded.

'Jack! Jack!' Robert was shouting his name. The lieutenant had tailed behind him through the fight, and now he plucked at Jack's sleeve.

From somewhere Jack summoned the strength to turn to see what was needed. Robert was pointing up the slope, his arm shaking. Jack looked at the brow of the hill. The broken regiment had cleared away. Instead of their ragged and terrified ranks, he found himself staring at a line of Confederate reinforcements. And there were thousands of them.

He looked at them and saw defeat. McDowell's plans were done. Somehow the enemy had found more men to plug the gaps torn in their flank. They could only have come from the Shenandoah Valley. The troops facing Jack's tired and battered regiment were not supposed to be there, but their presence meant only one thing.

The Union had just lost its first battle.

'Form line!' Jack's voice cracked as he shouted. His mouth was parched and his throat felt half closed. From somewhere he found enough moisture to repeat the order. 'Form line!'

His instruction was echoed almost immediately by the handful of officers still on their feet. He looked down the line. Bridges had been hit in the arm, the sleeve of his uniform coat ripped and torn just above the elbow. Standing with his left hand clasped to the wound, he repeated Jack's order, his mouth working furiously to give it enough force to be heard by every man still standing.

The men obeyed. They were exhausted, their strength long since spent, yet somehow they formed something that at least resembled a line and faced the enemy that outnumbered them by dozens to their every one.

'Load!' Bridges took his mauled regiment in hand, his voice just as calm as it had been all those hours before when he had ordered them to load for the first time.

'Take cartridges and caps from the dead if you need them.' Jack gave the advice as he stalked along the front of the company. He looked every man in the eye, holding their gaze as they started to reload their rifles one last time.

He turned to Robert. 'Take your place behind the line. When it breaks, run like fun.' He hissed the words, speaking quickly and urgently in a tone that only Robert could hear.

Robert stared back at him. For a moment, Jack thought he would argue. Then he took one glance at the bodies of the fallen that littered the ground all around the ragged Union line and nodded. He moved away immediately, doing as he was told without a word.

'Aim!' Bridges gave the order.

Jack forced himself into the front rank, watching as the enemy line advanced steadily down the slope. Their ranks were ordered. Their faces and uniforms were clean. These were men who had spent the day being transported by railroad, and they were fresh to the battle. Their ranks had not been gutted by enemy fire and their weapons were not fouled by a dozen or more firings. He knew they would be looking at the filthy creatures standing to their front with disdain.

'Fire!' Bridges shouted the order.

The men from Boston flung a defiant volley into the face of the enemy advance. They had learned to fire low and the storm of bullets cut into the Confederate line, killing men all along its length. Their introduction to battle was brutal.

'Load!' Bridges gave the order out of habit.

The men let their rifle butts drop to the ground. Hands reached to pouches for fresh cartridges that not one man expected to fire.

The enemy line had halted. They were no more than fifty or sixty yards away, close enough for the Union troops to hear the Confederate officers shout for their men to aim. Then they fired.

Jack heard men scream as they were hit. For one dreadful, bowel-wrenching moment, the air was filled with the snap and crack of hundreds of bullets tearing past. Then there was nothing but the inhuman shrieks of the men with freshly broken bodies.

He had turned his head away from the enemy volley. Every muscle in his body had tensed, the expectation of being hit so strong that his legs had nearly buckled as the bullets tore past. Then it was over. He raised his head and roared in defiance as he realised he was still whole. The Union line stood, but great gaps had been ripped along its length. Men died at the feet of those left standing, their anguished cries filling the ears of soldiers still trying to reload.

'Load!' Jack shouted the encouragement. 'One more volley!' He strode along what was left of the company's line. 'We stand and we fight.'

He looked for Bridges. The major was still on his feet, but the regiment's Irish colour had fallen, the corporal who had been holding it aloft, one of the last survivors of the colour guard, now lying dead at Bridges' feet.

It was the man Jack had half forgotten who picked it up. He had lost sight of Rowell when the line advanced up the hill. In the chaos of the fight, he had not spared the captain a thought. Yet now Rowell raised the flag high, showing it to the men who refused to break.

It was a fine display, a moment's courage that would almost certainly be rewarded with death. A dozen men had carried the flag that day. All had been shot down. Yet now Rowell, hateful, spiteful Rowell, moved it from side to side to stir the colour in the still air. The green silk rippled around its staff as he forced it to life. It reminded the men who they were, displaying their pride for all to see.

'Aim!' Bridges gave the order.

Any man still able obeyed, lifting their rifles to their shoulders one last time. It was a futile gesture. What was left of the regiment stood no chance of stopping the enemy advance. Yet the men from Boston held their ground, refusing to break, flaunting their desperate courage so that the troops coming against them would remember this moment for all time.

'Fire!'

It was no crisp volley. It rippled out, each man firing when he could. It crashed into the enemy line, nearly every bullet striking a man down.

'Stand your ground!' Jack lifted his chin and glared at the

enemy. They had been hit hard by the volley, but they held fast. Around him, some of his men started to reload, the action now so deeply ingrained that they did so despite not one officer shouting the order. Most, though, just stared at the Confederate line. Waiting.

Jack heard a Confederate officer shout at his men to aim. The Southerners' line seemed to make a quarter-turn to the right as the troops raised their rifles.

'For the love of God.' An Irishman to Jack's left muttered the prayer.

Then the enemy line fired once more.

Jack shouted then. It was an incoherent roar, and it lasted as long as the enemy volley.

The bullets whipped through the Union line. Men died in droves. Some still stood, but the cohesion of the line was gone. The praying Irishman to Jack's left was dead, his head smashed by a well-aimed bullet. All the regiment's colours were down, Rowell and the other men carrying the flags drawing the fire of dozens of Confederates.

Jack looked for Robert. To his relief, the lieutenant was still standing, even though the men in the files to his front had all been downed. Bridges was still alive too, the major already moving forward to pick up the fallen national flag.

There was time for one last glance at the Confederate line, then Jack was moving. There was nothing left to be done.

It was time to run.

Chapter Thirty-seven

'**P**ull back!' Bridges gave his last order. 'Pull back!'

Jack moved through what was left of the front rank. The regiment had stood their ground when others would have broken, but now the time for defiance was past.

'Pull back! Stay together.' He repeated Bridges' order. 'Pull back.'

The men did not turn tail and run. Instead they faced the enemy and walked backwards, retreating with some vestige of order. Jack watched them go, then moved fast, weaving through the men until he reached Robert.

'Come on, time to go.' He reached out and took the young lieutenant by the arm.

'We can't!' Robert shook off Jack's grip. 'Rowell is hit.'

Jack looked over his shoulder towards the remains of the colour party. A sergeant from B Company had retrieved the state flag. Bridges had ripped the Stars and Stripes from its pole and was bent down, the flag bundled awkwardly under his damaged arm as he tried to drag Rowell's body down the slope.

'Shit!' Jack spat the word. 'You want to help that bastard?'

'We have to.' Robert shoved his sword back in its scabbard,

then grabbed Jack by both forearms. 'He's still my sister's intended.'

Jack saw the resolve in Robert's expression. He was tempted to knock the younger man down just to spare them the ordeal. Robert must have seen the thought in his gaze and glared back at him, defiant and determined, even as the men pulled back leaving them exposed and alone.

'For God's sake.' Jack put his own weapons away. 'Come on then, you fool.' He forced his body into motion, his flesh as reluctant as his mind. He did not wait to see if Robert followed.

'Bridges!' He hollered for attention as he ran towards the major. They were in front of the men now, the remains of the regiment moving slowly back down the slope. The enemy were walking forward, but the regiment's defiant volleys had dented their enthusiasm and they advanced slowly, many stopping to help the wounded. 'Bridges!'

Finally the major looked up. 'Go back, you fools!' he shouted. He had managed to drag Rowell from underneath the fallen Irish colour, but he was struggling to move him more than a few inches with every tug.

'Shut up!' Jack skidded to a halt and looked down at Rowell. He had been hit in the gut. Blood smothered the lower half of his body, his blue tunic turned black. It was a horrible wound, a man killer. 'Leave him.' Jack straightened up, then took a pace backwards. He reached out to grab Bridges by the shoulder. 'He's going to die.'

Bridges looked at him, his eyes narrowed. 'You go.' He bent down and pushed his hand under Rowell's shoulder, moving him another half-foot.

Jack couldn't watch. He turned away and busied himself tearing the Irish colour from its pole. The green silk was smothered with Rowell's blood, and a dozen tears and rents in the fabric told of the bullets that had cut through the flag that day. Yet it was no rag to be discarded and Jack stuffed it inside his jacket before turning back to see that Bridges had managed to progress no more than two or three yards.

'For the love of God.' Robert muttered under his breath as he looked in horror at Rowell's wound. Yet the gruesome sight did not deter him, and he took Rowell under the other shoulder then nodded to Bridges. 'Let's go.'

Together the two men started to drag Rowell back. Neither looked at the snail trail of blood left on the crushed grass. Jack did not move. He had seen enough wounds to know that Rowell would die. It was inevitable.

Then Rowell screamed. The sound escaped his lips then died away quickly as he fought against the pain. He looked up at Jack. His eyes were bright in a face encrusted with the dirt of battle. Blood was smeared across one cheek.

'Don't you dare leave me here, you son of a bitch,' he hissed, his face contorted as the pain took hold. 'Don't you dare leave me.'

Jack saw the rabid fear in the captain's eyes. It transported him to another battlefield, to another moment when he had watched a man facing the oblivion of death without hope of survival. That man had begged for mercy, his final words a desperate plea to be spared hours of agony. Jack had delivered it, killing Sergeant Thomas Kearney of Le Douzième Régiment Étranger with his own blade. Now a man he had come to despise faced the same fate, yet begged for his life. Jack would not do him the same kindness as he had done for his friend.

'Get out of the fucking way,' he growled, then shouldered Bridges aside, nearly knocking him from his feet. He bent low, scooping Rowell up like a father picking up a child. Pain flared white-hot as his back took the strain, then he was moving, lumbering clumsily down the slope with the captain held in his arms.

Rowell was heavy. His right hand clutched at Jack's shoulder, fingers digging in like claws. Jack could hear the breath rasping from the other man's lungs, the gasps washing across his face. He focused on the pain. Every step was agony, his back on fire and his legs straining to hold him upright. He could feel Rowell's blood hot against his hands and he could taste it in every mouthful of air that he dragged into his tortured lungs.

Behind came the yips and yells of the rebel advance. The sound was louder now, the enemy moving across the plateau where they had bludgeoned the Union advance to a bloody halt.

'Go left!' It was Bridges. The major was staggering along at Jack's side, his left hand reaching out every few steps to steady Jack as he tottered on. His right arm hung useless at his side, the regiment's flag still clutched under his armpit. Robert trailed in their wake, the young officer watching the enemy troops behind them.

Jack glanced to his right, where more enemy troops were advancing. Some were stopping to snap off a shot, but most just came on at a steady pace, their officers urging them forward so that they could take the Union men in the flank. A quick glance to the left showed still more enemy reinforcements swarming across the southern reaches of the plateau. The regiment was nearly surrounded, the enemy line advancing on every front and swallowing up any men in their way.

'Shit.' It was more a gasp than a word. Still he angled left, moving away from the closest threat. He heard the familiar whip-crack in the air as Confederate sharpshooters maintained a constant withering fire. He kept his legs moving, forcing strength into his aching muscles, keeping up the pace.

Rowell was silent in his arms. Jack had no idea if he was still alive, but he had no intention of stopping to find out. His only thought was to keep moving and to keep Robert with him. He would not stop. Not for anything.

He was moving steadily, and already the remains of the regiment were a good hundred yards away. The pace of their retreat was slowing, the men looking around for orders. None came, and so they hesitated, the knot of beaten, frightened men stumbling to a halt.

'Go on!' Bridges saw what Jack had seen. He gave Jack one last steadying push, then turned to head towards the regiment. 'Get him away.'

Jack glanced at Bridges as he walked away. The major's face was dreadfully pale, his lips pressed together and eyes narrowed as the pain of the wound to his arm fought for control of his mind. Yet Jack also saw the determination in his expression.

He was still looking at Bridges when the sharpshooter's bullet hit the major in the temple, driving through skull and brain before exploding from the other side in a gory eruption of blood and bone. Bridges dropped like a stone. He was dead before he hit the ground.

Jack staggered, his momentum carrying him on. Somehow he brought his body to a halt and twisted awkwardly on the spot. Bridges lay face down on the grass. Jack forced his legs to hold him in place, his awkward burden nearly toppling him over. He looked across to the remains of the regiment. The men had stopped moving altogether and were huddled together, leaderless as they faced thousands of fresh Confederate forces.

Robert was staring at Bridges' body. He had not moved since the major had fallen.

'Grab the bloody colours and come on!' Jack shouted, then staggered onwards. His spine shrieked in pain, but he mastered the agony and started to move back down the slope. It was time to get away. He was not there to lead the men. He was there to keep Robert safe.

No one would blame him for carrying a wounded officer from the field of battle, and once Robert was safely delivered back to his father, Jack would get paid. With money in his pocket, he would be able to leave the war far behind and forget the bloodstained hillside where he had abandoned a group of beaten and bloodied soldiers to their fate.

He stumbled and nearly lost his footing. It was enough to stir Rowell, and he cried out, his body shuddering in Jack's arms.

'Shit!' For the second time, Jack lumbered to a halt. 'You have to take him,' he hissed at Robert.

'What?' Robert had been trailing after Jack, the Stars and Stripes carried like fouled laundry.

'Take him!' Jack lurched towards him, pushing Rowell's body against the younger man's chest.

'I can't!' Robert backed away from the bloody bundle in Jack's arms.

'You fucking have to!'

'I'm not strong enough.'

'Then dump the bastard on the ground. I don't care what the fuck you do as long as you get the hell away.'

Robert recoiled from the venom in Jack's voice. 'The men need someone to lead them.' He lifted his chin in defiance and spoke firmly. 'You take him; you're stronger than me. I'll see to the men.'

'They need me, not you.' Jack stopped Robert in his tracks. 'They need a fucking leader, not a boy who'll piss in his fucking breeches.' He took another step towards Robert. 'Now take him and fuck off.'

'The men—'

'Shut your fucking mouth.' Jack pushed Rowell's unconscious body into Robert's gut, not caring that he smeared blood across the other man's tunic. 'Take him, goddam your fucking eyes.'

Robert nearly buckled under the weight, but Jack managed to get Rowell's body into the younger man's arms. He wrapped Rowell in the Stars and Stripes as best he could, then he stepped back and looked at Robert. 'Now fuck off!' He roared the instruction with such force that spittle was flung onto the young lieutenant's cheeks.

Robert staggered under Rowell's weight. For a second he held Jack's gaze, revulsion showing in his eyes. Then he moved, taking the first awkward steps down the hill and towards safety.

Jack watched him go. Only when Robert was half a dozen paces away did the Englishman turn to look at the huddle of men that was all that was left of the regiment. He had made his choice. He had not enjoyed being cruel, but it had been necessary; Robert would not have gone any other way.

Jack was free of the burden he had taken on for money. He was free to do what he did best.

Rose tied off the bandage then rocked back on her haunches to inspect her handiwork. Her mistress's cloak had once been a pretty dusky pink. Now it was stained with blood, but it was slowing the bleeding from the young soldier's belly, and that was a much better use for the fabric.

She rose to her feet, ignoring the cramp in her legs, wiping blood from her hands on a napkin that had once been the softest white cotton, but which was now so stained and ingrained with filth and ordure that it had the texture and feel of thick card.

The man she had bandaged had not made a sound all the while she had treated him. He lay still, hands flat on the ground by his sides, fingers digging frantically into the dirt. Now he looked up at her, his blue eyes crazed with pain, his body giving a great shudder of agony from the brutal wound that would surely kill him.

There was nothing more she could do for him. She turned, looking for the next person to help. The wounded were coming back in ever-increasing numbers. The first ones to reach the hillside had been lavished with care. Men with light wounds had been treated like kings as those left on the hillside plied them with the finest provisions and bound their wounds with tablecloths and cotton napkins.

Such luxuries had not lasted for long. After the first hours of the battle, the men coming back had been more grievously wounded. Now they lay in long lines, most of their wounds left open to the elements as the handful of civilians who had stayed to help ran out of cloth to bind them.

An officer wearing the grey uniform of the New York militia galloped up the slope on a bay mare lathered in sweat. Rose saw the way the horse laboured up the hillside, its strength long since spent.

'What's happening?' she shouted across.

'We are pursued by cavalry; they have cut us all to pieces!'

The officer reined his horse in, holding it back for a couple of seconds before ramming his spurs in and forcing it back into motion.

It was the last confirmation Rose needed.

She glanced across to her mistress. Elizabeth was squatting on the ground next to a sergeant, pouring the contents of a bottle of fine Bordeaux wine into his mouth. Her face was dirty and one cheek bore a single streak of blood the width of a finger. Only the path cut through the grime by her tears was clean.

Rose strode over. 'Ma'am, we must leave.'

Elizabeth looked up and scowled. 'We cannot. We're needed here.'

Rose shook her head. 'It's too late now. We have done all we can.'

As if to emphasise her words, a salvo of shells landed on the far northern edge of the hillside. They were too far away to hurt, but both women flinched as they tore great crevices in the hillside.

'Come on, missy.' Rose grabbed Elizabeth by the arm and hauled her to her feet. She prised the bottle from her mistress's hand and passed it to the wounded sergeant before frogmarching Elizabeth towards one of the few coaches still parked near the trees where they had picnicked earlier that day.

'Is it over?' Elizabeth took one look at Rose's face and hissed the question.

'The battle is lost.' Rose turned to look anxiously over her shoulder, as if expecting to see the rebel host come storming into view. All she saw were hundreds of men streaming back through the fields below the hillside. There was little order to the retreat, and men were dumping their equipment as they fled from the battlefield. The fields were littered with clothing, rifles, musical instruments, edibles and water, the troops stripping away anything that would slow them down.

Elizabeth paused, looking around her, taking stock. 'We'll give our carriage to the wounded; Senator Ashby's too, seeing as he is not back to use it for himself. We can travel together in the servants' carriage.' Her assessment was swift. She took Rose's arm in a tight grip. 'Will you find my father?'

The maid nodded. There was no need to say anything further.

As she moved away from the trees, Rose was nearly knocked from her feet by Senator Ashby, who was heading for his carriage, one of the last left on the hillside.

'Stop!' She could only shout after the senator, who was moving briskly.

Ashby paid her no heed whatsoever. His legs pumped furiously as he bolted for the carriage.

Rose moved quickly. She was much younger than the aged senator and it took her a few short seconds to run past him and block his way. 'You will not take that carriage.'

Ashby strode towards her, his hand raised as if about to cuff her across the face. 'Damn you. Do not dare to speak to me in that tone, you damn N—'

'Ashby! What the devil is going on?'

Rose had not shied away as Ashby raised his hand to her. She had held her ground, glaring at the man in defiance. Now her master intervened, shouting at the senator as he limped towards them across the hillside.

'Control this confounded woman.' Ashby jabbed his walking stick in Kearney's direction. 'Get her out of my way before I take my stick to her.'

Rose snapped her arm forward and held the stick in a firm

grip. 'You beat me with this, master, and so help me I'll beat you back.'

Ashby pulled hard, trying to free the stick. He failed.

'Ashby!' Kearney arrived breathless and flushed.

'Father!' Elizabeth had caught up, and spoke before Ashby could reply. 'The worst of the wounded must go in the carriages. Ours and Senator Ashby's.'

Kearney looked at his daughter. 'Very well, have them loaded this instant.'

'Now look here, Kearney.' Ashby was still trying to free his stick from Rose's grip.

'No, you listen to me.' Kearney shouted the senator down. 'My daughter has this situation under control. I suggest we leave it to her.'

'Damn you and damn your precious trollop of a daughter.' Ashby finally freed his stick. He took no more than a single step.

'Stay where you are, Senator.' Kearney had pulled the pistol from his waistcoat. It was a single-shot derringer, the kind a gentleman or a lady would keep about their person as protection against some unforeseen villain. It might have held only the single bullet, but it was aimed directly at Ashby's heart.

Kearney held the gun still as he looked at Elizabeth. 'Tell Henson your plan. Have him load Ashby's carriage first, but leave a single seat for the senator.' He glanced at the maid. 'Well done, Rose. That was bravely done.'

But Rose was not looking at either her master or Ashby. Her gaze was fixed on a man wearing a dark blue uniform who was staggering up the hillside carrying the bloodied body of a man wrapped in the bright red, white and blue of the Stars and Stripes.

Chapter Thirty-eight

—◆—

'My God.' It was Kearney who spoke first. 'Robert!'

Robert staggered to a halt as he heard someone shout his name. He stared at his father in shock.

Rose moved first. She ran to Robert's side, her arms reaching out to try to help him carry Rowell's body. Kearney had not taken a single step. He was staring at his son as if unable to believe his eyes.

'Father!' Robert struggled up the slope. Whatever astonishment he felt at finding his family was quickly forgotten.

'Is that Ethan?' Kearney was struggling to make sense of what he was seeing.

'He's hurt bad.' Robert had kept moving. He staggered past his father, his gaze fixed ahead.

'Take him to the carriage.' It was Rose who gave the instruction. She had slipped her arm under Rowell's head, supporting it as best she could. 'Ma'am! Get Henson.' She snapped the order at Elizabeth, who had neither moved nor spoken since Rose had first spotted her brother.

'Elizabeth!' Robert shouted. There was the snap of authority in his voice and it awoke Elizabeth from her shock.

'This way.' She moved quickly, ushering him up the slope. She looked down at her fiancé's bloodied and unconscious body. 'Is he dead?'

'How the hell should I know?' Robert hissed the words. He had no breath for more.

The three of them struggled up the slope as best they could. Rose was the first to spot the Kearneys' driver. 'Henson! Over here.'

Henson needed no urging. He rushed over and hauled Rowell's body from Robert's arms.

'Put him in the servants' carriage, then tell the servants to load up our carriage with as many wounded as they can.' Elizabeth fired off the instructions before turning her attention to her brother, who had collapsed to his hands and knees the moment Henson had removed his burden. 'Where's Jack?' she asked him urgently.

'He's back with the regiment.' Robert managed to force the words out in between gasps for breath. His head hung down as he dragged air into his lungs.

'You left him?'

'He made me.' Robert took one last lungful of air, then forced himself to his feet. 'Now come on.'

'What's happening?' Elizabeth stared at her brother as if she no longer recognised him.

'We're running, that's what's damn well happening.' Robert turned to his father, who had limped up the slope behind them. 'Father, all hell is breaking loose.'

Kearney reached out to clasp a hand to his son's shoulder. 'Are you all right?'

'Yes. Jack saved me. Just like you damn well ordered.' Robert wiped a hand across his sweat-streaked face. 'Now we need to get away whilst we still can. The whole damn rebel army is coming this way.'

Kearney looked around him. 'There is not room in the carriage for us all.' He glanced once at Elizabeth, then reached out and took hold of his son's forearms. 'You must get her away from here. I entrust her to your care. You are better able to steer her safely through this chaos than I.'

'What about you, Father?'

Kearney looked across to the carriages that were being loaded with wounded. 'I shall claim a place in Ashby's carriage. Then at least I can ensure that he does not abandon the charges in his care.'

'You are sure?'

'I am.' Kearney looked his son in the eye. 'You are changed.'

'No man can come alive through that and not be.' Robert snapped the reply. 'I shall not let you down, Father.'

'No. I see that now.' Kearney held his son's arms for a moment longer, then he let them go and headed towards the senator's carriage.

It would be down to his son to get Elizabeth safely away from the rebel army.

The turnpike was blocked by a long line of carriages and wagons.

Robert sat alongside Henson and tried to spy a way through. He saw none. He could just make out the wooden bridge that spanned the Cub Run Stream. He was not certain, but it looked like a heavy wagon had taken a direct hit from a Southern shell and had slewed around to block the road. Men were swarming around it, but he had no idea if they stood a chance of dragging it clear.

'You see any way through?'

'No, sir.'

'Fuck it.' Robert swore under his breath. He saw Henson's eyes widen at the pithy oath. The driver's expression was nearly enough to make him laugh. He had clearly spent too much time around Jack.

He looked around, trying to spot Senator Ashby's carriage amidst the chaos. There was no sign of it, and he could only presume they had tried another route. It would be typical of his father to somehow avoid such a disaster. He would likely be waiting for them in Washington with a sly smile on his face and a dry remark as to what had taken them so long.

Ahead, he saw a family abandon their carriage, the father deciding to try to find a way through on foot with his wife, small son and two servants trailing in his wake. Robert turned to look behind him. Elizabeth and Rose were trying to bind the wound to Rowell's stomach with the 1st Boston's colour. Blood had stained the white stripes so that the flag appeared to have been made from a sheet of red silk.

It made his decision easier. He could not hope to try to mimic the family in front of them. They would not stand a chance on foot. They would have to find another way.

A file of Union soldiers rushed past the line of stalled carriages. Not one carried a rifle. None was wounded. He opened his mouth to shout at the men, his first thought to try to get them to clear the broken wagon from the bridge.

Before he could utter a single sound, a salvo of shells smashed into a wood to the left of the turnpike. The noise of their impact was dreadful, the crack of trees being torn apart loud enough to drown out the terrified shouts and cries of the men and women stranded on the road.

'We need to get moving.' Elizabeth was cradling Rowell's head in her hands, but now she turned to look up at her brother.

'There's no way through. We need to get off this damn road.'

Elizabeth bent forward and kissed Rowell on the forehead, then stood up to survey the scene. Her dress was covered in dirt and blood, and her hair was wild where it had been bared to the ravages of the wind. 'There, to the west. Henson, get us off the road. It's the only way.' She gave her instructions quickly.

'You heard her, Henson.' Robert clapped his hand on the driver's shoulder. It was as good a plan as any, and they could not stay where they were.

Henson nodded, then stood up to study the ground to the west of the road. As he did so, a pair of hands grabbed hold of the side of his seat.

'What the devil!' Robert saw the soldier haul himself up. He was wearing the twin stripes of a corporal. His uniform was nearly pristine and his face was clean and free of the stain of powder. 'Get down this instant!'

The man ignored Robert's command. He was wrestling with Henson for control of the reins. Another soldier was trying to climb up the rear of the vehicle. Still more swarmed around the wheels. It would only be moments before the carriage was overwhelmed.

'Get down!' Robert gave the order as he levelled his revolver. He had not fired it that day and every chamber was loaded. 'Get down, or so help me, I will shoot you down.'

The corporal stopped his struggle with Henson and looked at Robert nervously. 'You going to shoot one of your own men, Lieutenant?' He licked his lips, the gaping maw of the Colt revolver no more than six inches from his face.

'If I have to.' Robert saw the fear flash in the corporal's eyes. He lifted the gun a fraction of an inch, then snapped out his left fist. It was not a great punch, but it landed squarely on the corporal's jaw, knocking the man's head back with enough force to snap his teeth together. He released his grip on the reins long enough for Henson to shove him over the side of the carriage.

'Get away.' Robert changed his point of aim, directing the gun at the soldier halfway up the rear of the carriage. The man let go, falling away to join his mates by the wheels. It gave them an opening.

'Go! Go! Go!' Robert grabbed hold of his seat and urged Henson to get them moving.

The carriage bucked as it scrabbled over the edge of the turnpike and onto the grassy field by its side. The ground was soft this close to the river, and the carriage's wheels dug great grooves in the soil, but Henson knew his job and he worked the horses hard, flicking the reins and geeing them up so that they hauled the heavy carriage away from the turnpike, the wheels showering the fleeing soldiers with great clods of earth.

Jack peered through the powder smoke. He could see a regiment moving along in good order, but he had no idea whose side they were on.

'Ours?' James Thatcher appeared at his shoulder and joined him staring into the smoke. Behind them, a few hundred men stood in a rough column. They looked nothing like the soldiers who had formed up that morning. The companies were hopelessly mixed and just three of the captains were still on their feet. None contested Jack's right to command.

'I have no idea.' Jack turned his head and looked hard at the young man at his side. It was odd hearing James Thatcher speak, but they had all been altered by that bitter day and he did not have the strength of mind to dwell on the change. 'West. We go west.'

He turned and waved at the regiment, then signalled the direction he wanted them to take. It took them away from the Bull Run, but also away from the unknown regiment, and that was good enough for the moment.

The men followed his instructions, moving obliquely across a slope, their tired legs hauling them on. They were surrounded by rifle fire. At one point they heard the ordered sound of a regiment firing volleys, but most shots came singly, or in short flurries, the fighting breaking down into a disordered scramble.

Jack looked at the men as they trudged across the slope. They had been on their feet for more than fourteen hours and they were done in. If the Confederate army pursued hard, the disordered and exhausted Union soldiers could be broken beyond repair. With few other troops between Manassas and Washington, the Southern army had the chance to win the war within their grasp.

Yet as far as he could tell, the Confederate army was as fatigued as the men they had beaten, and he had seen little indication of further reinforcements reaching the battle, nor any sign of rebel cavalry sent in pursuit of the beaten Union troops.

'Lieutenant!' Captain Sanders of D company called across to Jack. 'You see them?' He was pointing ahead. Another body of men was standing in line around two hundred yards away behind a split-rail fence. They were the first formed troops Jack had seen for some time.

'They ours?' Jack shouted back. He could not see them well enough to be sure.

'Look like regulars to me,' Sanders answered confidently enough.

Whoever the men were, it was clear that they were still formed and fighting. Even as Jack watched, they poured out a volley, his glimpse of them immediately hidden by a rush of smoke.

'Keep moving!' He had no intention of re-forming the remains of the 1st Boston into a battle line. They had done enough.

They pressed on, step by weary step. The walked past great swathes of corpses, the dead lying in groups that marked out where individual fights had taken place. The men barely looked at the twisted, broken bodies. The day had hardened them to such horror.

They came off the sloping ground, crossed the turnpike where they had waited for so long to fight, then started to climb once again. As they left the road behind, the sounds of fighting slowly disappeared into the distance. Jack felt strangely peaceful, as the shouts, roars and screams of men fighting to the death receded into the depths of his mind.

They crested the hill, the men plodding along, keeping moving as best they could. The bodies of the dead littered the ground, the scene of the morning's fighting no less grotesque for being hours old. Jack saw one man who had crawled a fair distance despite having had both legs blown off, a grisly trail of blood marking his path. Another man who had been shot in the face sat bolt upright, his eyes staring into nothing above the ruin of his mouth and nose.

'Keep moving.' Jack paused and stepped to one side so that

he could check the men over as they passed. He did not recognise many of the faces, the remains of the ten companies now mixed together. A few men wore the uniforms of a different regiment altogether, stragglers who had attached themselves gratefully to one of the few groups quitting the battlefield in some sort of order.

The high ground gave Jack a chance to see the rest of the retreating Union army. Some were running in complete disorder, the hillside and beyond covered with retreating men. A handful were moving back in more formed groups, the remains of a regiment or a company still banded together.

From his vantage point he could also see a carriage scrabbling across a distant field. Even from a distance he could make out the bright flash of a lady's dress, colour that had no place amidst the drab greys, blues and browns of the soldiers' uniforms. He cursed them then, those foolish civilians who had stupidly come to watch a battle as if it were a spectacle laid on for their enjoyment. Any notion of celebrating a victory had been lost as the Union army broke itself on the resolute wall of Confederate defenders. Now those fine ladies and gentlemen found themselves joining the broken army in a desperate bid for survival.

'Isn't that Mr Kearney's coach?' James Thatcher had followed Jack out of the ranks and now peered at the distant coach from under a hand that shielded his eyes from the glare of the afternoon sun.

'What?' Jack was not sure he had heard correctly.

'I reckon that's the Kearneys' carriage. Amos and I helped my uncle work on it a year ago.' Thatcher lowered his hand and looked at his lieutenant. 'I'm sure of it.'

'Shit.' Jack felt a rush of fear. If the man was correct, then the flash of colour he had seen had to be Elizabeth Kearney. And if Elizabeth was there, he could only assume that Rose was too.

'Here, take this.' He pulled the Irish colour out of his jacket and bundled it into Thatcher's arms. 'Keep heading north. Tell Captain Sanders he has the regiment.' He looked at the younger man's face. 'And tell him I made you first sergeant. A Company is yours now.'

Thatcher looked at Jack as if he had gone mad. 'Where the hell are you going?'

Jack had a wild grin on his face. 'Over there.' He nodded at the carriage that was flogging its way through the field at no more than a snail's pace.

'You coming back?'

Jack shook his head. 'I reckon not.'

Thatcher held his gaze, then nodded. He did not say a word before he turned and ran after the rear ranks of the regiment.

Jack forced his worn-out, aching body to move. He had done all he could for the regiment. Now it was time to look out for someone he had not allowed himself to think about since they had parted the night before. It was time to take the first steps towards a future of his own choosing.

Every breath burned as Jack hauled it into his tortured lungs. Every moment was a torment, every lurching step an agony to be endured. He had fallen once, his legs buckling as he tore down a slope. The landing had been painful, the jarring contact with the ground awaking the pain in his back so that he ran with spasms shooting up and down his spine. Yet he kept going, plotting a path that would intercept the carriage, refusing to listen to his body, refusing to quit.

The vehicle was moving slowly by the time he got closer, its wheels churning great furrows in the soft ground near the river. No matter how hard the driver lashed the exhausted horses that pulled it, it could go no faster than an old man's stagger.

'Hold there!' Jack called out as soon as he was close enough for them to hear him. He saw heads turn. He recognised Elizabeth at once. Robert was there too, the blue of his uniform marking him out well enough. There appeared to be more people in the carriage, but they were screened from his view.

None of them appeared to recognise him.

He saw Robert brace himself at the front of the carriage. At first, Jack's brain was too exhausted to work out what the younger man was doing.

Then Robert fired for the first time.

'Shit!' Jack was well past flinching, but he still tensed as the bullet cracked through the air over his head. 'It's me, you fucking fool!' He tried to shout to Robert, but the breath wouldn't come and the words emerged as little more than a gasp.

Robert's second bullet was lower. It spat into the ground a yard in front of Jack's boots, burying itself harmlessly into the damp sod.

'For fuck's sake!' Jack ploughed on, dragging the air into his abused lungs as best he could. He managed to wave an arm in a clumsy gesture that he hoped would persuade them to stop shooting for long enough to look at him and know who he was.

He was getting close. He could see Robert preparing to fire again.

'Don't shoot, it's Jack!'

Jack was never more relieved to hear his own name. As

he plunged on, he saw a third person's face. Rose was busy with something on the floor of the carriage, but she had glanced up for long enough to save him from getting a bullet in the head.

'Hell fire!' Robert lowered his gun and peered at Jack. 'I thought you were a damn secher! Stop here, Henson!'

Jack had no breath for a reply. He just put his head down and ploughed on until he managed to catch up with the now stationary carriage. He hauled himself up, then reached out to snatch the smoking revolver from Robert's hand.

'My God.' Elizabeth spoke for the first time. She was looking at Jack like he was something from a nightmare.

Jack did not care to reply. Seeing no room in the carriage, he jumped back down and worked his way round, using the time to catch his breath, then clambered up next to Henson. Only then did he look at the faces that were turned his way.

'Is he still alive?' He fired the question at Rose, who was squatting on the floor of the carriage next to Rowell's bloodied body.

'Barely.'

Jack nodded. He looked around at the people in the carriage. Elizabeth's face and clothes were covered in grime and worse, a testament to her having done more than just spectate. Robert's blue tunic was soaked in gore, a reminder of the bloody burden he had carried and which now lay on the floor of the carriage. Then there was Rose.

'You all right, love?' He could not hold back the question.

'Better than you, by the looks of things.' Rose glanced at him for no more than a second. There were grey circles around her eyes and her face was covered with a crust of dirt, but there was such life in her bloodshot eyes. The sight of her lent him strength. He would bring them through safely, no matter what it took.

'Henson! Get us moving.' Robert gave the order.

The driver needed little urging, but despite his whipping, the horses struggled to make any progress in the heavy ground.

Jack was half turned towards the rear of the carriage when he heard the dreadful roar of a salvo of shells. The first hit the ground twenty yards away, the field erupting in a great fountain, heavy clods of earth thrown high into the air. A heartbeat later and a second shell landed no more than ten yards away. The cascade of earth that rained down on the barely moving carriage was just as spectacular. It was still falling when a third shell hit the ground five yards from the rear left wheel.

The carriage was thrown sideways as if it weighed no more than a child's toy. Jack had no idea how it stayed upright as it lurched and twisted like a small boat caught in a rip tide. He saw Elizabeth's mouth open, but her scream was lost in the roar of the explosion. The horses plunged and reared, their shrieks of terror loud in the aftermath of the blast, before there was the snap of breaking wood. The carriage gave a great shudder then came to a halt, the driver fighting the pair of horses to a standstill.

'Anyone hurt?' Jack turned and shouted the question. He had held on for all he was worth and had somehow maintained his seat. But those in the back had not been so lucky and had been thrown down. Robert had fallen half out of the carriage, whilst Rose had been flung forward so that she smothered Rowell's body.

'No!' Robert forced himself up. 'Elizabeth—'

'I'm fine.' She did not let him finish the question.

'He's dead.' Rose's voice cut through the others. She was pulling herself upright, but her eyes were riveted on Rowell's face. Elizabeth's future husband was staring at the sky through sightless eyes.

Jack shared a look with Robert. 'Come on, let's move. Out of the carriage.' It was the only option. The vehicle was going nowhere. The explosion had torn the rear left wheel nearly completely off its mount. All that remained was a twisted mess of broken spokes and shattered rim.

He did not wait to see the others out. Instead he jumped down, his boots hitting the ground with a squelch. As soon as he had his balance, he looked around, trying to find the best route to safety. They were on low ground far from the turnpike. A heavily wooded slope looked down on them from the far side of the river. It promised sanctuary, if only they could reach it. Crossing the river on foot would not be easy.

'Which way?' Rose emerged from the far side of the carriage. She walked to Jack's side, then reached out to grab his right hand, holding it tight, binding him to her.

'We have to cross the river.' Jack felt the urge to pull her to him. But then Robert came around the side of the broken carriage, followed by his sister.

'You think we can?' Robert did not so much glance at the intertwined hands.

'We'll have to.' Jack turned on the spot and looked for Henson. 'What do you think?'

Henson shrugged, then turned to free the horses from their traces.

'We could ride.' Elizabeth offered the suggestion.

Jack quashed the idea. 'We have no saddles.'

'And there are five of us.' Robert reached out and laid his

hand on his sister's back. 'You ever learn to swim, Lizzy?'

'What about Ethan?' Elizabeth turned to face her brother. 'We cannot leave him behind.'

'We can and we will.' Jack was cruel. 'He's dead. Just like thousands of other poor bastards.'

Elizabeth looked at him. 'You would leave him here?'

'You have a better idea?'

She paused. She could not hold his gaze, her eyes flickering from his face to his hands. 'No.'

'We need to get moving.' Jack took control. 'We'll head downriver. Find a place to cross.' He turned and looked over his shoulder. The Confederates could not be far behind. If they had any sense, they would press on with everything they had. They had their boot on the Union army's throat. All they had to do was keep it there and the war would be done in a single day.

Chapter Thirty-nine

Henson led the way. Once he had cut the horses from the traces, the driver had produced a short-barrelled carbine from under his seat. Elizabeth went next, with Robert behind his sister, his reloaded revolver held ready and the bloodstained Stars and Stripes bundled under his left arm. Rose followed, with Jack bringing up the rear. He walked with two loaded revolvers, one held in each hand.

From her place further ahead, Elizabeth turned to glare back at him. It was a look of such disdain that Jack felt it hit him like a physical thing. He glanced away, unmoved, hefting the unfamiliar weight of Rowell's ivory-handled revolver in his left hand. He had reclaimed the weapon as they walked away from the broken carriage and the body of the man left inside. Elizabeth had protested at what she had called theft. Jack had ignored her, just as he ignored her glare. He'd be damned if he would leave the weapon behind for some bloody rebel soldier.

They were making good time, moving more quickly than they had in the carriage. They had left the sodden ground near the river and were heading west into a thickly wooded area. Jack intended to put a good few miles between them and the battlefield before turning them north once again and trying to find a place to cross the river.

It was cool under the trees, and almost peaceful. After hours in the sweaty, stinking heat, the fresher air came as a blessed relief. The only sounds were the scuffing of their boots through the undergrowth and the gentle sound of the wood's canopy moving back and forth in the breeze.

But they were not alone. Every few minutes they heard voices, or the noise created by a body thrashing through the wood at speed. They were not the only fugitives seeking refuge amongst the trees, and it made Jack anxious. Any encounter could be dangerous, whether it was with the enemy or their own side. He had seen soldiers after battle. Men pushed to breaking point were unlikely to think of anything but their own survival. They would let nothing stand in their way.

Henson brought them to a halt, then hissed a question over his shoulder. 'Which way?'

They were in the gloom now, deep in the woods. Above their heads the canopy had thickened, blocking out the late-afternoon sun and leaving them in almost complete darkness.

Four faces turned to look at Jack.

He paused. Keeping a sense of direction was impossible. He was no woodsman; just a boy from the narrow streets of a metropolis.

'I don't bloody know. Just keep damn well moving.' He waved his hand.

They moved off again, Henson plunging ahead, his carbine held across his body. No one spoke. They just plodded along, exhausted and drained by the day's events.

They had walked for no more than ten minutes when Henson stopped them again. 'What's that?'

'For God's sake,' Jack growled. 'What now?' His temper was fraying.

'You hear that?'

He stopped moving and listened. He heard the sound that had stopped Henson immediately.

'Shit.' He knew what it meant. It came from their left and was the sound of an ordered group of men moving purposefully through the wood. He heard the tramp of boots and voices giving orders. He had no idea if he was listening to a body of Union soldiers or a formed unit of Confederates, but he had no intention of waiting to find out.

'That way!' He gestured to the right. 'Move! Quickly now.'

Not one person disobeyed. They turned and forced their tired bodies into a run, the notion of the column lost immediately, stumbling on as a group, keeping together as best they could.

Jack heard cries from behind them. They had been heard.

They increased their pace, kicking a way through the undergrowth. Jack angled his path, making sure he stayed behind Rose. He would not lose sight of her. The sound of men moving followed. He had not caught a single glimpse of any pursuer, but he had the feeling of being chased.

The wood opened out, the dense undergrowth giving way to little more than moss and tree roots.

'Come on!' Jack urged them on. If they picked up the pace in the more open ground, they might get away before the men behind them could fight their way free of the denser woodland they had just left.

Henson moved ahead, leading the way. The others followed, lungs heaving with the strain of moving so fast.

'Lord of mercy!' It was Rose who spotted the man first. He

was sitting against a tree directly in their path. He wore a dark grey uniform with the bright blue stripes of a corporal on his sleeve. His jacket was pulled open to reveal his guts, which hung out of his stomach and lay blue and glistening in his lap.

Jack was sure the man was dead. He was wrong.

The corporal's head turned to look at the mismatched group running towards him. 'Help me!' he called out with surprising strength to his voice. 'You there, in the name of the Lord, help me.'

'Keep moving.' Jack answered for them all. The sight of the man did not move him. He had seen the same wound a dozen times already that day.

Rose alone disobeyed. He saw her change direction the moment the soldier cried out, then drop to her knees beside the man, her hands already tearing at the stained hem of her skirt.

'Rose! Leave him!'

'I will not leave a man to die like a dog.' She turned her head, throwing the words back at him, then busied herself preparing a rudimentary dressing.

'Jack?' It was Robert. The others were slowing, their hopes of escape fading fast.

'Shit.' Jack stood over Rose. He could hear the men behind them. Every instinct told him that they were Confederates. It meant their only chance lay in moving as fast as they could without stopping, no matter what they saw.

'Rose. You have to leave him.' He tried to reason with her.

'You go if you must.' Rose did not so much as look at him. She had torn a thick strip of fabric from her skirt and was trying to slip it around the man's waist.

'Bless you, miss.' The soldier turned his eyes to Jack. They were the pale blue of fresh ice, and were lucid and alive. 'Why don't you go to hell?' He asked the question mildly.

'Damn it.' Jack ground his teeth in frustration. Precious seconds were ticking by, and they would need every one.

'Jack?' Robert had stopped now, his sister at his side. Even Henson had paused, licking his lips anxiously and staring back at the woodland from where the noise of pursuit was coming.

Jack took one last look over his shoulder, half expecting to see Confederates bursting through the trees.

There was only one solution.

He raised his own revolver and aimed it squarely at the wounded soldier's head. The man was going to die anyway, his grotesque wound worse even than the one that had killed Rowell. A swift death now would be a mercy.

His finger curled around the trigger.

'No!'

Rose slammed her hand into his gun the very instant before he fired, knocking it to one side. 'Go! Now!' She glared at him then, eyes filled with anger. Then she turned back to her gory task.

'For Christ's sake.' Jack spat out the words. A new decision was made. He waved at Robert. 'You go, quickly now. We'll follow.'

Robert stared back at him for no more than the span of a single heartbeat. Then he was plucking at his sister's sleeve and they were off, Henson leading the way, Robert and Elizabeth following. The wood swallowed them in moments.

'I hope you know what the hell you are doing.' Jack checked over his pair of revolvers, speaking to Rose without looking at her.

'You can go.' She replied even as she bound the soldier's guts back into his belly.

'And leave you?' Jack tucked Rowell's revolver under his arm and made sure his sabre was loose in its scabbard. He would need it soon enough. 'Where would the fun be in that?'

The first Confederates came into sight. There were half a dozen of them and they were spread in a skirmish line. Jack had no idea if these were all he faced, or if they were just the lead element of a much larger force. Whichever it was, it did not matter. There was only one thing he could do; one course of action he could take to keep them safe and free.

He attacked.

His breath roared in his ears as he started to move. It deadened all other sounds so that he barely heard Rose shout at him not to be a fool. The pain in his body fell away, the aches and the tiredness lost as the wild desire to fight thrilled through him.

The first Confederate saw him coming. He was fat, with a great roll of blubber around his belly. He did not look like a soldier, his uniform little more than a wide-brimmed hat, brown homespun trousers and a shirt that might once have been beige, but which was now grey and stained with sweat. His face was covered with a thick growth of beard, but Jack still saw his mouth open in shock as a Yankee officer came charging towards him.

Jack fired. He used his own revolver, the weapon so familiar that it felt like an extension of his own body. His first bullet took the fat Confederate in the throat.

'Come on!' He released the demons.

He darted to one side, dodging past a tree, and fired fast,

barely aiming, at a man in a brown plaid shirt who raised what looked to be an ancient smoothbore musket. The man died with two bullets in his chest before he could pull the trigger of his outdated weapon.

The last three bullets were fired in quick succession, all aimed at a Confederate who stood and stared at Jack as if he were some creature from the depths of hell. The man died when the final shot pierced his brain, the Colt's heavy bullet taking him in the eye.

Jack roared then, shouting his war cry for all he was worth. Three men were dead, all killed by his hand. He was a god of war and he thrilled with the knowledge that he would not die here, not at the hand of farmers and labourers who knew nothing of how to fight, how to kill.

The next man turned to face him. Jack saw the fear on his face as he aimed his musket. He heard the familiar cough of the older gun, then the snap in the air as a musket ball whipped past him. He laughed, the sound braying and harsh. Then he raised the ivory-handled Colt and fired it for the first time.

He missed, the feel of the weapon in his left hand unfamiliar and strange. The bullet cracked into a tree behind the Confederate's head, so he fired again. The second shot took the man in the heart.

He whooped and moved on, not even looking as the man crumpled to the ground without a sound. He caught a glimpse of another Confederate and fired on instinct, cursing as he saw the bullet gouge a thick splinter from the edge of a tree trunk.

The two men left had gone to ground. Jack kept moving, crashing through the undergrowth, daring them to show themselves. Neither did, but he fired anyway, smothering them with violence so that when he found them, their fear would slow them and make them an easier target for Rowell's Colt or his own sword.

'Come on!' He shouted the challenge, then fired again and again, snapping off the last shots in the gun's chambers.

One man stepped out from behind a tree, his musket already held at his shoulder. Jack saw the movement and ducked away, twisting to one side then darting around a thicker tree trunk. He dropped his own revolver and drew his sword, the action instinctive, then burst from behind the tree no more than five yards in front of the man with the raised musket. He saw the weapon twitch in surprise, the barrel moving as the man tried to aim. Jack was on him before he could fire.

It was easy then. His sword battered the musket upwards. The Confederate fired, the ball blasting harmlessly into the sky, then staggered backwards, the recoil knocking him away from Jack, who simply stepped forward and punched the guard of his sword into the man's face.

It was a cruel blow, driven by all his strength. The guard cut deep into the soft flesh above the man's beard and pulped his nose. Defenceless and hurting, he could do nothing to defend himself. Jack pulled back his sword arm, then drove the point of the sabre into the man's throat, twisting the steel the moment it went deep so that it would not be stuck in the suction of flesh.

For one dreadful moment, the man gazed back at Jack, eyes wide with terror as death came to claim him. Jack held his stare, then ripped his sword free and turned away, barely registering the feel of blood hot on his hand. He did not look at the man, who slid to the ground, hands clasped around the ruin of his neck.

Jack had seen six men. Five were now dead. He could hear

others, more Confederates, deeper in the wood. But they were far enough away to ignore. He moved, ducking under a branch then crashing through the undergrowth, his eyes never still as he looked for the sixth man. The fight had taken him away from Rose, so now he doubled back, retracing his steps past the bodies of the men he had slain.

He saw the man almost immediately. He was standing near the wounded soldier, his musket pulled tight into his shoulder. And he had Rose in his sights.

Jack had no bullets left. He could do nothing but pound along, forcing the strength into his legs.

'Heh!' he shouted, forcing the words out. 'Over here!'

It was as if he was wading through treacle. He strained every fibre of his being, trying to find extra speed. Nothing he did made a difference, the ground passing with stubborn slowness under his boots.

The rebel was shouting at Rose; he could hear that much over the roar of his breath in his ears, even though the words themselves were lost. The man's anger built as Rose stayed on the ground, her hands never still as she bound the wounded soldier's torn flesh.

The rebel took a step back. The shouting stopped. He pressed his cheek against the stock, taking final aim.

Jack saw the puff of smoke as he fired. The cough of the ancient musket echoed through the wood a moment later. The kick of the weapon jerked the rebel's shoulder back, the man shuddering as he absorbed the recoil.

The passage of time changed. The ground flew past in a rush, every second searing by in a blur. The rebel was lowering his weapon, his head thrust forward as he looked to see if his aim had been true.

Jack charged. The rebel's head turned in time for Jack to see the shock register on his face. Then he hit him.

He cared nothing for finesse. He threw himself at the man, bludgeoning him to the ground. They came down together, bodies jumbled. Jack's teeth snapped together as he hit the ground with bone-jarring force, and his sword went flying. He lashed out regardless, catching the rebel on the side of the head with the ivory-handled Colt that he still clutched in his left hand.

The blow glanced off the man's skull, but it was enough to hold him on the ground for a moment longer. Jack pushed himself up, then lashed out, smashing his fist into the rebel's face. The blow gave him a moment to find purchase, and he swung his leg over the man so he could straddle him and pin him down.

There was a moment's struggle, then he knocked the man's arms away. It gave him the opportunity he needed and he punched down hard. The blows flowed from him then, one after another, a punch with his free right hand followed by his left smashing the Colt into the rebel's unprotected face. Blood smothered his right hand and stained the ivory handle of the Colt crimson. Still he punched on, blow after blow; every emotion, every hurt fuelling an insatiable rage.

He stopped suddenly. The rebel's face was little more than a mash of gore and bone, unrecognisable as being human. He pushed down on the man's chest, levering himself up, forcing himself to his feet.

He did not turn his head. He could not bear to see her lying in the dirt.

The rebel had fired at point-blank rage. At that distance, even the ancient musket was a deadly weapon, and he knew with utter certainty that Rose had been taken from him. Guilt and grief washed through him. He closed his eyes against the agony, the horror of the moment complete. Once again, he had lost everything.

When he opened his eyes, Rose was sitting on her haunches staring directly at him. She was totally unharmed. Somehow the rebel had missed.

'He's dead.' Her voice was calm, her tone even.

Jack looked down at the man he had beaten to a merciless death. He could not comprehend what had happened. He did not know how she was still alive.

'Not him.' Rose stood up and carefully brushed the dirt from her knees. 'Him.' She pointed at the man she had been treating.

Jack looked at the soldier sitting against the tree. Rose had closed his eyes so that his face looked peaceful.

'We can go now.' She spoke carefully, as if he were incapable of understanding.

The last of the madness left him. What was left was cold, his soul emptied of all emotion. Save for one.

'You're alive.' It came out as little more than a whisper, the feeling of relief strong enough to steal his voice.

'Of course I'm alive.'

'I thought . . .'

'I know what you thought.' She paused. She looked at him then as if seeing him for the first time. 'I watched you kill them. I watched you kill them all.'

Jack had no words. He looked down at the man he had beaten to a pulp. He felt nothing. No revulsion. No guilt. He looked back at Rose. 'You should go.'

'I'm not going anywhere without you.'

'You saw me. You know what I am now.' He forced the bitter words out.

'I see you, Jack Lark.' She stepped towards him, holding out her right hand. 'And I know what you are.'

He was smothered in gore and had beaten a man to death in front of her eyes. Still she came to him, taking his free hand, pushing hers into it so that it nestled in his palm.

'Come on.' She paused and looked up into his face. 'We'll go together.'

Epilogue

Somewhere in Virginia, Monday 22 July 1861

The barn was quiet. Jack peered out of the opening in the centre of the gable end. The moon was up and it cast an eerie light across the fields. It showed a group of Confederate soldiers going about the business of setting up camp no more than five hundred yards away. Muskets had been stacked and the men had got a dozen fires going, the crackle of burning wood carrying through the quiet of the night to reach Jack as he counted heads and calculated odds.

'They still there?' The question was whispered.

Jack shivered as he felt Rose's breath wash against his cheek. 'Yes.'

'Then we'll stay here. Move in the morning.' She was close enough for him to feel the touch of her lips against the soft flesh of his ear.

He did not have the strength to argue. They had run until the last light of the day had faded. There had been no plan, no notion of direction. They had just steered a course between groups of Confederate troops, their only intention not to get caught.

Twice they had seen Union soldiers. The first had been a group of four men working their way in the opposite direction. Neither of them had been tempted to call out, to try to join them. They wanted to be alone.

The second time had been a group of twenty Union soldiers under guard. Dressed in the grey of the New York militia, they had been sitting in a rough circle surrounded by men with guns trained on them. It was a reminder of the fate that awaited Jack and Rose if they allowed themselves to be caught. Or at least the fate that waited for Jack. Rose would face a very different one. As an escaped slave, and one who had committed at least one murder, she would likely be tortured and executed. It was a fate worse than being a prisoner of war. Much worse.

He turned from the opening. The Confederate soldiers had men standing picket. There was no chance of getting away without being seen.

Gingerly he sat down, resting his back against the bales stored in the barn's loft. The place smelled of hay and animals. It was warm and comfortable. It would be hard to leave here.

'You hurting?' Rose kneeled beside him and looked at him, her face lit by the moonlight shining into the barn.

'I'm fine.' Jack tried not to grimace. Every muscle hurt, his body only now awakening to the dozens of bruises it had taken in the day's fighting. He craved the oblivion of sleep, but he dared not close his eyes, for to do that would be to stir the memories of the day. Then the faces of the dead would come back to haunt him, allowing him to relive the dreadful events with complete clarity.

'You're lying.'

'Perhaps.' Jack let his head rest back against a bale, then released a long breath he did not know he had been holding.

'You think they all made it?'

'The Kearneys?'

'Who else.'

'I've no idea.' Jack was too tired to think. He hoped they had. Henson had seemed a capable fellow, and Robert knew what he was about. He wondered if he would ever go back to Boston, if he would ever find Kearney and claim his reward for saving his son.

'I reckon they did.' Rose seemed more certain. 'You stopped those sechers. That gave them time to get away.'

'Let's hope.'

'You don't want to talk, do you?'

'No.' Jack blinked hard, fighting against the exhaustion.

Rose sat where she was. He could feel her gaze on him.

'You going to take off your boots?' She reached out to lay her hand on his shin.

'No.' Jack caught a hint of something in her voice. He could not see enough to be sure, but he detected mockery.

'That an English thing?'

'What?'

'Doing it in your boots?'

'Doing what?'

'Doing what, he says.' Rose came closer. 'Like you're a damn innocent, Jack Lark.'

Historical Note

At the very start of this project, I faced a difficult decision. I could, if I wished, use the history of one of the Union regiments that fought at Bull Run and take it as the basis for my story. Alternatively, I could create a fictional regiment, as I did when writing Jack's first outing *The Scarlet Thief*. In this instance I was guided by a source much closer to the men who had fought on that steamy day back in July 1861.

In his preface to *The History of the Ninth Regiment Massachusetts Volunteer Infantry*, (E. B. Stillings, 1899), its author, Daniel George Macnamara, writes, 'The writer is deeply impressed with the great responsibility which he incurs in the undertaking. A history . . . should be truthful, unbiased and accurate.' I was very aware that I was most certainly not writing a history, yet my story, if it was to succeed, must be welded to the events that I was covering. It was with this in mind that I chose to use a fictitious regiment, and so the 1st Boston Volunteer Militia came into being.

Having made that decision, I must now mention any area where I strayed from the path of real events.

I was much inspired by existing speeches from the period, in particular that given by Massachusetts Governor John Andrew. I felt these words expressed the sentiments of the time perfectly and offered a brilliant insight into the moment. To suit the narrative of this story, I had Andrew give his speech a few weeks early. Other great speeches of the era inspired some other sections of dialogue elsewhere in the novel and I hope they are more authentic for it.

The departure of the 1st Boston and 6th Massachusetts Volunteer Militia is based on the parade given to the 9th Massachusetts when they left the city later in June 1861. To fit the timeline of *The True Soldier*, I've had them depart early on 18th April rather than late on 17th.

The Baltimore riot happened; however, the seven hundred men of the 6th Massachusetts Volunteer Militia fought through the city on their own. The brutality of this riot demonstrates quite how divided the country was at the start of the war. The division between North and South was not as clear-cut as I had naively imagined, and it was most certainly not marked simply by a line drawn on a map. It was Lieutenant Leander Lynde of the 6th who tore the mocking flag from the hands of a rioter, a cool and brave act considering the pressure the 6th were under at that time. The rest of the events happened much as I described, and it is a sobering thought that the riot claimed so many lives before the war had truly begun.

At the fight at Blackburn's Ford, Brigadier General Tyler did exceed his orders; however, of the Union side, just the 1st Massachusetts and the 12th New York were involved in the fight. The two regiments lost eighty-three men, with nineteen killed, thirty-eight wounded and twenty-six listed missing. The Southern regiments involved lost seventy men, with fifteen killed, fifty-three wounded and two missing.

For the Battle of Bull Run itself, I chose to concentrate on my fictitious 1st Boston, whilst leaving all notions of an overview of the battle to other writers. Here the 1st Boston follow a likely path through McDowell's ambitious flanking attack, which ultimately failed in the face of stubborn, and brave, Southern resistance. The swift delivery of reinforcements from the Shenandoah Valley through the Confederate generals' use of the railroad is a great example of their using modern technology to their advantage.

Anyone wishing to read more of the events covered in this novel will discover a great wealth of resources. As ever, the fantastic Osprey books are my first port of call. I heartily recommend *First Bull Run 1861 – The South's first victory*, from the campaign series, as a great overview to the battle. For those looking for something more in-depth, I would suggest *Battle Cry of Freedom* by James M. McPherson. I found this book fascinating reading and I shall certainly be revisiting its pages as I write Jack's next adventure.

The Boston in which Jack arrives will be largely familiar to visitors to the city today. Anyone wishing to see what it looked like in 1861 should peruse *Old Boston in Early Photographs 1850–1918*, from the collection of the Bostonian Society. For tales a little more earthy, *Venus in Boston* was a great resource and one that really captured the somewhat seedy delights of the former Ann Street (renamed North Street by the time of Jack's visit in an attempt by the authorities to clean up that part of the city).

I have already mentioned *The History of the Ninth Regiment Massachusetts Volunteer Infantry* by Daniel George Macnamara. Every regiment has its own account, but this is

Frances Br..Kate
Shackleton as..ripts
for television and three sagas, one of which won the HarperCollins
Elizabeth Elgin Award................ Unknown was short-listed for the

Theatre, the Gate and Nottingham Playhouse. *Jehad* was nominated
for a *Time Out* Award.

Frances lived in New York for a time before studying at Ruskin
College, Oxford, and reading English Literature and History at
York University. She has taught in colleges and on writing courses
for the Arvon Foundation.

Visit Frances Brody online:

www.francesbrody.com
www.facebook.com/FrancesBrody
@FrancesBrody

Praise for Frances Brody:

'Frances Brody has made it to the top rank of crime writers'
Daily Mail

'The 1920s are a fascinating and under-used period for new crime
fiction, so it's a particular pleasure to have Frances setting her story
at that time. Kate Shackleton is a splendid heroine . . . I'm looking
forward to the next book in the series!'
Ann Granger

'Kate Shackleton joins Jacqueline Winspear's Maisie Dobbs in a
subgroup of young, female amateur detectives who survived and
were matured by their wartime experiences. As self-reliant women
in a society that still regards them as second-class citizens, they
make excellent heroines'
Literary Review

'Brody's winning tale of textile industry shenanigans is shot
through with local colour'
Independent

By Frances Brody:

KATE SHACKLETON MYSTERIES

Dying in the Wool
A Medal for Murder
Murder in the Afternoon
A Woman Unknown
Murder on a Summer's Day
Death of an Avid Reader
A Death in the Dales
Death at the Seaside
Death in the Stars
A Snapshot of Murder

OTHER NOVELS

Sisters on Bread Street
Sixpence in Her Shoe
Halfpenny Dreams